JON LAND

THE LAST PROPHECY

FORGE®

A TOM DOHERTY ASSOCIATES BOOK
NEW YORK

NOTE: If you purchased this book without a cover you should be aware that this book is stolen property. It was reported as "unsold and destroyed" to the publisher, and neither the author nor the publisher has received any payment for this "stripped book."

This is a work of fiction. All the characters and events portrayed in this book are either products of the author's imagination or are used fictitiously.

THE LAST PROPHECY

Copyright © 2003 by Jon Land

All rights reserved, including the right to reproduce this book, or portions thereof, in any form.

A Forge Book
Published by Tom Doherty Associates, LLC
175 Fifth Avenue
New York, NY 10010

www.tor-forge.com

Forge® is a registered trademark of Tom Doherty Associates, LLC.

ISBN-13: 978-0-7653-6110-3
ISBN-10: 0-7653-6110-8

First Edition: April 2004
First Mass Market Edition: December 2004
Second Mass Market Edition: May 2008

Printed in the United States of America

0 9 8 7 6 5 4 3 2 1

"Land's series seems to gain momentum with every installment, and his latest is as timely and extravagantly plotted as ever. . . . The breakneck pace and chockablock plotting leave protagonists (and the civilized world) constantly teetering on the brink of destruction. Highly entertaining from start to finish, this is prime escapist fiction . . . riveting." —*Publishers Weekly*

"Engaging heartstuff about lovers divided by religions loyalties . . . Moves hellbent—just as fans want and as Land loves to deliver." —*Kirkus Reviews*

"Should appeal to fans of *The Da Vinci Code*." —*Booklist*

"Land's pacing is incredible. . . . What makes Land's thrillers so enjoyable is his brilliant mix of fiction with undertones of current events. . . . While this book moves at lightning speed, it is paced well and the crescendo to the ending is perfectly timed— all of which makes it a must read for Jon Land's fans and thriller-readers generallly." —*The Providence Sunday Journal*

"He is the indisputable master of the post 9/11 thriller in which both the stakes and the standards have risen markedly. . . . Jon Land remains the best thriller writer alive today and nobody shows any signs of catching him anytime soon." —*Bookviews*

"Once again Jon Land delivers an action packed thriller that takes events from today's headlines and weaves them into a terrific story. . . . *The Last Prophecy* is an outstanding one-sitting reading experience." —*The Midwest Book Review*

"Land delivers yet another action-packed thriller, integrating the continuing conflicts between Arabs and Jews with the terrorist backlash of the U.S. occupation of Iraq. . . . Reading *The Last Prophecy* is like navigating the twists and turns of a cliffside road at 90 miles an hour, leaving the reader furiously turning the pages." —*The Jewish Voice and Herald*

"Land is superb at his labyrinthine plots within plots, especially when huge action scenes erupt out of nowhere and keep us on the edge of our seats. . . . *The Last Prophecy* is a taut, tense thriller that erupts like an explosion—fierce, furious, ferocious." —*East Side Monthly (Providence, RI)*

BOOKS BY JON LAND

*Published by Forge Books

DEDICATION

February 20, 2003

The Station nightclub fire in West Warwick, Rhode Island

For the 100 lost

Music taught me lessons a classroom never could,
To love with your heart, and unleash your soul.
—Nick O'Neill

ACKNOWLEDGMENTS

It's been a while since last we met. But it's that time of year again, and I've been looking forward to this moment as much as you. There's no greater feeling for me than seeing a book of mine in print for the first time, except, of course, *reading* it for the first, which is where you come in.

Before we get to the business at hand, some thanks are in order. I'm sorry to start on a down note but *The Last Prophecy* marks the last appearance of my wondrous agent, Toni Mendez, on this page. Toni passed away earlier this year at the age of ninety-four. She'd been my agent for twenty-three years at the time and she will always will be. I met Ann Maurer through Toni, just one of the great gifts she gave me, in this case one of editorial strength and resolve that continue to make my books better.

This and the others never would have become books, though, if not for the terrific group at Tor/Forge led by Tom Doherty (a terrific editor in his own right!) and Linda Quinton. My Forge editor, Natalia Aponte, never ceases to amaze me as she wields her red pencil with as much sensitivity as insight and continues to treat me to innumerable lunches at Bolo, where great ideas and great food go hand in hand. And how about *The Last Prophecy*'s knockout cover, thanks to Irene Gallo, or another award-winning production job, thanks to Eric Raab? Kudos also to the publicity department, especially Jodi Rosoff and everyone else who suffered through my company at trade shows and the like.

The Last Prophecy also found me blessed with a typically

large stable of readers and advisers, including Rabbi James Rosenberg (who outdid himself on this one), Nancy and Moshe Aroche, Emery Pineo, Daniel Oron, and Matt Alder, among numerous others.

Meanwhile, the first Jon Land film is looming closer in the offing. (Don't I say that every year? But I really mean it this time.) You can still reach me at jonlandauthor@ netscape.net to hear more about that and what's coming next, as well as to give me your feedback on *The Last Prophecy*. If you don't hear from me right away, it just means I've packed up, sold out, and gone Hollywood. No, just kidding. That would leave you without next year's book. As for this one, here's hoping you have as much fun with the reading as I did with the writing. So make yourself comfortable and let's get started.

Finally, my deepest thanks to the members of the 120th Evacuation Hospital (the model for this book's 121st) for sharing their stories with me last year for what I hoped would be a fitting nonfiction tribute. Although that project never materialized, their experiences have stuck with me in a time when true heroes are in short supply.

If you can look into the seeds of time,
And say which grain will grow and which will not,
Speak then to me.

—Shakespeare, *Macbeth*

P R O L O G U E :

BUCHENWALD, APRIL 1945

"Seventy-eight bodies and still counting, sir," the corporal's voice crackled, muted slightly by the surgical mask that covered his mouth.

Colonel Walter Henley switched the walkie-talkie from his left ear to his right. "Keep me informed, Corstairs."

"Yes, sir."

Henley did a rough count in his head. Since its arrival two days before, his unit had exhumed nearly a thousand bodies from the trenches that littered Buchenwald, the process as physically exhausting as it was spiritually draining. Henley replaced his own surgical mask and started back toward the wing of a wrecked bomber a dozen of his men were cutting up to convert into morgue tables. The job of transporting the survivors, once they were made fit to travel, to medical facilities far better equipped to treat them, was monumental. Henley had ultimately accepted the recommendation of his motor staff to convert the holds of their two-ton transport trucks into makeshift mass ambulances.

Two days, Henley reflected. *Is that all it's been? . . .*

He recalled the cryptic orders that had dispatched his unit here from Frankfurt, vague yet suggestive enough to lead Henley to temporarily transfer all forty of the 121st Evacuation Hospital's nurses to another unit. Like everyone else, Henley had heard of the Nazi death and labor camps, but had difficulty believing the substance of the tales, the whispered rumors and hushed action reports cloaking their existence in a surreal fog. Still, the reality of Buchenwald had dwarfed anything his imagination could conjure up.

It had started with a faint odor drifting through the beech wood forests of Weimar that swelled to a pastelike thickness by the time the 121st's trucks pulled up to the camp's front gate. There, a sea of fetid humanity garbed in soiled striped uniforms greeted them with gaping stares of grateful relief mixed with lingering hopelessness—as if those prisoners lucky enough to survive had forgotten how to smile or lacked the capacity.

A truck driver had given one of the starving, emaciated figures a chocolate bar. The disembarking members of the 121st then watched in horror as the prisoner, after gobbling up the candy, writhed and spasmed toward death, his body thrown into toxic shock by the sudden burst of nutrients into his system. It was in that moment that Henley first grasped the gravity of what his unit was facing. As the first medical personnel anywhere to enter one of the Nazi camps, they had no protocol to call upon, no textbook to consult, no procedure to follow.

Then again, the very nature of the 121st was new in warfare: a completely self-contained, totally mobile four-hundred-bed hospital that could be on the move with minutes' notice and equipped to handle anything the battlefield had to offer. Four hundred beds, of course, was hardly sufficient to care for the twenty-one thousand prisoners they found waiting for them in Buchenwald.

In the early hours, medics washed and deloused inmates too weak to lift their own arms; poor souls suffering from dysentery, typhus, tuberculosis, pneumonia, and malnutrition. Flattened tents became makeshift hospital beds. The stacks of corpses outside the trenches were carefully unpiled and personnel raced about with stethoscopes glued to their ears in search of possible heartbeats.

Henley learned that Buchenwald was actually a transfer center from which inmates were shipped to other locales, including death camps. Nearly 250,000 prisoners from thirty different countries passed through its gates on their way elsewhere, a fifth of whom died before they could be moved.

After two days, though, the 240 men of the 121st had finally managed to reverse the trend that awaited them at the gate. The death rate was falling by the hour, and the first patients were being prepared for transport atop stretchers made of planks stripped from the decaying buildings. The stench, though, lingered. Something worse than death; the dirt, the world itself maybe, gone sour and spoiled.

"Colonel Henley, this is Corstairs again. Do you copy?"

Henley pulled off his surgical mask and raised the walkie-talkie back to his ear. "Come in, Corporal."

"I'm still at Trench Delta, sir," Corstairs said breathlessly. "You're needed here stat."

"We've just begun transport, soldier. Can this wait?"

"No, sir, I don't think so." A rustling sounded as Corstairs lowered his surgical mask, his voice strained and slightly broken when he resumed. "Under the bodies, Colonel . . . we found something else."

DAY ONE

THE PRESENT

CHAPTER 1

LOGON COMPLETE
ALL STATIONS CONFIRMED ACTIVE ON-LINE
ENCRYPTION PROCEDURES IN EFFECT

MESSAGE RUNNING

From: UNITED STATES
X-Priority:
Sensitivity: Company-Confidential
To: ALL
MIME-Version: 1.0
IM secure status: active
X-MailScanner: Found to be clean

THE SITUATION HAS BEEN CONTAINED AS OF TODAY. ALL PROCEEDING AGAIN ON SCHEDULE.

From: GREAT BRITAIN
X-Priority:
Sensitivity: Company-Confidential
To: ALL
MIME-Version: 1.0
IM secure status: active
X-MailScanner: Found to be clean

DISCUSS POTENTIAL COMPLICATIONS.

From: UNITED STATES
X-Priority:
Sensitivity: Company-Confidential
To: ALL
MIME-Version: 1.0
IM secure status: active
X-MailScanner: Found to be clean

LIMITED.

From: RUSSIA
X-Priority:
Sensitivity: Company-Confidential
To: ALL
MIME-Version: 1.0
IM secure status: active
X-MailScanner: Found to be clean

SPECIFY.

From: UNITED STATES
X-Priority:
Sensitivity: Company-Confidential
To: ALL
MIME-Version: 1.0
IM secure status: active
X-MailScanner: Found to be clean

EXPECT MANDATED INVESTIGATION. EASILY CONTAINABLE.

From: JAPAN
X-Priority:

Sensitivity: Company-Confidential
To: ALL
MIME-Version: 1.0
IM secure status: active
X-MailScanner: Found to be clean

**CONTAINMENT CRUCIAL. OTHERWISE
SUGGEST PUSHING BACK TIMETABLE.**

From: UNITED STATES
X-Priority:
Sensitivity: Company-Confidential
To: ALL
MIME-Version: 1.0
IM secure status: active
X-MailScanner: Found to be clean

**AGENTS ACTIVATED. ALTERATION OF
TIMETABLE NOT PRACTICAL. ANY
ALTERATION THREATENS PROJECT GOAL.**

From: FRANCE
X-Priority:
Sensitivity: Company-Confidential
To: ALL
MIME-Version: 1.0
IM secure status: active
X-MailScanner: Found to be clean

HOW MANY DEAD?

From: UNITED STATES
X-Priority:
Sensitivity: Company-Confidential
To: ALL

MIME-Version: 1.0
IM secure status: active
X-MailScanner: Found to be clean

REPEAT MESSAGE.

From: CHINA
X-Priority:
Sensitivity: Company-Confidential
To: ALL
MIME-Version: 1.0
IM secure status: active
X-MailScanner: Found to be clean

HOW MANY KILLED TO CONTAIN SITUATION?

From: UNITED STATES
X-Priority:
Sensitivity: Company-Confidential
To: ALL
MIME-Version: 1.0
IM secure status: active
X-MailScanner: Found to be clean

**34. ACCEPTABLE NUMBERS. PRIMARY THREAT
ELIMINATED. COLLATERAL DAMAGE
EXPECTED.**

From: GERMANY
X-Priority:
Sensitivity: Company-Confidential
To: ALL
MIME-Version: 1.0
IM secure status: active
X-MailScanner: Found to be clean

ARE WE CERTAIN PRIMARY THREAT ISOLATED PRIOR TO CONTAINMENT?

From: UNITED STATES
X-Priority:
Sensitivity: Company-Confidential
To: ALL
MIME-Version: 1.0
IM secure status: active
X-MailScanner: Found to be clean

NO EVIDENCE OF SHARED INTEL.

From: JAPAN
X-Priority:
Sensitivity: Company-Confidential
To: ALL
MIME-Version: 1.0
IM secure status: active
X-MailScanner: Found to be clean

SECONDARY TARGETS?

From: UNITED STATES
X-Priority:
Sensitivity: Company-Confidential
To: ALL
MIME-Version: 1.0
IM secure status: active
X-MailScanner: Found to be clean

ONE. NO COMPLICATIONS EXPECTED.

From: RUSSIA
X-Priority:

Sensitivity: Company-Confidential
To: ALL
MIME-Version: 1.0
IM secure status: active
X-MailScanner: Found to be clean

CONFIRM COUNTDOWN TO PROMETHEUS.

From: UNITED STATES
X-Priority:
Sensitivity: Company-Confidential
To: ALL
MIME-Version: 1.0
IM secure status: active
X-MailScanner: Found to be clean

TEN DAYS.

MESSAGE TERMINATED

DAY TWO

Y ou're not needed here, señor," Colonel Riaz said stiffly. "Everything is under control."

Ben Kamal trained the binoculars one of Riaz's men had provided on the school. "How many hostages still inside?"

"Fourteen."

"That doesn't qualify as under control."

"We have gained the release of thirty-one, señor."

Ben pulled the binoculars from his eyes and looked at Riaz. The stiff wind blew some of his neatly combed hair onto his forehead and he brushed it aside. Like his father's, Ben's hair had actually thickened with age even as the first tinges of gray dappled the dark mane. He was past forty now, and crow's feet dug deeper around his eyes, seeming to dim their radiant shade of blue. Ben had never liked the color of his eyes, wishing they were darker, just as he wished his stomach was as flat and his build as powerful as Riaz's.

"Does that include the three killed when the gunmen took the school?" he asked the colonel.

Riaz stiffened. His dark brow was creased with sweat, and now beads of it had formed on both deeply pockmarked cheeks. He mopped at the right cheek with a forearm. "One of those three was my man: the security guard."

"And one of them was the U.N.'s: the principal. Which means there was one child among the three." Ben's stare hardened. "Who does he belong to, Colonel?"

Riaz scowled. "We did not ask for the U.N.'s help."

"You didn't have to. It's our school."

Ben had been in New York for security strategy meetings at United Nations headquarters when Alexis Arguayo personally pulled him out. Arguayo, head of the U.N.'s Safety and Security Service, was Ben's direct superior. Arguayo had lured him into the organization with a promise of excellent pay and the opportunity to travel to exotic locales in primarily an advisory capacity. That all changed with the bombing of the U.N. compound in Baghdad at the former Canal Hotel. Suddenly Ben was thrust into the limelight as the lead United Nations representative involved in the investigation. For everyone else involved, the results of that investigation were as clear as the culprits were obvious. While others were busy holding press conferences, Ben squirreled his way into the bowels of the compound where he ultimately unearthed a hidden warren of storage chambers that led to the basis for a conclusion to which he alone subscribed.

Ben followed procedure and filed his report through the proper channels, a report that was swiftly denounced as outlandish and totally lacking in fact or evidence. Before he could prove his point, Ben was pulled from the investigation and returned to advisory status where he languished for six months, until that morning. Two hours after Arguayo had pulled him from the meeting, Ben was on a plane to Bogotá. After arriving, he was driven ninety minutes south to the town of Macerta where Colombian rebels had taken students hostage at a school operated under the auspices of the United Nations education division.

Riaz leaned closer and lowered his voice. "I'm going to tell you something, Inspector," he said. "You see that man over there, standing behind our line?"

Ben followed Riaz's eyes, grateful to be out of reach of the colonel's foul-smelling breath, and focused on a well-dressed man with high cheekbones and powerful Indian features.

"I see him."

"His name is Pablo Salgado, Inspector. He is a top official in what's left of the Medellín cartel. Salgado's son is among the hostages."

"What does that have to do with anything?"

"This is a personal matter, a *drug* matter. This was a kidnapping gone wrong. What it becomes now," Riaz added with a shrug, "it becomes."

"Salgado's son is in first grade, Colonel. I doubt very much he even knows what drugs are."

"This is Colombia, Inspector. Sometimes it is better to let these things work out by themselves."

"Do you think the parents of the other thirteen children would agree with you?"

"Their opinions are unimportant," Riaz said.

Ben nodded tightly. "So the gunmen kill Salgado's son and Salgado takes his revenge. . . ."

Riaz's eyebrows flickered. "That's what the Americans want, isn't it?"

"I'm American."

"I'm sorry. You look . . ."

"*Palestinian*-American."

"Oh," Riaz said, and left it there.

"This has been going on for seventy-two hours now, Colonel. They ran out of food and water twelve hours ago, which means you're running out of time."

"That's the idea."

Ben looked toward Pablo Salgado, struggling to light a cigarette in a trembling hand, his own soldiers who had accompanied him powerless to do anything but hold the match. He saw Salgado as a man, a father.

Ben turned back toward Riaz. "They've asked for food."

"Yes."

"And you've refused."

"Of course. My troops are in position, señor. I expect to receive the okay to storm the building once night falls."

Ben's mouth tightened. He checked the sky. Another

ninety minutes of light, two hours at the outside. Riaz wouldn't be too concerned about casualties; he had already made that clear. Ben looked toward Salgado, a father about to lose a son to another kind of senseless war.

Ben yanked the cell phone from Riaz's belt and thrust it toward him. "There's been a change in plans. Tell the men inside the food is coming."

Riaz gave Ben a long look and snickered, flashing a set of yellowed teeth. "You have no authority here, Inspector. You are strictly an observer."

"And right now I'm observing a man on the verge of causing the United Nations to pull out of his country in total," Ben said, counting on the chance that Riaz didn't see through his bluff. "How do you think your government would feel about that, Colonel?"

Riaz's face reddened. "What do you want, señor?" he asked, barely able to contain his anger.

"To deliver the food they've been asking for."

Riaz caught the look in Ben's eyes and nodded slowly. "My men will not help you. You're on your own."

Ben continued holding the phone out until Riaz snatched it from him. "That's nothing new."

CHAPTER 3

Mohammed Sahib yanked open the warehouse door and, smiling, beckoned the woman to follow him inside.

"Is better than what you were expecting, yes?"

Danielle Barnea eyed the huge stacks of flour, foodstuffs, and seed.

"You wish to inspect? Please, please . . ."

Danielle moved closer to the sacks, each of them clearly stamped with the United Nations insignia. Outside, the last of the Somali day was fading fast, leaving behind steam-baked air that smelled to Danielle like burning rubber. In these same Mogadishu streets, eighteen American Special Operations troops had lost their lives more than a decade before. That reminded Danielle of some of the ill-fated missions she had been lucky to survive during her days with Israel's Sayaret Matkal, the elite Special Ops force responsible for actions undertaken outside the country. That seemed like a lifetime ago now. So much had come and gone that had led to this operation, brought her here not on behalf of Israel, but the United Nations. Ten months and at least that many assignments for the U.N.'s Safety and Security Service, and it still felt odd.

"You like?" Sahib asked, startling her. He had drawn up close while her mind had been wandering and the smell rising off him was a combination of onions and cheap tobacco.

His face was thin, depressions worn into the center of both cheeks that deepened each time he flashed a smile.

She stepped lithely to one side and he tapped one of the sacks, as Danielle watched. He had what looked like a .45 caliber pistol shoved down his baggy pants that billowed over his gaunt frame.

"Is perfect arrangement, yes? United Nations sends for people. We steal before it gets to people. Sell low to brokers who sell high. Everybody win. Makes me feel like capitalist."

Sahib smiled again, his teeth blindingly white.

Danielle ran her eyes about the warehouse, cataloging everything for her report. She counted four armed guards in addition to Sahib, none of them paying much attention, their assault rifles shouldered. The missing shipments had been plaguing the United Nations for years, boatloads of goods that never reached the poor and needy they were supposed to aid. It was estimated by some that fifty percent of all U.N. shipments to Third World countries like Somalia ended up in the hands of black marketeers, corrupt government officials, or a combination thereof.

"I have medicines too, antibiotics. Good ones. You like?"

Danielle turned back to Sahib. "Not this trip."

"We ship anywhere, by boat or plane. Just like FedEx. Plane costs more."

Danielle kept scanning the room, counting the sacks in her mind for her report. Her job here was done. Her cover had held and she had made contact with Sahib, something no other United Nations operative had managed to do. Now she would give Sahib a deposit and provide him with shipping instructions. The balance, of course, would never be paid. The shipping instructions were a sham. U.N. peacekeeping troops stationed twenty miles to the north would seize the stolen goods as soon as she provided the location of the warehouse and security posted in the area.

A high-pitched horn honked behind her and Danielle

turned to see an ancient, weathered cargo truck waiting outside the warehouse.

"You will excuse me, yes?"

With that, Sahib trotted away from her and reverently greeted a stout man who had emerged from the passenger side of the truck, preceded by a figure who was clearly his bodyguard as well as driver. The stout man embraced Sahib lightly and then stepped back into Danielle's line of vision.

She felt something shift in her stomach. The stout man was Sharif ali-Aziz Moussan, an Iraqi terrorist with strong links to al-Qaeda. Rumors that he had been killed during the American invasion had been unfounded, leaving him as one of Iraq's most sought-after fugitives still at large.

Moussan spoke softly to Sahib. The Somali smiled tensely, his gaze drifting briefly back to Danielle as he explained her presence here. Moussan nodded, apparently satisfied, while Danielle bemoaned the fact she had come here unarmed in the guise of a conduit and broker. After all, this was purely an intelligence-gathering mission; her job was to turn over whatever she learned for further action and no more.

But Sharif ali-Aziz Moussan would be long gone by the time that further action transpired. She watched Sahib lead Moussan toward another section of the warehouse. The bodyguard who had emerged from the truck ahead of Moussan stepped out of the shadows and fell into step behind them.

Danielle's heart fluttered. She recognized him as well. The man's name was Hassan Tariq, a colonel in Iraq's Special Republican Guard, a man who had personally supervised the guerrilla war waged against American and British troops that had been raging since Baghdad fell.

Across the warehouse, Danielle watched Sahib yank back a thick canvas divider to reveal stacks and stacks of weapons ordnance. Too far away to discern anything more specific than that, she drifted closer, keeping behind some semblance of cover as best she could. The language denoting the contents of the crates was French, not a total surprise considering France's propensity for selling to anyone who could pay. So far as she knew, though, the French arms traders had never done business in this part of the world, meaning this particular shipment must have come from somewhere else or been stolen in transit. Then again, it was also possible the shipment had been smuggled out of Iraq in the early days of the war and brought here for safekeeping until such time as the weapons were needed.

Danielle could read French well enough to recognize the markings on the various crates and boxes: ammunition, assault rifles, grenades, antitank weapons—the crates contained everything a small army needed to wage war, she realized, as Moussan swung suddenly and thrust a finger in her direction.

CHAPTER 4

Ben wheeled the cart loaded with sandwiches and drinks across a gravel playground toward the school. He passed a set of swings which swayed in the light wind and a seesaw flopping slowly up and down. One of the cart's wheels kept sticking against the gravel and the extra weight of the bucket of ice on the lower shelf made the effort more cumbersome than he had expected. Still, the fact that the school's electricity, and with it the air conditioning, had been turned off hours before would make the ice very welcome indeed.

A door was thrust open when Ben drew within ten feet of the building. He veered the cart slightly, having aimed it toward a larger set of double doors closer to the classroom where the hostages had been gathered. There was a slight incline the last stretch of the way, and a few of the sandwich trays shifted, nearly sliding over the cart's small raised lip. Ben held them in place with one hand as he drew near the door, then had to shimmy the cart carefully over the doorjamb to get it into the building.

Ice cubes rattled, jangling against each other. The door slammed closed. Ben felt a pistol barrel smack against his temple. He was torn from the cart and pressed up against the wall.

"Who are you?"

"I don't speak Spanish."

"What then?"

"English."

A powerful hand spun him around. "Who are you?" a dark face set against the even darker hallway demanded in English.

"United Nations! I'm from the U.N. An observer."

The man looked him over and snickered. "Too late to make peace."

"It's never too late," Ben said, as the gunman riffled through the sandwiches stacked atop the trays.

Ben held his breath and started to slide back toward the door. Almost instantly, the gunman's hand lashed out and pinned him against the wall again.

"Where you going, Mr. U.N.?"

"I got you the food you requested. My job is done."

"Not anymore, Mr. Observer," the gunman said, his mind working. "You come with me and we find a new job for you."

He smiled, clearly pleased with himself, and prodded Ben back to the cart, pushing him forward when Ben began to wheel it down the white concrete floor.

The classroom was five doors down, darkened save for a few candles and stray flashlight beams, the windows covered by a combination of blinds and black construction paper. The gunman shoved Ben into the room and the cart nearly spilled over.

"¿José, quién es este gringo?"

José offered his explanation to a tall, thin man dressed in army fatigues. The tall man nodded at the mention of the United Nations, seemed to approve. Then he reached down and grabbed a sandwich in a filthy hand.

"You eat," he ordered Ben, thrusting it in his face.

Ben took a bite. The luncheon meat, whatever it was, tasted awful, but it wasn't poisoned. Ben chewed slowly, scrutinizing the scene around him. The other two terrorists were positioned in opposite corners of the darkened room. The children, terrified and sobbing but hopeful at the sight of the food, sat at their desks, which had been clustered into a circle in the center. The room stank of sweat and fear. Ben noticed a few pools of urine on the floor.

He swallowed, took another bite.

"Enough," the tall man said, snatching up a few sandwiches for himself. "Children come up and you give them."

"I brought drinks too. Soda," Ben said, and watched the tall man's eyes move to the cart's lower shelf too. "It's warm."

"No shit."

"But I have ice."

The tall man gave the cart's lower shelf a closer look before diving his hand down into the bucket of already melting cubes. Ben sucked in his breath, fearing the tall man would find the pistol concealed in a plastic bag amidst the ice. But he came away only with a handful of cubes and swabbed them along his face, leaving streaks of dirt behind as he moved away and left Ben alone near the cart.

José, meanwhile, herded the kids from their chairs into a stiff, single line. Ben searched the young faces for Salgado's son, couldn't decide which one he was.

Just a little closer, he willed. *A few more seconds . . .*

Ben reached down and dug some ice out into the first plastic cup. Handed it to the first boy in line, along with a soda can and a sandwich. The two terrorists in either far corner were both eating now, the tall man halfway back to the cart when Ben finished serving the second boy and reached down to get the third a cup of ice along with a drink.

Now! It has to be now!

Ben thrust his hand into the ice, deep to the bottom of the bucket, and closed it around the plastic bag containing the nine-millimeter pistol Colonel Riaz had reluctantly provided. His fingers sloshed through more water than he had expected, making him fear the possibility that the gun would jam once he tore it free of the plastic. In the shadow of an instant, he hesitated, then focused again on the two guards in the room's rear corners busy with their sandwiches. Ben's eyes had adjusted well enough to the murky light now, the positions of his targets etched onto his mind.

Ben peeled the plastic bag open and slipped the nine-millimeter free. Then he drew the gun from the bucket, squeezing hard to keep the frigid water from turning his fingers slow and stiff. He brought it up ready to fire, turning it on the tall man first since he appeared to be the leader.

The roar was deafening and the gun's kick was greater than he had expected. The tall man's eyes bulged in shock as he was pushed backward into the wall, hands clutching for the jagged hole that had appeared in his shirt.

Ears still ringing, Ben twisted and shot José in the face. He could hear the children screaming now, even while he opened fire on the terrorist in the nearer corner, catching him between mouthfuls and before he could trade his sandwich for the assault rifle slung behind him.

The terrorist in the opposite corner, though, had time to bring his rifle around and start shooting before Ben could resteady his pistol. The staccato burst of automatic fire burned through his already clouded hearing and Ben hit the floor in time to hear the chalkboard at his rear explode under the fusillade. He rolled once and came to a halt firing.

Click.

The trigger felt like a lead weight. The pistol had jammed and Ben discarded it. Over his head another spray of fire dug chasms from the wall. He heard the familiar rattle of a spent clip ejecting, followed by the clack of a fresh one being snapped home, and rolled toward the tall man he had shot in the chest.

The tall man still had his submachine gun shouldered and Ben went for it, realizing too late it was pinned under his body. No way he could wrench the barrel any way but straight up. He pulled the trigger instantly, doing his best to hit the overhead lights.

The sound of glass breaking joined the childrens' screams and the din of the gunshots reverberating through the room.

The glass rained down on the final gunman, distracting him long enough for Ben to tear the submachine gun from the leader's shoulder. He hit the trigger again and watched the bullets spin the final gunman around in his tracks, resembling a twisted marionette as he smacked into a desk and toppled over on the floor. At that very instant, the door to the room burst open and Colombian soldiers flooded in, led by Colonel Riaz who quickly assessed the situation and ordered his men to stand down.

"I see you did exactly as I instructed, Inspector Kamal," Riaz said, reaching a hand down to help Ben up from the floor. "Very good work."

CHAPTER 5

"W hat is she doing here?" Moussan demanded, fixing his piercing eyes on Danielle.

"I'll take the whole shipment," she said to Sahib, ignoring Moussan, Tariq, and the weapons supply they had come to procure. "How fast can we arrange for—"

"This will have to wait," Sahib interrupted. "Something else has . . . I am sorry. You understand, yes?"

He grabbed her arm and began to usher her from the warehouse, toward Sharif ali-Aziz Moussan's truck that would soon be packed with enough weapons to destabilize Baghdad anew. Hassan Tariq watched her the whole way, suspicion dawning in his eyes.

"I will have you taken to a local hotel to wait," Sahib continued. "I will come for you once this business is complete."

Sahib whistled for one of his guards. The man hurried over, shifting his rifle from his right shoulder to his left. Sahib jabbered some terse instructions and the man nodded his understanding. Then Sahib forced a smile and jogged back toward Moussan, leaving Danielle alone with the guard.

She followed him out of the warehouse toward a dust-covered sedan parked down the street. The man moved to the driver's door, paying her no heed, and started to ease himself inside.

Danielle pounced, the moves unfolding before she had a chance to contemplate them, instinct taking over. She saw herself slamming the door when he was halfway in the car, catching the man partly on the hip and partly on the gun he had forgotten to strip from his shoulder.

He grunted, more in surprise than pain, and twisted toward Danielle. She cracked him in the face with an elbow, slammed his face down on the steering wheel, then yanked his limp frame backward and let it slump toward the console.

Next Danielle pried his assault rifle free. She felt the surge of adrenaline slow, leaving cold reason in its place. Sahib still had three guards in the warehouse, not to mention Moussan himself and the deadly Tariq. Danielle didn't like the odds of a shoot-out, considered the more explosive option of setting the warehouse ablaze. Burn the weapons and think of all the lives that would now be spared as a result. She could live with that.

But in that case Moussan and Tariq would both likely escape, and that she could not live with.

Danielle reached back into the car and swept her palm across the guard's bloodied face. Her fingers came away wet and warm, and she splattered the blood across her own face. Its acrid stench turned her stomach as she felt along his belt for the pistol she remembered seeing there.

Nothing. And nothing on the seats or floor either. It must have been a different guard she was thinking of, and now a key element of her plan was forfeit. Danielle refocused her thinking and circled round to the passenger side of the car. She stuck a hand through the window and popped open the glove compartment.

A semiautomatic pistol lay there, rusty black and dull from poor upkeep. Danielle took the pistol in her hand, checked its heft. She had never heard of the maker before and didn't like the feel. But the clip was full and she jerked the slide backward to chamber the first round before jamming the pistol low on her hip, easily hidden by her sweat-soaked shirt.

Danielle started back toward the warehouse, staggering, bloodied, and seemingly in a panic.

"Help me," she gasped to the first pair of Sahib's guards to emerge from inside, collapsing to her knees. A third emerged and began scanning the street.

All three skirted past her, not stopping, and darted into the street. Sahib emerged next, followed closely by Moussan and Tariq, who had drawn and steadied his own weapon.

"My God," Sahib said, crouching when he saw her bloodied shape on the ground.

As he leaned toward her, Danielle reached up and grabbed him round the throat, spinning him before her as she lurched to her feet. Danielle shot Sahib's three guards in rapid succession first, then swung toward Tariq. Tariq opened fire just as Sahib attempted to flee, his route taking him right into the path of the bullets, the force of which threw him into Danielle.

Ears ringing madly, Danielle shed Sahib from her. When she looked up she saw Tariq dragging Moussan back inside the warehouse. But Moussan stumbled and fell. Tariq had leaned over to help him when a fresh barrage from Danielle chased him into the half-light of the cluttered warehouse. Moussan rolled across the pavement, trying to regain his feet. By then, though, Danielle was upon him. She grabbed his collar and jerked him to his feet by the scruff of the neck, all the time holding her gun on the doorway in case Tariq reappeared.

Moussan looked at her with a mixture of hate and shock and spat out something in Arabic. Danielle smacked his temple with the butt of her pistol, just as Tariq lunged out from inside the warehouse. She fired, yanking Moussan backward toward his truck, keeping his body between herself and the sliding door. Tariq hesitated, got off a single wild barrage before Danielle heard the click of his magazine being expended.

She chose that moment to shove Moussan into the truck's cab ahead of her. He lurched across the seat, trying to force her back into the street. Danielle fastened one hand tight on the steering wheel and struck Moussan with the pistol again, hard enough to knock him unconscious this time.

Moussan flopped against the passenger-side window, as she twisted the key and gunned the engine. Screeched into reverse, then ground the gears with a too-fast shift into first. The truck's tires spun, then grabbed. She caught sight in the side-view mirror of Tariq charging after them, opening fire anew, and shoved her foot down on the accelerator. The increasing gap between them sent his bullets sailing harmlessly off target, and Danielle sped off into the heat of the Mogadishu day.

She had already memorized the routes of the back and side roads, just in case she needed to make use of them. The United Nations force to which she was supposed to report was stationed twenty miles to the north, expecting a simple intelligence briefing.

They were about to get much more, Danielle thought, gazing at the limp form of Sharif ali-Aziz Moussan slumped next to her in the front seat.

DAY THREE

The Israeli soldier slammed Ben Kamal against the side of the truck, holding him there while a second soldier frisked him roughly.

"Maybe you should check my identification again," Ben said, as calmly as he could manage.

"The name would still be Arab."

Ben turned just enough to look one of the soldiers in the eye. "Palestinian actually."

"Even worse."

"It's a United Nations identification."

"Worse still," one of the soldiers said, and they both laughed. "We were told to expect you."

"Told you used to be a detective in the West Bank."

"Then you should have also been told to clear him through the checkpoint."

The voice startled the soldiers and they swung to see a tall woman leaning against the side of a Humvee with United Nations markings. The sleeves of her shirt were rolled up past the elbows to reveal a pair of forearms once perpetually tan but now forever pale. Her dark hair shifted about her shoulders, tossed by the stiff crosswind that swirled over the hilltop.

"I'm Inspector Danielle Barnea, also attached to the United Nations."

The soldier holding Ben let go and stepped away from the

truck. "Yes, Ms. Barnea. We were told to expect you as well."

"That's *Commander* Barnea. I still retain my rank in Israel."

"Of course, Commander," the sergeant said, nodding sheepishly. "There's an escort waiting for you at the top of the hill. He'll lead you the rest of the way into the village."

Ben joined Danielle at the Humvee. She opened the rear door for him and he climbed in ahead of her.

"I'm glad they didn't ask what I was doing here," Ben said, as their U.N. driver eased the Humvee past the soldiers and continued up the hill.

"I don't know any more than you," Danielle told him. She had arrived at an airstrip reserved for Israeli military and United Nations personnel less than an hour earlier, having been rushed by helicopter out of Somalia after turning Sharif ali-Aziz Moussan over to U.N. authorities north of Mogadishu. Based on what she knew about procedure these days, Moussan would already be on his way to Guantánamo Bay, Cuba, where he would join the bulk of al-Qaeda and top Iraqi prisoners detained there. "A massacre in a Palestinian village, that's all I was told."

"But, of all people, why send us to investigate it?" Ben wondered, shoulders stiff against the seat back.

They'd been aching ever since his escapade at the school in Colombia. It felt as though he'd been in a car accident. Unlike Danielle, he had been whisked to the airport and placed on a commercial flight bound for New York City where he transferred to an El Al flight into Tel Aviv. The irony of traveling on Israel's national airline was not lost on him; in his role as a Palestinian detective, just a few years before, it would have been unthinkable. Still, once arriving at Ben-Gurion Airport he'd been detained for three hours in a windowless cubicle while Israeli officials confirmed his identity and U.N. visa.

"Why bother sending any U.N. personnel?" Danielle added.

In the ten months she and Ben had been working for the U.N.'s Safety and Security Service, neither had investigated a single murder, never mind a massacre. The service was normally called into action when serious crimes were committed on territory either controlled or administered by the U.N. Most often these crimes involved U.N. peacekeeping troops or relief workers, either as victims or perpetrators. And the investigations were inevitably contentious, riddled by jurisdictional squabbles with host governments. What had been proven so true at the local level seemed equally true on the international level: nobody likes a cop.

Danielle looked at Ben and smiled tightly. "I heard about Colombia."

"I heard about Somalia. Nice work."

"Likewise. It's good to see you out from behind that desk."

"If they'd assigned you to Baghdad with me . . ."

"Then they wouldn't have listened to either one of us, instead of just you."

"No one ever considered the possibility I was right, what that might mean Saddam's regime was storing beneath the U.N. compound when it was still the Canal Hotel."

Danielle's eyes scolded him gently. "The United Nations has no power, Ben. You were assigned there as window dressing, a respected name to use in photo captions."

"That didn't come with the job description."

"It never does. Now tell me about Colombia."

"Window dressing was better."

Danielle looked at Ben quizzically, waiting for him to continue on his own.

"I've never walked into that kind of situation knowing how it was going to end before," Ben said, once the tale was complete.

She shook her head. "You've lost me."

"I entered that school knowing I was going to start shooting."

"You didn't like the feeling."

"Not at all."

"I'd like to say you get used to it, that it gets easier with time. But I can't, because it doesn't. You do what you have to do—that's all," Danielle said, thinking of her own experience in Mogadishu. "You did what you knew you had to, just like Baghdad."

Ben thought of the look on Pablo Salgado's face when his son emerged from the building. All the while he embraced the boy, he kept his eyes locked gratefully on Ben's. Ultimately they nodded at each other and Salgado led the boy off out of the reach of the authorities and Colonel Riaz. Ben, too, was hustled away before being questioned, and at first he blamed the U.N.'s desire to avoid a diplomatic incident.

Then an attaché had delivered the emergency orders that had brought him back to Palestine. He felt a welter of mixed emotions since he had resigned himself to never again seeing his homeland after he departed two years before. He had not missed it as much as he thought he would. Just the smells mostly, except for the now all-too-common stench of gunpowder.

"This is your first time back, too," Ben said, running the calculations in his head once more. "What's it been, a year?"

"Eleven months." She sighed. "You wouldn't know I left here commander of National Police."

"Maybe they think you've come back here to collect your pension."

Danielle forced a smile. "My name has probably been expunged from every database in Jerusalem. When I found out they were sending me here, I tried to think of people to call and couldn't think of a single one. Sad, isn't it?"

Ben shrugged. "A way of life for me."

"Sorry."

"No need to apologize."

He reached out and squeezed Danielle's hand. They'd spent barely a week together in the past six months at the London apartment they shared. Strange, since they had accepted the U.N. Security Chief Alexis Arguayo's offer because they thought it would afford them more opportunity to be together. That hadn't proven the case yet, though, and they both found it painfully ironic to be brought together now in the part of the world they had been forced to flee.

"Do you know anything about this village?" Danielle wondered.

"Bureij consists of olive farmers mostly," Ben told her. "A thousand hilly acres of the finest groves in the West Bank. Lots of problems with water, though. Accusations a few years ago they were stealing from a pipeline that ran through a neighboring Israeli settlement."

"True?"

"Probably. But the pipeline rerouted a supply deeded to Bureij after Oslo."

"Lots of things have changed since Oslo."

"Including the village's population, as I recall. Down to less than a thousand, I think."

"To farm a thousand acres of olive trees?"

Ben stared at her flatly. "The settlers burned half of them just over a year ago. Could be they're the ones to blame for the massacre. These things have a way of getting out of hand."

"If this were a settler issue, the army would have assumed jurisdiction. The U.N. would have sent observers, not investigators."

"Meaning?"

Before Danielle could answer, their Humvee braked to halt on the crest of a hill alongside a cream-colored Mercedes SUV. The Israeli soldier behind the wheel cocked his head backward.

"They will take you the rest of the way," he offered simply and turned away again.

Ben and Danielle climbed out of the Humvee and approached the Mercedes, watching the rear left window slide down.

"Why us?" Ben repeated. "That's what I still can't understand."

"Then permit me to explain," greeted Colonel Nabril al-Asi, as he threw open the door.

I t's been too long, Inspector," al-Asi said, hugging Ben tightly. "And you, Chief Inspector," he followed, turning to Danielle, "it looks like working for the U.N. has agreed wonderfully with you." He kissed her lightly on the cheek and held her hands briefly before stepping back so he was centered between the two of them. "Just like old times, eh?" he quipped.

Al-Asi had once headed the powerful Palestinian Preventive Security Service, the equivalent in its heyday of Yassir Arafat's secret police. In that position he had been among the most feared and respected of any Palestinian official, until a combination of Israeli incursions and Palestinian Authority impotence destroyed his organization and stripped him of his power. From a hunter, the colonel became the hunted, especially when his antimilitant stand ran him afoul of just about all his former enemies and allies alike.

But the transitional process that had begun with the appointment of a Palestinian prime minister brought al-Asi back into the government as minister of the interior, giving him the unenviable task of organizing the Palestinian Authority's twelve disparate security agencies into a coherent whole. The only correspondence Ben and Danielle had had with him was a Christmas card featuring the colonel with his wife and three children, together again and all smiling. There was no return address. Ben still wondered how the colonel had managed to track down theirs in London.

"Now I know why we're here," Ben said, looking at Danielle.

"I don't," she followed. "U.N. detectives called in to investigate a massacre in a Palestinian village?" She shook her head. "The Israeli government would never allow it."

A familiar sparkle appeared in al-Asi's deep-set, hooded eyes. "Unless they had no choice. Unless two of the victims of the massacre were U.N. relief workers."

Ben and Danielle glanced at each other. The UNRWA, United Nations Relief and Works Agency, was one of the primary factors in the festering and increasingly contentious relationship between Israel and the United Nations. Ever since a U.N. resolution had effectively created the State of Israel in 1948, the common thinking among Israelis was that the organization had evolved into nothing more than a mouthpiece for the Palestinian viewpoint, lacking in both credibility and objectivity. And those here under the auspices of the UNRWA were believed to be the prime offenders, offering up a biased and one-sided view of both Israeli-Palestinian relations and the Palestinian predicament.

"In that case, finding two detectives to represent the United Nations who were both qualified and reasonably acceptable to both sides would be a virtual impossibility." The colonel's thick hair was now evenly mixed black and gray, and Ben noticed his mustache had begun to gray as well, making him look older. But his cool demeanor, so quashed during his period in effective exile, had returned. "I thought immediately of you, of course," al-Asi continued. "Who better suited to conduct such a sensitive investigation? Besides, it gives us the chance to work together again."

"Of course, Colonel," Danielle started, "since we're here on your recommendation, it assures your continued involvement in the investigation."

Al-Asi's eyes flashed devilishly. "That thought did cross my mind, Chief Inspector. Now, let us review the facts."

He moved toward the edge of the hill, Ben and Danielle

quickly falling in behind him. Below lay a rolling expanse of green olive groves amidst which rested the village of Bureij. Almost directly across from them, on a twin hillside, stood the sprawling Israeli settlement of Nabokim.

"We know that yesterday morning," al-Asi continued, "an Israeli troop detachment stormed the village in search of a suspected militant named Rahim Naddahr. In the process of searching for this militant, many of the village's residents were rounded up and herded into the street under great protest. We know at some point these protests became heated and shots were fired. When the firing stopped, thirty-two Palestinians and two UNRWA teachers were dead."

"What does the Israeli army say?" asked Danielle.

"They categorically deny everything. Claim they had no movements in this area yesterday and that all their troops were accounted for."

"A rogue unit?"

"They claim to be looking into that possibility. I don't believe it will lead anywhere."

Danielle followed al-Asi's gaze across the olive groves, considering the prospects. If true, Bureij would rival the infamous 1948 massacre in Deir Yasin, a Palestinian village just outside Jerusalem, as a dark blotch on Israel's history that would haunt the nation for years to come. The international outcry would be catastrophic, further isolating Israel from the international community and severely straining relations with even the United States. But that was nothing compared to the Palestinian response, which could incite unprecedented levels of violence and require an equally unprecedented Israeli response, negating the slim progress achieved over recent months.

Ben drew up alongside the colonel, ignoring the valley beyond. "You think the Israelis are covering up?"

"It is something they are very good at, Inspector."

"Not this time," Danielle insisted flatly. The harshness of her tone surprised both al-Asi and Ben, and they looked at each other before turning toward her. "I still have some sources in Israel, Colonel, and they claim the IDF is as baffled by this as everyone else."

Al-Asi shrugged. "I'll grant you the fact that your countrymen haven't circled the wagons, as the Americans say; nor have they paraded out a slew of officials to offer the typically alternate version of events. That says we're facing a very complicated scenario here."

"And what does the evidence on the scene say?" Danielle asked.

Al-Asi smiled and gazed at both of them. "That I should call the two of you."

CHAPTER 8

You need to understand the gravity of what we're facing here," the colonel said, as he drove the Mercedes SUV toward the village, his driver left on the hill above. "Under our new prime minister, Israelis and Palestinians have made some strides over the past months, or let us say things have not regressed further. But it's fragile and the situation is more volatile than ever." He glanced at Danielle in the passenger seat, Ben in the rear. "This massacre is sure to embolden the militants to launch a new wave of suicide bombings. And, as we speak, Israel is massing forces in unprecedented numbers, prepared to quell any uprising through whatever means are necessary." Al-Asi paused and took a deep breath. "I'm told those means may include the forcible expulsion of all Palestinians from the West Bank."

Ben leaned forward. "That information came from a reliable source, I assume."

"Absolutely. The first four times he told the same tale over the years, it was disinformation meant to scare me. This time it's not."

"How do you know that?"

"Because this time, it was he who was scared."

On the roads before them, Israeli troops rimmed the perimeter of Bureij, enforcing a general curfew to keep all residents in and all other parties, including the media for now, out. Ben and Danielle's U.N. IDs were examined yet again at checkpoints both on the outskirts and inside of the village, passed back to them on both occasions accompanied by a scowl that was becoming rapidly familiar.

It seemed as though the soldiers were less bothered by Colonel al-Asi's presence here than that of two U.N. investigators—not a total surprise given the fact that United Nations officials were held in even less esteem than Palestinians. At least, it was said, Israel knew what to expect from Palestinians, while the U.N.'s agenda was more complicated and obtuse. There had been talk in Parliament for a while of expelling United Nations representatives from the West Bank and Gaza, discussions that were extinguished only when prevailing legal opinion indicated Israel did not have the authority to do so.

Once they were allowed through, al-Asi drove Ben and Danielle to a central square that in better times had served as the village bazaar. Bureij for years prior to the current ongoing conflict had enjoyed a good relationship with the neighboring Jewish settlement, as well as a number of nearby Israeli towns. The village had relied on these to patronize the bazaar, and many of the villagers had relied on the bazaar to supplement their meager livelihoods. But it was empty today, the lines of pushcarts, kiosks, and tables full of wares and market produce present only in memory.

"This is where the bodies were found," the colonel explained as he drew the Mercedes SUV to a halt. "There were well over a hundred in the square at the time, all rounded up by the soldiers."

"Or men posing as soldiers," Danielle reminded.

"Of course," al-Asi said, with just the slightest hint of sarcasm, as he climbed out. "I forgot."

Danielle and Ben followed him from the SUV, instantly noticing a number of well-spaced Israeli soldiers hanging discreetly back along the adjoining streets.

"No reason to doubt the identity of those," Ben noted.

"Or their purpose in being here," Danielle added. "Right, Colonel?"

"I was warned the movements of the U.N. investigative team would be closely monitored," al-Asi told her.

"And if the U.N. had dispatched different investigators?"

"Then, Chief Inspector," the colonel responded, still addressing Danielle by the rank she'd held with the National Police when they first met, "I suspect there wouldn't have been any movements worth monitoring. That's precisely why the two of you are here."

Danielle turned her eyes from the windblown dust of the square and brushed aside some stray hairs that had wandered across her face. Along the street, she caught glimpses of frightened faces pressed against windowpanes or narrow slits in wooden shutters, all chased inside by the Israeli curfew.

"Has anyone spoken to potential witnesses?" Ben asked.

"The Israelis have."

"Not you?"

"The witnesses have been taken into what the Israelis are calling 'protective custody.'"

"We'll need to interview them."

"You might find access extremely difficult to obtain."

"Then we'll build our case elsewhere." Danielle twisted to face Colonel al-Asi straight on, her eyes harsh and relentless. Looking at him as anything but the close ally he had proven himself to be over the years. "What can we be sure of, Colonel? What isn't open to interpretation?"

Al-Asi sighed and glanced about to make sure all the posted Israeli soldiers were well out of earshot. Still, he lowered his voice. "That the perpetrators spoke Hebrew to each other. That their uniforms were Israeli army issue, their weapons American-made M-16s."

"The ballistic reports have already confirmed that?" Danielle asked him.

"There are no ballistic reports, Chief Inspector. The Israelis took possession of the bodies and are holding them at an undisclosed location. I, though, was able to recover some errant bullets from the sides of buildings. They were 5.56-millimeter, consistent with American-made M-16s carried by the majority of IDF forces."

"Lots of weapons take 5.56-millimeter load."

Al-Asi's expression didn't change. "There is also the matter of the boot prints," the colonel continued. "The grid design was consistent with a line manufactured in the factory district south of Tel Aviv. Palestinians used to make up the primary workforce at that plant. Now, I understand, Russian immigrants have taken their place. I'd be worried about quality control if I were you, Chief Inspector."

"What were the names of the U.N. teachers killed?" Danielle asked him.

"David Lister and Franklin Salemme," al-Asi replied. "I left their files in the car."

"All right, so here's what we know," Ben said, and began walking the perimeter of the central square, careful to skirt the white tape strung round waist-high stakes that cordoned off the actual crime scene. Inside, fluorescent tags flapped like flags atop tiny poles driven into the street to denote the positions and identities of the massacre's victims. "The soldiers, or those dressed like soldiers, rolled into town in search of this wanted militant Naddahr. In trying to find him, they herded the villagers out of their homes and brought them here."

"What did this Naddahr do?" Danielle asked suddenly.

"He is accused of orchestrating simultaneous suicide bombings six months ago," al-Asi told her.

"Guilty?"

"Almost certainly, Chief Inspector. Naddahr was born in Bureij. The soldiers claimed to have hot intelligence that he had returned to the village to visit his parents."

"You, or the Israelis, have looked into that, I assume."

"I can't, Chief Inspector." Al-Asi pointed toward a pair of fluorescent tags flapping ceaselessly in the relentless wind. "Both Naddahr's parents were killed in the massacre."

Ben turned once again toward al-Asi. "How many villagers did you say were gathered here?"

"Nearly two hundred at the time the shooting began."

"Packed loosely in a circle," Danielle concluded from the dispersal of bodies. "Not the way I would arrange them if I intended a massacre."

"No one is gauging intent here, Inspector, only results."

"Does that include us, Colonel?" Danielle asked him sharply.

Ben shifted sideways to position himself between them. "This is how your army conducts such an incursion, isn't it, Danielle?"

She followed his gaze into the cordoned-off portion of the square and nodded. "Pretty much, yes."

"Then something had to spark the shooting. What do the witnesses say about that, Colonel?"

Al-Asi glanced toward Danielle before responding. "That the soldiers simply started firing."

"Without any provocation whatsoever?"

"None."

"Any weapons found among the victims?"

"Israeli officials haven't said. Those who tended initially to the bodies say no."

"Which means nothing," Danielle insisted, sounding even more caustic. "If there was provocation, shots fired, it could have come just as easily from others in the crowd who managed to get away."

"The Israelis searched the homes and confiscated all weapons they could find," al-Asi reported, "intending to test them to see if any had been fired recently."

"Don't tell me," said Ben. "Results still pending."

"I was thinking the two of you would prefer to have your own tests conducted, anyway."

Danielle frowned. "On weapons we don't have?"

Al-Asi smiled slightly. "The Israelis didn't find all the weapons, Chief Inspector."

I managed to locate the rest," the colonel continued. "But there's no reason for you to test them."

"Why?" Danielle asked him, as Ben drifted off toward the contingent of media that had just been allowed in to witness the U.N. investigators on scene, doing their job with no interference by Israeli authorities. Cameras flashed and whirred. A media truck for a network pool feed was the only vehicle on the street other than army issue and the colonel's Mercedes SUV.

Al-Asi's eyebrows flickered. "Because I already have, and none of them have been fired, Chief Inspector."

"That doesn't prove anything."

"It proves the guns I recovered from hiding weren't used to provoke the soldiers. That's all," the colonel said calmly.

"You know how my country works, Colonel," Danielle said, her tone icy.

"Intimately."

"Then you should know that if the IDF was responsible for this, there would already be a cover story, at least the semblance of one, in place. Israelis make very good shots, Colonel, but we make even better storytellers. When we say nothing, it's because we're confused, caught off guard by something."

"I'd say something like this qualifies there."

"Twenty-four hours ago it did. But now, more than a day later?" Danielle shook her head. "They'd have everything in place by now. No, the absence of a lie concerns me more than your boot prints and bullets."

"I trust you're not speaking from experience, Chief Inspector."

"Oh, but I am, Colonel: twice with National Police I arrested soldiers or government officials involved in fabricating tales to cover their own asses."

Al-Asi and Danielle held each other's stares, neither seeming to breathe. Ben looked back at Danielle from his position near the media contingent. She was wearing her auburn hair cropped slightly shorter than it had been. Her khaki slacks and white shirt looked perfectly tailored to a frame no less lean and muscular than the last time he had seen her, evidence of many hours spent in the gym. Working out for Ben, on the other hand, had become too much of a memory as of late. Passing forty in itself had not sparked any internal crisis, other than the realization that he had now outlived his legendary father. There was something cruel and unjust about that. Too often lately Ben found himself gazing into the mirror to compare himself to the great Jafir Kamal, hoping to find a resemblance where none had previously existed. He couldn't say why the lack of one had been bothering him so much lately, unless he had foolishly expected that reaching his father's age would somehow make him more like Jafir Kamal.

Ben strolled back and immediately sensed the tension between Danielle and al-Asi. "Were any children among the victims?" he asked the colonel.

His question had the desired effect of allowing the colonel to break off his taut stare at Danielle. "No, Inspector. They were confined to the school, never evacuated by the troops."

Ben's eyes flashed, his mind working fast. "Which building is the school?"

The colonel pointed away from the square, past the line of Israeli soldiers and cluster of reporters. "The two-story white-stone one diagonally across from the square."

Ben squinted into the sun. "With a clear view of the massacre, especially from the second floor."

Al-Asi nodded, his familiar smile returning. "I see your point, Inspector."

"The question," Ben began, "is whether any of the children saw more than that."

CHAPTER 10

Franklin Winters stood rigidly before the desk of the secretary of state, watching him read the letter that consisted of a single paragraph.

The secretary looked up grimly after completing it. "I don't suppose there's anything I can say to make you change your mind."

"I'm afraid not, sir."

"We go back a long way, Franklin. You can call me by my first name."

Winters's stance remained erect. "I'd rather not, sir."

"And I'd rather not lose you, old friend. You're the best damn ambassador to the U.N. this country has had since Albright."

"I appreciate the compliment, sir."

"Then stay on."

"I can't, sir."

The secretary of state sized Winters up from behind his desk, trying to match this man with the one who'd won the Silver Star, Purple Heart, and Medal of Honor in Vietnam. "How many administrations have you served, Franklin?"

"Seven, sir."

"This one needs you most of any of them, Franklin. This *country* needs you, for Christ's sake."

"My decision is final, sir."

The secretary of state eyed Winters warily. "How much of this is because of the death of your son?"

"Disappearance," Winters corrected.

"Pardon me?"

"You said death. That's never been confirmed. My son remains missing in action," Winters insisted, feeling his mind drifting in an all-too-familiar direction.

OUTSIDE BAGHDAD: MARCH 2003

SPECIAL FORCES *Team Bravo moved with the night. The twelve men approached from the north where they had entered the country through the Kurdish region. A native had guided them through the mountainous region south, but they had proceeded alone for the last several hundred miles to the outskirts of the city. Moving mostly at night, they wore civilian clothes to better blend in during the day on the chance they were spotted.*

They had spent the bulk of their time over the previous seventy-two hours relaying positions of "hidden" Iraqi air defenses to command headquarters in Qatar in preparation for the coming war.

Tonight Team Bravo was moving in single file, dressed in desert camouflage uniforms. With the start of war now a given, their final assignment was to infiltrate Baghdad in preparation to direct precision-guided missiles to hard targets inside the urban arena.

As the lights of the city twinkled before him, Team Bravo Commander Jason Winters signaled his team to stop as they neared a ridge. From that point their route into the city would be over flatlands providing little cover. Winters checked his GPS screen to make sure their position and heading were exactly as planned. Each member of the team wore a transmitter in his belt that continually broadcast his precise position back to SIT-COM in Qatar. The commandos carried customized M-16 assault rifles, Heckler and Koch submachine guns, Glock 21 pistols with sound suppressors, Gerber MK2 killing knives, and night-vision goggles that instantly adapted to a sudden light source to prevent shock blindness.

Winters raised the palm-sized satellite radio to his ear. "CentCom, Team Bravo. In position."

"Team Bravo, CentCom. You are cleared for entry."

"Roger, CentCom. Cleared for entry." Winters reclipped the radio to his belt and whispered into the microphone that amplified the vibrations emerging from his vocal cords. "We move. Recon at Site Y."

Winters was the first over the ridge, the other eleven members of Team Bravo falling in line behind him in perfectly synchronized rhythm, their progress followed at CentCom Headquarters as flashing specs moving across a terrain computer generated to replicate the northern pass into Baghdad in near perfect detail. For the past several months, there'd been only a token amount of technicians and intel analysts on duty at this hour. With the start of the war looming, though, CentCom was packed solid. The voices remained hushed, though, the officers living on black coffee, anxious but confident.

The duty officer watched Team Bravo's approach to the city and reached for his own coffee, which had gone lukewarm. He nearly spilled the cup and took his eyes off the screen for the moment it took to right it.

When he looked back, the twelve flashing lights were gone.

The duty officer waited a few seconds to make sure it wasn't a glitch before changing modes and enhancing detail on the chance that Team Bravo had entered some sort of dead zone; ground depressions and mineral deposits caused them sometimes, though not often. When this failed, he decided to break radio silence.

"Team Bravo, this is CentCom. Please acknowledge."

No response.

"Team Bravo, this is CentCom. Repeat, please acknowledge."

Nothing.

"Team Bravo, this is CentCom, requesting status update."

By this time a number of those new to the command center had clustered around the duty officer's screen, sensing something was wrong and finding confirmation of just that fact in the empty screen before him.

Team Bravo had disappeared.

"I'M SORRY," the secretary of state said. "Poor choice of words on my part."

"Understood, sir."

"All the same, walking away won't bring him back."

"I'm not expecting it to."

"So your resignation . . ."

"Has nothing to do with my son, sir. That's correct."

The secretary of state rose and walked out from behind his desk. "Then tell me why, Franklin. We've been friends a long time. You owe me that much."

"I have my reasons, sir."

"I'd like to hear them."

"I'm afraid they don't concern you."

"Don't concern me? When I lose the best man I've got, you can be damn well sure it concerns me."

Winters started for the door, his gait rigid and heavy. "I'll have my personal papers and files transferred, sir."

"I hope you know what you're doing, Franklin," the secretary said, shaking his head. "I sincerely do."

Winters looked back at him one last time. "So do I, sir."

CHAPTER 11

The girl's name was Raifa Assir. She was eleven years old, attending the equivalent of American fifth grade. Hers was the eighth door Colonel al-Asi had knocked on, but the only one at which the parent claimed her child wasn't home.

"This won't take long," al-Asi promised, brushing lightly past the woman into a well-kept home surprisingly cramped with furniture. All the upholstered pieces were wrapped in throw covers, though, evidence of their age and desperate need of repair. The wooden chairs and tables were scratched and marred by divots, discolored in irregular patches by the unforgiving sunlight. The stench of burned bread hung in the air, mixing with the scent of a fresh loaf baking in the oven.

He found Raifa Assir in the cramped bedroom she shared with two sisters and one cousin. She had squeezed herself between the room's one small bed and the wall. The colonel emerged from the room guiding the little girl before him.

"I have a daughter her same age," the colonel said to Raifa's mother as much in apology as reassurance. The door opened again and Israeli officials barged their way in until Danielle blocked their path.

"Let us do our job," she told them forcefully.

"Our orders are that you're not allowed to conduct interviews outside of our presence," one of the men said, clearly flustered.

"My orders are to investigate this massacre, through any means at my disposal."

"I'll keep them company," Colonel al-Asi offered, stepping outside to join the Israelis. He closed the door behind him, after stealing one last look at Danielle and leaving her with a smile.

"We don't want trouble," the young girl's mother said when the four were seated around the tiny kitchen table. "My daughter didn't see anything. Why are you here?"

"Stop it, Mamma! I want to tell them!"

The mother covered Raifa's mouth with her hand. "She saw nothing, I'm telling you. Now get out of here, get out of my house!"

"It's too late for that now," Danielle told her.

"It will only be too late if my daughter speaks a word. That's why we lied when the Israeli soldiers came. If they ever found out we lied . . ."

"They won't," Danielle promised.

"Yes, they will," the woman said grimly, "once they find out what really happened."

BEN SLID his chair closer to the woman's. "You're frightened."

"Of the Israelis, yes."

"And the U.N.?"

The woman shrugged. "They try, do what they can."

"We represent the U.N. and you have my word the U.N. will protect you," Ben assured.

"The U.N. cannot even protect their own people. Two dead for daring to teach Palestinian children. Such a waste."

"Then let your daughter help us punish those responsible."

The mother looked to her daughter and nodded reluctantly. Raifa Assir sipped from a cup of lukewarm mint tea. Her hands trembled as she raised it to her lips, then replaced it on the table.

"I should have hidden under the desks, like the others, as we were told by our teacher," Ben translated, after the young girl began to speak, *"before he was taken outside."*

"Before who was taken outside?"

"Our teacher, our new teacher."

"Who took him?" Danielle asked and waited for Ben to repeat the question in Arabic.

"The soldiers."

"Israeli soldiers?"

Before Ben could repeat the question this time, Raifa Assir nodded. *"They came in trucks like the ones in the street now. We all saw them from the windows. We weren't really scared at first, until they began going into all the buildings and dragging people out with them."*

"When did they come to the school?"

"I don't know what you mean. . . ."

Ben reformed the words in his head. "How many people from the village were already in the square when they came inside the school?"

"A lot. More than a hundred. As soon as the soldiers came near the building, our teacher ordered us under the desks. Told us to stay there no matter what happened." Raifa looked down into her tea. Her voice began to tremble, break. *"I wish I had listened. I didn't."*

"What did you see, Raifa?" Ben posed as gently as he could.

The little girl swallowed hard. For the first time, Ben noticed a handmade rope bracelet she was wearing and thought of his own daughter, long dead now, making one for herself at summer camp.

"What did you see?" he repeated.

"The teachers were brought out to join the others in the square. The soldiers poked at them with the barrels of their

machine guns. One teacher argued with them and they poked at him harder."

"You saw all this?" Danielle said, mustering her best Arabic.

"Yes," Raifa Assir said, and cleared her throat. *"The other children stayed under their desks, hands covering their heads. Outside the soldiers were demanding to know where someone was—I couldn't hear the exact name. They went up and down through the lines of people, asking each one. Their voices got louder. There was a lot of shouting. Then I heard the firecrackers."*

"Gunfire . . ."

"I didn't know that then," Raifa said, not waiting for Ben to translate. Her voice grew soft, sank lower. *"I didn't know it until the first bodies began to fall."*

The woman took her daughter's hand, sobbing softly to herself.

"But you saw where it came from," Danielle said, and waited for Ben's translation.

"Yes."

"Where?"

"The soldiers. The same machine guns they had used to poke the teachers. The barrels were still smoking when people screamed and tried to flee. Then there was more smoke, and fire, coming out of the barrels. I saw the bodies falling, stains spreading beneath them. And I looked for my mother among those running. I looked for my mother. . . ." Sobbing uncontrollably, Raifa collapsed in her mother's arms.

Danielle reached out and grabbed Ben's elbow. "Ask her if she remembers anything else about the soldiers. Markings on their uniforms or vehicles, even names."

"She would have told us if she did."

"Ask her," Danielle insisted.

Ben posed the question softly, then waited for Raifa Assir to complete her thought before translating. *"They returned*

to their trucks when the people ran. A few tripped over the
bodies before running away."

"They let the survivors go, made no effort to pursue them?"

The little girl nodded. "Just went back to the trucks," she said, speaking in English for the first time.

"You speak English well," Danielle said. "How did you learn?"

"My teacher at the school, the new one. Mr. Lister. He made us practice every day." She looked down and muttered something.

"One of the two relief workers who was killed," Ben elaborated.

"Did the soldiers run?" Danielle asked.

This time Raifa answered in Arabic, Ben translating as soon as she was finished.

"They hurried."

"None stayed behind?"

"No."

"No prisoners were taken?"

Raifa shook her head, said something so softly Ben had to lean forward to make it out.

"They just left the same way they came. Very fast. One of
their trucks ran over a goat. That's when I reached up and
stopped the camera."

"Camera?" Danielle repeated.

Ben leaned forward to better hear Raifa's next response. "A tape," he said. "She says she has a tape."

CHAPTER 12

How could she have made it?" Danielle asked.

"She didn't," Ben answered. "Her teacher, this David Lister, was filming the class. When the soldiers arrived, he turned the camera to face the square through the window. Raifa only removed the film from the camera." He stroked the little girl's hair, drawing the slightest of smiles amidst her trembling. "She's been hiding it here ever since."

Ben and Danielle accompanied Raifa into her bedroom and watched her retrieve the tape from beneath the mattress. She seemed only too happy to give it up, handing it to Ben. He tucked it into his jacket pocket and moved back through the house to the front door. Danielle opened it ahead of him and found their path blocked by an even larger complement of Israeli soldiers nestled around Colonel al-Asi.

"Commander Barnea," a captain said, after offering a stiff salute, "you are wanted in Jerusalem."

"Inform whoever wants me that his *request* must go through United Nations channels."

"It has, Commander. I am authorized to tell you that you are wanted in Jerusalem on U.N. business."

Danielle looked toward Ben.

"My orders are to escort you and you alone, Commander," the captain said without even eyeing him.

"Go ahead," Ben said, twisting away so as not to reveal

the bulge the videotape was making in his pocket. "I'll catch
up with you at the hotel."

Danielle nodded and walked off with the captain.

WATCHING JERUSALEM sharpen in the shrinking distance
felt almost surreal to her. Danielle had been born in the
city's Hadassah Hospital and for the first thirty-two years of
her life never went more than a day, it seemed, without seeing it again. There were numerous assignments carried out
for Sayaret Matkal that meant longer stretches of a life led in
utter secrecy, as well as extended periods of training at bases
in Israel few knew existed. Even then, though, Jerusalem
seemed close, if not in mind, at least in heart.

Joining National Police as the youngest woman ever to be
named *pakad*, chief inspector, gave her an office with a view
of the Old City from her window. After a brief stretch working for a private security firm in the United States, she returned to Jerusalem as commander of National Police with
the promise of becoming *Rav Nitzav*, commissioner, within
the year. But desperate circumstances had conspired to end
her tenure prematurely. Publicly, Danielle was lauded in her
absence; privately, it was made clear she was not welcome in
Israel ever again.

Being recruited almost immediately, along with Ben, to
join the Safety and Security Service of the United Nations
helped ease the pain of that somewhat. The work was emo-
tionless and procedural, each day vanishing in the vapor
stream of the last. But she embraced that work as a welcome
alternative to the conflicted and vindictive world of Israeli
politics she had bought into until it finally sold her out.

Still, she missed Jerusalem—the sights and sounds, but
mostly the smells. Of fresh produce and grilling meat, and
the sticky brown dust that follows the wind. Danielle

watched Jerusalem grow before her from the back of a Humvee seated next to the captain who had escorted her from the village of Bureij. Her heart pounded. Eleven months away and she felt like a stranger in her own land.

She expected the Humvee to take her to the nest of government buildings that rimmed the Knesset, an audience with someone of influence with a mind to intimidate her. Danielle knew how the game was played. It was just strange being on the other side.

But the Humvee bypassed the government complex and proceeded instead to the four-story limestone headquarters of National Police. There, the captain brought her to a private entrance she had used countless times herself and into an elevator that opened directly to the suite of offices operated by the innermost cadre, including the commissioner she never became.

The captain remained inside the compartment when the doors slid open. Danielle stepped out into a reception area that served the trio of offices contained in this wing.

"Welcome back," said David Vordi from the doorway of the commissioner's office.

"AREN'T YOU going to congratulate me on my new position?" he asked, eyes wide with an ironic glare.

As deputy minister of justice, Vordi had brought Danielle back to Israel as commander of National Police nearly two years before. Not surprisingly, her fall from grace must have led to an equally precipitous drop for him.

"I never knew you held an affinity for law enforcement," Danielle told him.

"I don't. But I'm going to have plenty of time to develop one now."

Danielle swallowed hard, realized her mouth had gone

bone dry. She gazed past Vordi into the office beyond, occupied by her mentor, Herschel Giott, until his death a half dozen years before. Things had seemed so simple then, though equally sad.

"That should have been mine," she said, as much to herself as Vordi. His hair was shorter and thinner, making his face look gaunt. His midsection had gone to flab, although Danielle remembered him as a man compulsive about fitness ever since he had served as one of her trainers in Special Ops. Vordi must have been approaching forty-five years old now. He looked as if he had aged a decade in the months since she had last seen him.

"I guess you could say both of us have you to thank for where we are now."

"I don't have any regrets."

"I do," Vordi said. "For trusting you to do this job to begin with."

"You brought me back here to destroy me."

"No, Danielle," he said quite calmly, taking a single step toward her. "I brought you back here because I thought both of us could prove the others who wanted to destroy you wrong." Vordi looked around him, as if seeing his surroundings for the first time. "As you can see, I've paid a price for that misjudgment, too."

Danielle looked into his eyes and saw that the attraction she had once sparked in him was gone. In its place was a narrowed gaze and lingering sneer that fixed upon her hatefully.

"U.N. officials know nothing of this meeting, do they?"

"You're clever as ever, I see, Danielle."

"And you're just as predictable."

"In any case, there's a good reason for this meeting."

"And that is?"

"First, tell me what the perpetrators were apparently looking for in Bureij."

"A terrorist named Rahim Naddahr."

Vordi started to slide past her. "Then you need to accompany me somewhere."

"Why?"

"So I can prove to you that Israel had nothing to do with the massacre."

CHAPTER 13

The picture was grainy, out of focus, and further blurred by the proximity of the camcorder's lens to the window after Raifa Assir's teacher, the late David Lister, had turned it around to capture the complement of Israeli soldiers dispersing through the town. Minutes later, the tape caught the soldiers herding residents into the square, the throng increasing gradually until the school's teachers were escorted into the frame to join them.

"I count a dozen soldiers," noted al-Asi.

"Look at the way they're holding their weapons," Ben added.

The colonel leaned closer to the screen. "Fingers on the triggers. They intended to open fire all along."

From the village, Ben and al-Asi had driven to Ramallah, bypassing the leveled complex of Palestinian government buildings for a residential neighborhood on the outskirts of the city. The colonel's driver stopped in front of a tight cluster of concrete homes and pulled away quickly as soon as the two of them had climbed out.

"We've learned to improvise, Inspector," al-Asi had explained as they headed up the walk. "Welcome to the new headquarters of the Palestinian Ministry of the Interior."

Inside Ben saw that walls connecting the three homes had been knocked down to create an officelike effect for the colonel's staff.

"We have limitations, of course," al-Asi continued. "To

put any communication antennas or satellites on the roof, for example, would invite a punitive Israeli attack, so we make do with what we can."

That included a single twenty-seven-inch television and ordinary VCR, hardly the sophisticated video equipment required to adequately analyze the tape Raifa Assir had made. Ben rewound the tape in Search mode and froze the frame on the two soldiers who walked into the square with their rifles already unslung.

"A massacre was their intention from the beginning," Colonel al-Asi said again.

"The right equipment can zoom in on the soldiers' faces and enhance the frames. That would enable us to identify them."

"With the help of the Israeli government and army, you mean, Inspector."

"That is, if the soldiers were Israeli at all."

Al-Asi turned his gaze on the screen, his smooth face half-lit by the soft glow emanating from it. "This tape would seem to offer all the proof we need. The uniforms, the weapons, the vehicles—it's all there."

"Unless that's exactly what the real perpetrators wanted us to think."

"You're not thinking like a Palestinian, Inspector."

"No, I'm thinking like a detective."

Ben pushed Play and watched the teachers being absorbed into the mass herded into the square. Then, suddenly, he pressed Freeze again.

"What is it?" al-Asi asked him.

Ben focused on a still frame of the soldiers who had escorted the teachers from the school into the square, caught from the rear. "The soldiers who came out of the school haven't moved to rejoin the others. They're holding their positions near the teachers. Look at their weapons," he added. "Fingers on the triggers, ready to shoot in attack, not self-defense."

Ben ran the tape forward again in slow motion. The three soldiers he had pointed out opened fire into the crowd, which scattered in all directions as bodies dropped like dominoes, clogging the street. The picture then filled with the fleeing crowd, their screams drowning out the muted sounds of gunshots. The throng jolted to the right, and the camera caught another pair of soldiers firing into the mass as if it were target practice. More bodies fell.

The tape ended.

Ben hit the Stop button. "The massacre wasn't provoked, Colonel, it was premeditated. The gunmen came to Bureij to kill as many as they could and then leave. But why this town?"

"If we knew that, we'd be a lot closer to catching the perpetrators."

"Exactly," Ben said and pressed Rewind.

"What is it, Inspector?"

"Something I just realized."

CHAPTER 14

"What are we doing here, Commissioner?" Danielle asked again.

"As I told you, you'll see soon enough," David Vordi said evasively.

They had been driving for nearly two hours, Danielle in the SUV's backseat next to Vordi while a plainclothes National Police officer drove.

"I should think that you wouldn't want a U.N. official to see what goes on inside this place, Commissioner," she noted.

"We're here looking for the truth, Inspector," Vordi said impersonally. "Not further complications."

Even up close, Ketsiot Prison in the Negev Desert was virtually indistinguishable from the desert that surrounded it. Everything, including the steel perimeter fence, was painted a sand color to help disguise its presence. Within, Danielle knew, there were four separate one-story buildings where prisoners were held in individual cells. Those held at Ketsiot never mixed, the idea being to forcefully construct a new routine out of anything that passed for ordinary.

Sleep deprivation blurred the distinctions between night and day. When prisoners shed their clothes and begged for relief from the overpowering heat, powerful air conditioning compressors would drastically reduce the temperature and humidity, leaving them chilled and shaking from the sudden wash of cold. The prisoners were fed well but not on a regular schedule to further mask the passage of time. Reward for talking could be as simple as restoring a normal routine coupled with a trip, however brief, outside.

The gate was manned by a quartet of Israeli soldiers, one of whom activated it remotely after checking Vordi's and Danielle's credentials. She knew Ketsiot had been closed down years ago, an event that drew praise from the world community and was greeted with celebration by the Palestinians. Now she realized that had been a sham. The government she had been part of for nearly half her life had mastered the art of misinformation. Informing the world that Ketsiot had been shut down, even providing pictures of its supposed demolition, provided a public relations coup along with the perfect dumping ground for the most serious of Palestinian prisoners.

Contrary to that, though, Danielle saw ample evidence of new and ongoing construction, as they drew farther into the compound.

"You were never here," Vordi said, following her gaze. "Not officially."

"What's going on?"

"It was the Americans' idea," he told her. "Guantánamo's running at capacity and operating a prisoner-of-war camp is not to their liking politically. So we entered into an agreement to handle the overflow and all new prisoners. I suppose the Americans decided they wanted something for all their foreign aid."

Vordi had meant that as a joke, but the remark didn't even draw a smile from Danielle. Their driver halted the SUV in a parking area so sand-strewn that the asphalt was barely visible. Other than theirs, all the vehicles were military issue.

Climbing out, Danielle shielded her eyes from the sand, noticing a captain in the Israeli army approaching from the direction of a nearby building. The captain saluted Vordi, eyed Danielle derisively, and pursed his lips.

"If you'll follow me, sir," he said, purposefully ignoring her.

The inside of this particular building was just as she remembered it on the few occasions when circumstances drew her to the most brutal of all Israeli prisons. Dark and quiet, save for the hum of fans fighting to circulate air through the desert-heated bare walls. Danielle noticed that the air smelled of sweat and dried urine, as the captain led them past an endless series of steel doors outfitted with old-fashioned key locks. Soldiers were posed every fifteen yards or so, apparently oblivious to the visitors' presence.

They stopped in front of the last cell on the right, manned by a mammoth soldier. Vordi nodded to him, and the soldier unclasped a single key from his gun belt, then jiggled it into the ancient lock. He pulled the door open and shouted coarsely in Arabic before shifting his massive frame enough to provide space to pass by, never taking his eyes from the prisoner within.

Danielle entered the cell just behind Vordi, saw a bearded Palestinian man seated on a bed cot with his elbows resting on his knees.

"Inspector Barnea," Vordi said, "may I present Rahim Naddahr."

CHAPTER 15

Watch this part again," Ben said, pointing at the screen.

He started the tape from the point the teachers walked into the frame, herded toward the square from the direction of the school.

"I'm watching," al-Asi said. "What am I supposed to be seeing?"

"There should have been some provocation to set off the shooting. There wasn't."

"We've already been over that."

"But not this." Ben stopped the tape just after the teachers were absorbed into the front of the crowd gathered in the square. "The gunmen here," he started, touching the screen with his finger.

"The Israeli soldiers, you mean."

"The *gunmen*," Ben persisted, "right here were the ones who started the shooting. The rest joined in to cover up the truth."

"Which is . . ."

"This wasn't a massacre, it was a murder. Those teachers from the school were the targets."

Colonel al-Asi squinted toward the screen. "Four of them were killed."

"Two being members of the United Nations relief team. Doesn't make a lot of sense, does it, Colonel?"

"None, Inspector. But I have their files right here. If there's any sense to this, perhaps we'll find it inside them."

Al-Asi produced a pair of manila folders and watched Ben read them quickly.

"Salemme was American," he noted. "Twenty-six years old. Signed on with the United Nations Relief and Works Agency right out of college and re-upped for a second two-year stint. Attended Brandeis University and requested assignment to the Palestinian territories."

"Palestine," al-Asi corrected.

"That's not what he wrote on his application."

"All the same, Inspector, they must not have taught him much at this Brandeis University."

"He thought he could make a difference."

"My point exactly. What about the second man?"

"David Lister, age thirty-two. Another American. Veteran of the Peace Corps. Joined the United Nations Relief Agency as part of a plea agreement following repeated arrests for antiwar and anti-Israeli protests in the United States."

"Interesting, don't you think?"

"Not especially, Colonel. Israel would've had no idea of his identity. Host governments are not permitted to vet U.N. employees and representatives."

Al-Asi reached over and switched off the television. "Anything else in either man's background that stands out?"

Ben scanned the files again and shook his head. "Not a thing," he said, just before his satellite phone rang.

"Kamal. . . . *What?* . . . You're sure? . . . No, hold him there. I'm on my way."

Ben pocketed the satellite phone and looked back at al-Asi, clearly stunned.

"What is it, Inspector?"

"David Lister. They found him."

"His body?"

Ben shook his head slowly. "Very much alive. He's waiting for us at United Nations Relief Agency headquarters in Nablus."

CHAPTER 16

M r. Naddahr was transferred from the detention camp on the outskirts of Ramallah just last month. Isn't that right, Ramir?"

Naddahr looked up hatefully at Vordi. One of his eyes was swollen closed and Danielle could see all of his front teeth were either missing or broken.

"This following an escape he orchestrated in which three prisoners managed to get away briefly before they were tracked down and killed," Vordi continued, staring down at the man seated on the cot. "Mr. Naddahr was recaptured before he was able to leave the grounds, but not before he killed a twenty-three-year-old sergeant with a wife and two children. We thought he might find spending the rest of his days here at Ketsiot a bit less stimulating. Isn't that right, Ramir?"

Vordi leaned over and Naddahr recoiled fearfully. Danielle noticed his right arm hung limp and useless. She studied the man now cowering against the wall more carefully. The bruised and puffy patches on his face still left it whole enough to make him recognizable as the terrorist the Israeli army troops were hunting when they stormed the village of Bureij.

"I think you can see my point," Vordi said when they were back in the hallway.

Danielle heard the door of Naddahr's cell rattle closed behind them, remain silent.

"It's quite clear, Inspector," Vordi continued. "If the parties responsible for this massacre were truly Israeli troops, they wouldn't have come to the village on the pretext of arresting someone the military knows is already in custody."

Danielle tried not to show how relieved she felt. The thought that Israelis, her people, could behave that way sickened her.

Her people . . . Strange how quickly she fell into her old thinking patterns.

"I must ask you to keep this visit secret, of course," Vordi was saying.

"Then why bring me here, if I can't use the information as part of my investigation?" Danielle challenged.

"Because clearly you must take that investigation in another direction." Vordi stopped before they reached the door at the end of the hall. "After all, Inspector, if we weren't behind this massacre, then who was?"

CHAPTER 17

C hief Inspector Barnea is certain?" al-Asi posed.

Ben tucked the satellite phone back into his pocket. "Naddahr's been in Israeli custody for months. She just came from seeing him."

Al-Asi eased his head back against the SUV's rear-seat headrest, as his driver slowed to let an Israeli patrol zoom past. "This is most disturbing, Inspector, most disturbing."

The driver accelerated again after the patrol had passed by uneventfully and, minutes later, the city of Nablus came into view. United Nations Relief Agency headquarters for the West Bank was housed in a bunkerlike slab of a building on the outskirts of the city. It had been built originally in 1984, one of several diplomatically sensitive public relations steps taken by Israel to mend its image following the disastrous invasion of Lebanon. The government had supplied all building materials free of charge and allowed the U.N. to hire a Palestinian construction crew to perform the work. The headquarters was originally constructed to blend in with the rest of the structures in the area. But a huge UN had been painted in red atop the roof to make the building easily visible from the air in the hope of keeping it safe from retaliatory Israeli air strikes launched on Nablus.

"What's troubling you, Colonel?" Ben asked al-Asi.

Al-Asi kept his eyes fixed forward. "That the Israeli military might have had nothing to do with the massacre."

"And that *disturbs* you? You've been one of the strongest advocates for peace all along, behind the scenes anyway."

"My point exactly, Inspector. Because I hesitate to think where the investigation might go now, where the finger of blame may be cast."

"Palestinians killing Palestinians?"

"Hoping to cast the blame on Israel, why not? The furor over this incident is already sending ordinary Palestinian citizens into the streets. Israeli forces are clamping down again, tighter than ever. I fear this could scuttle what remains of the peace process forever and silence those of us who support it." Al-Asi finally looked toward Ben again. "You will be under great pressure not just to find who is responsible, but also to prove who is not. This theory of yours . . ."

"That's all it is, Colonel: a theory. It doesn't tell us anything."

"One of your U.N. victims was here in the guise of someone else, Inspector. That tells us something."

THE REAL David Lister was waiting for them in what passed for a lounge inside U.N. regional headquarters. The furniture was covered in faded and worn brown fabric, wrong for the region and ill suited to the room. Obviously surplus from another U.N. facility.

Lister paced the room nervously, buzzed on the caffeine from a half dozen Diet Cokes that littered various tabletops and armrests. He had learned of his apparent death through a U.N. memo to all relief workers advising caution in the rest of the region. Tall and lanky, he seemed to talk with his elbows more than his hands, his narrow face drooping between words.

Ben handed him the file on the massacre victim who had taken his name. "Recognize this man?"

Lister kept shifting the pages from hand to hand. "His face, no. His background, yes. Because it's mine. Everything in this file is mine, except the picture." He handed the pages back to Ben. "How could this happen?"

"Where were you posted prior to Palestine?" Ben asked him.

"Guatemala. For the past five years."

"The man posing as you took your identity because he thought it would be safe. Forged the transfer documents and showed up for assignment in the West Bank."

Colonel al-Asi turned away from the window. "Having no way to anticipate that the person he was impersonating would end up being sent to the same region himself."

Lister popped open another can of Diet Coke and chugged a hefty swig. "And the anomaly doesn't show up in anybody's records?"

"Different regions, different databases," Ben explained. "It may have been caught, or would have been soon, except the anomaly probably would've been blamed on poor record keeping, not identity theft."

"After all," said al-Asi, flashing the slightest of smiles, "people are more apt to want to sneak out of this area, not in."

Lister drained the rest of the can and laid it down on the table between them. "Man must have had his reasons."

Ben glanced at the real David Lister's file. "You're here to supervise a construction crew."

"Reconstruction, actually. Of a hospital the Israelis blew up. It hasn't been easy, let me tell you."

"Because of the Israelis?" from al-Asi.

"Because of the language. I speak fluent Spanish, not a word of Arabic."

"Our victim spoke fluent Arabic," Ben recalled to al-Asi.

"Man must've done his homework," Lister said, and reached for yet another can of Diet Coke.

"INTERESTING," AL-ASI noted, after he had closed the door to the room behind them. "Because if the U.N. worker murdered in Bureij wasn't David Lister . . ."

"Then who was he?" Ben completed.

anielle Barnea soaped up a second time and let the steaming hot water gush over her. The first washing had been to cleanse her of the grime from the road and the long hours of travel. The second was to wipe away how she felt.

Dirty at returning to her home country as something other than an Israeli. She had missed Israel more than she had ever confessed to Ben in their months with the U.N.'s Safety and Security Service, avoiding the issue since it was abundantly clear he had left far less behind. Whenever Danielle grew nostalgic, though, she simply summoned the memories of how her last days had been riddled with betrayal and isolation. Israel would always be her home, but there was nothing left here for her anymore. She had seen too much, knew too much. The very attributes that should have made her a great asset had turned her into a tremendous liability. Those who should have embraced her experience and loyalty instead chose to see her as a threat. Too powerful and visible to go quietly into a life of political exile, even if she had been willing to. Too stubborn and headstrong to play by their rules, even if she remained in the system.

Now she was home, carrying a United Nations visa instead of an Israeli passport. She had become, in the mind of her country, part of the enemy.

The United Nations . . .

She had hated the organization herself for all its hypocrisy. Now, instead, she felt like a hypocrite herself. She never believed in her work for the U.N. the way she'd believed in her work on behalf of Israel. In becoming a pariah, an outcast, though, that belief had been stripped away, leaving her with . . .

With what?

Nothing.

It hurt to form the thought, the reality of it dawning hard and fast. Danielle finally reached up and turned the water off, then grabbed for the towel she had slung over the shower rod.

For nearly a year she'd been able to run from her past, the pain and anguish that dominated it. Returning had brought it all back, confronting her all at once with an undeniable reality: whatever conclusions her investigation reached would lack credibility to both sides. To the Palestinians because she was Israeli and to the Israelis because she had fled the country as a fugitive. The Israelis had agreed to her participation because it provided the government with an excuse to deny everything in the event they didn't hear what they wanted. She had been duped. Again.

Danielle yanked back the curtain and stepped from the shower, a cascade of water trailing her across the tile. The phone rang and she padded quickly into the bedroom for it, expecting it was Ben with a report on whatever he and Colonel al-Asi had found in Nablus.

"Yes," she answered.

"Ms. Barnea?" A female voice. "Danielle Barnea?"

"If you're a reporter—"

"I'm not. I'm a sister. Matthew Henley's sister."

"Never heard of him," Danielle said, stopping just short of hanging up the receiver.

"You know him by another name, Ms. Barnea. David Lister—one of the U.N. personnel massacred in Bureij."

VICTORIA HENLEY sat at a corner table in an overstuffed chair in a tiny area set off from the rest of the hotel lobby that featured Starbucks coffee. The trays of danish, muffins, and cookies were free and, for the most part, uneaten. Victoria Henley was alone and, Danielle noticed, positioned as far as possible from sight of anyone passing near while still keeping the hotel's main entrance and lobby in view. She held a mug of coffee in her hands, paying little attention to Danielle's approach.

"Ms. Henley?"

The woman smiled slightly. "I wasn't sure it was you. I didn't know what you looked like."

"But you knew my name, that I was here."

"Because you've been assigned by the U.N. to investigate my brother's murder."

Danielle sat down in a matching overstuffed chair but left it discreetly away from the table. "Something not commonly known."

"I have sources."

"In the U.N.?"

"Several places," Victoria Henley said, and took a sip from her coffee.

Danielle guessed her to be in her late twenties, a young woman who could have been very attractive if she had worked at it at all. Instead her hair hung limply past the baggy blazer draped over her shoulders. She wore no makeup and her eyes drooped from fatigue. Danielle noticed her coffee showed no trace of steam, evidence she had been nursing the mug for some time.

"My brother was the reason that massacre happened," Victoria Henley continued, looking down into her cooling coffee. She uncrossed her legs and Danielle noticed she was wearing worn, faded jeans. "They found him, somehow they found him. . . ."

"The Israeli army?"

The woman frowned at her. "If you're half as good as I've heard you are, you've already figured out it wasn't the Israelis."

"Assume I have. Why would this other party stage a massacre just to assassinate your brother?"

Victoria Henley took a deep breath, didn't finish it. "Matthew was a linguistics expert, one of the foremost in the world. Pioneered software programs designed to translate one language into another contextually using rudimentary principles of artificial intelligence." Victoria Henley stopped, perhaps anticipating a question. When Danielle remained silent, she continued. "That's why they killed him."

"Because of something he translated."

Henley leaned forward and jarred the table slightly. "I don't know who they are."

"I didn't ask you that."

"They killed my father too. That's where it started. And I'm next now, as soon as they find me." She spoke matter-of-factly, as if resigned to her fate.

"What do you want from me, Ms. Henley?"

"Vicky. Please."

"Vicky."

Victoria Henley stretched her elbows farther across the table. "I want you to believe me, Inspector Barnea. I want you to believe that my father and my brother aren't the only victims. There are at least a dozen others, probably more by now. All members of my father's unit in World War Two. Because of something they found, something they found sixty years ago in Buchenwald."

CHAPTER 19

Ben lay next to Danielle in the double bed of his Jerusalem hotel room, two floors down from hers.

"How long has it been?" she asked softly, pressed up against his side, her head resting on his chest.

"Six weeks, no seven. And then only for a night."

Originally he had been booked in a room one floor down. But twenty minutes after checking in, he had called down to request a room change on the chance that the one he'd been given was wired with more than cable television. Given the animus between the U.N. and Israel, Ben expected as much, especially since he was Palestinian. He could only imagine how much it irked Israeli authorities to have him staying in Jerusalem in the block of rooms on permanent reservation by the United Nations. Still, since the odds of his movements being tracked were better, it was easier for Danielle to come to him.

Ben stroked her hair, enjoying the scent of her drifting softly upward. Something sweet, like lavender. She'd purchased it during a trip to Geneva, he remembered.

"When are you meeting this Victoria Henley next?" he asked.

"*We're* both meeting her first thing tomorrow morning."

"You believed her, didn't you?"

"I haven't had time to check out her story."

"But you believed her."

"I believe she was terrified. That's enough for now."
"Terrified of what?"

VICTORIA HENLEY hooked a strand of her long hair behind one ear. She laced her fingers together to still their trembling.

"They were all members of an Evacuation Hospital unit. Do you know what that is?"

"The first generation of mobile army surgical hospitals," Danielle said.

Victoria Henley nodded. "Yes, a whole new concept for the battlefield. My father's unit was the 121st. They'd barely set down in Germany when they were sent to Buchenwald."

Danielle's eyes coaxed Victoria Henley on.

"They were among the first Americans, the first *people,* to set foot inside a German concentration camp. Two hundred and forty of them, all men. The women, nurses, had been temporarily reassigned to spare them the—"

"I know about the heroic work done by the liberators," Danielle interrupted, not wanting to further rehash this painful part of Jewish history.

"The 121st weren't liberators. They were ... Never mind, that doesn't matter. What matters is that twelve of these men have died in the past two months, including my father."

"Old men in their eighties, seventies at the very least. I don't see what—"

"They didn't just die, Inspector. Like I told you, they were murdered," Victoria Henley insisted. "Sixty years after the fact."

The conviction in the woman's voice made Danielle rethink her initial judgment. "What was it they found in Buchenwald?"

"I don't know. I overheard my father talking on the phone a few times, once to Matthew. He cursed the day they dug it up. He always repeated that."

"How did you learn about Matthew's death?"

"A colleague of his, one of the teachers in the village school who survived, contacted me. Told me."

"That means he knew who your brother really was. Matthew must have confided in him."

Victoria Henley hedged. "In me, actually. This teacher and I had been . . . together for a while years ago. He knew how the U.N. relief bureaucracy worked. I asked him to help. He set up the entire ruse, just to help my brother. Not that it did him much good," she added, almost too softly to hear.

"When was this ruse set up?"

"After my father's funeral. Three weeks ago."

Danielle gave her a few seconds to compose herself. "How did your father die, Vicky?"

"He was shot outside an ATM."

"What did the police say?"

"What do you think? They called him a victim of random street crime, never seemed particularly bothered by the fact that the surveillance tape for that period was mysteriously damaged."

Victoria Henley fished a five-by-seven photo from a worn leather shoulder bag and handed it to Danielle. The photo was contained within a folding cardboard sleeve, and Danielle opened it to find a photo of a smiling older man with his arms around a young man and woman on either side of him.

"That's the last picture taken of the three of us," Henley explained. "About six months ago."

Danielle studied the picture some more, comparing the radiant face of the young woman pictured to the haggard expression that claimed Victoria Henley now.

"I haven't slept in two days," she said. "I close my eyes and all I see is what's left of my father's face and skull."

Danielle gave her a few more seconds, looked at Henley's

fingers for the first time and saw no wedding or engagement ring. A woman in her late twenties, early thirties maybe, losing the only family she had left.

"I'm going to find who killed your brother, Vicky. I promise."

"Unless they kill us both first."

"I'm pretty good at this sort of thing."

"So are they."

Danielle waited for Victoria Henley to drain the rest of her coffee before resuming. "What was it your brother translated?"

"Something my father—"

She stopped suddenly, eyes widening at the sight of something across the lobby. Danielle turned in that direction and saw a plainclothes Israeli security detail making a routine sweep.

"It's all right," she said calmly.

"No," Henley told her, clearly unsettled. "I can't talk anymore right now. I'll tell you the rest later. Tomorrow."

"Where are you staying?" Danielle asked. Victoria looked utterly exhausted, barely able to keep her eyes open.

"I keep moving around, so they won't be able to find me."

Danielle slid one of her room's access cards across the table. "You can use my room tonight."

Victoria Henley reached down for the card but didn't take it. "What about you?"

"I won't be needing it."

"OKAY," BEN said, fitting the story together in his head. "These twelve old men, members of an Evacuation Hospital unit, were murdered because of something they found in a concentration camp sixty years ago."

"Something Victoria Henley's brother must have translated."

"Did she say anything else about him?"

"Only that he was here hiding out from whoever killed his father."

Ben chuckled softly.

"What's so funny?" Danielle asked, raising her head to try and see his face.

"Only that someone would come to Palestine to hide."

"You did once," she reminded.

"I was lucky; you found me."

Danielle lowered her head to his chest once again. "Like somebody found Matthew Henley. His sister's terrified the same thing is about to happen to her."

Ben reached over her to switch off the light and drew Danielle closer to him. "Did you adopt stray animals as a child?"

"All the time."

"I thought so."

And he kissed her deeply, losing himself in Danielle as he always did in these moments. The only time when he felt safe and secure, when the pain of the past didn't blot out whatever good might lie ahead. He felt her mouth over his and felt himself floating in a pillow-soft world where nothing could hurt him, where the serial killer who'd killed his family vanished into a past from which he could at last turn away.

Then a sound like a car backfiring hammered Ben's ears an instant before the room itself shuddered, and chunks of plaster rained down off the walls. A fire alarm began to wail, and Danielle rolled off Ben in the same moment he lurched off the bed. Both of them pulling their clothes on, charging into the hallway together.

The shrill alarm was more piercing in the corridor and guests had already begun to spill from their rooms. A pair of exit doors at opposite sides of the hall burst open almost simultaneously, Israeli soldiers flooding out along with plain-clothes United Nations security personnel.

"Move away from the door, Inspector Kamal!" one of them shouted, freezing in his tracks when he saw Danielle. "Inspector Barnea?" he managed, eyes glassy with shock.

Danielle looked back at Ben; his untucked shirt, her half-buttoned top. "What's going on? What happened?"

"The explosion, Inspector," the U.N. man said to her, looking more relieved now, as others on both sides of him jabbered into their radios. "It was your room."

CHAPTER 20

No, dude, you're doing it all wrong," Jake Fleming said to the freshman seated next to him on the couch. "You gotta hold the smoke in your lungs longer. Let an expert show you."

Jake lifted the bong, purchased in Jamaica during spring break, off the coffee table.

"Now, watch," he said to the freshman, whose name he'd once again forgotten. Tom, maybe, or Tim. Something like that.

Jake flicked the lighter and touched the flame to the bowl. Then he formed a seal with his mouth against the top of the bong's glass chute and sucked in deeply. Instantly the bong's central chamber filled with smoke. Jake kept sucking, as he pulled the slide from its slot. He felt the rush of smoke fill his lungs, fought down a cough, and squeezed his mouth closed. Finally, when he could hold it in no longer, he opened his lips and let the smoke out. Slowly, watching waves of it float upward toward the ceiling.

"Now that's what I call a hit," Jake said raspily, handing the bong and lighter over to Tim or Tom. "I think it might be kicked. Give it a try, Tim."

"Tom."

"Yeah, right. Whatever."

Tom lowered his mouth to the bong and flicked the lighter.

"No, wait," Jake said, pushing himself off the couch.

He moved to the door, certain he'd heard something out in the dorm hallway. Brown University police were usually cool about smoking pot, long as the smell didn't filter out into the hallway. Jake made sure the towel was stuffed tight under his door, then checked the dead bolt.

"Okay," he told Tom. Or was it Tim?

Tom tried again with much better results until he started coughing up a storm again and dropped the slide onto the floor, scattering the bowl's remaining contents over the rug.

"Not cool," Jake said, dropping to his knees to fish the slide from underneath the couch where it had rolled.

He'd just clamped his hand on the hot glass when the door burst open. His first thought was his drunken fraternity brothers coming back from the bars. But the sight of dark uniforms pouring into the room made him think it must be Brown cops on a serious mission. Only Brown cops didn't carry guns and these dark shapes were wielding big ones.

"Stay down!"

"Let me see your hands!"

Jake tried to raise them and realized one was still lodged under the couch holding onto the slide.

"Let me see your hands!" one of the shapes repeated again and Jake realized the shape had no face. No, it was just covered in a ski mask or something.

Jake finally got his second hand out and cowered back against the couch, stretching both into the air. More masked shapes pushed into the room; there must have been a dozen of them, so many Jake couldn't even see out into the hallway where a few more kept yelling, "Clear! Clear!" like a scene from some fucked-up movie.

On the couch, Tim or Tom was still coughing. Across the small dorm room a smaller masked shape was lifting Jake's computer off his desk, not caring what he dragged with it. He bumped into another of the intruders who was busily emptying the contents of Jake's drawers into a box marked EVIDENCE.

On the couch, Tim or Tom was still coughing.

"Oh, fuck," was all Jake could think to say.

DAY FOUR

CHAPTER 21

Ben and Danielle refused to leave the hotel for safe refuge, insisting they be allowed to remain through at least the initial course of the investigation that stretched into the early morning hours.

Israeli army personnel secured the hotel and cordoned off the floor where the blast had occurred. Guests who had descended on the lobby had been rapidly evacuated to the hotel's parklike entry area and kept back behind hastily strung crime scene tape to keep them from the path of emergency vehicles. Danielle heard that Commissioner David Vordi of National Police was already en route to take charge. She insisted on seeing the blast site and Ben accompanied her up the stairs, since the elevators were still being checked for more explosives.

The smell struck her as she was climbing the stairwell a good half flight before the closed-off floor. Sour and smoky at the same time, something like metal singed in a microwave.

Semptex or C4, she concluded. Some form of high-tech plastic explosive.

A guard at the top of the stairwell reluctantly let them pass through the door. Harsh acrid smoke continued to drift down the hall with thin ribbons of cloudy mist. It thickened along with the smell as Ben and Danielle drew closer to the blast site. Their feet kicked past debris in the form of chunks and shards torn mostly from the ceiling. A white flourlike dust permeated the air, sticking to their skin and leaving its chalky residue across the walls and doors.

As they neared her room, Danielle saw a pair of Israeli paramedics carrying out a single black body bag, an all-too-familiar sight in Israel. They placed it atop a dolly and started to wheel it down the hall until Danielle stopped them, reached for the zipper.

"I wouldn't do that if I—"

Danielle's hardened gaze froze the paramedic and she returned her attention to the body bag, opening it just enough to see a face not recognizable as Victoria Henley at all. Still, Danielle reached down and parted the corpse's charred lips enough to peer into the mouth. Then she closed the bag up and continued toward the jagged hole blown out where her door had been. The blast had collapsed a good portion of the walls on either side, while inside the room itself there was . . . nothing. Just blown-out remains and an overheated stench rising off the residue of burnt fabric and glowing fibers of mattress stuffing dancing in the air like fireflies. Nothing was recognizable, save for the television, which lay perfectly straight on the floor with a spiderweb crack down the center of its screen.

"It was the mattress," Danielle surmised from the blast pattern. "The explosives must have been packed into or under it."

She wondered if Victoria Henley had been lying atop it when the blast erupted. It would explain the nature of her wounds. Sometimes those closest to the center of a blast were actually left most whole, an anomaly that had long confused Danielle.

"You're not safe here," Ben said softly.

"Henley was the target, not me," Danielle insisted.

"You gave her your key card and she was up here what, an hour later? The room was always occupied until you came down to my room. How could anyone have set the explosives?"

"You should have looked into her mouth, Ben."

"What?"

"Victoria Henley's mouth. There was no charring."

"Meaning . . ."

"She was dead before the explosion. They killed her and covered up the truth by staging the explosion."

"To make it appear as if you were the target the whole time."

"Exactly."

"Inspectors," an Israeli captain called from just behind them, "I have an urgent call for you."

He held a satellite phone forward, ignoring Ben in favor of Danielle.

"Barnea," she said. Several seconds passed before she spoke again. "We'll be waiting."

Ben looked at her, as she handed the phone back to the captain.

"That was Alexis Arguayo," Danielle told him. "He's on his way."

I was in Germany when word reached me," Arguayo said, as soon as he closed the office door behind Ben and Danielle. Once powerfully built, most of his muscle was now covered in dense layers of fat. His face carried a sheen of sweat and splotches of it had bled through the white dress shirt beneath his blue suit coat.

Arguayo, head of the United Nations Safety and Security Service, was Peruvian by birth but had spent most of his life in Venezuela where he eventually became a citizen. An army veteran, he had taken over as police chief of Caracas when that city was infested with crime. Six years into his tenure, crime had decreased eighty percent and Arguayo had moved on to politics, becoming Venezuela's delegate to the United Nations. He returned to personally take charge of the army's brutal crackdown on the rebels who had brought Venezuela's economy to a standstill. Both Ben and Danielle wondered if he had trouble reconciling the legendary ruthlessness that ultimately helped bring the rebels down with the far more bureaucractic position of head of the U.N.'s security division.

In that capacity Arguayo had personally recruited Ben and Danielle, impressing them with both his organizational skills and surprisingly pleasant demeanor that belied his reputation. But Arguayo seemed neither pleasant nor gentle today. He looked from Ben and Danielle to David Vordi, who sat pensively behind the hotel manager's desk.

"I like to think my people are safely under the protection of the host country," Arguayo said accusingly. "Apparently I thought wrong."

"You insisted on your Security Service conducting its own investigation, General," Vordi shot back, "instead of letting us do our jobs."

"Your jobs? And if we can't trust you with the simple task of keeping a hotel in the middle of Jerusalem secure, how can we trust you with anything else?"

"Perhaps if you stopped ignoring the terrorists operating from the refugee camps you administer, things would improve."

"As you are well aware, the U.N. does not administer them, we merely feed the population of these camps. At least we did until your government began obstructing the movements of our relief workers."

"The restrictions are necessary for our own security," Vordi insisted. "Your drivers are almost exclusively Palestinian."

"Were, Commissioner. We're using truck drivers supplied by the Swedish government now, a fact apparently lost on your military patrols."

"I'll pass the word along."

"And you might also mention that our relief agencies are now feeding over a million Palestinians, up from a hundred thousand when the most recent conflict began."

"We did not start this conflict, General."

"But you are determined to finish it, through any means at your disposal, Commissioner, even if that includes the murder of innocent villagers."

Vordi held his expressionless gaze on Arguayo. "Apparently Inspector Barnea has not yet briefed your office on her findings, that the Israeli Defense Forces were not involved in this massacre," he said, ignoring Ben altogether.

Arguayo swung toward Danielle. "Is this true?"

"Indications point to that, yes," Danielle acknowledged, not wanting to elaborate any further in front of Vordi.

"I see. But you're not certain."

"Not yet," Danielle told Arguayo. "Not conclusively."

"Still quite a bit accomplished in only twenty-four hours. Unfortunately, Inspector Barnea, Inspector Kamal will be left to complete the investigation on his own."

"I don't understand, General."

"A woman was killed in your room last night, in an explosion clearly meant for you."

"I'm not convinced of that."

"You believe this other woman was the target?"

"She had information that may have proven vital to the investigation."

Arguayo narrowed his gaze. "Why was I not apprised of this earlier?"

"We'd only spoken once. I haven't had the opportunity yet to substantiate her claims."

"And yet you gave her your room."

"She believed she was in danger."

"And assuming she was correct . . ."

Danielle exchanged a glance with Ben. "It may take the investigation in another direction."

Arguayo continued to stare at Danielle. "Inspector Kamal, do you concur with Inspector Barnea's findings?"

Ben didn't hesitate. "Yes, General, I do."

Arguayo frowned. "I'd hoped you would've learned your lesson."

"In Baghdad or Colombia?"

"Take your pick. I'm still waiting for your report on Colombia."

"I wasn't sure anyone read the one I wrote on Baghdad."

Arguayo glared at Ben. "You wanted us to blame the *Russians* for orchestrating the bombing of the compound."

"It was a hotel before the U.N. appropriated the building, General. And the evidence I gathered indicated KGB and GRU documents were stored there following the collapse of the former Soviet Union."

"Documents indicating what exactly?" Arguayo challenged.

"I wasn't given an opportunity to find out."

"Toward what end? Embarrassing the Russian government at a time we can least afford to?"

Ben held his ground. "Someone in Russia ordered the bombing once the hotel was turned over to the United Nations because they couldn't take the risk something they had hidden there would be uncovered."

Arguayo shook his head in mock disbelief. "Some*one*? Some*thing*? You really should listen to yourself, Inspector."

"Feel free to banish me back to my desk, General."

"Oh, I'd like nothing better." Arguayo turned toward Danielle. "But that would leave me with no one to coordinate this investigation, since Inspector Barnea is being recalled."

Danielle's eyes bulged. "If I may, General—"

"No, Inspector Barnea, you may not. Instead you will be driven to an Israeli military airfield where you will board a jet that will take you back to London. Consider yourself on leave. You can use some time off. Your plane's waiting. I want you in the air in thirty minutes."

ARGUAYO HAD his private car, a Mercedes, drive Danielle to the airfield. Ben followed her there in a U.N. vehicle and joined her on the Tarmac near a small jet sitting on the runway, its engines revving.

"Arguayo wants you out of here very badly," he noted.

"I don't care. What I'm looking for now isn't in Israel anyway."

"He'll be monitoring calls in and out of my phone," Ben reminded, "to see if we speak."

"Then we won't, at least for a few days."

"This might all be wrapped up by then."

"You really believe that, Ben?"

"Not for a second."

They hugged briefly, then Danielle walked off to the jet alone. Ben watched her climb on board, shielding his eyes from the sun. As soon as the door closed behind her, he drew his phone from his pocket and dialed Colonel Nabril al-Asi.

"So glad to hear you weren't injured last night, Inspector," al-Asi greeted.

"How'd you know it was me, Colonel?"

"I figured I'd be hearing from you as soon as Chief Inspector Barnea exited Israel."

Ben watched the small jet begin its taxi down the runway. "You never cease to amaze me."

"Now what can I do for you?"

"Whoever was behind the massacre in Bureij has authentic Israeli military vehicles, Colonel. I'd like to know where they got them."

So you see, Inspector, even though I am a cabinet minister," al-Asi told Ben, as they approached Nablus, "most days I am not permitted to enter our largest city."

His voice sounded more pained than bitter, and he looked at the city rising up beyond the approaching Israeli checkpoint almost nostalgically. The difficulty in traversing short distances was a memory Ben had left behind. It was the one that stood out above everything else in comparing life in Palestine to the rest of the world.

"This isn't good," al-Asi commented, as Ben braked the U.N. vehicle to a halt near the Israeli soldiers who had finally waved him on.

"It never is."

"Not this bad. There was rioting in the streets of Nablus last night. Ramallah too. The massacre in Bureij set the mobs off. They might not be quelled this time."

"Giving the Israelis the excuse they need to expel the entire population, annex the West Bank once and for all."

Al-Asi looked as low as Ben had ever seen him. "The end of our dream, Inspector."

"So if the Israeli army is proven to be behind the massacre . . ."

"The mob mentality is further fed."

"And if the Israeli army is absolved . . ."

"Those in the street won't believe the report."

"Unless it comes from a Palestinian."

"Apparently," the colonel told Ben, "Alexis Arguayo understands that as clearly as I do. Otherwise you'd have been banished along with Chief Inspector Barnea. But it's a good thing you weren't. I think you'll find what you're looking for here in Nablus."

The soldiers came to either side of the vehicle before al-Asi could elaborate further, starting yet another thorough examination of documents and identification papers likely to stretch far into the afternoon. They seemed to recognize Colonel al-Asi, both by face and position, affording him considerably more respect than Ben. Perhaps because of the colonel's presence, it was only a half hour before they were sent through the checkpoint and an Israeli military jeep led them down the road into Nablus, past security patrols posted vigilantly at random intervals.

"I wonder if the Israelis truly realize what they've done," al-Asi asked distantly.

"What do you mean?"

"These past four years, the number of Palestinians they have turned against peace forever."

"I don't think they care," said Ben. "Or, perhaps, that's what they want."

"Slide your window down, Inspector."

Ben touched the control and felt the oppressive heat surge into the cabin.

"Now tell me what you smell in the air."

They reached the outskirts of the city and the Israeli jeep pulled off to the side, allowing them to proceed on alone.

"Something rancid," Ben answered and slid the window back up.

"Garbage," explained al-Asi. "It's been nearly a month since anyone in Nablus had theirs picked up. It's become a symbol to Palestinians of what their lives have become. And where are they to turn? Many, too many, have turned to conservative Islam. It's impossible to keep head scarves for women on the shelves. Older men have to pray outside because the mosques are packed with so many of those younger. They have turned toward the only thing that offers them hope even as it preaches that for Palestinians to survive, Israel cannot."

Their SUV passed a pair of bombed-out buildings that stood like fallen sentinels at the entrance to the city.

"There can never be any real peace now, Inspector," al-Asi said, almost too softly to hear. "Both sides have realized that."

Ben followed the line of concrete barriers, creating makeshift routes along once-bustling roads and avenues. A bit closer to the city center, he could see Nablus had been split in half by a six-foot dirt barrier. The other roads were cordoned off and a tank stood ominously at the edge of the main north-south thoroughfare, leaving the east-west route as the only passable one in the city. A pair of Israeli soldiers leaned against the tank smoking cigarettes while another pair rotated their eyes and assault rifles in tandem.

This road and the adjoining ones looked otherwise deserted, Ben noticed, although the source of the rising stench was clear. Garbage that had been piled futilely for pickup had been strewn across streets that had become asphalt patchworks riddled with ruts and jagged holes. Evidence of a people so lacking in hope that it would readily deface its own world.

"Once I managed to convince the Israelis to pick up the garbage," al-Asi told Ben. "They came in a long line of trucks under heavy military escort. The residents booed the soldiers but applauded the trash haulers. I don't think the Israelis got the point."

They passed the now-shuttered building that had housed the Palestinian stock market. Structures that had held fledgling businesses were dark, empty tombs, power long shut off within them.

Ben thought they were headed toward the refugee camps

that rimmed the northern half of the city: the two Askars, Old and New. But a second tank blocked the only route in and out of them, and al-Asi continued to follow the berm, his plans apparently unruffled. Here, even the centuries-old factories that made olive-oil soap and formed the only still functioning industry in the city had been closed down. But the thin warrens and alleyways were open and al-Asi signaled Ben to pull into one of the latter where he parked behind a burned-out husk of a sedan.

"The auto repair shop of Abu Kishek," al-Asi explained, stepping out into the street. "He used to fix many of the government's cars for us. Now that we have no government . . ."

"Don't tell me: he's found other ways to occupy his time."

"Exactly, Inspector."

CHAPTER 24

Upon arriving at Heathrow Airport outside London, Danielle moved straight from the diplomatic area of the international terminal toward departures and purchased a ticket for the first flight bound for New York. She produced her U.N. visa but paid for the ticket with her personal credit card.

She still had nearly two hours before her flight left, and she flashed her identification at a security checkpoint to gain access to a private lounge reserved for diplomats. A separate more leisurely area of the lounge contained soft drinks, snacks, and four televisions each closed-captioned in a different foreign language. Beyond the modular sofas and chairs stood a door manned by a plainclothes security man to make sure no one unauthorized entered the private offices and conference rooms.

Danielle lacked such authorization but, fortunately, the diplomatic lounge itself was outfitted with a bank of six computers, each contained in its own partitioned work space. All were vacant, and she settled herself into one nearest the center.

The machine was already on, and she clicked on the Internet icon. She thought of Victoria Henley, the fear in the young woman's eyes as she told the tale of her brother and father. A few hours later she was dead, leaving Danielle to follow whatever trail she could uncover back to the United States and the 121st Evacuation Hospital.

Danielle watched the screen spring to life with the colorful graphics of a Web provider. She thought of Ben, off trying to find the true party behind the massacre in the village of Bureij. Separated from her again.

So what else was new?

Nothing. That was the problem. London for Ben and Danielle was no different from their time together in the United States, or the Middle East for that matter. More obstacles keeping them apart than reasons to stay together.

Danielle had started to key in the U.S. Army's Web site in search of information about the 121st when another thought occurred to her. Many veterans groups maintained their own Web sites. Perhaps the 121st was one of them. She ran a search under "121st Evacuation Unit" and hit Enter.

Seconds later, a dozen listings filled the screen, the first directing her, as hoped, to the unit's official Web site. She clicked on it and watched as the screen emptied and almost instantly began to fill again.

The 121st's Web site was slick and professionally produced, its cover page full of impressive graphics and colors. A number of subheadings lined the left-hand portion of the screen from "Reunion Report" to "Buchenwald Revisited." Danielle clicked on the heading labeled "Roster."

A small clock icon appeared in the top right corner, as the screen dissolved and reformed again, this time into a listing of bios and contact addresses headlined by recent deaths of unit veterans. Danielle imagined a killer searching out his victims this very same way, heroes of World War II who had survived that and everything since only to make themselves terribly easy targets.

The Web site was not up-to-date, at least a few months behind judging from the brief listing of recent deaths: four of the twelve Victoria Henley had alluded to, all of them easily explicable through means other than cold-blooded precision murder.

A death in surgery.

A car accident.

A heart attack.

A private plane crash.

Danielle clicked on the profiles page and scrolled down, counting as she went. Over three hundred personnel had been part of the 121st originally. Only thirty-seven remained listed on the site, of which a dozen had not updated their entries for several years, meaning their contact info could easily be out of date. The section finished in a listing of those for whom no bio was present along with a call to contact Jerry Nadler with any information.

Danielle realized why the Web site had not been updated for several months. Jerry Nadler was one of the dozen members of the unit to have perished in the past few months.

She went back to the head of the list and scrolled down more slowly, studying the current addresses in search of those closest to New York City. There was a Scarsdale, an Albany, a Stamford, Connecticut, and a Honesdale, Pennsylvania. Danielle was about to jot them down, then decided to just hit Print instead. Instantly she heard a whirring sound and saw a Hewlett-Packard humming to life on a stand to her right.

Who knew how many of these four were dead by now too? But Danielle only needed to find one still alive, one who could tell her what the 121st had uncovered in Buchenwald sixty years ago.

W hat makes you think this man is ready to help us?" Ben said, as Colonel al-Asi raised his hand to knock on the repair shop's side door.

"Because Abu Kishek wants something, Inspector, something I can't give him that you can."

"What's that?"

"A visa for his son to attend the Olympic Games this summer. The young man's a champion boxer, capable of bringing Palestine our first medal ever. He used to train at the athletic center near the old Casbah before the Israelis closed it. Now he trains here in the auto repair shop, when the curfews allow."

"Have you seen him fight?"

Al-Asi nodded. "An exhibition match with the Israelis when he was just a boy. Good, fast hands. Strong jaw. A Palestinian who deserves a chance."

The door opened and a midsized, slightly overweight man with a receding hairline looked out nervously.

"Quickly," Abu Kishek greeted, peering out to the edge of the alley. "Come in."

He closed and locked the door again as soon as they were inside. The repair shop was larger than it looked from the outside, the air laced with the scents of motor oil and rubber. Ben noticed a corner of the floor had been cleared of all cars and supplies to make room for training equipment. A heavy punching bag dangled by a chain from a ceiling beam. A speed bag had been installed into the wall. Dumbbells and barbells were squeezed against a wall near an ancient tread-mill a mechanic had turned on its side to better access the damaged controls.

"My son cannot run in the streets or the hills anymore," Kishek explained, when he saw Ben eyeing the equipment. "He must do all his training in here."

"Inspector Bayan Kamal," Ben said, extending his hand.

Kishek removed a workman's glove to shake it, then looked humbly toward al-Asi. "Thank you for bringing him, Minister."

"You said it would be worth our while."

"So long as you make it worth my son's, yes." He looked toward Ben again. "The minister has explained my son's situation?"

Ben nodded.

"Are you able to help?"

"Given a reason to, yes."

Kishek led them forward across the center of a shop packed with broken-down cars. With no money to purchase new vehi-cles, Palestinians had no choice but to hold on to their old ones, even as they advanced well past their effective life spans. Then again, few had anywhere to drive to these days. And, judging by the layers of dust accumulating on many of the cars, Ben guessed they had been here for a very long time.

They stopped at a far wall lined with tool-bearing shelves. The topmost held a wide assortment of tires, all of them used and few of them, by the look of things, that matched.

"I need assurances," Kishek said anxiously.

"You want a special United Nations compensatory visa for your son to attend the Olympic Games this summer," Ben told him. "I want information about the massacre in Bu-reij. I get what I want, and you get what you want."

"I meant assurances that I will be kept out of your investi-gation, that what I'm about to tell you remains here in this shop."

"You have my word."

But Kishek looked toward al-Asi. "Minister?"

The colonel nodded a single time.

With that, Kishek took a deep breath and reached up to the wall as if to grab for a ratchet set. But he bypassed all the tools for a secret latch that gave with a click. Then he pushed open a door hidden against the wall.

"Remember your promise," he said to Ben before leading the way through.

Al-Asi entered next, followed by Ben whose nose had already detected the pungent aroma of fresh auto paint. He found himself in a section of the shop about a third the size of the primary area beyond, lined with a smattering of military-style vehicles in various stages of alteration to make them appear authentic Israeli army issue.

"I want you to understand something," Kishek said, while Ben continued to run his eyes about the collection, cataloging what he saw. "I don't work for terrorists. I don't do business with murderers. We use vehicles like these to travel between towns, reunite families, and transport vital supplies—food and medicine. You need to know that."

"Whatever you say."

"You are Palestinian."

"Yes."

"Then you must understand."

Ben moved up to a truck drying under a set of heat lamps. "I understand vehicles like these have been used in attacks on several Israeli settlements."

"I know nothing of that! Nothing!"

"But you know something about the massacre in Bureij."

Kishek sighed deeply. "Some young men came to me last week seeking very specific vehicles. I needed the money for my son's training. No one has any cash to pay for repairs. They tell me keep the car as collateral. What am I supposed to do with them all?"

"Get back to these men who came to you last week."

Kishek took several breaths to steady himself. "They were looking for one transport and two Humvees."

"Israeli military patrol," al-Asi noted. "Standard deployment."

"I told them I could handle the transports, but that I had no access to Humvees. They would have to settle for older-style Jeeps. They agreed. I named my price. They didn't argue."

"You met these young men in person?"

Kishek nodded. "Twice. Little more than boys really, three of them. They picked up their vehicles four days ago."

"The day before the massacre."

Kishek shrugged.

"How were you paid?"

"In cash. American dollars."

"Do you still have the money?"

"Some. Hidden."

"What did these Palestinian boys look like?"

Kishek scowled. "Who said they were Palestinian? You see, my son followed them when they left. They were Jews."

ow is she today, Ruth?" Franklin Winters asked his wife's aide, stepping into the kitchen.

"Having one of her better days, Mr. Winters," Ruth replied, her white nurse's uniform stretched by her ever increasing weight. "She's in the backyard. Don't worry," she continued, before Winters could voice his concern. "I've been keeping an eye out."

Winters moved through the sliders onto the deck and then down the stairs into the backyard. Before the Alzheimer's, the yard had been his wife's pride and joy, tended to with love and care that made it a landscaping showplace. Mary would prune, trim, and weed for hours, fashioning every individual part toward achieving a perfect whole.

The gardens were run down now, dying of neglect, barely recognizable from what they had once been. Several times Winters had hired gardeners and landscapers to tend them, abandoning the process when it agitated and unnerved Mary to a degree that aggravated her condition. There was no real hope for improvement, only an attempt to slow the process slightly.

From the deck, Winters could see his wife kneeling in a rock garden amidst the withered remains of flowers and shrubs. Mary's nightgown was soiled at the knees and streaks of dirt marred the fabric where she had wiped off her hands. She looked up when she heard him coming down the stairs.

"Hello, Franklin," she greeted happily.

At least she recognized him. One of the good days, then. Not telling the secretary of state the truth behind his resignation, trying to keep his wife's illness a secret, had been meant to preserve her dignity. Now, though, gazing down at the woman whose entire world consisted of this yard and the four walls beyond, Winters wondered whether it was his own dignity he was out to save.

"Spring's coming," Mary continued. "I thought I'd get a head start on things this year. The roses look beautiful, don't you think?"

In point of fact, they were long-dead stems and nothing more.

"Beautiful," Winters told his wife, forcing a smile.

She climbed awkwardly to her feet and wiped more dirt onto her nightgown. "I'd better get lunch ready. It's Wednesday, you know."

It was Tuesday.

"And Jason comes home early from school on Wednesdays. Do we have milk?"

"Plenty."

"Boy's gotta have his milk. I think tuna fish today. Yes, tuna. That's my husband's favorite." Mary narrowed her gaze at Winters, as if noticing him for the first time. "Do you know Franklin?"

Winters could barely manage a nod.

Mary peered toward the house. "He must be inside. I'll go and get him. Did he invite you for lunch?"

"Yes," Winters said, the word nearly catching in his throat.

"Tuna fish for three, then. I like the brand packed in water not oil. The oil's too heavy. Upsets my stomach."

Mary stopped when she came to a hoe wedged into the ground and leaned over. For the first time, Winters noticed that she had started tiny holes all through the yard, as if digging for something she'd never be able to find. When she stood back up with the hoe in hand, she looked different, suddenly more alert.

"Franklin, when did you get home?"

"A few minutes ago."

"You drop Jason off at school?"

"Yes."

"Did I tell you his teacher called? He got into another fight." Mary shook her head. "You're not firm enough with that boy, Franklin. You spoil him rotten."

She came up and gave him a hug before plodding up the wooden steps to the deck. Winters watched his wife lean the hoe against a cast-iron bench en route to the door. The disease had robbed her of everything, but life had robbed Winters of almost as much. He watched her stop suddenly, swing round, and retrace her steps to the railing. She placed a pair of withered hands atop the finished wood and peered into the once beautiful backyard gardens. Winters found himself envying her a little. Living in the past, happy at least in those few moments when life flashed back and froze happiness.

Winters would never be happy again, and he knew it. Mary might be happy, but wouldn't remember it.

Which was worse?

Winters would give anything to wake up one morning and believe, with all his heart, that Jason was coming home. He longed for the undoubting simplicity of that notion. Mary would prune nonexistent roses, dig holes for flowers she'd never plant, and return to the process the following day unimpeded by her ravaged mind.

"Better times are ahead," Mary said suddenly and strongly, a phrase she had used often before the disease had stolen her sense of reason. "Better times are ahead."

"Yes," Winters said, even though she was paying no attention to him, "they are."

D anielle slowed the rental car to a jogger's pace, consulting the street map doubled over and creased on her lap. According to the directions Charles Corstairs had provided over the phone, the turnoff she was looking for should be coming up any moment.

Night had already fallen when she began her drive from New York City and now a thick blanket of fog had settled over the Pocono Mountains of Honesdale, Pennsylvania. Charles Corstairs, one of the remaining survivors of the 121st Evacuation Unit, was the third person she had called on her list, having received no answer at the first two. She had remained cryptic about the reason for the call, saying only that she had information vital to the 121st.

Corstairs, according to the brief bio on the unit's Web site, was a rose farmer and had been for twenty years. He had sold his original, much larger spread in New York State three years back and downsized himself here following the death of his wife to cancer.

Fearing she was lost, Danielle tried his number on her cell phone, only to discover no signal was available. So she pulled over and flipped on the car's dome light to better study the map. A glance up at a hand-scrawled street sign told her she had found the route she was looking for. She turned off the dome light, tossed the crinkled remnants of the map to the passenger seat, and took a right down a flattened but unpaved road. A quarter mile up, she saw a white mailbox and turned into Corstairs's driveway.

He had told her to meet him at the house, but she saw lights on in a long, rectangular greenhouse and movement flickering about the rows. So she parked closer to the greenhouse and moved toward a rear entrance.

The door flew from her grasp when she eased it open, banging against the inside wall with a rattling clang.

"Mr. Corstairs?" she called, as she closed it, much more carefully. The pungently sweet smell of roses assaulted her. Their scent, so beautiful in a bouquet, was overwhelming in such a vast multitude. "Mr. Corstairs."

"Over here," a voice greeted from the other side of the greenhouse. Slightly hoarse, but sounding powerful and much younger than Corstairs's seventy-seven years. "You must be Ms. Barnea."

Corstairs emerged between two rows of long-stem roses, wearing a rubber apron and matching gloves. He was tall and still fit, looking a decade or more younger than his actual age. Beyond the glass of the greenhouse, the fog continued to flow in waves, obscuring the world beyond.

Danielle met him halfway up the row, between symmetrical plantings of white and red long-stem roses. She kept breathing through her mouth until she grew accustomed to the powerful aroma that permeated the room. "Thank you for seeing me so soon."

"You mind if I see an ID?"

Danielle produced it, still not used to the cumbersome size of the United Nations identification wallet. Corstairs took the ID, checked the face against hers, and then handed it back, apparently satisfied.

"United Nations Safety and Security Service," he then said.

"That's right, Mr. Corstairs."

"Call me Charlie, please. I'm a farmer, Inspector Barnea. No one's called me mister in longer than I want to remember."

"They called you corporal in World War Two, though, didn't they?"

Corstairs seemed to tense a little, recalling the reason for Danielle's visit. "Inspector Barnea—"

"Danielle, please."

"Danielle, you mind telling me what my old unit has to do with U.N. security?"

"Nothing directly. It's something that came up in another investigation I was pursuing."

"Something that came up," Corstairs repeated.

"Your commanding officer was a man named Walter Henley."

Corstairs nodded sadly. "He died a few weeks ago. A robbery or something. I . . . couldn't make the funeral."

"His daughter believes he was murdered, along with a dozen other members of the 121st."

Corstairs remained expressionless, waiting for Danielle to continue.

"Because of something your unit found in Buchenwald."

Corstairs stiffened. His upper lip crimped slightly upward. "Vicky tell you that, too?"

"In Jerusalem. Before she was killed as well."

Charlie Corstairs started to walk away, then stopped, leaving his back turned to Danielle.

"Was she right, Mr. Corstairs?"

He turned and shook his head sadly, then looked at Danielle again. "Charlie, remember?" He pointed to the right. "Come this way, Danielle, there's something I'd like to show you."

Three rows over Danielle found herself staring at beautiful plantings of peach-colored roses. At first she didn't even think they were roses, so broad and thick were their petals.

"Ever seen roses like this before?" Corstairs asked her.

"No," Danielle said, reaching out to touch one.

"Of course not, because I created them. They're hybrids, formed by crossing different species of roses."

Corstairs reached out and plucked one from its pot, handing it to Danielle who took it gently in hand.

"I like to think when I do this I'm creating life," he continued. "I started crossbreeding just after my wife died, for therapy I guess. But now I realize it wasn't therapy for her death so much as for Buchenwald. What we saw there, how unprepared we were." Corstairs shivered slightly. "You said on the phone you were Israeli."

"Yes."

"Then you understand."

"All too well."

"My wife and I went back there not long before she died. The memories all came back. I couldn't get them out of my head."

"What about sixty years ago? What was it the 121st found hidden in Buchenwald?"

Corstairs cleared his throat and began to speak.

"FOUND WHAT, Corporal?" asked Colonel Walter Henley.

"You'd better come over here, sir."

"On my way."

Henley came on foot to the other side of the camp where Trench Delta was located. He fit his surgical mask over his face and peered down at where Corstairs was standing, shovel in hand. In the process of searching for more bodies, he had cleared away the dirt in this portion of the trench, exposing something dull and gray.

"It's metallic, sir," Corstairs said, tapping the object with his shovel.

Henley heard the pinging sound and leaned farther over

the edge. He nearly slipped and only a private's quick grasp saved him from tumbling into the muck and collected lime.

"I've dug a little around the outside," Corstairs continued. "I think it's a storage case for papers, documents."

"Belonging to the camp's occupants, perhaps."

"Perhaps, sir."

"Then we should remove it and find out. We might learn more about those poor souls we're trying to save. At least reunite them with what little we can."

"Colonel?"

"Yes, Corporal."

"There are other cases, at least two more in this same trench."

Henley thought for a moment. "I'm going to send you a detail of men. I want those cases removed and I don't want them damaged."

"THERE WERE three cases," Corstairs finished, his mind sliding back to the present. "Each about three by five feet. Solid steel, almost like safes, and locked tight as a drum. A fourth we found last was smaller, more like a lockbox. I carried that one to Henley myself. The others we put on the back of a truck."

"What else?"

"That's all, at least from my end. Except, well . . ."

"What, Charlie?"

"A day or so later two armed guards had been posted at the truck, and a few days after that, it was gone. I don't know where. Colonel Henley never mentioned the cases again and neither did I."

"He never opened them."

"Not to my knowledge he didn't. Henley was my commanding officer. The truth is I don't know what happened to whatever was inside those cases from the time we loaded them on the truck."

"But we can assume they didn't contain the possessions of the camp's residents."

"Clearly not."

Danielle looked down at the hybrid rose in her hand. "And in all the years since you never asked Henley what those contents were?"

"I don't think I wanted to know," Corstairs told her. "Besides, we were out of touch for decades after the war. It was only a few years ago that the unit started holding reunions and I've missed all of them."

"By choice?"

Corstairs looked down at a floor speckled with stray droplets from a recent watering. "It helps some of them to get together and talk about Buchenwald. It doesn't help me." He looked around at the vast array of roses. "This does."

"Who else in the unit might have seen what was in those cases?"

"Henley's second in command, a captain named Jack Phills."

"Phills?" Danielle tried to recall that name from the roll of the 121st's living and dead, but couldn't.

"He doesn't go to reunions either, but for altogether different reasons. You see—"

Glass shattered. Pots tipped over and smashed to the floor. Danielle barreled into Corstairs and took him down an instant before the next barrage of fire blew apart the plantings directly over their heads.

CHAPTER 28

D anielle could feel Corstairs trembling beneath her, his body otherwise stiff as a board.

"Are you all right?" she asked in his ear. "Are you all right?"

"Yes, yes. I think so. . . . Yes."

Another barrage shattered more of the greenhouse's windows. Flowerpots exploded and debris rained down upon them.

"Do you have a gun?" Danielle asked, starting to ease herself off Corstairs.

"Yes, but not here. In the house."

Danielle tried to recall the layout of the property. Too much ground separated Corstairs's home from the greenhouse to make his gun of any use to her. She looked up at the fog wafting into the greenhouse through the broken windows, softening the bright light.

Light . . .

"Where's the switch?"

"What? I—"

"The light switch!"

"Front wall," Corstairs answered, pointing tentatively from the floor. "Right side of the door."

Danielle calculated the distance. Fifty, maybe sixty feet. "What about weapons? Tools, insecticide—anything."

Corstairs stretched a hand beneath his apron and extended a spade to Danielle. The spade had three sharp, curved prongs currently crusted with soil and it fit neatly in her palm.

"Roll under the planting table behind you," she told Corstairs. "Stay there until I come get you."

Danielle crawled fast across the floor, holding the spade before her. This wasn't the first time she'd traveled weapon-less and been forced to improvise. Back in her days with Sayaret Makal in the Israeli Special Forces it was often a way of life, but it was something she had never liked or grown used to.

Another burst of gunfire sent more glass spraying throughout the greenhouse. Danielle could feel the cold moistness of the fog now, mixing with the heat burst rising off her body. She felt surprisingly calm, everything sharp and in focus. Little things suddenly standing out, like the light shimmer of sweat that coated the surface of her skin.

She reached the front wall and studied the bank of light switches briefly before lurching upward and drawing all of them down at once in a single swipe. The greenhouse was plunged instantly into darkness, evening the odds somewhat. The gunmen had no choice but to come inside now, into the darkness where their superior numbers could be more easily dealt with.

Danielle retrained her grip on the spade to make sure it was ready to use as a weapon, then moved to the green-house's far back corner where the little light shining in from the house was least available. More glass shattered, as a pair of gunmen hurdled through the already weakened windows, spraying the room with gunfire that flashed through the thickening fog. The door banged open, and Danielle thought she recognized another two sets of footsteps barging their way inside.

Four men in total, then. Just what she had suspected.

Stay under the table, Danielle thought, as if Corstairs might hear her.

She stood motionless in the corner, waiting for the separation she needed to launch her first strike. Her heart thudded with practiced anticipation, not fear. Ten months without any action and now twice in the same week. Doing what she did best, what she had been trained to do for so long.

Danielle saw one of the gunmen heading toward her, turning slowly from one side to the other as he made his sweep. That meant his eyes were poised her way barely a third of the time; ample opportunity for her to choose her moment to pounce.

In the end, instinct dictated her move. She sprang because something inside, like an internal clock, told her it was time. She caught the man at a moment when he was turned all the way around, facing the opposite direction. Danielle felt herself grabbing his hair and jerking his head back as she raked the prongs of the spade across his throat. There was little sensation after that. Just a splash of warmth and the coppery stench of blood as it gushed from his wound. Danielle had stripped the submachine gun from his grasp before he touched the floor.

Three attackers left, all separated in the same darkness that was now hers to blend into. She crouched low and tried to pick out any of the remaining gunmen amidst the indistinct shapes lost to the thickening fog and endless rows of multicolored roses.

Danielle ducked still lower and tried to spot her targets under the planting tables. But the meager light spilling in from the main house didn't reach the floor.

"Over here," a hushed voice called across the greenhouse. "I think I heard something."

The speaker must have been closing on Charlie Corstairs's position. Danielle heard a brief clatter of footsteps, followed by another. Then she angled her submachine gun slightly upward, aiming for a still-whole portion of the greenhouse's windows, and squeezed off a rapid burst.

The submachine gun jumped in her hands, the percussion of the shots stinging her ears and drowning out the sound of more glass shattering. A pair of shapes in the greenhouse's center spun toward the sound and opened fire.

Danielle studied their muzzle flashes, programming the positions into a part of her brain that acted on such things subconsciously. She rose to an upright position and fired twin, evenly spaced bursts at the spots where the gunfire had flared. One man screamed and took a section of potted roses with him to the floor. The other was punched backward into a support beam from which he slowly slumped down.

Danielle heard the final man's footsteps pounding across the floor. He was almost to the door when she locked him in her sights, aiming low for the legs to make sure she took at least one of them alive. Pulled the trigger.

Click.

She tossed the empty submachine gun aside and leaped up on the nearest table, feeling her shoe sink into freshly watered soil before she leaped to the next. Four tables later, she dropped to the floor with her gaze locked on the final man fleeing into the night. Almost to the door, she heard a gasping sound and swung to find Charlie Corstairs kneeling on the floor clutching his chest, face pale white against the churning fog.

He was having a heart attack.

Danielle rushed to him, left the final man to the night. She eased Corstairs down to a lying position atop a bed of shattered glass, soil, and the remnants of roses, and cradled his head in her lap to keep it elevated.

"Breathe easy, Charlie. You're going to be all right."

Suddenly he began gasping for breath, his hands flailing through the air as if for something to grasp. One of them struck Danielle in the cheek as she maneuvered to lie his body out flat. Then his hands stiffened and flopped to his sides, the old man's eyes locked open.

Danielle tilted Corstairs's head backward and tried CPR, alternating her breathing with chest compressions. Minutes passed, how many she couldn't say before she sat down next to the body, breathless and exhausted.

Danielle tried a few more minutes of CPR before finally giving up and exiting the greenhouse, as the distant wail of sirens fluttered through the night air.

CHAPTER 29

W hat's going on?" Ben asked al-Asi, as they neared a military blockade erected before the entrance of an Israeli settlement.

The colonel half-smiled. "That's right. You've been away from our country for a while. You are witnessing an eviction, Inspector."

"By *Israelis*?"

Al-Asi nodded. "Of another outpost manned by what we've come to call the Hilltop Youth. The brainchild of one Sammy Barr. Ever heard of him?"

"No."

"Call him a fabulously wealthy rogue settler. Famous for buying land from Palestinians in the occupied territories to create more settlements. Infamous for planting bombs in the cars of Arab mayors and plotting to blow up the Dome of the Rock."

Ben could see some sort of ruckus going on just short of the top of the hill. Israeli soldiers, it looked like, dragging and carrying teenage boys and girls toward a waiting bus.

"What does he have to do with all this, Colonel?"

"A few years ago, one of Barr's grandsons was shot and killed. While the family was mourning him, a few of the boy's friends set up camp with tents and sleeping bags on a hill facing Barr's estate on the other side of Nablus. That was the beginning of the Hilltop Youth. Thanks to Sammy

Barr's financial support in the years since, over seventy of these small encampments have been built illegally, manned almost entirely by radical Israeli youths. The Israeli government has finally become more proactive in dismantling them. But every time one outpost gets taken down, another rises up, usually erected by those just evicted."

Ben watched more children being herded forcefully onto the bus. "So their incarceration doesn't last very long."

"They receive a slap on the wrist and are told to never do it again. Make no mistake about it, Inspector, these are dangerous children; not so much for what they are as for what they're going to grow up to be. They represent the first generation of Israelis to be born on the settlements. They feel their right to this land transcends everything else and they are not of a mind to compromise."

Ben gazed again at the Israeli boys and girls swiping at soldiers with their fists and imagined them grown up, in a position to wield power. He looked back toward al-Asi and could tell from the colonel's grim expression that he had been thinking the same thing.

"Do you trust Kishek?" Ben asked, stopping his U.N. vehicle well short of the Israeli blockade.

"He is a man with something to gain, Inspector. Often that is the best reason to trust anyone."

Ben and al-Asi approached the roadblock with arms extended before them and identifications held open in their hands. The soldiers seemed to be regarding them casually until one of them, a captain, emerged from behind the cover of a tank with his palm extended into the air.

"That's far enough," he ordered.

He approached and checked Ben's ID, then al-Asi's, letting his stare linger for a longer time on the colonel.

"What's going on here has nothing to do with the United Nations," the captain finally said to Ben.

"We're here on another matter."

"You mean *you* are," the captain shot back. He pointed toward al-Asi. "He's not. He has no authority here. In fact, I don't see a travel pass stapled to his papers."

"This man is minister of the interior for the Palestinian Authority."

The captain smiled. "Then he's out of his territory, isn't he?"

"I'd like to question the leaders of this outpost."

"Farm."

"Pardon me?"

"Farm. They call it a farm. Meitza Farm, after one of their friends who was shot to death while taking a walk."

"You'd rather leave them in place, wouldn't you, Captain?"

The officer shrugged. "I don't know. The more we evict them, the madder they get, so you tell me. In any case, they're now in Israeli custody. You'll have to wait until they're processed to file a request for an interview."

"Do you know why I'm here, Captain?"

"Can't say that I care."

"I'm investigating the massacre in Bureij. As you'll note in my . . . papers, the Israeli government has granted me the authority to interview anyone I see fit when I see fit." Ben hardened his stare, hoping it added to the substance of his bluff. "I'd like to interview the leaders of this farm, Captain, and I'd like to interview them now."

CHAPTER 30

A pair of soldiers drove Ben up the last stretch of hill-side in a jeep open to the descending night. The wind was crisp and cool and he longed for the jacket he had left in the U.N. vehicle back at the blockade where Colonel al-Asi was being held until he returned.

Drawing closer to the outpost, Meitza Farm, he saw a pair of ramshackle tireless trailers plopped down on the ground not far from what looked like a rusted trash Dumpster, fitted with makeshift roof and window cutouts so it might serve as living quarters. As he watched, another pair of boys were dragged out of the Dumpster, the second grasping the jagged cutout of a doorjamb for effect more than anything.

The youth of Meitza Farm looked more like American hippies than young religious zealots. They had wound their drooping side curls into what passed for dreadlocks and their brightly colored knitted yarmulkes looked like the shapeless caps worn by urban youth back in the U.S. Their baggy pants billowed in the breeze and their bare feet, kicked free of san-dals in their struggling, were brown with dirt and grime.

One of the soldiers who had escorted him to the hilltop moved to talk with the officer orchestrating the eviction, while the other stayed back, staring caustically at Ben the whole time.

"You may speak with the leaders," the soldier explained when he returned, "only if they wish to speak with you."

"Tell them I'm Palestinian," Ben suggested. "They won't be able to resist."

HE WAS right, of course, but given only five minutes for his interview. The boys' names were Moshe, Ari, and Gilad. All rail thin, their pants riding very low on their hips. Moshe wore glasses. Ari had on a T-shirt emblazoned with the logo of some American hard rock band. Gilad had clubbed his hair back into a ponytail, leaving only the side curls dangling free. They were sequestered inside one of the dilapidated trailers, an Israeli soldier posted just outside the open doorway. The trailer smelled of must and mold, but was reasonably clean, which made Ben realize he had not seen a single speck of garbage outside.

So the Israelis hauled away trash from this isolated hilltop encampment, while down below amidst the flickering nightlights of the city of Nablus, no garbage had been picked up in months.

"You have a cigarette?" Moshe, the bespectacled one, asked him.

"I don't smoke."

"All Palestinians smoke."

"When they're not fucking," Ari said, and plucked an acoustic guitar from its stand against the wall. He strummed a few wild notes. "Making more Arab babies they can't feed."

"Yeah," echoed the ponytailed Gilad who, Ben noticed, had a black eye.

"Where'd you get that?" Ben asked him, pointing to the bruise.

"Another Palestinian punched me in the olive grove. I punched him back harder."

Ari hit a harsh riff on the guitar to enunciate his friend's point.

"Some members of Meitza Farm were seen in Nablus," Ben told them, lowering his voice, "buying vehicles painted to look like Israeli military issue. I'd like to know who they are."

Ari stopped strumming the guitar.

"We don't know what you're talking about," claimed Gilad, toying with his side curls.

"I think you do. In fact, I think you were the ones who arranged to obtain the vehicles, vehicles that were used by men impersonating Israeli soldiers when they massacred thirty-four innocent people in the Palestinian village of Bureij. I'm willing to overlook your part in this, but only on the condition you tell me where I can find the men you're working with."

"We can't tell you what we don't know," Moshe told him.

"You're being used," Ben said.

"You're full of shit."

"Listen to me, whoever's behind this can't afford to let you live," Ben said, rotating his gaze between the three of them. "You know too much. Your only chance is to help me find them before they come after you."

"You think we're scared? You think we're scared of anyone?"

"You would be if you were smart."

"Jews aren't cowards like Arabs."

"Being afraid to die doesn't make you a coward."

"What makes you a coward?" pestered Gilad.

"Is Sammy Barr involved in this?" Ben asked them.

The three boys exchanged glances, smiling.

"Who?" one of them asked snidely.

"Never heard of him," another followed.

Ben climbed to his feet. "I guess I'll have to ask him for myself."

CHAPTER 31

Jake Fleming woke up with a start, figuring it must all have been a dream. But he found himself seated in a stiff chair in a room he didn't recognize. His head throbbed. His mouth felt pasty and dry. He massaged his neck, realized he must have been lying with his face on the Formica table in front of him because his right cheek was asleep. He swept the long sandy brown hair, now gnarled and tangled, from his face, held it briefly behind him, and then shook it over his shoulders again.

The door to the room opened and a man wearing a suit entered. But the suit didn't fit right, as if the guy had lost lots of weight since he'd first bought it. There were bags under the guy's eyes and frown creases worn into his cheeks. He sat down and opened up a folder he must have had tucked under his arm.

"My name's Fisher, Jake. Can I call you Jake?"

"What am I supposed to call you?"

"Del."

"Del?"

"Short for Delbert."

"You're the one who drove me here," Jake said, the foggy parts of his mind starting to clear.

"That's right."

"So where's here?"

"Office of Homeland Security."

"We in Washington?"

Fisher shook his head. "Not exactly. We maintain a dozen regional offices."

"Never heard of them."

"Nobody has. The idea is to spread them out through the country to assure the fastest, most secure response. Right now you're at the Sector Three facility just outside of Nashua, New Hampshire."

"Not exactly a hotbed for terrorist activity."

"That's the point."

"What?"

"You go to Brown, Jake. Why don't you tell me?"

Jake let go of his smugness. "Okay. You'd want to keep your regional facilities away from the most likely targets, including large centers of population." He twisted to better face Delbert Fisher. "Look, I'm not saying I don't smoke. I do, but I don't deal, and last time I checked I wasn't much of a threat to homeland security."

"What's your major at Brown?"

"Computer science, but I haven't declared yet. You don't have to until you're a junior." The boy's eyes widened. "Hey, is this about that hack into the FBI mainframe I pulled? That was a joke, man. I already apologized to the school and—"

"Are you familiar with al-Qaeda, Jake?"

"The terrorist group? Sure."

"Are you a member of al-Qaeda?"

"Am I *what*? Hey, do I need a lawyer? Can I at least call my parents?"

Fisher just sat there, not even his face moving. "Are you familiar with the Patriot Act?"

"Sorry. No."

"Basically, it gives us the right to hold anyone suspected of terrorist activities without counsel and in secret."

"Terrorist activities? *Me?*" Jake raised his arms and held them before him. "Del, you really have the wrong guy. The closest I ever got to a terrorist was watching CNN."

"You operate a Web site."

"Whole bunch of them."

"And you're unaware that known terrorist operatives have been posting, receiving, and exchanging messages on this Web site?"

Fisher took a piece of paper from his folder and slid it across the table. Jake saw it was a copy of the e-mail inbox from one of his Web sites. A number of messages had been highlighted.

"I didn't open most of those. They had virus written all over them."

"We opened them, came up with fifty distinct user identities. But the messages are coded." Fisher leaned a little forward. "You could help yourself by helping us."

"How am I supposed to do that?"

"Tell us what the messages say."

"Would if I could, but I can't."

"Have you ever been to Afghanistan?"

"I'm from California, for Christ's sake!"

"Do you understand the severity of what you're being accused of?"

"What am I being accused of?"

"Conspiring to commit terrorist acts."

"Me?"

"I'm giving you a chance to cooperate."

"Wait, this is about one of my Web sites, right? The hempfest one's been up the longest," Jake said, examining the e-mail list lifted from his computer, "but these came off my party site."

"Party site?"

"I run reviews of raves and dance clubs. Just got it up and running maybe three weeks ago."

"Three weeks," Fisher repeated, his voice dropping an octave, the brash confidence slipping from his expression. "Could it have been twenty days?"

"Yeah, I guess so."

Fisher moved back through the doorway.

"Hey, where you going?"

"I need to check on a few things," Fisher said.

"I could use some food when you come back," Jake called after him, as the door closed tight.

DAY FIVE

T *here were three cases. Each about three by five feet.
Solid steel, almost like safes, and locked tight as a
drum.*

Danielle ran Charlie Corstairs's words through her mind,
trying to recall the ones that had followed.

*The fourth was smaller, more like a lockbox. I carried that
one to Henley myself. The others we put on the back of a
truck.*

Corstairs had not had the opportunity to elaborate on any
of those words before he died, meaning Danielle would have
to find that elaboration elsewhere along with information on
the man Corstairs had called Jack Phills. Not only was the
elusive second in command of the 121st Evacuation Unit not
listed on the unit's roster, but his name appeared nowhere on
the entire Web site in any form.

By five o'clock the next morning, after a few hours of
sleep at a cheap roadside motel, Danielle was on the road
again, heading toward Washington and wanting to reach
the Pentagon as near to its opening as possible. Along the
way she stopped only long enough for coffee and to use the
e-mail feature on her cell phone to send her request for information.

Everything had to be done, at least initiated, by e-mail
these days in information areas of the Pentagon. No more requests presented in person for immediate action. The e-mails

were handled in the order they were received, unless there was a priority coding or a personal contact.

In Danielle's case, it was the latter. Tom Spears had once been attached to the U.S. embassy in Israel until one day he got too close to a bomb and lost both his legs in the blast. Danielle was the lead investigator on the case and, when the terrorist responsible was killed by an Israeli missile, she had brought a picture of the aftermath to Spears in the hospital. He lay there, looked at it, and then laid it down atop his chest. Danielle stayed with him for a time in silence. They never actually spoke until months later. Spears called from his new post at the Pentagon just to say thank you. That was all.

They had met once during Danielle's brief tenure with a private security firm in the U.S., then again when she first took the job with the United Nations. She knew Spears got to work early and left late. So his receipt of her e-mail request was not in question, only his ability to fill it.

Upon arriving at the Pentagon, it took nearly an hour to process the paperwork required to grant Danielle access to the military intelligence section. Finally she centered the pass dangling from her neck and proceeded down an aisle dividing the two halves of a room lined with office cubicles. The two previous times she had met Spears had been on the outside, never inside this, his personal domain. He was waiting for her in his office doorway, hands on the armrests of his wheelchair, wearing his uniform with the pant legs clipped off just below his stumps.

"Long time, Danielle," Spears greeted.

She grasped his hand warmly between both of hers. Danielle noticed Spears's arms were thick and knobby with muscle from extensive workouts and wondered if he might have been compensating for the chopped-up trousers he wore to work every day.

"It wouldn't have been quite as long if they hadn't kept me waiting for an hour."

"That's because you're U.N. The U.N.'s not very popular around here."

"I haven't been many places where it is."

"Come on in," he said, and wheeled himself inside the office after her, closing the door.

Danielle gazed about, studying the surroundings. Not much of note other than the lack of a desk chair and the sight of a familiar picture hanging on the wall behind Tom Spears's desk: the picture Danielle had given him of the terrorist who had taken his legs being blown up.

She made sure her cell phone was turned off before she sat down. Alexis Arguayo had left a number of messages on her voice mail since last night. He sounded worried initially, but the latter messages must have come after he learned she had gone on from London of her own volition. The messages insisted that she return his call posthaste, which, of course, she hadn't.

Spears wheeled himself behind his desk and laid his fingers over his keyboard. "Okay, where do you want to start?"

"How about these steel cases the 121st Evacuation Unit found in Buchenwald?"

Spears worked the keys quickly, fingers dancing across them until he had found what he was looking for. "Reported recovered on April 17, 1945. Turned over to military intelligence on April 20. Three heavy steel cases. Three and a half by five feet in size, each weighing approximately two hundred pounds, including contents."

"Three days passed between recovery and pickup?"

"Could be. Could also be that the April 20th date refers to when they were logged in at military intelligence headquarters, not picked up in the field."

"Is that standard operating procedure?"

"Depends. They were kind of making up the rules as they went along at this point."

"What happened to the cases after they were logged in?"

"There is no after."

Danielle narrowed her gaze across the desk. "Pardon me?"

A trace of a smile flickered across Spears's lips. "I thought you'd like that. I can't find anything else filed about these cases from the day they were logged in. Almost as if they just disappeared."

CHAPTER 33

H ere, take a look," Spears continued, after giving Danielle a moment to digest his revelation.

She came out of her chair and Spears angled his computer screen so she could view it.

"You can see the routing numbers the cases were given upon check-in here, here, and here," he resumed, pointing to them one at a time. "Theoretically I punch in those routing numbers and I can get a complete report on the history of the cases and their contents. Like chain of evidence in a court trial."

"Theoretically."

Spears punched in one of the numbers and the screen displayed NO FILE ON RECORD. Entered the next two with the same results.

"Are you saying the army lost the cases?" Danielle asked, settling back in her chair.

"That happens sometimes."

"And other times?"

"They get lost on purpose, especially with sensitive documents or materials the army, or some other higher power, figures are better not left to public consumption, or even knowledge. Anything more you can tell me?"

Danielle tried to recall if Charlie Corstairs had said something else she had neglected to pass on to Spears, but ultimately just shook her head.

"I ran some other general checks," Spears told her, turning his wheelchair so that the picture of the terrorist's car ablaze was centered directly over his head. "Comparisons to see how similar materials were handled. Found plenty of examples, but the trouble was they were different, weren't really applicable."

"Why?"

Spears slid his chair under his desk. "Because your cases were found in Buchenwald, buried in a trench beneath the remains of bodies. Typically most of the materials and documents recovered from the Nazis were hidden *after* the war was lost. But yours, clearly, were buried before the war began."

"And were never seen again after the 121st dug them up."

"I didn't say that. Somebody saw them, but that somebody didn't want anybody to know that they saw them or what it was they saw."

Danielle nodded to herself. "You're saying I need more clearance."

Spears shook his head. "I'm not saying that. You could be the president of the United States and you still couldn't access this info. That's how deep somebody buried it. These cases of yours could be sitting in a storage warehouse in Bethesda right now or their contents could have been destroyed, for whatever reason, sixty years ago in Germany."

"Wait a minute," Danielle said, remembering something. "What about the fourth case?"

"Fourth?"

"According to Corstairs, four cases were dug out of the trench. Three large and one small, like a lockbox."

Spears looked back at his computer. "Sorry, only three were logged in at pickup."

Danielle frowned, frustrated over hitting a dead end. "Anything on Phills?" Danielle wondered, changing the subject to the 121st's second in command.

Spears keyed in a new site on his screen. "Career army.

Saw duty in Korea where he won a chest full of medals. A major by the time Vietnam rolled along. His last posting."

"Things didn't go well."

"Vietnam derailed a lot of careers around here. The halls are full of stories . . . and a few of the remains, if you catch my drift."

"We have them in Israel too, Major."

"Not like John Henry Phills you don't. He was a Special Forces commander, way before it was fashionable. Helped coordinate the Phoenix Project. Ever hear of it?"

"Vaguely."

"You should," Spears continued. "It's right up your alley. The Phoenix Project's prime directive was to knock off members of the Vietcong cadre. In areas where their assassins were active, we were actually winning the war."

"They weren't assassins, Tom."

Spears gave her a long look. "I guess your knowledge of Phoenix was a little sharper than you suggested."

"Like you said, it's right up my alley."

"Yeah, well, anyway, Phills went out with a team one night and was the only one to come back. Nobody ever got the whole story straight, but whatever happened was enough to get him sent home. He insisted he was okay, wanted to be returned to duty, but the brass was hearing none of it. Then the day he was shipping out, he showed up at the airport naked except for his boots, carrying his duffel bag."

"Section Eight?"

Spears nodded. "Two years in a veteran's hospital pysch ward. He dropped out after that. Went to live in the woods somewhere."

"Explains why his contact info's not listed on the 121st Evacuation Hospital's Web site."

"Fortunately, the Pentagon keeps better records. He's got a cabin in the Blue Ridge Mountains of West Virginia." Spears handed Danielle a detailed map that she saw had been printed off a computer. "You drive your car in as far as you can and then walk the rest of the way."

Danielle took the map, tried to estimate how long the walk would be.

"That doesn't mean he'll remember anything that can help you, though. Or even that he'll talk to you if he does."

"Leave that to me," said Danielle.

ammy Barr lived in a castlelike, Mediterranean-style home built of white stone and stucco that rose dramatically out of a West Bank hilltop overlooking Nablus. Stone statues of roaring lions flanked the main doorway visible from the road beyond the chain-link fence that surrounded the property. The chain-link was rimmed with barbed wire, but other than that there seemed little attention paid to security. No Israeli military presence was evident, surprisingly, as if this sprawling estate built on land purchased from Palestinians was more like an outpost of the Hilltop Youth and less like the home of an Israeli multimillionaire.

The gate was locked shut, and Ben rattled it a few times to see if he could gain anyone's attention. He imagined himself being watched on the most advanced surveillance system money could buy. Figured that the grounds within were either mined or wired with electrical fields to discourage invaders, maybe both.

Ben rattled the gate again. He looked inside the fence at landscaping that looked more like a picture postcard growing out of the desolation surrounding it than a real home. But Sammy Barr wasn't making a home here, he was making a point.

Ben rattled the gate harder.

"Who the fuck are you?" The booming, nasal voice

seemed to resonate from nowhere and everywhere at once, echoing slightly. *"Leave my fucking fence alone."*

Ben finally pinned the voice to one of two circular parapets that bracketed the massive structure on either side. Leaning out of the topmost window was a man with just a memory of curly hair fading back over his scalp, below which hung a pale flabby face on an outsize head, and a torso that looked small by comparison. Sammy Barr wore a white, short-sleeved button-down shirt opened at the collar. He was holding something Ben couldn't clearly make out against the parapet window's sill.

"Mr. Barr?"

"Ain't you a fucking smart one."

"I need a few minutes of your time, Mr. Barr," Ben said loudly, his voice punched back at him by the wind blowing in his face.

"You a lawyer, come to serve me with more papers? Fucking forget it. My land deals were a hundred percent aboveboard. People took my money of their own fucking volition. No one stuck a gun to their head, just stuck cash in their pockets."

"Really? I understand some of the contracts were falsified."

"Prove it, shyster."

"Can't. Some of the Palestinians you did business with have been killed as collaborators. The rest aren't about to come forward out of fear of being labeled the same thing."

"Ain't that a shame, shyster."

"I'm not a lawyer, Mr. Barr," Ben shouted up to the man in the tower. "I'm from the United Nations."

Barr leaned forward and Ben saw the object he was holding against the windowsill was an assault rifle. He raised it and fired a wild burst into the air well over Ben's head, making him flinch. "I gave at the office." Another barrage sailed skyward. "Now get the fuck out of here."

"I'd like to talk to you about the massacre in Bureij."

"Sure, come on up. We'll have a drink to celebrate."

"I'm Palestinian, Mr. Barr."

"Yeah, it figures. You're also U.N., if what you say is true, and neither of you has any authority here. You're on Israeli land."

"Depends who you talk to," Ben called back at him.

Ben turned and gazed down the hill, at the city of Nablus shimmering in the early-morning light. From this angle the pitted streets, the bombed-out buildings, and the barriers slicing the city into a labyrinth that led nowhere weren't visible. Nablus circa 1995 when hope accompanied freshly paved streets and new construction projects. It was a pleasant view until thoughts of what lay beyond the distant façade intruded.

"So get your ass back to your refugee camp," Barr continued, his voice seeming to grow more nasal, "and leave me the fuck alone."

"It'd be better for you if we talk."

"Or I could just shoot you and save myself the trouble."

"You have a grandson serving a two-year term in an Israeli prison for throwing a grenade into a Palestinian school yard."

"Grenade didn't go off. It was a dud and the boy knew it. I'll have him out in six months."

"No, Mr. Barr. Terrorist acts now fall under a new heading of Crimes Against Humanity being heard by the International Criminal Court, administered by the U.N. I don't think you want us to seek extradition, do you?"

Barr fired another burst, close enough to Ben this time to buckle his knees. "Israel doesn't recognize this court, never signed the agreement. Good luck getting him extradited, you fuck."

"I wasn't talking about him, Mr. Barr, I was talking about you."

"Hah, hah, hah!"

"It's not funny. I understand your fingerprints were found on the grenade too," Ben said, repeating what he had learned from Colonel al-Asi.

Barr stopped laughing and the sound's echo drifted past Ben into the hills beyond.

"Good luck making it stick."

"I don't plan to. I just want to open an investigation. See how your adoring public feels about their hero trying to kill children."

"My adoring public would love it. Besides, I knew the grenade was a dud."

"But your grandson didn't, and I think the publicity might just be enough to get the Israeli military to knock you down from your mighty world and off your high horse."

"What's your name?"

"Inspector Bayan Kamal."

"Well, Inspector Bayan Kamal, come back in a couple hours and maybe we can have a chat."

CHAPTER 35

"Thing is," Sammy Barr said from the other side of the fence, "I like to know who I'm talking to before I talk to them."

He keyed open all three padlocks and yanked the gate inward. Ben gazed about, figuring there must be security guards patrolling the grounds. But none were visible anywhere. Just Sammy Barr, who liked to call himself the King of All Settlers, living just beyond rifle range of a million Palestinians who wanted him dead.

Up close Barr looked small and meek. His outfit, white shirt and dark slacks, was the same one he had been wearing earlier that morning. So, too, Ben guessed, was the assault rifle he was holding.

Ben stepped through the gate and watched Barr fasten it behind him, angling the locks back into place.

"Inspector Bayan Kamal, more frequently referred to as Ben—and appropriately so since you hold dual citizenship in the United States." Barr spoke from memory as he struggled a bit to fit the locks home. "Born outside of Ramallah on the West Bank, but lived in the Dearborn area of Michigan from the time he was six until he was thirty-two, shortly after his wife and children were slain by the serial killer he was pursuing. Returns to West Bank where—"

"I get the point."

"I don't think you do," Sammy Barr said, and picked up where he had left off. "Returns to the West Bank to help train a Palestinian detective force and ends up making waves everywhere he turns. Accurate assessment?"

"Pretty close."

Barr finished relocking the gate and turned from the fence. "Can't trust those Palestinians, Benny. You see my point. Come on, let's take a walk."

Barr slung his assault rifle around his shoulder and led Ben onto his property. "Only thing worse than Palestinians is the fucking U.N. Means I got two reasons to hate you, and that's two reasons too many."

"Your fingerprints on that grenade wouldn't win you a lot of love either, Mr. Barr."

Barr smiled broadly, coming up just short of giving Ben a friendly slap on the back. "You're a fucking great detective. So's your friend Barnea."

Ben speared him with a look.

"You think I wouldn't find out, put two and two together? You find out about the grenade business from her?"

"No," Ben said, thinking of his conversation regarding Sammy Barr with Colonel al-Asi the night before.

"So what happened? She was running National Police, right?"

"Second in command, actually."

"Under whom?"

"No one. She was promised the job and—"

"Don't tell me: she got royally fucked."

"In a manner of speaking."

"I know all about that shit, Benny. Israelis aren't the easiest people to deal with and your friend Barnea ran afoul of lots of the same ones that would like nothing better than to see my ass in a sling. Know how I get by? I don't give a shit about them. Anyone doesn't agree with me, I say fuck 'em."

"I don't agree with you."

Barr stopped and gave him a closer look. "I'm big on taking homes away from your people. You'd be an asshole if you did agree with me."

"At least you admit it."

"Know why I'm talking to you, Benny? Because you're as stubborn an asshole as I am. You just won't learn your lesson. Not with the Palestinian police and not with the U.N. either. They send you to Baghdad to play tenth fiddle in the orchestra and you end up leading the band. Too bad nobody followed. Russians blowing up the U.N. compound to destroy Cold War documents? Shit, where was your evidence?"

"Blown up. That's the point."

"You must've had something."

"Just a few shreds. Nothing to make anyone look twice."

"Didn't stop you from pushing things, though, did it? I like a man who pushes. Right or wrong. The truth, Benny, is I'm one of those people who believes Israelis and Palestinians can't coexist together. It's just not in our nature. Means one of us has to go, and it's not going to be the Israelis. But, hey, you don't see me advocating forced expulsion like some do."

"No, you just arrange to have grenades tossed into Palestinian school yards."

"A dud grenade."

"What about the next one? You're inciting this Hilltop Youth to become a new generation of Jewish terrorists."

"I'm teaching them to keep what's theirs."

"You mean, take it."

"I mean, take it back. Read your Bible, Benny. The West Bank belongs to us. Share and share alike sounds good before the United Nations General Assembly, but it's not worth shit when Jewish kids get blown up on the way to school."

"So the grenade was your version of, what, a dry run? See if your young fanatics were up to spraying innocent villagers with machine gun fire?"

Ben had hoped to get a rise out of Sammy Barr with that. What he got instead was that familiar broad smile. "You'd like that to be true, wouldn't you? Make it so you could tie this thing up all nice and neat for your bosses at the United

Nations. Sorry to disappoint you, though, Benny. I had nothing to do with that massacre."

"What about your Hilltop Youth?"

"Same thing."

"Then why would they need to acquire Israeli military vehicles?"

Barr shook his head, the smile gone. "Give it a fucking rest, will you?"

"I can't. See, we don't know who fired the guns in Bureij, but we know the vehicles that brought the gunmen there were purchased by three residents of Meitza Farm."

"That's fucking bullshit! What, you think making us look like assholes is enough to make your point for you? Well, let me tell you something, Benny. I don't give a shit about that either."

Ben's cell phone rang and he excused himself to take the call when he saw it was from Colonel al-Asi, marked 911.

"You think I had something to do with that massacre?" Sammy Barr continued. "Forget it. Not my style. And if somebody says I did, they're a liar. Maybe I better talk to these little pricks myself on your behalf."

Ben finished his call and snapped his phone shut. "You can't."

"Why the fuck not?"

"Because a bus carrying them to the detention center in Jerusalem was struck by a rocket twenty minutes ago."

CHAPTER 36

"We owe you an apology," Delbert Fisher said, entering Jake's room with a box of doughnuts tucked under his arm.

"I told you I wasn't a terrorist. Just drive me back to school and we'll call it even," Jake said, and sat up on his cot. There wasn't much else in the windowless room to speak of. Just a bathroom about the size of a small closet containing a sink and toilet, but no shower. The bathroom didn't have a door and Jake had been doing his best to avoid using it, considering he was certain some hidden camera had him under surveillance 24/7. He saw the box held in Fisher's arm. "Hey, those for me?"

Delbert Fisher nodded and handed the doughnuts to Jake. The boy split open the top of the box and grabbed a chocolate frosted.

"Let's talk about that latest Web site you set up."

"I already told you. It's about raves and dance clubs, reviews and listings—that sort of sh—, er, stuff. Not the kind of thing I'd expect you'd be interested in."

"It's been up and running for just over three weeks."

"That's right."

"And that's the problem."

"Huh?"

Fisher sighed audibly. "Three weeks ago the German police raided an al-Qaeda stronghold in Hamburg. The men inside had enough warning to wipe out or erase all their computer files and records, before they went for their guns. There weren't any survivors to interrogate. You understand what I'm saying here?"

Jake nodded.

"The very next day your Web site goes on-line, with a URL identical to the one belonging to the Web site the terrorists had shut down."

"Uh-oh," Jake said.

"The leaders had time to destroy their records but not to warn the cells, the operatives, they were controlling. So the operatives continued business as usual." Fisher stopped and stared at Jake for a moment. "Updating reports as to their mission status."

"Mission status?"

"That's right, because something was about to go down. Something big."

Jake looked down at the floor. "I was wondering why I was getting so many hits. . . ."

"They left encrypted messages on your chat board."

"That explains why every time I tried to open them, all I got was gibberish. Figured it was a virus and trashed them."

Fisher's expression grew even more somber. "We figured you for the new conduit, picking up where the Hamburg cell left off."

"You don't figure me for that anymore, right?"

Fisher shook his head twice. "Not once we figured the coincidence out, no. But that left us with another problem, Jake: the terrorists are still out there and we've got no way to find them."

Jake leaned back against the wall and stuffed the rest of the chocolate frosted into his mouth. "What's that have to do with me?"

"We need to track them down, Jake. We need you to help us."

"*Me?* Don't you guys have a hall full of computer experts or some-thing?"

"Sure, we do, and none of them can replicate whatever it is you did that kept the operatives posting."

Jake started to reach for a second doughnut, then changed his mind. "Maybe something I did made them stop."

"We don't think so. And we can't take the chance that we're wrong because if we scare them off, we lose them for good." Fisher knelt down so he was eye to eye with Jake Fleming. "Our tech people identified fifty distinct electronic signatures. You know what that means."

"You keep asking me that," Jake said, pursing his lips and blowing the shaggy hair from his face.

"It wasn't a question, because you do *know* what that means. Fifty rogue cells prepared to launch an operation against this country."

"Just take me back to school. I want out of here."

"You can do that if you want," Fisher replied, quite calmly. "I'll drive you down myself. All you have to do is say the word."

"I just did."

Fisher nodded, looking sad. He straightened back up, knees cracking, and retreated toward the door. "Okay, let's go."

But Jake didn't move. "Wait a minute."

"Okay."

Jake cocked his head to the side, worked his teeth over his upper lip. "What exactly is it you want me to do?"

CHAPTER 37

The first thing Danielle saw when she stepped into the clearing was a man wearing a Confederate army uniform aiming a shotgun square at her.

"Avon don't usually venture this far out, pretty lady."

Major John Henry Phills stood on the porch of a perfectly crafted A-frame log cabin formed of wood identical in shade and texture to the surrounding trees.

"I'm Victoria Henley, Major Phills," Danielle said, forming the lie she had settled upon back in Tom Spears's office. "Colonel Walter Henley's daughter."

Phills tipped the shotgun's barrel downward. "Didn't know he had a daughter."

Danielle came a few steps closer, then stopped. "Did you know he was dead?"

"Nope. Sorry to hear it, though. If you came here to tell me, you done your part. Now be on your way."

"I need your help, Major. I need your help to figure out who killed him."

Phills eyed her suspiciously. "You a Yankee or a Reb?"

"Yankee."

"Too bad."

"I'm also here because you might be next."

"Not if the killers are as sloppy as you, pretty lady."

"You knew I was coming?"

"Got me a very sophisticated early warning system." With that, Phills slid a foot over to a barely visible wire and jiggled it with the toe box of his boot. Unseen soda and vegetable cans jangled together somewhere.

"I'm also here because I'm afraid I might be next," Danielle told him.

"Then you better come inside, Yank. We'll call ourselves a truce."

THEY SAT facing each other at a heavy wooden kitchen table. Inside the cabin smelled strongly of pine and cedar, and all of the furniture was built of heavy wood.

John Henry Phills had traded his shotgun for a pair of Colt pistols, one of which he laid before him on the table. "You ain't Walt Henley's daughter. You're too pretty."

"Then why'd you let me in?" Danielle asked.

Phills eyed her suspiciously. "You really a Yank?"

"Nope. Israeli."

Phills narrowed his gaze further. "You come here in one of the black helicopters? They can run silent, you know."

"I work for the United Nations, Major. The Safety and Security Service. My name is Danielle Barnea."

Phills eased his hand a little closer to the pistol planted near him. His other hand sneaked down to his hip where the second Colt was waiting. "What call's the U.N. got trespassing on my property under false pretenses?"

"I'm here because the real Victoria Henley came to me for help after her father and brother were killed. Now she's dead too and I'm trying to find out why."

"Not my problem."

"It is if the same people come gunning for you."

"Let them. A little war's good for the soul. Hardens it, I reckon."

"Walter Henley wasn't the only one," Danielle told him. "Neither was Victoria or her brother. Thirteen members of your Evacuation Unit have been murdered in the past two months, the most recent only last night."

"And just how do you know that?"

"Because I was there. At Charlie Corstairs's greenhouse."

Phills's face lost a degree of intensity, eyes growing suddenly furtive and darting. "Damn flower farmer."

"I think you know more about the other veterans of the 121st than you've been alleging."

"Only good thing about Charlie Corstairs was that he was a Reb too. Kind of man I used to be able to talk to."

"He's dead, they're all dead, because of those steel storage cases your unit found in Buchenwald."

Phills mouthed that word under his breath. He yanked off the jacket top of his Confederate uniform, revealing a sleeveless shirt below. He was short, yet incredibly well built for a man his age. He had so much mass that his skin seemed to have lost its elasticity. The result was a knobby, unnatural look that featured long knotted bands of muscle pressing up against his flesh. His head was shaved bald and his face was lean to the point that his cheeks angled inward, hollowed where they met bone. His blue eyes were powerful and piercing, relentless in their intensity.

"Charlie Corstairs told me he had those cases hoisted out of the ground and into a truck," Danielle explained. "But they weren't picked up for three days afterward. What happened to them in the meantime?"

PHILLS AND Colonel Henley opened the cases together, using the expertise of a surgical technician in the 121st who was a locksmith by trade. Reams and reams of documents and photographs were found on four separate shelves in each of the three larger cases. Both Phills and Henley immediately sus-

pected an intelligence bonanza, though it was impossible to say for sure since neither of them spoke German. Neither did anyone else in the unit, at least not well enough to adequately translate what it was exactly that the Nazis had squirreled away in Buchenwald.

But they had another day before military intelligence was coming to pick the cases up, coincidentally the same day General George Patton ordered the residents of nearby Weimar to be paraded through the camp's grounds to see the atrocities perpetrated by their countrymen. The locals had steadfastly denied knowledge of what was transpiring in the camp. This wasn't the case, of course, but their reactions clearly showed that the level of depravity caught even them off guard.

Colonel Henley told Phills to select three of the locals, who also spoke English, to translate a few of the documents prior to the material being handed over the following day. It was the next logical step since clearly standard procedure had already been violated when they opened the cases themselves. They expected secret war plans, material sensitive to the Third Reich if nothing else.

They were wrong.

"WHAT WAS inside?" Danielle asked John Henry Phills.

"Documents. And not just any documents either. What do you know about Hitler, Yank? His fascination with the supernatural, the occult, foretelling the future?"

Danielle frowned. "Not very much."

"Then try this. For years Hitler had sent agents scouring the world for artifacts believed to have magical, at least majestic properties. The Holy Grail, the Ark of the Covenant, Pandora's Box, the goddamn boogeyman and Frankenstein's monster for all I know."

"You're telling me you found something like *that* inside those cases?"

"Not at all. What we found, according to our Kraut translators from Weimar, were the reports on the progress made by various agents in filling the shopping list Hitler had sent them out with."

"Anything pertinent?"

Phills shook his head and Danielle saw for the first time how tense his neck muscles had grown. "There were maps, some historical documents, transcriptions of interviews conducted with experts, records of every find uncovered at the archaeological digs they financed. Testimony of experts in the field promoting their own theories. Some near misses. A few of the teams believed they were getting close. One was convinced the Lost Ark was in Ethiopia of all places. Others had filed massive reports just to appear they were doing their job."

"Only the material was never delivered in Berlin."

Phills got up from his chair and moved to the bar where he poured himself a glass of whiskey. "Or if it was they dumped it into the shitter."

"Because someone didn't want Hitler to see it."

"That would be my take."

"Even though, according to these translators, it didn't amount to much, if anything."

"True enough," Phills agreed and took a hearty sip from his glass. "But maybe the connection in Berlin didn't know that. For whatever reason, he didn't want Hitler to get his hands on the contents of those three cases."

"Four," Danielle corrected. "The three larger cases were transferred to military intelligence. There's no record of the fourth, a smaller one, anywhere."

"Some things are better off going unrecorded, I suppose."

Danielle took a step closer to Phills and watched him take a smaller sip of his drink. "What was in that last case, Major?"

"Not for me to say, Yank."

"Then who can?"

"Me," a voice announced from the loft that ran the length of the rear portion of the A-frame.

Danielle turned toward the stairs and saw a man descending from the darkness, his face hidden until he came into the spill of the first-floor light.

"I can," said Colonel Walter Henley.

CHAPTER 38

Walter Henley walked down the stairs slowly, as if bearing a weight far greater than the steel lockbox held under his right arm. He looked terribly worn and sad. Danielle recalled the photo his daughter Victoria had showed her picturing a vibrant older man standing proudly between his two children, an arm over each of their shoulders. This man bore little resemblance to that one.

"You said my daughter's dead," he said, his voice cracking as he reached the foot of the stairs. "Is it true?"

"Yes, I'm sorry."

"How?" Henley barely managed to say.

"An explosion at a hotel in Israel," Danielle said.

Henley fought to steady himself. "Then if you're here, she must've told you about Buchenwald, about the 121st."

Danielle nodded. "You had Major Phills let me in even though you knew I wasn't your daughter. Why?"

"I thought you might be one of . . ."

"One of *who,* Colonel Henley?"

Henley dabbed at his eyes with the sleeve of his jacket. "They won't stop until we're all dead. They couldn't be sure who knew anything, so they're killing everyone they can find."

"They didn't kill you."

"They tried," Henley said, his lips trembling.

"You let your daughter believe you were dead."

"To protect her, for God's sake! I thought she was safe. I thought Matt was safe. The massacre made me realize how wrong I was. I tried to reach Vicky, to tell her the truth, but I couldn't track her down." Henley sank down heavily on the bottom step. "What have I done? What in God's name have I done?"

Danielle stared at the steel lockbox now held on his lap. "Vicky told me you were dead, Colonel Henley. Mugged at an ATM machine."

"I was. I struggled with my attacker. His gun went off into his face. Large caliber. You understand?"

Danielle shrugged.

"He was about my same height and weight. I'd gone there to take enough money out to run anyway, and now I had the chance. I planned to contact Vicky eventually, but before I could they killed Matt and she took off across the world. She knew what I knew, you see. She knew that members of the 121st have been dying mysteriously all across the country for weeks."

"And she seemed to have a very good idea why your son was murdered. She was going to tell me the day before yesterday."

"Did my daughter tell you what my son's job was before he was forced to disappear?"

"A linguistics expert," Danielle recalled. "Pioneered a new software application."

"Specifically to be used to replace human beings in hard case translation. Right now, the F.B.I. has a six-month backlog of Arabic correspondence and files because they haven't got the manpower to handle it. My son's software will eventually change all that. It's groundbreaking." A soft sad smile crossed Henley's lips. "It will probably save thousands of lives someday."

"What does that software have to do with Buchenwald?"

"My son used it to translate what we found there, Inspector," Henley explained. "That's why my children and my friends are dead. But they're not alone. Plenty more, thousands and thousands, are about to join them."

Then he unclasped the lockbox and began to open its lid.

The scene looked like many other scenes played out in Israel all too often. The rocket had slammed into the bus broadside as it was moving down the road under military escort. The force of the explosion spun it around, then toppled it over, leaving it half on the road and half off, the back end angling down an embankment. The bus must have slammed into one of the escort Jeeps at one point because the Jeep's twisted carcass stood on the opposite side of the highway, roasting in the sun.

From their raided outpost, the Hilltop Youth had been taken to a military substation to be processed. Of course, they hadn't realized that the procedure was meant to help them, facilitate the misplacement of records and the like so these transgressions in behavior could be more easily "forgiven." Instead they had made such a show with their continued protesting that ultimately they were incarcerated at the substation to maintain a measure of calm while the processing continued through much of the night. The efforts of an Israeli lawyer finally convinced them that climbing on the bus was far more advantageous than staying off it.

Ten minutes later, the missile had slammed into the bus's side.

Sammy Barr jumped out of Ben's SUV before it had come to a complete halt and rushed toward the stretchers that had been laid across the now closed road, the shapes upon them all covered by plastic sheets. The wounded had all been taken away by now, only the dead left behind.

Ben counted twenty-one bodies, tried to recall how many Hilltop Youth had been staying at Meitza Farm. Then he thought of his interview with the outpost's young leaders and wondered if their bodies were among those lined up neatly on the pavement.

Colonel al-Asi met Ben near the United Nations SUV. "This is not good, Inspector."

Ben frowned and shook his head at the sight before him. "I'll say."

"It's even worse than it looks. Already this is going to be called Palestinian retaliation for the massacre in Bureij. The Israeli army is preparing to roll into the West Bank in unprecedented numbers and to utilize unprecedented force."

Ben looked at the still-smoldering remains of the bus, the charred and blackened side where the rocket had impacted facing the sky now. He could see part of the jagged hole the rocket had left behind. Moving tentatively closer with al-Asi, his shoes crunched over glass that must have been from the bus's blown-out windows.

Ben noticed a trio of unarmed, white-uniformed United Nations observers talking to a pair of Israeli officers, one of whom looked to be taking copious notes.

"The observers were the first on scene," al-Asi noted. "Their outpost is on the other side of that hill. According to the observers' story, they heard the sound of the rocket firing. On their way outside they heard the bus explode and then the screaming. Two men wearing masks were already rushing off down the hill into the olive groves on the other side. Two of the observers gave chase, while the third called for help and went to the bus to see if there was anything he could do." Al-Asi paused and focused on the charred husk of the bus again. "There wasn't very much."

Ben saw Sammy Barr approaching and excused himself. What was left of Barr's hair blew wispily in the wind. He looked determined and remorseful at the same time, his eyes still watery and red-rimmed. Barr brushed past Ben, slowing just enough to direct a few words at him.

"We need to talk."

I t's my fucking fault," Sammy Barr said, seated in the passenger seat of Ben's U.N.-issued SUV. Beyond them, more stretchers were laid next to the dead lined up across the center of the road.

"Were you involved in the massacre, Mr. Barr?" Ben prodded.

"No! I mean, well, yeah, three kids from Meitza Farm came to me. Said they wanted to avenge a friend who was beaten to death outside Ramallah. Stupid fucking kid had an e-mail relationship with some Arab girl. One day they finally decide to meet. He shows up and gets his skull bashed in." Sammy Barr shook his head, blew his nose. "You can't blame them."

"There's plenty of blame to go around for everyone."

"You should know."

"Me?"

"If it couldn't work for you and your Israeli girlfriend, how's it supposed to work for anyone else?"

"We're doing just fine," Ben said, more defensively than he had intended.

"Sure, because you hightailed it out of here. Hey, don't get me wrong, I don't blame you."

"Neither of us had much of a choice."

"And what does that tell you? You try to make a difference, look where it gets you. Don't bother's what I say. The only difference I want to make is one that helps Israelis find peace, with or without Palestinian help."

Ben felt his pulse starting to race, forced himself to stay calm. "And that's why you gave these kids the money they needed?"

Sammy Barr continued to focus his gaze out the windshield. He looked numb. "They were talking about forming an outpost militia."

"Kids with guns."

"There are kids with guns on both sides, Kamal."

"I'm all too aware of that. So they asked you for money," Ben said to Sammy Barr.

"Not just money. What they really needed were details on troop deployments, so they'd have freedom of movement. Kind of stuff my contacts can provide."

"And you gave it to them. . . ."

"Hey, we're at fucking war here."

"Is that what you call it?"

"You got a better word, Inspector?"

Ben gestured out the window toward the last of the bodies. "You're looking at it."

"Revenge for Bureij," Sammy Barr said softly. "That's what it must have been."

"You think *Palestinians* blew up that bus?"

Barr turned away from the road long enough to spot Colonel al-Asi standing by himself in the meager shade of some thin trees. "You tell me."

"That's not the way he works."

"You tell him about the kids?"

"I may have mentioned it."

"Could have just as easily been you, I guess. Doesn't matter a fucking bit, though, because I'm putting a stop to it. I didn't approve this massacre. Killing innocent people's not what we're about."

"No, you prefer stealing their land."

"I'm trying to work with you here, Kamal. I had those kids watched. I had their calls monitored. I'm going to make some myself, set up a little meet for the two of us. Put an end to things before they get out of hand."

"Things been out of hand for a long time."

"Lots more villages in the West Bank, Kamal."

"And lots more buses, Mr. Barr."

Barr nodded, accepting Ben's point. "That's why I'm going to hand over the leaders of this outpost militia to you tonight."

CHAPTER 41

This is the very same box we found buried under that trench in Buchenwald, Inspector Barnea," Henley said, looking down at his lap as if visualizing its contents for the first time.

"The one you never turned in to military intelligence."

"It would've been of no value to them."

"They might have seen things differently," Danielle said.

"If it had been a gold bar, would there have been anything wrong with us keeping it?"

"Wrong? Yes."

"I meant, would anyone be hurt by it?"

"What's the difference? Unless you found Hitler's long-lost gold under that trench."

"Not gold, Inspector Barnea, but something that may have turned out to be just as valuable."

COLONEL WALTER Henley had jimmied open the lockbox in the camp building the 121st was using for its headquarters. He sat at a desk that in all probability had been occupied by Buchenwald's commandant, or a similarly high-ranking figure, until barely a week before.

Immediately he saw the contents of this smaller lockbox

were different; specifically a black leather case, zippered closed. Henley opened the case and pulled out a plastic pouch that was both air- and watertight. Henley slit the pouch and slowly removed a thick wad of irregularly shaped heavy parchment paper. The paper had yellowed and grown brittle with age. A piece of one page's corner came off and Henley thought for a moment about sliding the contents back into the pouch. But they were more than halfway out and reversing the process now would probably do more harm than good.

So Henley continued to ease the pages from the pouch, curious as to why they had been segregated in a separate container. His rough count of the pages put the number at fifty-two, all of them containing two, three, or four four-line verses written in a language he didn't recognize. Mostly French, it looked like, with other languages or dialects sprinkled into the mix.

The next morning, prior to contacting military intelligence, he and Major John Henry Phills had similarly opened the larger three cases. The contents of these cases, though, were considerably different from those of the smaller one: what looked like field and mission reports accompanied by maps and other historical documents.

U.S. military intelligence didn't rate retrieval of the documents highly. It was severely backed up as the Nazi war machine continued to fall. They could not possibly arrange pickup for another two days. Henley's orders were to secure the material until he was otherwise instructed.

That had been the only order Walter Henley had ever violated in his entire military career. He had retained the services of German locals from Weimar who shocked him with their quick and often cursory translations of a sampling of the documents contained in the three larger cases. The fact that they had been buried here in Buchenwald, which opened in the late 1930s, indicated to Henley that Hitler had never

laid eyes on their contents. Someone, either a spy or a person
working against Hitler from the inside, had conspired to
make sure he never had a chance to review the materials,
fearing what the madman might do with some supernatural
talisman on his side.

This made Henley especially curious about the contents
of the pages segregated in their own lockbox and written
mostly in French instead of German. As near as he could
tell, the smaller case contained the only original documents
of the entire lot. Henley hadn't brought the 121st's personnel files with him and tried to recall from memory who
among its members might have some degree of fluency in
French.

There was only one he could think of: Mildred Hayes, a
nurse who had joined the 121st after a stretch of working for
the Red Cross in occupied France. Although Henley had
barred women, nurses, from accompanying the 121st to
Buchenwald, Mildred had shown up at the front gate the day
before, having hitched a ride on a convoy from Frankfurt.
She was well aware of what was going on and wanted to be
a part of it. Having spent the better part of her nursing career working in a burn unit, she figured she could handle the
rigors of Buchenwald.

And for the most part she was right. Henley found her
tending to patients in one of the unit's makeshift medical
wards well past the end of her shift. He was honest with her
about the origins of the lockbox, stretching the truth only
when he said he needed her help in preparing a preliminary
report of their findings for military intelligence.

Mildred accompanied Henley to his office and settled in
behind his desk. He repeated the process of carefully easing
the pages from the weather-sealed pouch and positioned
them in front of her. She slid a pair of reading glasses from
the rucksack containing all she had brought with her to
Buchenwald and settled them upon her nose. Positioning the

desk lamp, she began to study the top page, the only one to be written in prose instead of verse.

Almost immediately, Mildred turned back to Henley.

"Is this some kind of joke, Colonel?"

"Of course not. Why?"

"You're telling me these documents are real, originals?"

"As far as I know."

"And you really have no idea what they are?"

"That's what I needed you for."

Mildred shook her head and returned her attention to the pages before her.

"SHE WAS the one who organized our first reunion," Henley said, interrupting the flow of his tale. "That was eight years ago. She spent months tracking down as many of us as she could. It became her life's work, and she even mastered e-mail to make the process easier."

"What happened to her?" Danielle asked, fearing the answer.

"She died," Henley told her. "Peacefully, of natural causes two years ago at the age of eighty-five. I guess you could say she was one of the lucky ones. I never told her I kept the contents of the lockbox. She was under the impression, as everyone else was, that I turned it over to military intelligence when they finally showed up."

"What was it Mildred Hayes realized, Colonel?" Danielle asked, staring at the steel case still held in Henley's lap. "What was in those pages you asked her to translate?"

"The future, Inspector Barnea. The lost prophecies of Nostradamus."

CHAPTER 42

I 've got the tapes, Mr. Ambassador," Major Jamal Jefferson said to Franklin Winters once the front door was closed behind him.

Winters eagerly took the department-store shopping bag from Jefferson's grasp. It was a long way from the diplomatic pouches both of them were accustomed to, but more fitting in this case.

"Thank you, Major," Winters offered gratefully, as he made his way into the corner den, which contained his entertainment center.

"These are the last ones, Mr. Ambassador," Jefferson told him. "I've been through the inventory. All the rest were taken in different sectors."

Winters had known Jefferson since the younger man was a full-scholarship cadet at West Point, ultimately graduating at the top of his class. Took him under his wing and became his mentor, not because he was black but because Winters saw in Jamal Jefferson the raw abilities that made great men. Although Jefferson had left for a high-level position in the Department of Defense two years earlier, the two men had remained close.

Winters was barely conscious of Jefferson's presence in the room, as he fit the first of the tapes into his VCR. Winters switched on the television and hit Play, still standing when the screen came alive. It showed a picture of the streets of Baghdad taken with concealed cameras by Special

Ops troops during the war with Iraq. The footage was random, entirely worthless to most. To Winters, though, somewhere amidst it might lie some clue, however opaque, to his son Jason's fate. He studied every frame of such footage, devoured it, in the fleeting hope that somewhere, somehow he would catch a glimpse of his son. It wasn't much but it was all he had.

The tapes he had watched in the past year would fill a closet. A few shots, only a few, offered enough detail to be enhanced, studied. None had panned out. But short of going to Baghdad himself and turning the city upside down, this was all Winters could do.

"May I speak plainly, Mr. Ambassador?" Major Jamal Jefferson asked him.

"As of two days ago, I'm not an ambassador to anything anymore. You can call me Franklin," Winters said, without taking his eyes off the screen.

"Let me help you, sir."

Winters's finger stiffened over the VCR's remote control. "What are you talking about, Major?"

"I know something's wrong, sir. Just tell me what it is, see if I can help you work it out."

Winters still didn't turn from the television. "What's wrong is that my son is still MIA. Was there anything in the latest Sit Reports from the field?"

"A few leads. Nothing concrete."

Winters turned toward Jefferson again. "Leads?"

"Nothing concrete, as I said, sir."

"What then, Major?"

"Indications, innuendo, rumors. Please, sir, as soon as anything of merit crosses my desk, any fact at all, I'll bring it to your attention."

"Tell me about these indications, the rumors."

"Unreliable sources, sir," Jefferson said, regretting he had even raised the subject.

"I'd like to judge that for myself, if you don't mind."

"I'll see what I can do, but . . ."

"But what?"

Jefferson realized he was still standing at attention. "I'm looking into things further, sir. If anything checks out, anything at all . . ."

Winters turned back to the television, sighing deeply. "I understand, Major. Thank you."

Before Winters could speak again, his wife Mary entered the room and shuffled toward the television, blank stare locked on the screen.

"John Wayne," she muttered. "Is John Wayne in this one?"

"No, Mary," Winters said patiently.

"I so like John Wayne war pictures. Except the one he died in. *The Sands* of something. Can we watch one?"

Winters kept his attention trained on Major Jamal Jefferson. "Maybe later, dear."

Mary looked at Jefferson, then back at the screen. "Are the two of you staying for lunch?"

"Major Jefferson was just leaving."

"Because I made tuna fish. And I really should get your names so I can introduce you both properly when my husband gets home. Now, I have the tuna in water and oil. Or I could make both."

"I think I'll be going now," Jefferson said.

"Thanks again, Major," Winters told him.

"I'll get back to you as soon as I learn something more, sir."

Jefferson turned and walked out of the room, leaving Winters and Mary alone.

"He's black, you know," she whispered and then refocused her attention on the Baghdad street scene.

Winters realized he'd have to rewind, probably run the tape from scratch when he could give it his full attention. Another twenty or so remained in the bag Jefferson had delivered.

"What happened to John Wayne?" Mary said, staring at the screen again.

CHAPTER 43

W hat's the matter, Inspector?" Henley asked, after gauging Danielle's reaction.

"You're telling me all these people died for *that*?"

"You don't believe, I see."

"In a bunch of prophetic mumbo jumbo? No, I don't."

"Neither did I, for a long, long time," Henley said distantly. "But the Germans must have. We had it all wrong, you see. Oh, someone had hidden these documents from Hitler to keep him from seeing them all right, but not for the reasons we thought. No, they kept them from him because these pages predicted his fall. Cryptically, yes, but the insinuation was there in a few of the prophecies Mildred Hayes was able to translate to a certain extent."

"Is that why you never turned the manuscript in to army intelligence?"

"You said so yourself, Inspector: why bother when they wouldn't have believed anyway? The war was ending. We'd all be going home before too much longer. I told you before, I got greedy. If Mildred Hayes was right, and the documents weren't forgeries, I knew how valuable they might be. Once back in the States, I could get them authenticated and get some rough estimates on their worth. But I never did. I just held on to them. I never even bothered trying to have the prophecies translated." Henley stopped and took a deep breath. "Then something changed."

"Your son," Danielle recalled. "A linguistics specialist who wrote software code for translation programs."

Henley's gaze had grown as distant as his voice. He seemed to look past Danielle, at the wall, into nothing. "I'd become quite an expert on the prophet Nostradamus already. Those verses I had noticed were actually four-line stanzas called quatrains. Nostradamus wrote all of his prophecies in that form. Plenty know that, but very few know that he scrambled both the order and the meaning of his quatrains so that humanity would not be able to decode them until they had outgrown the savagery and violence of the sixteenth century."

"If Nostradamus could see the future, he'd have known that was never going to happen."

"I was just like you," Henley told her flatly. "Until my son's translation changed my mind. He was tops in his field in the entire world," he continued, his tired voice starting to crack with emotion again. "I finally showed him the manuscript and he wrote an encryption program designed to identify repetitive images and extrapolate their meaning. The computer discerns meaning by studying a large number of examples to isolate patterns and tendencies. What he found was truly amazing, terrifying in another sense. The manuscript foretold dozens of major events from the modern era. But the ones yet to happen were scariest of all, one in particular."

Henley pulled an ordinary piece of copy paper from the case and handed it to Danielle. She took it and read the one stanza, what he'd called a quatrain:

In an age of two's four, in a land of many
An army rises from midland afar on a day of equal light and dark
Beneath the flames of the bringer of fire, a darkness will reign eternal

"You said quatrain," Danielle noted. "What happened to the fourth line?"

"This was the last prophecy in the manuscript. Nostradamus never completed it. He must have died or fallen ill before he had the chance. But those three lines were enough to cost my children their lives, not to mention more than a dozen other good people, heroes who deserved far better."

"What did you mean before about far more lives about to be lost?"

Before Henley could answer, a shrill alarm began to blare through the A-frame.

"We got us some company," said John Henry Phills.

CHAPTER 44

John Henry Phills yanked open the cabin's lone closet and wheeled a Civil War–era cannon out from it into a position directly in front of the door.

"This ought to discourage them," he said, looking back. "But you better come with me first."

Henley clutched the lockbox tighter against his chest, as John Henry Phills lifted a flashlight from a shelf and handed it to Danielle.

"This way," he said.

Phills kicked a tattered carpet aside to reveal the outline of a hatch cut into the knobby pine floor. He reached down, found the handhold, and hoisted the hatch open. The cabin's murky light was enough to reveal a ladder below.

"Escape tunnel," he explained. "I built it for the day the black helicopters showed up. Runs a half-mile beneath the woods. Follow the back road until you come to Route Four. I'll hold them back long as I can."

Danielle lowered herself onto the ladder first. She felt a chilly draft, smelled air rich with moisture and rot. She touched down on a bed of soft dirt and held the ladder steady for Henley's descent. The latch above them closed abruptly as he neared the bottom. Once Henley was beside her, Danielle shined the flashlight down John Henry Phills's tunnel, which ran straight for a brief stretch before forking sharply to the left.

"It's them, isn't it?" Henley asked, sounding more angered than scared. "The ones who killed my son, my daughter. . . ."

"Tell me why, Colonel Henley," Danielle said, and began to head down the tunnel with Henley just behind her.

"Because I know what they're up to, their plan. Nostradamus predicted it and that knowledge is the only thing that can stop them."

In an age of two's four, in a land of many
An army rises from midland afar on a day of equal light
   and dark
Beneath the flames of the bringer of fire, a darkness will
   reign eternal

"The first line," Henley said, after reciting the quatrain again. "According to my son, 'two's four' refers to the year 2004. 'A land of many' is the United States."

A roar reverberated above them. Seconds passed, during which Danielle pictured John Henry Phills reloading his antique cannon. Sure enough, a second roar followed, shaking the tunnel walls with enough force to cough dirt downward.

Danielle picked up the pace, alternating her gaze between the black tunnel ahead and Henley. His voice was weakening, his breathing labored.

"In the second line," he resumed, " 'a day of equal light and dark' refers to either the autumnal or vernal equinox when there are exactly twelve hours of both day and night, signaling the onset of fall and spring."

"And an army rising from midland afar?"

" 'Midland afar' is Nostradamus's term for a particular region of the world: the Middle East, Inspector."

"And the bringer of fire?"

"Prometheus," Henley said, "according to Greek mythology. As for a darkness that will reign eternal, symbolically in the prophecies of Nostradamus, darkness refers not necessarily to death but to a demarcation point. An end of things as they are currently known. Forever."

"In the United States."

Henley drew even with her in the narrow tunnel. "That's why my son and daughter are dead, along with a dozen members of my unit." The flashlight caught Henley's utterly blank expression. "Because I brought the manuscript to our reunion this year, a grand unveiling, almost like geriatric show-and-tell. My son had just completed the translation. I didn't realize the stakes involved. I didn't believe all this any more than you do right now. If only I had, maybe, just maybe . . ."

Danielle could feel his eyes seeking her out in the dirt-stained air. More than a dozen murdered because of an incomplete prophecy? She didn't want to believe it. Henley's claims defied reason. Then again, what if the plot *was* real? If the perpetrators somehow learned that the existence of their plan had been betrayed, they would strike at all those who could expose them.

Coincidence, Danielle told herself. Just coincidence. But even that left a problem.

"There's something else, Colonel Henley," she told him. "How did whoever's behind this plot learn you had uncovered this prophecy?"

"I've racked my brain trying to figure that out. As soon as the killings began, as soon as it became obvious it wasn't coincidence or old age, I contacted everyone I could to find out who they had spoken to about the manuscript or the prophecy. I did my best to trace the connections. There weren't many and none of them added up to anything."

"That still leaves the members of your own group. How many were in attendance at the reunion?"

"Just over thirty including wives and a few children. You think . . ."

"What if one of them was involved in this plot somehow?"

"We're talking about men and women in their seventies, eighties even."

"You said there were children of 121st members there as well."

"Pushing wheelchairs, Inspector."

"How many veterans of your group who attended the reunion are still alive, Colonel?"

"Including Phills and me, only six."

"I'll need a list of the other four."

"All my lists are in this box," Henley said, still clutching it close to him.

Danielle felt a surge of fresher air, signaling they were nearing the end of the tunnel. "No clue to the substance of the plot, though."

"True," Henley agreed. "It must have been specified in the missing line. That's why we've got to find it before it's too late, and we're running out of time: the vernal equinox, the first day of spring, is only six days away."

"How can we find a line that doesn't exist?"

"I've spent the past month reading everything I could find on Nostradamus. There may be more undiscovered prophecies out there somewhere that give some hint as to what the missing line might have said. But where to look? I realized the answer lay in Germany, with figuring out how the team Hitler dispatched located the manuscript in the first place." He stopped speaking long enough to settle his breathing. "I contacted a man there, an expert on the writings of Nostradamus named Klaus Hauptman, just after my son completed the translation. But the murders began before I could make arrangements to see him. I'd actually planned to leave the morning after that trip I made to the ATM machine. I've been hiding out ever since."

"How'd you find this man?"

The percussion of an explosion rattled the tunnel's walls and sent dirt showering downward before Henley could answer. A rumble followed and then a sound like a churning engine.

"Run!" Danielle ordered, shining her flashlight ahead of them.

Henley stumbled at first, and she grabbed hold of his arm to help drag him on. Behind them, the tunnel was collapsing, caving in on itself. But Danielle could see the end just a few yards away, the smell of clean air stronger against the backdrop of the rampaging curtain of earth that continued to close on them.

She slammed into the door at the end of the tunnel and twisted the knob in the same motion. In that same instant Henley dropped the lockbox that held the lost prophecies of Nostradamus. She turned back and saw him reaching down for it.

"No!" Danielle screamed.

Henley had just managed to close his hands on the box when the wave of earth overtook him. Danielle threw herself back into the doorway and clamped a hand on Henley's arm. She dragged and pulled until his head and arms, clutching the case anew, came free. They were covered again just as quickly, and Danielle tried again until her own thighs were swallowed by dirt and rocks.

"Take it," Henley gasped before the dirt covered his mouth once more.

He managed to extend the steel lockbox but Danielle ignored it and desperately tried to free him. The weight of the collapsed tunnel defied her efforts. She heard Henley retching, gasping for breath.

"Take it," Henley managed again before the tunnel totally swallowed him and left Danielle scrambling to escape herself.

She plunged through the door, coughing dirt from her lungs, realizing only then she was holding the lockbox containing the lost prophecies of Nostradamus in her arms.

CHAPTER 45

The Qalqiliya Zoo had once been one of the most popular attractions in the West Bank. Ben recalled Israelis from nearby Tel Aviv mixing easily with Palestinians in the crowds before the animal enclosures. Peace had still seemed possible then. Now even the thought of a mixed crowd of Palestinians and Jews was not.

Sammy Barr had reached Ben a few hours before with news that he had managed to make contact with the members of the outpost militia he believed must be responsible for Bureij. His plan was to lure them to the zoo that night on the pretext of an issue vital to them, and then use ex-soldier settlers loyal to him to take them into custody until Ben arrived.

"Be careful, Mr. Barr, these men might not be what you expect," Ben warned, recalling his own conclusions drawn from the videotape of the massacre along with Danielle's insistence that its origins lay in another place and time altogether.

"You're in my world now and nobody crosses me here, not a fucking soul."

"Those kids were in over their head. You might be too."

"Yeah, sure. You can tell me about it after I turn them over to you, Inspector," Barr had informed him over the phone.

"Why not just turn them over to the Israeli authorities yourself?"

"Bad for my image. These people, one way or another, are what I'm about. Better you get the credit . . . and the blame. So we'll escort you to U.N. headquarters outside Ramallah.

After that, the militia leaders are yours to do with what you want."

"Israel will never let us take them out of the country."

"That's what I was thinking."

"It might be different if you turned them in."

"Yeah, I was thinking that too."

"Your cause is going to be hurt by this, Mr. Barr. There's no getting around that."

"Sure, the army will send in more troops, shut down more of the hilltop outposts. Then next month, maybe the month after, they'll be up and running again. I can live with that," Barr added, after a pause.

The Qalqiliya Zoo itself, Ben knew, had once been as full of animal life as any in the region, a great boon to the Palestinian economy in general and that of Qalqiliya, a town with a sizeable population of forty-two thousand, in particular. But a combination of insufficient funds and too many bullets had robbed the zoo of its cherished animals. So the zoo's veterinarian, who had also been trained as a taxidermist, elected to salvage the situation as best he could by stuffing the animals so they could still be viewed. The counterpoint was insane and ironic, typical of the tragedy that had come to dominate the West Bank, the animals having become the latest and saddest victims of a never ending war.

Thanks to an interminable wait at the checkpoint at the one road leading in and out of Qalqiliya, Ben arrived at the zoo nearly an hour late. He had forgotten that the town was cordoned off on three sides, most prominently by a twenty-four-foot wall that Israeli authorities someday intended to extend along the entire West Bank.

Ben parked in a dark corner of the street shadowed by the crumbling stone wall that enclosed the entire zoo. The entrance was just a hundred yards beyond and there was no lock on the gate. Sammy Barr had said he'd be waiting with the leaders of the outpost militia in what had once been the lions' den, which Ben knew was located in the center of the complex.

He eased the nine-millimeter Beretta pistol Colonel al-Asi had provided from his belt and clung to the shadows just off the main path. There was no longer any electricity in the zoo, meaning the only light came from the half moon sliding in and out of cloud cover. Ben's eyes adjusted quickly enough to catch glimpses of stuffed antelope grazing forever in a field and baboons that would never leave the trees they had climbed into. A giraffe tending to a baby in a sprawling pen left him especially sad, making him wonder how anyone on either side had let it get this far.

The lions' den came into view at last, recognizable from the Arabic signs still posted to tree trunks, directing Ben toward it with arrows. There had been Hebrew signs posted once as well, but someone must have torn them all down. The lions' den was located in a natural depression complete with man-made pond and a smattering of trees and vegetation. It had been the Qalqiliya Zoo's most crowning achievement once, since an entire pride had been maintained for a few years during which time two cubs were born in captivity.

Ben neared the rim of the depression, still enclosed by a rail fence but with the safety wire that once topped it long ago pilfered to serve some desperate jury-rigged purpose somewhere else. He gazed about, concerned because he could find no indication that Sammy Barr had, in fact, managed to lure the militia leaders here, or perhaps he had not been able to trap them.

Ben leaned up against the rails and peered between them at three stuffed members of the pride lying or standing below. Three of the lions, including the cubs, had actually survived and been transferred to other zoos around the world; not Qalqiliya's counterpart in Israel's Ramat Gan, which had refused to take them.

Then Ben saw Sammy Barr sitting amidst the stuffed lions on the dead grass. As far as he could tell Barr was alone, but the farther reaches of the den were hidden by a rock formation and trees, meaning the militia leaders could be over there, inside the attached building perhaps. Ben wedged the Beretta back into his belt, slid between the rails, and moved as quietly as he could down the embankment into the den.

He imagined a male lion was looking at him, as he made his way through the center of the pride toward Sammy Barr.

"Mr. Barr," he whispered. "Where are they, Mr. Barr?"

Ben thought he saw Sammy Barr start to turn toward him, but there was no response. Crouching, he slid up next to Barr and touched him on the shoulder.

"Did something go wr—"

Ben stopped. His eyes fell on Sammy Barr's face and the breath seized up in his throat. The face was still and empty with eyes glazed like fat marbles. A thick line of stitches ran up the center of his entire midsection through his torn shirt, leaving a messy trail of dried blood and viscera.

Sammy Barr had been stuffed.

CHAPTER 46

B en's stomach quaked. A wave of nausea swept over him, and he doubled over feeling he might vomit.

The move saved his life; gunshots fired from the fence-line above singed the air just over his head. Ben rolled away and felt Sammy Barr's corpse fall over and smack into his legs as bullets punched into it. He reached the edge of the hill and rolled down the slope toward the man-made pond, mud-colored and only half-full now.

Halfway down, he spotted the first of the bodies. Casually dressed men with sidearms still in their holsters, six in all. Four lay on the embankment. Two more had ended up inside the pond. Clearly the men Sammy Barr had come here to meet had turned the tables on his forces. By the look of things, it was an ambush and had been over very quickly.

Ben heard the scramble of footsteps in the den above and stripped the Beretta from his belt. In his haste to get inside the zoo, he'd forgotten to pocket the spare clips al-Asi had provided, leaving him with sixteen shots and no more.

The footsteps above grew louder, joined by a brief exchange of hushed whispers. Ben tried to count the voices, the number of steps, get some idea of how many he was facing. He pulled himself between a pair of bodies for camouflage and used the raised shoulder of the nearer corpse as a prop for his pistol.

Ben had just steadied it on the rim above when another burst of automatic fire coughed mud from the embankment in the air. Then a second weapon joined in and Ben dug himself lower into the soft earth. Still clutching the Beretta, he angled himself downward and slipped into the pond. More bullets chased him and rivulets of water sprayed upward.

He dropped under the fetid pond surface and stroked to the other side. He emerged just a few yards from the entrance to a concrete walkway that led into the lions' enclosure. Ben pulled himself through the muck, speeding up only when another burst of gunfire bore down upon him.

Soaked now, he dashed along the brief length of the walkway and found himself inside the lions' cage. Since this part of the zoo had been long closed, the gate had been left open. Absurdly, Ben thought as he surged through it and entered the exhibit hall, the cage still smelled strongly of the animals that would never be using it again.

More stuffed and preserved animals stood on display inside the hall as well. A number of monkey species, Ben noted, and a sprawling display of animals that called the desert home; their natural habitat re-created, sand and all. He considered a sprint to either of the building's two exits, then gazed through the darkness again at the hall's desert habitat and opted for something else.

Ben hurdled the solid waist-high fence and felt his feet sink into sand. He cringed and nearly cried out when a few of the desert animals he thought were stuffed squealed and scattered in terror. Obviously the Qalqiliya Zoo still boasted at least a few surviving species.

The animals continued to scamper away from him as Ben burrowed into the sand, burying himself as best he could. There was only enough sand to cover him if he lay flat on his stomach. In the darkness, even under the spill of a flashlight beam, the ruse might work so long as he didn't act too fast. He held the Beretta ready, barrel protruding just above the surface, and positioned himself for a clear view of the gallery.

Footsteps pounded from the lions' cage, smacking the display room floor hard. Ben heard two distinct sets and stead-ied his pistol. His heart thundered against his chest. He tried to force himself to breathe evenly.

Ben squeezed one eye closed and held the Beretta steady. He could see the two men coming now, sweeping left and right with their assault rifles, wearing what looked like night-vision goggles. He willed himself to wait until they crossed the reach of the Beretta's barrel.

A million thoughts sped through his mind, so many situa-tions like this the past few years. What was it Danielle had told him? You never get used to it, but you learn to accept it. And at that point half the battle is won.

The men crossed directly in front of the pistol's front sight. Ben opened fire, rotating the barrel only slightly and firing off ten shots in rapid succession. He stopped only when he saw the two men go down, then lurched out of the desert animal exhibit, causing his reluctant neighbors to scurry once more.

The bodies were lying facedown on the floor, and Ben left them there. He swiped the sweat from his face with his sleeve and advanced down the middle of the hall, pistol held in both hands, ready to fire at the first sign of motion. The far door that spilled out close to the street was open and he picked up his pace toward it. The fresher smells of the night greeted him as he crossed over the threshold.

A shadow shifted on his right and Ben twisted that way. Before he could angle the Beretta, something dark and shiny slammed down atop his wrist. His fingers went numb and he heard his pistol rattle to the pavement. But he kept twisting to the right and clamped both hands down atop an assault ri-fle's stock and barrel before its wielder could angle it into firing position.

The gunman was huge, a giant, holding at least a six-inch and fifty-pound advantage on Ben. He shoved hard and thrust Ben back through the doorway into the hall. Ben clung stubbornly to the rifle as they wheeled left and right. The man had the advantage of reach on him as well, and Ben caught a glimpse of his face in the moonlight filtering through a nearby window. The gunman looked to be smiling slightly, sure of his advantage, and certain he was about to tear the assault rifle from Ben's grasp.

The man jerked the rifle to the left as he pushed down hard with his right hand. Ben knew his purchase was gone and didn't fight it. Instead he barreled into the bigger man, thrusting him backward toward a plateglass wall.

The impact was shattering. They both crashed through and Ben felt jagged shards of glass rip through his shirt and tear at his flesh. He landed on top of the bigger man but lost his senses long enough for the roles to be quickly reversed. The man didn't bother trying to find the assault rifle the jarring crash had stripped from him. Instead he grasped Ben by the lapels and hurled him back through what remained of the glass.

Ben felt his body crunch against the concrete floor, a flash exploding before his eyes. Then he was being hoisted upward, feather-light in the giant's hands, and tossed over a railing into an empty display case. Before Ben could move, the big man pounced, pummeling him with a pair of blows that rattled his teeth and left one of his ears buzzing. Ben managed to block the next punch and got lucky when a wild strike ended with a thumb lodging in the giant's right eye.

The big man grunted and clamped a pair of huge hands on Ben's throat. Ben felt his head begin to clog from lack of air. He heard a rasping gasp and realized after a long instant that it was his own. His hands flapped downward and scraped against some jagged shards of glass. Desperate, he closed a hand around them, gathering up smaller chunks that dug into the flesh of his palm. Then he jerked his hand upward, digging the glass into the big man's face.

The giant screeched in agony, loosened his grip on Ben's throat, and tried to pull away, but Ben stayed with him, continuing to grind the glass into his flesh, atop him now. The man's mouth opened to scream and Ben shoved the handful of jagged shards into his mouth, wedging them down as far as they would go.

The giant's face purpled. His eyes bulged. Ben clamped both hands over his mouth and held it closed. The big man flailed with his hands, raking Ben's cheeks with his nails. Ben turned his head away but held his hand firm, didn't look down again until the giant's struggling had stopped.

Ben rolled away from him and rose shaking to his knees. It took a few seconds to catch his breath and even then he still needed a nearby post to support himself while he stood up.

Where have I seen these men before?

Ben felt warm blood dripping slowly out of his arm, his torso, his hand. He hobbled back to the two men he had shot in front of the desert animal exhibit. Both lay on their sides and Ben kicked them over onto their backs, looked down at their faces.

Beams of light shot into the hall from both sides of the building. The light blinded him temporarily, but not before he saw a stream of Israeli soldiers pouring toward him.

"On your knees now!" one of them shouted in Arabic.

Ben swung toward the soldier instead. Another of the soldiers angled in from the right and smashed him in the side of the head with the butt of his assault rifle. The lights blazed briefly before dissolving into a milky haze, as Ben keeled over into unconsciousness.

CHAPTER 47

Delbert Fisher hovered over Jake as the boy's fingers danced across the keyboard, then stopped suddenly.

"It's like I've been telling you," Jake said. "Nothing."

"Tell me again."

Jake ran a hand through his hair. He'd spent practically every moment of his time for the past day and a half in this office Fisher had provided for him, stealing a few hours to nap and living off Jolt cola, Mountain Dew, and stale doughnuts. "I've got exams, you know."

"We've taken care of that."

"Sure, extensions. I just can't wait to get back to campus. . . ."

"Actually," Fisher told him, "you're getting straight As this semester."

"You're shitting me."

"Like I said, it's been taken care of." Fisher leaned closer to the screen. "Now, tell me again."

"Okay," Jake started, considerably more relaxed, "those fifty messages you're talking about all came in within like a day—"

"Sixteen hours," Fisher corrected.

"—three weeks ago now. It's not like my site gets a lot of hits, so it definitely stuck out. I figured it must have been something I posted, maybe a pop-up even. So I went back and reconstructed the page exactly as it had been up when the messages came in."

"And nothing."

"Not this time."

Fisher stood up, walked around the table, and sat on its edge. "Tell me about your site."

"Man, how many times you want to hear it. I post night-club listings and reviews of dance clubs and parties."

"How do you review a party?"

"You know, not really a party. More like a rave."

"I get it," Fisher said, even though it was clear he didn't. "And you reposted these same listings and reviews exactly as they appeared the first time."

"Right. Not that anybody cares. No one's even e-mailed to tell me I fucked up. Ran the same reviews and listings for dates that have already passed."

"Word for word."

"Yeah, sure. Well," Jake recalled, "I did fix a couple typos."

"Typos," Fisher repeated.

"Thing is, I post a lot of this shit when I'm wasted. Like to do it while things are fresh in my mind. But sometimes the fingers don't work like they're supposed to, if you know what I mean."

Fisher didn't say that he did.

"Anyway," Jake continued, "there was this mad rave at this new club called All After, 'cause it's an after-hours place opened one to seven."

"A.M.?"

Jake nodded. "It's the life, man. It was a great night. Deejay Steve Smooth opened for Bad Boy Bill. He's rated number seven in the country, you know."

"No, I didn't."

"But somebody must've slipped me a roofie or something because everything was spinning and I posted my review without even proofing it, if you can believe that."

"I'm shocked," Fisher said.

"Next day I look at what's up on the site and, man, I spelled everything wrong, even the name of the club. Called it Al Awdah, instead of All After."

Fisher popped down off the table and stiffened. "Al Awdah?"

Jake managed a laugh. "Can you believe it?"

"That's it," Fisher said, instead of answering.

"That's *what*, man?"

"*Al Awdah* is an Arabic phrase, Jake. It means 'The Return,' the name of an Iraqi plot to seek revenge on the United States."

DAY SIX

CHAPTER 48

LOGON COMPLETE
ALL STATIONS CONFIRMED ACTIVE ON-LINE
ENCRYPTION PROCEDURES IN EFFECT

MESSAGE RUNNING

From: FRANCE
X-Priority:
Sensitivity: Company-Confidential
To: ALL
MIME-Version: 1.0
IM secure status: active
X-MailScanner: Found to be clean

WE WERE GIVEN ASSURANCES. MUCH IS AT
STAKE HERE.

From: UNITED STATES
X-Priority:
Sensitivity: Company-Confidential
To: ALL
MIME-Version: 1.0
IM secure status: active
X-MailScanner: Found to be clean

AGREED. BUT RECENT DEVELOPMENTS UNFORESEEABLE. CONTAINMENT NOW AN ISSUE.

From: GREAT BRITAIN
X-Priority:
Sensitivity: Company-Confidential
To: ALL
MIME-Version: 1.0
IM secure status: active
X-MailScanner: Found to be clean

ELABORATE.

From: UNITED STATES
X-Priority:
Sensitivity: Company-Confidential
To: ALL
MIME-Version: 1.0
IM secure status: active
X-MailScanner: Found to be clean

THE MANUSCRIPT IS NOT SECURE.

From: RUSSIA
X-Priority:
Sensitivity: Company-Confidential
To: ALL
MIME-Version: 1.0
IM secure status: active
X-MailScanner: Found to be clean

WE WERE LED TO BELIEVE OTHERWISE.

From: UNITED STATES
X-Priority:

Sensitivity: Company-Confidential
To: ALL
MIME-Version: 1.0
IM secure status: active
X-MailScanner: Found to be clean

AN ERROR WAS MADE. UNFORTUNATE, BUT UNDERSTANDABLE. WE UNDERESTIMATED ONE OF THE ORIGINAL TARGETS.

From: JAPAN
X-Priority:
Sensitivity: Company-Confidential
To: ALL
MIME-Version: 1.0
IM secure status: active
X-MailScanner: Found to be clean

A FOOL'S ERRAND FROM THE BEGINNING, AS WAS WARNED.

From: FRANCE
X-Priority:
Sensitivity: Company-Confidential
To: ALL
MIME-Version: 1.0
IM secure status: active
X-MailScanner: Found to be clean

WE ALL AGREED THERE WAS TOO MUCH RISK IN LETTING THE MANUSCRIPT FALL INTO THE WRONG HANDS.

From: CHINA
X-Priority:
Sensitivity: Company-Confidential

To: ALL
MIME-Version: 1.0
IM secure status: active
X-MailScanner: Found to be clean

AND HAS IT?

From: UNITED STATES
X-Priority:
Sensitivity: Company-Confidential
To: ALL
MIME-Version: 1.0
IM secure status: active
X-MailScanner: Found to be clean

**REGRETTABLY, MANUSCRIPT HAS BEEN PASSED
ON TO OPERATIVE WE NEGLECTED TO ELIMI-
NATE IN ISRAEL. DANIELLE BARNEA. HER PIC-
TURE AND DOSSIER SHOULD BE
COMING UP ON YOUR SCREENS NOW.**

From: FRANCE
X-Priority:
Sensitivity: Company-Confidential
To: ALL
MIME-Version: 1.0
IM secure status: active
X-MailScanner: Found to be clean

**ISRAELI SPECIAL FORCES, SHIN BET,
INVESTIGATOR AND LATER COMMANDER IN
NATIONAL POLICE. WHY WERE WE NOT MADE
AWARE OF ALL THIS AFTER HER PRESENCE IN
ISRAEL WAS NOTED?**

From: UNITED STATES
X-Priority:
Sensitivity: Company-Confidential
To: ALL
MIME-Version: 1.0
IM secure status: active
X-MailScanner: Found to be clean

**CONSIDERED A NONISSUE UNTIL SHE WAS
IDENTIFIED AT LOCATIONS OF TWO 121ST MEM-
BERS WITH KNOWLEDGE OF
MANUSCRIPT'S EXISTENCE.**

From: ITALY
X-Priority:
Sensitivity: Company-Confidential
To: ALL
MIME-Version: 1.0
IM secure status: active
X-MailScanner: Found to be clean

**WE MUST DISCUSS ALTERATION IN
PROMETHEUS TIMETABLE.**

From: RUSSIA
X-Priority:
Sensitivity: Company-Confidential
To: ALL
MIME-Version: 1.0
IM secure status: active
X-MailScanner: Found to be clean

**IMPOSSIBLE. FINAL INSTRUCTIONS FOR
PROMETHEUS ALREADY RELAYED. NO
FURTHER CONTACT POSSIBLE OTHER THAN
TERMINATION.**

From: UNITED STATES
X-Priority:
Sensitivity: Company-Confidential
To: ALL
MIME-Version: 1.0
IM secure status: active
X-MailScanner: Found to be clean

BESIDES, IDENTITIES OF THE FIFTY NOT COMPROMISED.

From: GERMANY
X-Priority:
Sensitivity: Company-Confidential
To: ALL
MIME-Version: 1.0
IM secure status: active
X-MailScanner: Found to be clean

BUT HAS THE OPERATION BEEN COMPROMISED?

From: UNITED STATES
X-Priority:
Sensitivity: Company-Confidential
To: ALL
MIME-Version: 1.0
IM secure status: active
X-MailScanner: Found to be clean

NOT WITHOUT SPECIFICS THE MANUSCRIPT DOES NOT PROVIDE.

From: JAPAN
X-Priority:

Sensitivity: Company-Confidential
To: ALL
MIME-Version: 1.0
IM secure status: active
X-MailScanner: Found to be clean

**TO REPEAT, THIS ENTIRE OPERATION HAS
BEEN A FOOL'S ERRAND FROM THE START.**

From: UNITED STATES
X-Priority:
Sensitivity: Company-Confidential
To: ALL
MIME-Version: 1.0
IM secure status: active
X-MailScanner: Found to be clean

**UNLESS THE PREDICTION BECOMES PUBLIC.
RELEASE OF THE DATE AND GENERAL DETAILS
WOULD BE ENOUGH TO THREATEN
PROMETHEUS. OPERATIVES MIGHT
WITHDRAW. ENHANCED SECURITY SUCCESS.**

From: GREAT BRITAIN
X-Priority:
Sensitivity: Company-Confidential
To: ALL
MIME-Version: 1.0
IM secure status: active
X-MailScanner: Found to be clean

**THAT'S THE POINT. WITH MANUSCRIPT NO
LONGER CONTAINED, ADDITIONAL SECURITY
PROCEDURES COULD ROB TARGETS, CURTAIL
IMPACT ON HIGH ORDER.**

From: ITALY
X-Priority:
Sensitivity: Company-Confidential
To: ALL
MIME-Version: 1.0
IM secure status: active
X-MailScanner: Found to be clean

WE ALSO UNDERSTAND THE MASSACRE CAN NO LONGER BE CONSIDERED CONTAINED EITHER. HAS THE UNITED NATIONS INVESTIGATOR RESPONSIBLE BEEN ELIMINATED?

From: UNITED STATES
X-Priority:
Sensitivity: Company-Confidential
To: ALL
MIME-Version: 1.0
IM secure status: active
X-MailScanner: Found to be clean

REGRETTABLY, HE SURVIVED OUR ATTEMPT LAST NIGHT. THE THREE MEN WE DISPATCHED DID NOT.

From: RUSSIA
X-Priority:
Sensitivity: Company-Confidential
To: ALL
MIME-Version: 1.0
IM secure status: active
X-MailScanner: Found to be clean

OUR MEN.

From: UNITED STATES
X-Priority:
Sensitivity: Company-Confidential
To: ALL
MIME-Version: 1.0
IM secure status: active
X-MailScanner: Found to be clean

NOTHING TRACEABLE BACK TO US. WE MADE SURE OF THAT.

From: GERMANY
X-Priority:
Sensitivity: Company-Confidential
To: ALL
MIME-Version: 1.0
IM secure status: active
X-MailScanner: Found to be clean

ASSURANCES MEAN LITTLE AT THIS POINT.

From: FRANCE
X-Priority:
Sensitivity: Company-Confidential
To: ALL
MIME-Version: 1.0
IM secure status: active
X-MailScanner: Found to be clean

BARNEA AND KAMAL MUST BE ELIMINATED BEFORE FURTHER DAMAGE IS DONE.

From: UNITED STATES
X-Priority:
Sensitivity: Company-Confidential

To: ALL
MIME-Version: 1.0
IM secure status: active
X-MailScanner: Found to be clean

WE'LL FIND THEM.

MESSAGE TERMINATED

C H A P T E R   4 9

W here am I?" Ben asked when a man he recognized as Commissioner David Vordi of Israel's National Police entered the windowless room.

"The Megrash Haruseim police station in Jerusalem. A cell held for only the best your people have to offer," Vordi said smugly. "I've heard it was reserved for Arafat when we were considering taking him into custody."

Ben had just awakened for the second time to find himself lying on an aged cot in what he now realized must have actually been a cell that smelled of must and mold. He had noticed upon first waking hours before that the various glass wounds he had received at the Qalqiliya Zoo had been neatly stitched and bandaged. And he was wearing fresh clothes that smelled of some flowery laundry detergent.

"Why am I being held here?" Ben demanded.

Vordi held his ground. "You're not. I'm here to release you into the custody of your own organization."

"Release me?"

"Immediately."

"You have no questions?" Ben asked, utterly bewildered.

"None I expect you'd be able to answer."

"Then let me ask you one: what have you learned about the three men I killed at the zoo?"

"What three men?"

"The ones your soldiers found me standing over when they arrested me!"

Vordi frowned. "We found the bodies of Samuel Barr and six of his associates. That's all."

Ben stood up slowly, his muscles rebelling even at the slight motion. "What's going on here?"

"You're being released. You should be happy."

"Why are you covering this up? Who's pulling strings?"

"I don't know what you're talking about."

"You don't want to know what I was doing at the zoo."

"I don't care."

But Ben continued anyway. "I had come there to meet Sammy Barr. He was going to turn over to me the leaders of an outpost militia responsible for the Bureij massacre."

"There's a U.N. car waiting for you outside. . . ."

"Listen to me, Vordi! Sammy Barr must've had it all wrong. This outpost militia had nothing to do with the massacre. The real party behind the massacre set everything up so the militia group would be blamed. Then they blew up that bus to cover their tracks. And when Sammy Barr tried to trap the parties responsible, he had to die too."

Vordi started to back out of the cell and beckoned Ben to join him. "This sounds like a U.N. problem. You can explain everything to your superiors. General Arguayo, for one, is very interested in talking to you. He sounded extremely upset."

Ben held his ground. "What is it you don't want me to find out?"

"Let's go, Inspector. Your car's waiting."

A TRIO of armed guards escorted Ben from the jail to a parking lot outside. He squinted at the sudden exposure to sunlight, feeling his eyes water. He moved gingerly, the effects of the battle last night making themselves felt, it seemed, in every muscle. There was nowhere he didn't hurt, and the areas Israeli doctors had stitched while he was unconscious had begun to throb as well.

A minivan with U.N. markings sat idling between twin rows of cars. One of the soldiers opened the rear door and stepped back so Ben could enter. Still perplexed by the inexplicable turn of events, he climbed inside and watched the door slide closed behind him.

A man wearing the white uniform of a United Nations peacekeeper smiled from the seat next to him. In the front sat a driver and a second peacekeeper, his body angled so he could watch Ben.

"Good morning, Inspector Kamal," he said. "On behalf of General Arguayo, we apologize for not being able to expedite your release earlier. The general is in Brussels. A plane is waiting to take you there."

"I need to speak with him now," Ben insisted.

"In time, Inspector."

Ben was aware the van had started moving, edging into traffic on Jaffa Road and then crawling along in maddening stops and starts. "It's imperative that I make contact with Inspector Barnea, then. I need a phone."

The man in the front passenger seat exchanged a glance with the man sitting next to Ben in the back. "We are not authorized to allow you to contact anyone until you speak with General Arguayo."

"How did he arrange for my release?"

"We know only our own instructions, Inspector."

Ben shrugged, prepared to let it go for now, until the man in the front seat shifted his body back around, inadvertently revealing a semiautomatic pistol holstered on his belt. Strictly against the U.N.'s operating procedure inside Israel, and grounds for expulsion. Ben glanced at the man sitting next to him and saw a similar bulge along his right hip.

Something was wrong.

"I think I'm going to be sick," Ben said. "Pull over, please."

The driver looked to the man in the front seat, then slid toward the curb without waiting for instruction.

"Hurry," Ben urged, his hand feeling for the door handle.

The minivan nosed into a space too small to accommodate its full size and halted. Ben yanked on the latch, about to push open the door when the man next to him threw a hand across Ben's body and held the door closed. In the front seat, the man in the passenger seat had pulled his jacket aside, hand buried near his hip as he spoke, trying to sound reassuring.

"Maybe we should wait until—"

Ben smashed the man next to him in the face with an elbow, catching him totally by surprise. He felt the bridge of the man's nose shatter on impact as his head snapped backward. In the front seat, the driver was trying to twirl around, fighting the confines of his shoulder harness, and the passenger next to the driver had managed to free his pistol.

Ben threw himself across the console, between the two men in the front seat, and jammed a hand downward against the wrist of the passenger as he angled the gun forward. A shot exploded and Ben felt the heat of the bullet, actually *felt* it, surge past his ear. A thump and a gasp followed, the bullet having torn a hole in the driver's chest. The driver looked down at the wound in astonishment before his head sank and he slumped in his seat.

The passenger tried to right the pistol again, and this time Ben used his free hand to slam the man's head sideward into the window, which spiderwebbed on impact. Ben rotated his fingers upward, digging them into the man's eyes. The man wailed, relinquishing grasp of the pistol long enough for Ben to tear it free and hammer him in the face with both hands. Then he pulled himself back into the minivan's rear and jerked open the door.

He sensed movement next to him and instinctively tumbled from the car onto the pavement. The man in the rear seat he had smashed with his elbow fired three shots in rapid succession, shattering the window. Ben leaped to his feet and dove over the hood of a passing car as it screeched to a halt, then skirted between the bumpers of another pair of cars mired in traffic.

He was vaguely conscious of more gunshots spitting through the air, but kept moving forward. Staying low and using the wedged-in cars for cover until he came to an inter-section. Ben darted down the cross street toward an open-air market beyond.

He had just crossed into the reach of the sunlight when a trio of Israeli soldiers spun round the corner before him, as-sault rifles leveled.

"Hands in the air!" one shouted. "Drop to your knees! Do it *now*!"

Ben did as he was told, the scene oddly familiar to the one played out in the zoo's exhibit hall just a few hours earlier. But this time Ben heard a fresh set of footsteps approach from the rear, followed suddenly by an all-too-familiar voice.

"You can get up now, Inspector," said David Vordi.

Danielle had tried to reach Ben on his cell phone right up until her flight boarded to no avail, his voice mail triggered before it even rang, indicating the phone was switched off or somewhere lacking service. The trip to Berlin, to see the man Walter Henley had identified as an expert on Nostradamus, would be long and arduous, taking up the bulk of an entire day. That suited Danielle just fine, since it would give her ample time to catch up on her rest, if she could.

She had mounted several more attempts to dig her way through the tunnel to reach Henley, but it was no use. The force of the explosions from John Henry Phills's cabin had collapsed the walls as well as the ceiling. Even if she could have gotten to him, too much time had elapsed to give him any reasonable chance at survival. She had abandoned the task reluctantly and hiked down to the main road where a passing trucker picked her up only a mile into her walk.

He had dropped her off at a roadside motel that consisted of tiny individual cabins usually reserved for hunters and campers in season. Off-season, the motel remained virtually vacant. She had remained at the motel only long enough to shower and sleep for a few hours. With no fresh clothes, she had no choice but to once again don the ones hopelessly soiled by the trek through the tunnel, despite her efforts to brush and clean them. And, with no means of transportation readily available, she had no choice other than to steal a car parked in front of a door three cabins down.

Danielle drove straight to Dulles Airport. Booking the appropriate flights meant dealing with reservations clerks who would certainly note her haggard and unkempt appearance. So she did her best to replace her soiled clothes with new ones purchased at shops along the airport concourse. Then she used a stall in the ladies' room to change and pull her hair back into a ponytail.

Danielle's sole luggage once the flight boarded was a backpack in which she'd stuffed Walter Henley's lockbox. The original manuscript was inside, contained in a sealed pouch, along with the translation coded to the individually labeled quatrains. Information on Klaus Hauptman, the man she was going to Germany to meet, was inside as well, along with a pair of unmarked CD-ROM discs that could only be the translation software created by Henley's son.

She had always considered the apparent success of Nostradamus's predictions to be the result of so-called experts analyzing prophecies so general in nature they could be interpreted to mean almost anything. That, though, was no longer the issue here. The issue was that the existence of *someone's* plot had been revealed, threatened to the point where multiple murders became the only way to safeguard its continuance.

In an age of two's four, in a land of many
An army rises from midland afar on a day of equal light
   and dark
Beneath the flames of the bringer of fire, a darkness will
   reign eternal

Three of the four lines were intact. And if Danielle could uncover the fourth, then the plot in its entirety might be revealed and somehow preempted.

When sleep failed to come on the first leg of the flight, Danielle busied herself with a more careful reading of the rest of the lost prophecies, as much out of curiosity as anything. True to Henley's claims, the translations obtained through his son's linguistics software revealed a significant number of predictions that were clear in their meaning and even clearer in their accuracy. So much of recent history was contained here. Many of the prophecies seemed innocuous, yes, and others were too convoluted to decipher totally. At best, open to interpretation; at worst, so vague they could be applied to any number of occurrences. But Danielle's eyes kept coming back to a number of quatrains that, considered in the context of Henley's code, clearly foretold some of the most striking events in recent memory, not to mention one that might be soon to join them.

. . . a darkness will reign eternal . . .

And she had only five days left to stop it.

CHAPTER 51

W e have much to discuss, Inspector Kamal," Commissioner of National Police David Vordi greeted, as he ushered Ben into the spacious office on the limestone building's fourth floor. Ben watched him place a manila envelope atop the desk and then take a seat behind it.

Ben shifted his chair to better face Vordi. "What's going on?" He had first met Danielle Barnea in this very office and had not set foot in it since, which only added to his discomfort and confusion.

"I sent the officers in the alley to follow the van that picked you up outside National Police."

"Why?"

"To protect you, Inspector."

"Try again, Commissioner."

Vordi's expression didn't change. "They were three cars back when the fight broke out in your U.N. vehicle. I'm assuming your United Nations escorts provoked your actions."

"Two of the men were armed. Strictly against U.N. procedure."

"What else?"

"That's all."

"You're holding something back."

"And if I was, why would I share it with you?"

"Because this time, you should have realized by now, we're on the same side."

"Is that what you said to Danielle to get her to come back?"

"Don't blame me for the problems Commander Barnea encountered upon her return, Inspector," Vordi said, staring Ben straight in the eye.

Ben gazed around him dramatically. "This was supposed to be her office, not yours."

"Believe me, Inspector, I wish it were. Because in that case I would now be minister of justice."

"She spurned your advances and you made her life miserable. I'd say you got what you deserved."

"Danielle didn't need me to make her life miserable. The two of you seemed remarkably adept at managing that much completely on your own."

"You sound jealous."

"I've known her a lot longer than you have, Inspector. Danielle chose you because in her heart she knows you're someone whom she can never truly have. That's what I meant about her not needing my help to be miserable." Vordi raked the bushy hair from his forehead. "But for now you need to reconsider where you place your trust. It's your own people in the United Nations who appear to want you dead, not me." The commissioner of National Police leaned forward and crossed his hands over the desk blotter. "You asked me what I wasn't telling you about the incident in the zoo earlier. I told you there was nothing."

"Keep talking."

"That was a lie. We were able to identify the three men you killed: all members of the former Iraqi Special Republican Guard. The Israeli government has extensive files on all of them."

Ben tried not to show his confusion. "Those men didn't look like Iraqis. They didn't look like Arabs."

"Neither do you, Inspector. But in this case, it doesn't matter anyway."

"Why?"

"Because according to our files, all three were dead long before your visit to the zoo."

"KILLED BY the Americans in the war," Vordi continued after a pause long enough for his point to sink in. "Here, see for yourself." With that, Vordi slid the file folder he'd brought with him across the desk.

Ben opened it, skimmed the file's contents to satisfy himself that, on paper anyway, Vordi's claims were substantiated. "But you chose not to tell me this earlier."

"We believed it was an Israeli problem, Inspector. After all, Sammy Barr and the six men who accompanied him to that zoo were Israeli nationals."

"The thirty-four victims of the massacre at Bureij weren't, Commissioner. I was sent here to find their killers."

"And you're suggesting these Iraqis were responsible for that as well."

"It was Barr who suggested it. He thought he was meeting with the leaders of a radical settler militia. I imagine the truth caught him totally by surprise."

"And what about you, Inspector? Were you taken totally by surprise, or did you recognize those three men you killed at the zoo?"

Ben remained silent.

"Because my guess is they were the ones behind the massacre you were so intent on blaming Israel for. I already proved our innocence to Commander Barnea. Now I find myself doing the same for you."

"And expecting something in return. Otherwise, I wouldn't be here right now."

"There's something you need to know. We kept the U.N. team that picked you up in the van waiting outside long enough to match their faces through visual identification software."

"Don't tell me: more members of Iraq's Special Republican Guard. Also listed as deceased."

"That's right."

"Who else knows?"

"No one has heard it from me."

"You haven't filed a report?"

"Not yet."

"Why?"

"Something strange is going on here, Inspector, and I don't understand what it is. Even if it doesn't include Israel directly, anything involving remnants of the Saddam regime is cause for great concern in our world." Vordi looked closer at Ben. "But, under the circumstances, it's an even greater concern in yours."

"Mine?"

"Your current employer, Inspector. The United Nations. I don't have to tell you there is no love lost between my country and that organization. Finding evidence of U.N. complicity in the murder of Israeli nationals, never mind one as well known as Sammy Barr, would be a political coup."

"Definitely good for someone's career."

"As would bringing those responsible for the Bureij massacre to justice. That is what you came to Israel for, isn't it?" Vordi challenged, twisting Ben's words back at him.

"You want me to find who's behind these Iraqis."

"I believe it would be in both our best interests. I'm prepared to contact your friend General Arguayo. Tell him of your tragic passing at the hands of men impersonating U.N. officials who perished in the attack. That should provide you a few days of safe going."

"I'll need to get into the West Bank," Ben said, thinking fast.

"That can be arranged."

"Quickly."

"Just say the word, Inspector."

CHAPTER 52

The city of Berlin, Danielle knew, was half the size of New York. Three and a half million people belonging to nearly two hundred nationalities work and live there, many in the modern housing projects that have sprung up everywhere since the city's reunification. The city spreads out in seemingly haphazard fashion in every direction, crisscrossed by wide boulevards and elevated rail lines of arguably the world's most advanced public transportation system.

She had only visited Berlin twice before, but the memories were etched on her brain. On both occasions the city had seemed so much a dichotomy to her: compellingly up-to-date with the elegant spires of recently constructed corporate towers rising into the sky, and yet mired stubbornly in the past. The reminders of that past were everywhere, interspersed with the glimmering steel and glass.

Danielle had made it a point on her prior visits to stop by the plaque near Zoo Station that listed the names of all the concentration camps, including Buchenwald. There were other sights she had taken in as well, but somehow she had missed the Jewish Museum on both occasions.

The museum was located on Lindenstrasse in what used to be called the eastern sector, and contained the most complete history of Germany's Jewish community anywhere. Originally the museum was housed in a reconstructed eighteenth-century courthouse. But over the years a steadily rising inventory, coupled with ever-increasing attendance, led to the addition of more exhibit areas in a new building accessible to the old one by an underground tunnel that finished at the Holocaust Tower.

Danielle had figured her visit to the Jewish Museum, to meet its curator Klaus Hauptman, would have to wait until the following morning. After all, even under the best of circumstances, her flight into Berlin wasn't scheduled to land until nine o'clock that night. She had arranged for a hotel room within walking distance of the museum but, upon arriving, noticed lights burning in a pair of windows in the fourth floor wing housing the building's offices.

Acting on a whim, Danielle had the driver drop her off. The main entrance contained an after-hours call bell and she rang it, gazing up at the lit windows above for a trace of movement.

"You're late," a voice said in German through a tiny speaker. "I'm in my office."

Danielle heard a buzz, then the sound of the main entrance to the museum clicking electronically open. She slid through the door and proceeded straight for the elevator, touching 4 as soon as she was inside the compartment. The elevator whisked her upward and seconds later the doors opened again on the fourth floor.

The suite of offices where she had noticed lights burning was located a few doors down on the right. Danielle walked toward it and peered inside. The office suite was actually one large room, crammed with tables and shelves, all of them full to bursting with boxes and files. The shelves looked so overstuffed that several seemed on the verge of toppling and many sagged in the middle from bearing too much weight for too long. Against the near wall, a large wooden desk was all but buried beneath an avalanche of paper. The office smelled of must, linseed oil, and something else, something not easily identifiable but that reminded Danielle of the scent of sodden newsprint.

A small roundish man with his sleeves rolled up past his elbows to reveal plump forearms stood on a step stool sorting through the contents of a shelf crammed with notebooks.

"Herr Hauptman?" Danielle said finally.

The roundish man twirled on the step stool fast enough to ruffle the stiff hairs of an ill-fitting toupee. "Who are you? What are you doing here?" he asked in German.

"You buzzed me in."

"I buzzed in a FedEx man with a promised delivery that's already hours late," Hauptman responded, switching easily to English.

"I doubt whatever you were expecting is anywhere near as interesting as what I've brought with me," Danielle said, and held Walter Henley's lockbox up for Hauptman to see.

"What is it you've got there?"

"It's what's inside you'll find interesting. I believe you were expecting a visit from an American named Walter Henley. I've come in his place."

Hauptman's eyes widened as he gazed at the lockbox again, climbing awkwardly down from the step stool.

"And just who are you?"

"Inspector Danielle Barnea. Former commander of Israel's National Police, currently with the United Nations Safety and Security Service."

Hauptman folded the stool up and leaned it against the nearest shelf. "Barnea. The name is familiar. . . ."

"My father was on the Israeli consulting committee chartered prior to the Jewish Museum's founding."

"And how do you know Walter Henley?" Hauptman asked suspiciously, his eyes darting back and forth from the lockbox to Danielle's face. "Why could he not come himself?"

"He's dead, Herr Hauptman, killed for what's inside this box."

The breath seemed to catch in Hauptman's throat, but his gaze quickly regained its suspicious air. "Men are seldom killed over historical artifacts, Inspector."

"But this particular artifact is different, isn't it?"

"That's what Henley was trying to find out, as I recall, when we talked two months ago."

"He told me," Danielle said, calculating in her mind. It was two months back that Walter Henley's son Matthew had completed his translation of the last prophecy.

"Henley was seeking confirmation that the manuscript in the box was authentic," Hauptman explained. "Then I didn't hear from him again until three weeks ago, I think."

Just before Henley's untimely visit to the ATM machine, Danielle surmised. "Then he shared with you what he had found."

Hauptman stood there stiffly, his toupee shining in the naked spray of light. "He shared with me what he *believed* he had found. But plenty of professional collectors have been fooled over the years by clever Nostradamus forgeries, never mind amateurs."

"The circumstances of the box's recovery didn't intrigue you?"

"Of course they did. But taken on their own, they prove nothing. A firsthand inspection of the document in question is the only way to determine authenticity, Inspector."

Danielle proceeded further into the room and laid the lockbox down on a narrow ribbon of available table space. "In that case, Herr Hauptman," she said, lifting the box open, "why don't you take a look and tell me what you think?"

CHAPTER 53

The magnifying glass began trembling in Hauptman's hand before he'd read less than three pages of the manuscript recovered at Buchenwald sixty years before. But his eyes remained transfixed, almost unblinking for the next half hour as he paged through the manuscript. Finally, he leaned back and gazed at Danielle with a glazed expression.

"It's genuine, isn't it?" she asked.

Hauptman shrugged. "It would take days, even weeks to be sure. I'd have to analyze the paper, the handwriting . . ."

"It *is* genuine, *isn't* it?"

"Yes, I believe it is," Hauptman said reluctantly. "Genuine and yet, well . . ."

"What?"

"How much do you know about Nostradamus, Inspector?"

"Other than what he wrote in these quatrains and that he claimed to be able to see the future, not very much."

"I was skeptical too once."

"That's the same thing Henley said."

"He must have realized the same thing I did, that too many of Nostradamus's prophecies ring true to be coincidence or random strokes of fortune. His use of the word 'Hister,' for example, 'who by his speech will seduce a great multitude' and 'will launch thunderbolts—so many and in such an array near, and far, then deep into the West.' Or

'Mabus,' who is clearly Saddam Hussein or Osama bin Laden."

"Which one?"

"Either, maybe both. That's the point. Nostradamus's visions in the volumes of predictions that encompass his collection called *The Centuries* are seldom clear or precise. Instead they're vague, often obtuse. Complicating matters further was the fact that in his time the *v* and the *u* were interchangeable and the *f* was read as an *s*. That's why I find this manuscript so fascinating," Hauptman continued, running a finger down the top page almost reverently. "It may be genuine but it's markedly different from Nostradamus's other works."

"How?"

"For one thing, the lines of the quatrains are longer, as if Nostradamus's vision of the future sharpened during his final days on earth. For another, these quatrains are much more specific with regard to dates and places. For instance, I notice several of this lost manuscript's predictions mention Hitler by his actual name."

"And yet you're still convinced the manuscript is genuine."

"I didn't say I was convinced. I'm speaking of indications and instinct. For every Nostradamus expert, there's a different theory of the secret to unlock his code. Anagrams, reverse image word play, time patterns, synecdoches—either individually or in groups, all these have played a role at one time or another. Which is correct? All, maybe none, most likely a combination. It's a matter of interpretation. For instance, the fifth quatrain in the second book of *Centuries* includes the phrase 'When weapons and plans are enclosed in a fish.' This could be interpreted as 'When Mars and Mercury are in conjunction with Pisces' to set up a time sequence."

Hauptman gazed back at the manuscript in fascination. "But the prophecies in this lost manuscript seem to be much clearer in meaning, as if Nostradamus no longer felt the need to disguise or cloud what he saw. I've never seen anything like them before, even in the numerous fakes that have crossed my desk over the years."

"And how many years is that, Herr Hauptman?"

The curator held his gaze somewhere between the manuscript and Danielle. "Almost as long as I can remember. Because of my father, Inspector. You see, my father was the man responsible for finding this lost Nostradamus manuscript in the first place."

Danielle recalled Henley's tale of agents for Hitler and the Third Reich scouring the globe in search of supernatural and mystical artifacts. A large portion of what they found had ultimately ended up buried in a trench at Buchenwald. Clearly, Hauptman's father had been one of these men.

"Do not mistake what I am saying for pride," the curator continued. "I bear no esteem for what my father did or the manner, I learned later, in which he did it. I was born just before the war, about the time he embarked on his travels." Hauptman looked away from the manuscript cradled before him, seeming to forget it for the first time. "I have very little memory of him. He died when I was barely a toddler."

"Then how did you—"

"Learn of what he found on his travels? From my mother years later, at the same time she finally confessed his true fate to me." Hauptman stopped and stared into the thickly scented air before him. "She'd always told me he died heroically at the front. That's what everyone thought."

"Go on," Danielle prodded.

"My father was executed."

"For failing to complete his mission satisfactorily?" Danielle asked, recalling the mass of documents and findings no one had ever shared with Hitler.

"No, Inspector: for completing it too well. Henley must have told you that much, at least alluded to it."

"He told me the original assumption was that the documents had been buried in Buchenwald for safekeeping. Only later did they realize their placement likely indicated they'd actually been hidden there before the war even started, because people like your father had found something they didn't want Hitler to see."

"Precisely," Hauptman acknowledged. "Plenty of the materials men like my father gathered for Hitler were ultimately delivered to an information ministry overseen by Goebbels that was directly responsible for following them up. But the leads that hadn't panned out or, worse, were accompanied by news Hitler wouldn't want to hear, were hidden away."

"Like a series of prophecies foretelling his eventual fall," Danielle added.

Hauptman looked down at the ancient pages, then back up at her. "Even a brief inspection of Nostradamus's lost manuscript revealed that much, which made my father a threat since he may well have known the ultimate fate of the Reich." Hauptman studied Danielle's expression. "You think me a fool, Inspector? Even after you personally witnessed this manuscript cost another man his life, you don't believe?"

"It's not just Henley, Herr Hauptman. Someone is killing off the surviving members of his unit that uncovered the lockbox sixty years ago."

Hauptman's eyes widened in surprise. "And that wasn't enough to convince you?"

"It convinces me that someone is planning a strike that this manuscript seems to foretell."

" 'Seems,' Inspector?"

"The final line of the manuscript's last prophecy is missing. Henley wasn't looking for authentication. He was hoping you might have some knowledge as to what the missing line said."

Hauptman turned back to the table and carefully flipped the pages of the manuscript to the final page.

" 'In an age of two's four, in a land of many,' " Danielle

recited from memory, " 'an army rises from midland afar on a day of equal light and dark. Beneath the flames of the bringer of fire, a darkness will reign eternal. . . . ' "

"For someone who doesn't believe, you seem to have mastered a difficult translation," the curator said, still reading the original prophecy himself.

"Thanks only to the linguistics software created by Henley's son, Herr Hauptman. He was killed too."

Hauptman shook his head, frowning in disbelief. "All this for . . ."

"For what? A prophecy that can't possibly be real? Now who sounds like the skeptic?"

"You believe all these people died for nothing, Inspector?"

"I believe they were murdered because the group behind this panicked. Became terrified their plot was about to be revealed."

Hauptman nodded smugly. "But thanks to the missing line you don't know the substance of this plot, so you came to me."

"I'm after the only remaining clue, yes. I don't care whether I get it from Nostradamus, the Delphic Oracle, gypsies, or you, Herr Hauptman."

Hauptman rose and lumbered stiff-shouldered back toward the shelves that carried the sum total of his life's work. "I assure you, Inspector, Nostradamus belongs in a category all his own. Look around you. This entire room is filled with historical mysteries that defy logic and reason. Nostradamus is no different."

"Except he claimed to be able to see the future."

"And did his best to discourage the exploitation of his prophecies by casting them in confusing, contradictory, and even coded language. But it wasn't just prophecies. While in Italy, Nostradamus once walked toward a group of Franciscan monks, including one named Brother Felice Peretti. As he drew even with Peretti, he bowed and knelt to him. The friars, aware that Peretti had been born a peasant, were puzzled by such reverence and asked Nostradamus to explain, to which he replied, 'I must yield myself and bend a knee before his Holiness.' The friars walked off laughing, but forty years later Brother Peretti became Pope Sixtus V."

"That proves nothing. It's just hearsay."

"I've read three different testimonials of that same event. Does that prove anything? If you're looking for a logical explanation, Inspector, you won't find it here. Nostradamus had studied astrology extensively, and when the planets were aligned to his liking, he would lean over a bowl filled with steaming water and pungent herbs. Staring into a thin candle flame, he would empty his mind and slip into a trance. It was in this state that he claimed to see visions projected in the mist rising before the candlelight.

"His intention, Inspector, was to write a book of prophecy that would predict the future of mankind until the end of time. Ten volumes, *The Centuries,* were planned, each to contain one hundred quatrains."

Danielle gazed down at the pages opened on the heavy wooden table before her. "And where does the manuscript found in Buchenwald fit in?"

"It doesn't. That manuscript must represent some kind of addendum. It's known that Nostradamus had begun writing two additional volumes but they were recovered in raw, unfinished form years ago." Hauptman gazed down at the pages before him. "This manuscript represents, in effect, a thirteenth volume, written near the end of Nostradamus's life as his mind became filled with visions he hadn't seen before."

"But as you see he left his final one incomplete, Herr Hauptman."

"I'm sorry I cannot help you with your missing line, Inspector, but perhaps I can point you in the right direction."

"Where?"

"Salon, France, where my father found this manuscript," Hauptman told her. "The place of Nostradamus's death."

CHAPTER 54

S he's upstairs," the aide Ruth said, as soon as Franklin Winters stepped through the door. "I can't do a thing with her today."

Winters climbed the stairs and entered the spare bedroom that had been transformed into his wife's domain, rife with the smell of Lysol to cover that of stale urine. His wife, Mary, spent many of her days just lying on the bed or rocking in the chair alongside it, always with the dreamy vacant expression of middle-stage Alzheimer's, her mind in a place Winters would never understand.

But the hospital bed's rails were down and Mary was nowhere to be seen. Winters tried his room next, where Mary sometimes went believing she still shared it with him. That didn't happen much anymore, as if the retreat into the repressed world of her own making was becoming more complete.

He found his room empty as well, then heard a rustling sound down the hall. The only other room on this floor was Jason's, and Mary never entered it. Most days, she seemed to have forgotten their son even existed, continually asking Winters who the person was in all the pictures.

Today, though, he found Mary hovering over Jason's bed, smoothing the covers, seeming to mimic making a bed rather than actually doing it.

"Got to have the room ready now that Jason's home," she announced, noticing Winters standing in the doorway.

"Mary—"

"He likes his covers tucked in just a certain way. Three pillows, always three pillows. Sheets have to be cotton." She stopped and looked at Winters again. "That's right, isn't it?"

"As a matter of fact, it is."

"I'm going to make his favorite dinner tonight too," Mary continued, even though it was clear she had no idea what that meal was. "He's been away a long time, hasn't he?"

Winters could only nod.

"I saw him yesterday, but he said he couldn't stay."

Somehow that piqued Winters's interest. "You saw Jason?"

"He forgot his lunch box. Why else would he come home during school? I made him tuna fish, you know. His favorite. The kind in water, not oil."

Mary moved to Jason's credenza desk and began to dust it down with an edge of her nightgown, careful to avoid the computer that sat in the center. The room had not changed from the time Jason had graduated from high school and gone off to college. And it remained the same even after he had disappeared in Iraq.

"He looked sad when I saw him. I think it was the tuna fish. I should have made something else." She drifted over to the window, tried to open it and failed, not remembering how to operate the lock. "He was standing right down there, near the swing set. I went outside, and he asked me to push him. He's a good boy, Franklin."

"Yes, Mary, he is."

"He was gone for a long time, but he's back now."

"That's good."

"You missed him too."

"I did."

"It'll be nice to have him home again," Mary said, empty gaze drifting out the window.

"Yes," Winters said stiffly, "it will."

CHAPTER 55

I'm glad your Israeli friends have become so coopera-
tive," Colonel Nabril al-Asi greeted with a wry smile,
after an Israeli military patrol dropped Ben off outside
his headquarters in Ramallah.

"They have their own reasons, believe me," Ben said, and
recounted to al-Asi his recent adventures, especially what
had transpired at the zoo and in the U.N. van.

The colonel listened without surprise. "What now, Inspector?" he asked simply, once Ben was finished.

"We go inside and take another look at the tape of the
massacre made by that little girl."

AL-ASI TURNED off the lights in the television room upstairs
so both of them could focus more easily on the picture displayed on the twenty-seven-inch screen. Ben longed for the
equipment he had grown used to while working for the private security firm in the United States and, sometimes, with
the U.N. Computer-generated enhancement and digital
printers that could turn any frame into an eight-by-ten photo
in seconds. For now the best he could do was use a handheld
magnifying glass and a Freeze button, which he pressed
each time a face on the tape grew reasonably clear.

The distance from which the film had been shot provided

only two clear images in total, still enough for Ben to be sure of what he had suspected last night.

"These are two of the men I killed at the zoo last night," he told al-Asi, lowering the magnifying glass from the screen.

The colonel gazed over his shoulder. "Members of Iraq's Special Republican Guard?"

"According to David Vordi."

"And you believe him?"

"I believe my own eyes, Colonel. The question is how Iraqis thought to be killed by Americans during the war ended up in Israel and what's the U.N.'s connection?"

"I know someone who might be able to help answer that question."

"I was hoping you might say that."

"Then get ready for a long journey."

"Where are we going?"

"A place I'm afraid will bring back some unpleasant memories for you, Inspector. Baghdad."

DAY SEVEN

Danielle melded into the group of tourists halfway through the shattered Roman ruins known as the Temple de Diane in Nîmes. She had taken the first morning flight out of Berlin for Paris and then transferred onto a smaller commuter plane bound for Marseilles. From there she had rented a car and driven north along a beautiful road lined by cypress trees and manor homes adorned with red-tile roofs. The scents of lavender and thyme were heavy in the sun-drenched air and oleanders rose in full bloom.

Sixty-five years ago, Klaus Hauptman's father Erich had come to a small town twenty miles farther to the north, having followed the trail of the lost prophecies of Nostradamus to an ancient stone abbey. According to Klaus Hauptman, his father had traced the manuscript to the abbey's caretaker, a man named Henri Mathieu. Hauptman knew little more of how the manuscript that had ended up in Buchenwald had changed hands. In later years, though, he did know that Henri Mathieu's son Jacques had become one of the world's greatest Nostradamus scholars and interpreters of his work.

Jacques Mathieu, Klaus Hauptman informed her, had settled in the southern area of Provence not far from the abbey that had fallen victim to German bombing at the outset of the war. He was one of the region's foremost historians and gave regular tours of historical sites close to his home outside of Nîmes.

Hauptman professed to know little else about him, other

than by reputation. They had never met or even corresponded. But Mathieu had authored dozens of articles on Nostradamus and had been instrumental in debunking numerous misinterpretations of the prophet's work as well as exposing a number of artful forgeries.

He had been a very young boy in 1939, so Danielle doubted he would be able to add anything to what Klaus Hauptman had already told her about the acquisition of the manuscript itself. Having joined the tour group, she listened to Mathieu chatter on with great enthusiasm about the Temple de Diane's colorful history leading up to its ultimate destruction during the Wars of Religion. Numerous areas of the site were being freshly excavated by archaeological teams, rendering them off limits to tourists. But this did not stop Mathieu from bringing his small entourage up to the rope line and describing exactly what had once stood amidst the ruins.

Mathieu walked stiff-legged with the aid of a cane, every step over the uneven and rock-laden ground drawing a grimace from him. He was breathing hard and sweating through his shirt, neither of which detracted from the exuberant tones of his strong, baritone voice.

Danielle waited until the tour was over and Mathieu had returned to his car before approaching him. She watched him gulp down a bottled water from a cooler in his backseat and then twist the cap off a second.

"Monsieur Mathieu?"

"You joined the group late, mademoiselle," he said, hardly regarding her.

"You noticed."

"I'm a historian. It's what I do. Notice things." He took another hefty sip from his water bottle. "Along with the fact that you showed no interest in the temple ruins."

"That's not what brought me here."

"And yet we are speaking."

"I'd like to talk to you about Nostradamus."

Mathieu smiled slightly, lengthening his bulbous jowls even more. "If you want your fortune told, there's a gypsy camp a few kilometers up the road."

He twisted the cap back onto his second water bottle and then turned back to his cooler dismissively.

"Your father was Henri Mathieu, caretaker of an ancient stone abbey in Salon and something else: the lost prophecies of Nostradamus."

Mathieu stiffened and turned around slowly, putting the weight of his right side against his cane. "And where did you hear that?"

"From Klaus Hauptman, curator of the Jewish Museum in Berlin."

"I've seen his name on eBay. Selling history to the highest bidder.

"His father—"

"I know who his father was, mademoiselle, and what he did. Better than you can possibly realize."

Mathieu climbed awkwardly into the front seat, dragging his stiff leg in after him.

Danielle moved up to the open window and watched him fumbling with his keys. "I have with me the original manuscript Klaus Hauptman's father Erich obtained from your father."

Mathieu held the keys still. "Obtained. Is that the word Klaus Hauptman used?" Then, before Danielle could respond, "What is this about? If you expect me to pay you for this manuscript you say exists, I'd recommend you let Hauptman place it for sale for you on eBay."

"This is about one of the lost prophecies, Monsieur Mathieu," Danielle said flatly. "If it's correct, a lot of people are about to die and I'm here to stop that from happening."

Mathieu's expression tightened as he continued to glare at her. Then he nodded slowly. "We should go somewhere and talk, mademoiselle."

CHAPTER 57

B en and al-Asi left just after dawn, using the papers and identification badges David Vordi had provided to traverse checkpoints on their way to Jordan. Two miles beyond the border, they found the field where a helicopter was waiting to take them to a border crossing with Iraq. Air traffic over the still-occupied country was severely restricted, meaning they'd have to transfer to another car for the drive across the long stretch of desert road east toward Baghdad.

"Who is it we're going to see exactly?" Ben had asked the colonel back at the Ministry of Interior's headquarters before they set out.

"A man named Ibrahim al-Kursami."

"Never heard of him."

"Not by that name, anyway. Perhaps the one he's better known as: Massoud Takran."

"You're acquainted with the former head of the Iraqi secret police?"

"Not exactly. He was still Ibrahim al-Kursami when I knew him."

"Knew him how, Colonel?"

Al-Asi didn't hesitate. "He was my mentor."

THE FACT that Nabril al-Asi, almost certainly the closest friend Ben had in the world, had learned his trade from among the most violent and brutal men in modern history shocked and unsettled Ben. Then again, the colonel had always been full of surprises and this was just another in a long line.

They didn't speak of the issue again until they were speeding across the desert on the all-but-abandoned highway that linked Jordan with Baghdad. It was al-Asi who brought it up again after they'd been cleared through the second American checkpoint and no longer had to concern themselves with the bandits who still plagued the earlier stretch of the route.

"You're disappointed in me, Inspector."

"Surprised, that's all."

The colonel smiled tightly, humorlessly. "What, did you think I became head of the Preventive Security Service using only my charm and wit? No, first I needed to learn how the game was played. In 1974, at the age of fifteen, I found myself exiled. I wasn't alone; there were many of us. I was considered to be of no use to the resistance movement building in Jordan, so ultimately I made my way with a few others into Iraq. Ibrahim al-Kursami was a colonel in the Iraqi military back then, assigned to stop the flood of refugees streaming in from Jordan, of which I was a part. He ordered his men to fire into the crowd when his instructions to stop and turn around were disregarded."

"What happened?" Ben asked.

"I threw myself over the body of a smaller boy. I thought I was dead until a powerful hand hoisted me upward and I looked into al-Kursami's eyes for the first time. Black eyes. I had never seen a man with black eyes before. He smiled at me. Others around me were screaming, sobbing, and fleeing back toward the border. I could have fled too but something stopped me. Maybe it was the fact I had nowhere else to go or maybe it was the way he looked at me. But I stayed and spent the next decade in Iraq as one of al-Kursami's protégés, then moved on to Lebanon, before returning to Palestine with Arafat as a member of his inner circle."

"You're telling me you learned your stock and trade from a man who had women and children raped in front of a husband or father for being disloyal to the state."

Al-Asi frowned. "I had left Iraq before al-Kursami became Massoud Takran and sank to the levels of depravity of which you speak. I won't tell you I didn't see him do brutal things but I'll tell you this, Inspector: I never once saw him enjoy it."

"That doesn't make his actions any more justifiable."

"No, I suppose it doesn't. But a man in al-Kursami's position, and mine, must learn to evoke fear in his enemies as well as his friends."

"The fear you inspire has always been based on intimidation, not brutality."

"I became what I had to, just as al-Kursami became what he had to, in order to survive. And that's what he remains to this day: a survivor."

"I thought the Americans captured him."

"Actually, he turned himself in."

"You're telling me he's *not* imprisoned?"

"Not after he proved himself an invaluable intelligence source. Al-Kursami was always a master at knowing how to close a deal. A survivor, as I said."

"He gave up high-level Iraqi leaders and the Americans let him live," Ben presumed.

"Oh, much more than that, Inspector."

"What do you mean?"

"You'll see," al-Asi said, and gave the SUV more gas.

CHAPTER 58

Danielle followed Jacques Mathieu into the center of the Old Town section of Nîmes to a restaurant called the Vintage Café. The way he seized the menu from the waiter's hand helped explain his generous girth, his eyes aglow just from perusing the café's daily selections. Around them, all the tables were taken and a hefty line of patrons Mathieu had bypassed spilled out onto the sidewalk. The maitre d' had greeted him fondly by name, exchanged a smile with Danielle, and then led both of them to a reasonably secluded corner table.

"I would have preferred to speak somewhere less crowded, mademoiselle, but I'm afraid our town's annual festival, an homage to Spain, is under way, and the tourists are everywhere." Mathieu chuckled lightly. "Except enjoying my tours of historical artifacts, of course. In any case the food here is excellent."

Danielle studied the menu. "I don't read French very well."

"Then let me translate the key items. The hot lentil salad served with smoked haddock is superb, as is the goat cheese terrine. If you have a heartier appetite, I'd recommend the mullet crisped in olive oil and basil or the herb-crusted lamb."

Danielle hadn't realized how hungry she was, only now trying to recall the last good meal she'd had. "Either of those last two sound fine. Your choice."

"Very well," Mathieu said and summoned the waiter. After ordering, he returned his attention to Danielle. "You're Israeli," he said suddenly.

"Is my French that bad?"

"Let's just say your accent is . . . distinctive. You would prefer English."

"Please."

"And I am to assume you are here on the Israelis' behalf?"

"I work for the United Nations now."

"On their behalf, then?"

"My own, Monsieur Mathieu. And the United States', where I believe this threat I mentioned is aimed."

Mathieu gazed at the backpack still resting on Danielle's lap. "A threat you learned of because of an ancient prophecy."

"That's right."

"And just how did you come to be in possession of it?"

"Through a World War Two veteran whose unit uncovered it in Buchenwald."

"Buchenwald? So that's where it ended up after . . ." Mathieu's voice tailed off.

"It had been hidden there," Danielle explained, "along with numerous other historical documents."

"A pity," Mathieu said, shaking his head. "I should like to speak to this veteran."

"You can't, I'm sorry to say. He's dead, along with virtually all the others in his unit who were aware of the prophecy's message. All murdered in the last few months."

"I'm not surprised."

"No?"

"Nostradamus always feared his great gift could be used in the wrong way. It's why he blurred the meanings of his prophecies, sometimes making them all but unintelligible."

"Then why bother writing them down at all?"

"I'd imagine he felt it was God's will. Or, perhaps, he

could not keep what he saw bundled up inside. Imagine carrying such a burden alone."

"Imagine sharing it with the world."

"You've proven my point, mademoiselle: for Nostradamus, there was no simple solution. He felt he had been given a great gift, that it would be tantamount to sacrilege not to use it for what he hoped would be the betterment of the world."

"Unfortunately that hasn't been the case."

"Hasn't it? If not for this last prophecy you speak of, would you be in a position to stop the cataclysm you seem quite certain is about to befall the United States?"

Danielle remained silent.

"And my guess," Mathieu resumed, "is that you are exactly the kind of person Nostradamus hoped would grasp the meaning of his work."

"I'm afraid he'd be disappointed in me."

Mathieu studied her briefly. "He foresaw the Six-Day War, you know."

"No, I didn't."

"Quatrain Twenty-two from Centuries Three: 'Six days the assault is made in front of the city,'" Mathieu said, reciting the words more than speaking them. "'Freedom is attained in a strong and bitter fight. Three will hand it over and to them pardon. To the rest fire, and bloody slashing and slaughter.'" He took a sip from his water, then continued. "The city, of course, is Jerusalem. The 'three' Nostradamus speaks of are Egypt, Jordan, and Syria. The rest could be Libya, Iraq, and Iran."

"Could be," Danielle repeated, as if the phrase made her point for her.

"Nostradamus did not always deal in absolutes so much as indications, much the same as your own prophets."

"I don't see what—"

"Your heritage, mademoiselle, the Jewish heritage, is rich in this very tradition. You've heard of the Ro'eh?"

"I suppose," Danielle said, recalling the term from her studies years before.

"They were the *original* prophets. Seers who foretold the future in writings not much different from those of Nostradamus, although less poetically. The Jews of their time made nary a move without their council."

"Not a very long time, considering the length of Jewish history."

"You're right, of course," Mathieu conceded. "Around 850 B.C. the Ro'eh was usurped by another group of prophets known as the Navi: Amos, Hosea, Isaiah, Jeremiah, and Ezekiel to name some. The philosophy of the Navi made them more 'forth' tellers than foretellers, in that they spoke of the world as it was as opposed to how it was going to be. The Navi believed in a contingent future totally dependent on the actions of man. If this, went their writings, then that. . . ." Mathieu shoved his chair closer to the table and lowered his voice. "My point, mademoiselle, is that Nostradamus wasn't a fortune-teller either. His abilities, his talents, lie somewhere between your Ro'eh and Nivi'im, and his writings are best considered in that context."

Danielle lifted Walter Henley's lockbox from her backpack and placed it in the center of the table. Unlike Klaus Hauptman, who couldn't wait to lay his eyes on the manuscript unearthed at Buchenwald, Mathieu left the lockbox just where Danielle had put it.

"Don't you want to see the manuscript?" she asked him.

Mathieu left his eyes upon her. "I'm more interested in the person who brought it to my attention."

"I don't matter."

"I disagree. Do you believe in the Ro'eh, mademoiselle, the Navi?"

"I was taught to."

"Because of your faith, your education. And if that same faith, that same education, had substituted the words of Nostradamus, what then?"

"Do you believe?" Danielle asked Mathieu, instead of answering.

"I have to, mademoiselle," he said, gazing down at this stiff leg. "Otherwise, this was for nothing."

"I hadn't realized that. . . ."

"What, Hauptman failed to tell you how his father came into possession of that manuscript?"

"I'm not sure he knew."

"Well, I certainly do," Mathieu said, struggling to slide his chair farther beneath the table. "And it's time you heard the story too."

CHAPTER 59

THROUGH A third-floor window of the abbey, Henri Mathieu saw the car coming. Big and black, its headlights slicing through the afternoon fog and windows tinted dark to keep its passengers from the view of those beyond.

A tall, broad man with straw-colored hair and sharp blue eyes climbed out of the backseat and approached the Abbey de Sébastian in Salon. Mathieu had come here following the sudden, tragic death of his wife that had left him to raise his young son alone. He had shown up at the front door of the abbey in a drunken stupor with his son Jacques huddled against his coat, searching for no more than a place to spend the night. He had remained three years, staying on as caretaker of the property even after the Franciscan monks had been reassigned elsewhere. In essence, Mathieu had survived his saviors.

He had not taken a single drink in those three years, coming to enjoy the quiet lifestyle that proved the perfect remedy to his vast grief. Since the monks' reassignment, the abbey received no visitors and this car was the first to drive up the long approach in many months.

The tall man with the straw-colored hair looked around, as if to reassure himself no one was about, then continued up the walk to the abbey's majestic double-door entrance. He rapped the tarnished brass knocker hard and for just an instant Mathieu considered ignoring his presence and staying clear of the windows until he was gone. But the man could have come bearing a message from the monks or the heads of their order, and Mathieu did not want to shirk his responsibilities. Besides, by the third series of heavy raps, it was clear the tall man wasn't going anywhere until he gained entry.

The stranger greeted Mathieu with a warm smile as soon as the caretaker threw open the doors, instantly putting him more at ease.

"I hope I am not disturbing you, Brother," he greeted.

"I am not a brother," Mathieu returned. "Just a lowly caretaker."

"As am I, Mr. Mathieu."

How does he know my name? Henri wondered. The man's French, he noted, was laced with a heavy German accent.

"I believe the monks who once occupied this holy place left something here for me," the visitor continued.

"Six months ago?"

"Has it been that long?" The man shook his head in mock surprise. "My travels have taken me elsewhere."

"Who are you, monsieur?"

"My name is Hauptman, Erich Hauptman. But that's not important now. What's important is that you produce the manuscript that the monks left here in my name."

Mathieu felt a chill surge through him. The manuscript Hauptman spoke of could only be one thing. Mathieu knew little about it, other than the fact that the monks here had kept its existence secret even from the holy fathers of their order. Hence, upon being reassigned they could not take it with them and opted to leave it in place, accounting in large measure for Mathieu's continued presence. He never asked what it was, simply accepted the charge of preserving and protecting it at all costs in return for the brothers of the abbey giving him back his life.

"I know of no such manuscript," Mathieu lied.

Hauptman frowned unhappily. "A pity."

"They must have taken it with them when they were called to the north."

Hauptman's piercing blue eyes grew utterly cold. "The monk I spoke with yesterday said otherwise."

Mathieu could only stand there, silent.

"The monk I spoke with yesterday told me the manuscript still lay within these walls. He mentioned you by name before I killed him."

Mathieu shuddered, felt his bowels loosen. "I am sorry, monsieur," he said, wondering if he could get the heavy door slammed before Hauptman forced his way inside. "But I know of no such manuscript. The brothers never shared its existence with me."

Hauptman planted a large booted foot inside the doorjamb, as if reading Mathieu's mind. "He did not know where it was hidden and, I suppose, I could search this place for weeks, months even, and never find it. Since I do not enjoy the luxury of time, I trust we can find a way to expedite matters."

Hauptman looked back over his shoulder at the black car and nodded. The rear door opened and another man, shorter and stout but clearly layered with heavy muscle, emerged dragging something behind him.

Jacques!

Mathieu's eight-year-old son trembled badly, clearly sniffling and sobbing. They must have taken him out of school, or been waiting when he emerged from the building.

"No," Mathieu muttered.

The short, heavily muscled man dragged Jacques halfway up the walk, then kicked the boy's legs out from under him. Mathieu watched him pull some kind of club from his belt and raise it over his head.

"NO!"

The man crashed it down into Jacques's right leg. The

crack of the bone breaking was audible. The boy wailed in agony, writhing wildly on the ground. The short man raised the club a second time and sliced it down again.

CRACK!

Again Mathieu could hear the sound of his son's leg being broken. Enraged, he rushed forward only to be swallowed in Hauptman's powerful grasp.

CRACK!

And his son screamed once more.

"A few more strikes and the boy will be a cripple for life, but at least he'll live," Hauptman said, quite calmly. "That will change if you do not produce the manuscript immediately, forcing us to move on to his other leg and then his arms."

CRACK!

"I'll get it for you! Just leave my son alone. Please, I beg you!"

Hauptman nodded at the short man who stopped the next swing of his club in midflight. "You have five minutes," he told Mathieu.

Mathieu needed only three to retrieve the case in which the manuscript was stored from inside the bricks layered onto a false chimney wall on the abbey's third floor. He rushed back down to the entrance, his hands shaking as he handed the case breathlessly to Hauptman. He tried to look past the big man out to his son who was moaning in agony on the ground.

"You see," *Hauptman said, kneeling down to open the case, "that wasn't so hard."*

Mathieu yanked a pistol that had been tucked into the same hiding place as the manuscript from his jacket and shot Hauptman point blank. He aimed for the chest, but the gun's powerful kick pulled the bullet high and to the right, into Hauptman's shoulder. Still enough to punch him backward, clearing a path to the heavily muscled man beyond.

Mathieu ran outside firing and kept firing until the gun was empty and the short man had sunk to his knees with blood rushing from his chest and belly, his own pistol clamoring to the stone walk.

Mathieu scooped up his son, drawing a high-pitched shriek as he jostled the boy's shattered leg, and rushed toward the forest that bordered the abbey's property. He never looked back, even when shots erupted behind him. He expected to feel the hot, searing pain of a bullet piercing his back. Asked only that he be given the strength to get his son to safety before he died.

Gunshots continued to echo, but Mathieu ran on. He reached the forest safely and took cover amidst the trees and thick brush that raked his face even as he sought to protect his son's. He ran far into the woods and hid himself and his son deep in a thicket.

Mathieu stayed hidden there until nightfall, keeping Jacques as warm as he could. Emerging only when the temperature grew too cold to bear, with a prayer on his lips.

W hen we got back to the abbey," Jacques Mathieu continued after a pause, "Erich Hauptman was gone. The muscled man too."

"What happened next?"

"My father got me to a doctor. There wasn't much he could do," Mathieu said, looking at his stiff leg. "I remember the doctor recommending amputation and my father refusing to hear of it. After that, I remember very little. I know we spent a lot of time on the move, hiding out." Now, at last, his eyes turned to the case Danielle had placed on the table before him. "All because of what lies in this box. Now tell me how you came to be in possession of it, mademoiselle."

Danielle told him the story, starting with the massacre that had brought her to the Palestinian village of Bureij; then the tale told by Victoria Henley.

"Buchenwald," Mathieu echoed, when she had completed that part. "Of all the places . . . And so Hauptman's work was for nothing." Another angry glance at his stiff leg. "This was for nothing."

"Hauptman paid for it with his life. Goebbels must have ordered the manuscript and everything else Hauptman had uncovered hidden away . . . and everyone with knowledge of the manuscript's existence killed."

"That's small consolation at this point. You showed this manuscript to Hauptman's son?"

"Yes."

"And he believed it was authentic?"

"I think he did. Klaus Hauptman claimed these final prophecies were uncharacteristically clear and unambiguous. Much different from the ones that comprised the thousand or so contained in *The Centuries*. The translations are all in this lockbox, along with the original manuscript your father gave to Hauptman to save you. The problem is Nostradamus never completed the last prophecy. The quatrain only contains three lines. The fourth, the line that lays out exactly what the United States is about to face, is missing."

"Wrong again, mademoiselle."

"What do you mean?"

"The fourth line isn't missing at all."

Flabbergasted, Danielle reached out and tapped the lockbox. "The manuscript is in here. See for yourself."

"I don't have to. How much do you know about Nostradamus, mademoiselle?"

"A bit. Get back to the missing—"

"That he was born Michel de Nostredame into a family of Christianized Jews, for example. The religious duality came to typify much of his work since his prophecies are written in a baffling blend of French, Provençal, and Latin. That, together with the purposely blurred meanings of his predictions, is why so much of his work has been passed off as irrelevant through the ages."

"I'm not interested in the past. I've come here about the *future, America's* future. I've only got four days to find the final line of the last prophecy."

"It wasn't the last prophecy at all." Mathieu leaned back in his chair, his gaze drifting. "My father was a caretaker and, in many respects, so am I. A caretaker of history, mademoiselle. I came upon much of what I know while searching for the truth behind Nostradamus. That he never stopped writing prophecies, for example. He continued writing them until the very moment he died."

"Monsieur Mathieu—"

"In 1556 Nostradamus suffered a severe attack of gout. Not that this came as any surprise to him; he had already foreseen his own death. So, knowing it was near, he returned to his home in Salon. He insisted on being moved into his study and had a special wheeled bench built to allow him some freedom of movement. It was enough to reach his desk anyway, and he wrote with a feverish passion each of his last days until the pain overwhelmed him."

"And he died after completing only three lines of his last prophecy."

"Yes and no."

"Which?" Danielle demanded, losing her patience.

"Yes, he died in the midst of writing it. But, no, it wasn't his last prophecy."

"Make sense!"

"Nostradamus made two copies of everything he wrote. He was in the midst of copying his final volume when death finally claimed him. It was that copy, the very same one you've brought to me today, that my father gave to Erich Hauptman at the abbey. The completed original remains intact."

"How can you be so sure of that?"

"Because, mademoiselle," Mathieu told her, "I have it."

The new Baghdad, al-Asi remarked, was very much like the old, at least in form and function. The major difference, of course, was the continued presence of American servicemen on the streets, posted at regular intervals never far from their Humvees, tanks, or armored vehicles. But the United Nations presence had increased gradually, easing Ben and al-Asi's passage through spot checkpoints, thanks to the identification Commissioner of National Police David Vordi had returned to Ben.

"You're telling me Ibrahim al-Kursami is still in Baghdad?" Ben asked.

"You're familiar with the Karada district, Inspector?"

"Newest and plushest of the city's residential areas just west of the city on the peninsula that runs between the Tigris and Euphrates Rivers."

"I'm impressed."

"I watch CNN, Colonel. That's all."

"It's also where we'll find al-Kursami."

"In hiding?"

"Under the protection of the Americans, Inspector. They never would've been able to capture the bulk of government officials who conveniently disappeared once Baghdad fell, including Saddam himself, without al-Kursami's help. He provided their locations, their plans and routes of escape. He was also instrumental in saving the lives of several prisoners of war by telling the American soldiers where they could be found."

"In exchange for his own freedom."

"As I said, Inspector. Al-Kursami is first and foremost a survivor."

Many of the city's streets were still blocked, forcing Ben to take a roundabout route to the Karada district. The road banked sharply and then flattened out through an upscale residential neighborhood of gated stone homes. The yards looked large by Iraqi standards, deep but narrow in width. The overall effect at first glance was an uncomfortably tight cluster of homes that on second glance revealed a high level of privacy. Even more interestingly, this section of Karada looked untouched by American ordnance, making Ben wonder if many of the exclusive residents hadn't made their deals with the Americans against Saddam well in advance.

Al-Asi directed Ben to pull into the slot set before a red steel fence. The colonel poked his face out before a tiny camera, smiled and, without any further elaboration, the gate swung mechanically open.

Ben drove on through toward a two-story stone house behind the steel security gate and inner wall that enclosed the property. As they climbed out of their vehicle, the front door opened and an older man appeared on the top step. Ibrahim al-Kursami's grin exaggerated the deep wrinkles that looked like narrow craters dug around his cheeks, eyes, and brow. Al-Asi explained earlier that he had gone back to using his old name, allowing him to lay the despicably evil Massoud Takran to rest forever. He must have been about sixty and looked all of it, thanks to a receding hairline he tried to hide by combing his gray hair straight forward and a thick mustache of the same shade. He wore wheat-colored linen pants and a matching silk polo shirt buttoned all the way to the top, both of which fit him to perfection. He held himself strong and erect, charged with confidence.

Ben gazed at al-Asi in the passenger seat. In twenty years, the colonel would likely resemble this man to an uncanny degree. The colonel had indeed learned much from his mentor, the coiled tension and power that lurked beneath the surfaces of both men further exaggerated by the striking way in which they presented themselves.

Al-Asi climbed the steps and embraced al-Kursami, kissing him on both cheeks.

"You're looking well, Ibrahim," al-Asi greeted.

"As do you, Nabril. Apparently, political life agrees with you."

"I am the minister of interior of a country that has none. Call me a champion of low expectations."

Ibrahim al-Kursami brushed al-Asi's comment off with a wave of his hand. "One day you will have your state and things will change. Who knows, you might even need to hire an old fossil like myself to help you."

"I doubt you'd want to leave all this."

"I doubt the Americans would let me anyway. I have apparently become invaluable to them. Still, to stay in their good graces, I'm forced to turn over one of my former associates from time to time."

"What happens when the list of former associates runs out?" al-Asi asked him.

"I'll make up some new ones," al-Kursami explained, flashing a devilish grin almost identical to al-Asi's. Finally the eyes of the former head of the Iraqi secret police turned toward Ben who was still standing at the bottom of the stairs. "And this must be the man you've told me so much about."

"Bayan Kamal," Ben greeted, extending a hand toward al-Kursami as he climbed the stairs.

Al-Kursami clasped both his hands over Ben's almost reverently. "You're an impressive man, Inspector."

Ben glanced at al-Asi. "The colonel has a tendency to exaggerate."

"My former pupil has nothing to do with the esteem in

which I hold you." Al-Kursami paused, seeming to size Ben up. "I followed your investigation into the bombing of the U.N. compound very closely."

"*My* investigation."

Al-Kursami nodded. "They should have listened to you, Inspector. You were the only one who had things right."

CHAPTER 62

You're talking about my theory that elements of the former Soviet Union were responsible for the bombing," Ben said once they were inside, seated in a spacious sitting room to the right of the main entrance. He and al-Asi sat on a couch, al-Kursami across from them on a divan covered in a black and tan printed fabric. "To hide something stored beneath the compound when it was the Canal Hotel."

"It's much more than a theory, I can assure you of that."

"How?"

"Because I supervised the process. Late 1991, I think, but the process stretched on for several months."

"You became caretaker of the material," Ben said.

"And nearly forgot about it myself until the bombing." Al-Kursami looked toward al-Asi. "When the colonel first contacted me, I figured that must be what this meeting was about. It wasn't, of course, but it might yet be."

"Still a man of riddles I see, Ibrahim." Al-Asi smiled.

"Indeed, Nabril. Now let's move on to the reason for your visit."

A maid entered the room with a tray holding three cups of sweet mint tea. She gave each man a cup and quickly took her leave.

"Dead Iraqi Special Republican Guardsmen who have risen miraculously from the grave," the colonel said when she was out of earshot.

Al-Kursami laid his tall glass of tea back onto the silver tray. The mint leaves poked up from the top, wrapping themselves over the edge. "A simple process when you think of it: all we had to do was leave their papers on other corpses. The Americans were indiscriminate about who they killed and didn't pay much heed when it came to properly identifying the bodies, so there was never any question that the ruse would work."

"Toward what purpose?"

"Revenge. The operation, known as Black Sands, was conceived to punish America after the inevitable fall of Saddam's regime as one of the primary components of Al Awdah, the Return."

"You told your American inquisitors the truth of what became of the soldiers of Black Sands?" al-Asi wondered.

"I did better than that. I gave them the name of the man in charge of the operation, the only one privy to all its details: Sharif ali-Aziz Moussan."

"The Americans have him in custody," al-Asi said.

Al-Kursami's eyebrows flickered. "But if the plot ended there, you wouldn't have come to see me, would you?"

"The soldiers of Black Sands were responsible for a massacre in a Palestinian village," Ben said.

"The question, then, becomes on whose behalf?"

Colonel al-Asi sipped his tea leisurely. "Your riddles are starting to try my patience, Ibrahim."

"Did I not teach you to push as far as your adversary will allow before he pushes back, Nabril?"

"You did at that."

"Another lesson learned well. I must've been a better teacher than I thought."

"Tell us more about these soldiers of Black Sands."

"We were able to get several hundred of them out of the country before the war began. There was a rendezvous point, a base from which they were to await further instructions."

"And this base?" al-Asi prodded.

Ibrahim al-Kursami remained silent.

"It is I asking the questions today, Ibrahim," al-Asi said, his voice taking on a threatening edge. "Tomorrow it will be the Americans. I think they would be most disappointed to learn that a small army trained to act against their interests was still loose in the world. They might have no choice but to deal harshly with the man who kept that information from them."

Ben had expected al-Kursami to lash out at al-Asi's thinly veiled threat. Instead, though, the former head of Saddam's secret police smiled.

"It seems I taught you too well, Nabril."

"These men murdered innocent Palestinians, Ibrahim, in the guise of Israeli soldiers."

"But I don't recall ever teaching you to care."

"No, *sidi*. That I learned on my own."

Al-Kursami nodded indifferently. "Black Sands was to be based in France, in Marseilles. But you'd better act fast if you expect to find them there."

"Why?" Ben asked.

Al-Kursami looked back at him. "Because Moussan's capture didn't end the plot. I didn't realize that for sure until now, until you told me about the murder of these Palestinians."

Ben felt a chill slide through him. "This has something to do with the bombing of the U.N. compound, doesn't it?"

"If only they had listened to you, Inspector. . . ."

"What was it the Russians had you bury under that hotel, Ibrahim?" al-Asi wondered.

"Relics, Nabril, relics of the Cold War and another age entirely. Only one of these relics is of any concern to you in the form of a plot to plant moles in high-level positions in governments, seats of power, all over the world."

"A wives' tale, Ibrahim."

"A wives' tale that took up several crates of documents. The agents were real, but after the Soviet Union fell they became pariahs. Unable to return to their homeland, stuck in the sham lives they had made for themselves. Still no doubt loathing the way of life they had been charged with eventually helping to destroy."

Ben set his tea down on the glass table before him. "You mean they're active again?"

"They never stopped being active, any more than they stopped hating. Given the opportunity, I expect they would most willingly complete their mission. Given the opportunity."

"You're saying somebody gave it to them."

"No, Inspector, you are. I realize that now. I should have seen it before, of course." Al-Kursami leaned back comfortably and took a deep breath. "But this sort of lifestyle tends to make a man soft."

"You never told anyone about these Soviet moles, about the files hidden beneath the Canal Hotel?"

"No one ever asked," al-Kursami told Ben. "And, besides, I didn't think they posed any real threat. The threat came from the soldiers of Black Sands and I made sure to tell one of my inquisitors everything I knew about them, which was everything that existed."

Ben and al-Asi exchanged a taut glance.

"Then how could they still be at large?" the colonel asked.

"Because the inquisitor was one of the high level moles left stranded with the collapse of the Soviet Union," al-Kursami said and turned toward Ben. "Someone you're well acquainted with I believe, Inspector."

The former head of the Iraqi secret police said the name and Ben felt his blood run cold.

"WHAT ARE you going to do, Inspector?" Colonel al-Asi asked when they were back in their SUV.

"Go to Marseilles."

"I meant about—"

"I know what you meant, Colonel, and the answer's the same. Marseilles is the only place where this can be stopped once and for all." Ben leaned back and massaged his eyelids, contemplating the task before him, made even more complicated now. "But I can't do it alone."

"I only wish I could accompany you myself," al-Asi said apologetically.

"I understand."

"I wish I did," the colonel sighed. "But in my new position . . ."

"Don't worry, Colonel. I've got a new ally I think will be more than happy to assist me."

Mathieu refused to elaborate on where they were going, suggesting they drive across town in his car since Danielle's was pinned on a street blocked by a parade of floats crawling by. They finished their meals, Danielle enjoying the bread and salad as much as the mullet Mathieu had ordered for her.

He promised the distance to their destination was short, but the street celebrations constantly stalled their progress, turning the drive into a maddening series of stops and starts. Finally Mathieu pulled into a handicapped space directly across from Musée Archéologique et d'Histoire Naturelle, Nîmes's Museum of Archaeology and Natural History.

"We'll have the whole place to ourselves," Mathieu explained. "The spring festival has closed it for the week."

"Then how do we get inside?" Danielle asked.

Mathieu dangled a tarnished key before her. "One of the advantages of being on the museum's board of directors."

They walked around the side of the building to a service entrance. Mathieu fitted his key into the lock and the door opened with a click.

"This isn't a very well-known museum," he explained, as he switched on a bank of lights, "and not well appointed by European standards. It mostly contains archaeological finds of local interest like statues, busts, friezes, tools, coins, and pottery."

"No manuscripts?" Danielle prodded.

Mathieu smiled. "Just one."

They wound their way through an exhibit hall. The display cases interested Danielle the most, since it was logical to assume that the completed manuscript to which Mathieu was referring would be contained within one. But he trudged past all of these in favor of a smaller wing of the museum that contained waxwork re-creations of famous area residents through history.

"This is the closest museum to Nostradamus's home in Salon," Mathieu told her. "As such we've adopted the prophet as one of our own. See for yourself."

He stopped before a glassed-in, sealed exhibit with a black curtained backdrop featuring an elegant reproduction of a sixteenth-century room. A wax figure sat at a writing desk, pen in hand, a quill pen touched to the top of a hefty stack of pages.

"Inspector Barnea, may I present Michel de Nostredame, captured in his thirties at the height of his powers."

The bearded figure wore a tie shirt and open vest, his captured pose appearing almost trancelike.

"The pleasure's all mine," Danielle returned. "But that's not what I came for."

"Oh, but it is, mademoiselle," Mathieu said, and moved to a door, the contours of which were disguised by the glass.

He slipped a key into a slot Danielle had first taken to be a chip in the glass and opened the door. Then he entered the room and beckoned Danielle to join him. She felt a gush of cool, dehumidified air and followed Mathieu to the writing desk. Once there, he gently removed the thick stack of pages from beneath the wax figure's pen and extended them toward her.

"I give you the lost prophecies of Nostradamus," said Mathieu. "In their entirety."

"INTERESTING HIDING place," Danielle noted, when they had exited the exhibit.

Mathieu locked the glass door behind them and laid the pages down atop a small table upon which rested a tablet outlining the life and works of Nostradamus. "I thought you'd like it. The last place, I'd venture to say, anyone would ever expect to find a priceless document."

"You've kept the manuscript all these years, since you were a boy, haven't you?"

"My father must have returned for it before we fled the abbey for good. He never actually told me about the manuscript. I found it among his possessions after he died. Even though the translation was difficult to manage, I knew it could only be one thing. I've been its keeper ever since."

"The condition of the pages . . ."

"I treat them regularly with a special preparation to make sure they are preserved."

"And you never considered sharing the manuscript with the world?"

Mathieu's gaze grew somber. "I had experienced what the prophecies could do in the wrong hands, Inspector. The only thing that kept me from destroying them altogether was their historical value, not their monetary worth."

"And you were never once curious about what they had to say?"

Mathieu shrugged. "Curious? Not really. I do not believe the future is meant to be known before it happens. But I can tell you over ninety quatrains are contained in the pages."

"I'm only interested in one."

MATHIEU LED her to an upstairs office that featured a PC workstation rigged into the museum's central server. Danielle had no idea how much memory was required to run Henley's encryption software but fully expected the capacity of the server would be more than enough.

She carefully removed the pages of the manuscript recovered in Buchenwald from the lockbox and laid it down next to the thicker pile Mathieu had removed from the exhibit. Danielle then quickly matched the last prophecy in her stack to one two-thirds down in the larger one. She switched the machine on and inserted Henley's disc into the drive. Seconds later the program was running, cueing her to enter the desired item. Danielle carefully typed in the fourth line of the prophecy exactly as Nostradamus had written it in the original manuscript. The machine whirred, a lightbulb icon flashing to indicate the information was being processed.

Danielle felt her heart thudding as she awaited the result.

In an age of two's four, in a land of many
An army rises from midland afar on a day of equal light and dark
Beneath the flames of the bringer of fire, a darkness will reign eternal

Danielle recited the three lines to herself while she waited, stopped when the computer had stopped whirring. The lightbulb icon no longer flashed. On screen the fourth line of the prophecy had been decoded and translated into English. Danielle leaned forward and read.

Went cold.

Because everything was clear.

"Do you believe now, mademoiselle?" Mathieu asked calmly, reading over her shoulder.

"We've got to go," Danielle said, ejecting the disc and then gently smoothing the original manuscript back into a neat pile. "Can I take this with me?"

Mathieu frowned, seemingly about to reject her request when he suddenly shrugged. "I suppose so. It's not doing the world any good here, is it?"

Danielle shook her head and they retraced their route downstairs, then through the exhibit halls, turning off lights on the way. Danielle focused on what she had just learned, contemplating the steps available to her now that the prophecy's translation was complete. She considered the plot in its entirety, the sheer simple madness of it lying in its utter simplicity. The fourth line holding the final key to why the old veterans of the 121st Evacuation Unit had to die, the roots of their deaths forged long, long before.

Finally she recognized the door through which they had entered the museum. Mathieu yanked it open and light flooded in, blinding Danielle long enough to keep her from seeing the four armed men standing directly in front of her.

"A pleasure to see you again, Inspector Barnea," greeted Klaus Hauptman, stepping between them.

CHAPTER 64

The four men now standing rigidly behind Hauptman looked oddly Western. Oddly because there was something forced and uneasy about the way they held themselves. But they were professionals; the way they held their pistols told Danielle that much.

"Ironic, isn't it?" Hauptman asked Mathieu. "First our fathers meet and now, in another age, we follow the same path in a virtually identical pursuit." The men behind Hauptman stiffened perceptibly, as he returned his attention to Danielle. "I assume you now have the complete manuscript in your possession. If you'd be so kind as to hand it over . . ." When Danielle held her ground, his eyes moved to her backpack. "I assume the lockbox is inside that, Inspector."

Danielle reached inside and removed the lockbox slowly, still weighing her options. "You're a part of this," she said, extending it toward him.

"I'm a part of something, yes. What it is, I don't really care." Hauptman snatched the lockbox from her grasp and stepped back beyond her reach and closer to his armed escort. "For me it's a simple exchange of merchandise. I'm just a broker."

"Bullshit. You got innocent people killed," Danielle accused. "Old men and women, war heroes in the United States."

"Who had the unfortunate occasion to stumble upon a relic of history uncovered by my father."

"You mean stolen from mine," Mathieu sneered, trembling with rage and fear.

"Alas, history repeats itself," Hauptman gloated. "I wonder if even Nostradamus could have seen such a thing as he gazed into the future. First Henley contacts me about his lost prophecies, then a second party offers infinitely better terms."

"What's your fee, Herr Hauptman?"

"Isn't it obvious, Inspector?" He held up the lockbox she had just handed him. "The contents of this. I can't even imagine what an original copy of the lost, final prophecies of Nostradamus might yield in the open market. Millions, tens of millions if advertised and auctioned properly." He stared Danielle right in the eye. "Not bad in exchange for the life of whoever delivered it to me. My employers will be most pleased. They wanted to take action in Berlin, move on you at your hotel, but I talked them out of it. Convinced them you might be able to uncover materials far more interesting to them in France."

"You knew I had the complete manuscript," said Mathieu, shaking his head in disbelief.

"I knew it existed somewhere and that a man like you would be stupid enough to hide it from the world." Hauptman turned his gaze on Danielle. "Inspector Barnea here was kind enough to aid me in this pursuit. I owe her quite a debt."

"My father should have killed yours when he had the chance," Mathieu threatened. "I won't make the same mistake."

And then he barreled forward awkwardly into Hauptman, throwing his entire weight into the smaller man as he lashed out with his cane toward the gunmen.

"Run!"

Danielle lurched away and rushed down the narrow street. She hated leaving Jacques Mathieu behind, but knew she had no other choice. The clack of gunshots echoed well before she reached Boulevard de l'Amiral Courbet, forcing her to run in a crouch and pin herself as close to the building as she dared without sacrificing speed. A pair of bullets cracked into the brick and showered her with dust and fragments. But an instant later she had swung onto the main road and was swallowed by the marchers in the parade.

Rat-tat-tat . . .

The sound stopped the breath in her throat, submachine gun fire surely. But another series of bursts made her realize it was nothing more sinister than firecrackers being set off by joyous revelers awash in celebration and alcohol. Both simply dressed and costumed parade participants jaunted along the street, a springy hop to their step courtesy of the hefty mugs of sangria wine each of them toted.

Danielle surged on, slicing her way through the crowd as her feet mashed orange rinds, lemon peels, and strips of ribbons and crepe paper—the residue of spilled sangria and marchers. She gazed backward in search of the gunmen who had accompanied Klaus Hauptman here, but could make out nothing through the cluster of revelers.

Who are these men?

Danielle had no doubt that they were part of whatever was about to befall the United States, dispatched by the force behind the strike. But there was something oddly familiar about the way they held themselves and their weapons, as well as the insolent glares plastered across their faces. They reminded her of the Hezbollah soldiers or Syrian secret police she had come up against so often through the years.

Danielle decided her best strategy was to retrace her steps as well as she could back to her abandoned car. Assuming the nearby streets were clear by now, the car would afford her the safest and quickest means of escape.

Passing the next cross street, though, showed her this was not to be. Partying tourists and locals had clogged roads and snarled traffic as far as the eye could see. With no other choice, Danielle continued to move with the flow of the parade crowd east toward the Arènes, or Arena, considered to be the best preserved Roman amphitheater in the world.

A miniature of the Coliseum in Rome, it was the size of nearly three football fields and still boasted a seating capacity of nearly twenty-five thousand. Legendary gladiator battles and wild-boar chases had once packed its bleachers full. More modern times, though, had left it as little more than a historical artifact except for occasional performances and this annual spring homage to Spain when fans packed its seats for *la corrida,* largely ceremonial bullfights that formed the highlight of these festival days.

Ahead, Danielle could see a steady stream of parade goers pouring into the Arena. The sounds of cheers and applause from within it rose above the revelry, drowning out another series of firecrackers.

Danielle heard a gasp and saw a man on her right tumble to the street, his hefty pitcher showering those around him with sangria the same red color as the blood that speckled the back of his shirt.

Not firecrackers this time, then: *bullets!*

Danielle quickened her pace, slicing through the drunken crowd for the Arena.

CHAPTER 65

Inside the cavernous Arena's dark underbelly, the air was rife with heat and sweat. The stench of urine drifted in the air, evidence of revelers using darkened corners and the cover of ancient columns to relieve themselves.

Danielle could see that the crowd, while mostly men, contained enough women so she wouldn't stand out terribly. The problem was that virtually all the women were dressed in the comfortable flowing skirts and print shirts of Spain, in stark contrast to her slacks and boots. She stayed on the move, hoping for a quick exit through which to duck back out, but quickly realized the ancient Arènes had not been constructed with such conveniences in mind.

The flow of the crowd banked upward onto a ramp that rose back toward the sunlight and spilled out on the Arena's lowest tier. Below on the dusty grounds that had once grown wet with blood, at least a dozen bulls jousted with brilliantly costumed matadors and handlers in the oddly restrained choreography that formed in this area the essence of *la corrida*. Danielle knew the men, professionals all, were in little danger. But the mere possibility of being gored by a razor-sharp horn, combined with the ever-dwindling space between man and charging beast, left the celebrating crowd in awe. At times, the fights crisscrossed with matadors exchanging bulls, or aligned so the beasts converged from two directions at once.

Danielle slid on with the crowd's flow, still in search of the nearest exit.

"Hey, watch the fuck where you're going!"

The protest, yelled in French, made her twist to the right in time to see the darkened barrel of a submachine gun appear. She dove sideways, just beneath a burst of gunfire which singed the air over her head as she fell to the ground.

Screams rang out. The crowd suddenly shifted en masse and seemed to surge mindlessly in all directions at once. Heavy footsteps nearly trampled her before Danielle somehow regained her footing. The surge of the crowd was downward now, toward the ground of the Arena itself, and Danielle was swallowed up by it, lifted briefly off her feet. Ancient Romans knew nothing of safety rails and she felt herself slammed into a short retaining wall. The force of the crowd spilled her over it to the dusty earth below, wet with a recent hosing and stinking of animal feces.

Danielle crawled for a brief time, climbing back to her feet just in time to see a charging bull further enraged by the chaos lower its head into a bystander immediately on her right and gore him straight through. The man's screams echoed in her ears, as handlers rushed to his aid.

Another burst of submachine gun fire sliced through the air and two men on Danielle's right collapsed, taking another half dozen drunken revelers down with them. Before Danielle could twist around in search of the gunman, the thundering of hoofbeats made her whirl just in time to lunge from the path of a rampaging bull. Another animal in the center of the Arènes gored a fleeing matador from behind, then pitched the man up and over its haunches. He landed hard alongside the sword from which he'd been separated and didn't move.

Danielle burst toward him, pushing her way through the panicked crowd. In one single swift motion, she reached down and swept the sword from the dirt, then immediately twisted back into the crowd and the approximate path of the gunmen pursuing her.

The flow of the panicked crowd was sideways now, heading for the exit, and she melted into it, bending at the knees to keep herself from view. She caught brief glimpses of two of the gunmen slicing toward her and angled herself to take full advantage of both human cover and the blind spots of her pursuers. She attacked from the side instead of dead on, positioning herself so that one man was between her and the other.

She lashed out with the sword's tip before her first target was even aware of her presence. Her aim, while slightly off, still raked across both his eyelids and brow, blinding him in an agonizing wash of blood. The second man twisted toward his screams, gun angling directly for her. But Danielle jabbed the tip of the matador's bloodied sword straight through the soft flesh in the center of his throat. She yanked it outward and saw a fountain of scarlet spray outward, as the man's hands clutched for the wound.

Danielle dropped the sword and rejoined the crowd. Its flow heaved her to the right, then back to the left when another bull charged, coming straight for her. She was saved only when an unfortunate drunk, pushed into its path, was catapulted up and over the back of the rampaging beast.

Danielle spotted an opening in the crowd that had parted in the bull's wake and surged forward, angling for the stalls at the far end of the Arena. They were built into the structure's underbelly, promising escape. She gazed back long enough to assure herself the final pair of gunmen were hopelessly mired amidst the panicked crush of humanity, and then dashed the final stretch of the way to the stalls.

To her right, Danielle glimpsed a young girl, barely more than a toddler, emerge from a panicked throng into a clear patch of ground. A bull had sighted down on that section of the crowd and was now pawing the earth sixty feet in front of the little girl. The girl was crying, her face and clothes both dirty, her nose bloodied. One of her sleeves was torn.

The bull launched itself into motion.

And so did Danielle.

She rushed straight for the little girl, risking a headlong strike from the bull. In the last moment, she could smell the stench emanating from the enraged beast, see the steam rising off its sweat-soaked hide, hear its gravelly snorts. But her hands latched onto the little girl and scooped her up safely. Danielle twirled sideways, taking her from the path of a deadly strike while leaving her vulnerable to the horn that dug into her back.

The sudden burst of pain made Danielle's spine arch and she placed the little girl down before staggering forward. She tried to twist back toward the stalls, but a numbness crept up her vertebrae, broken only by the sensation of something warm spilling out of her, as she collapsed.

CHAPTER 66

he replies started coming in an hour ago," Jake said before Delbert Fisher was through the door.

Fisher peered over the boy's shoulder at the mishmash of data scrolling across the screen.

"Shouldn't you call some of your tech experts in, let me explain it to them, too?" Jake asked him.

"Just tell me what this says."

"Not much really. Just a designation, followed by the word 'Confirmed,' and '3/20.'"

"A date," said Fisher.

"Four days from now," Jake elaborated.

"How many confirmations total?"

"The same number as the original series of messages that brought your Gestapo to my dorm room: fifty."

"The same fifty?"

"According to the designations, yes. Hey, Del, you ever smoke dope?"

"Not even once."

"You should. It relaxes you. Soothes the stress."

Fisher ignored the suggestion and ran his hand down across the screen in line with what Jake had called designations. "Any idea what these are?"

"Jumbled letters and numbers. Some kind of code."

"I'll get encryption people working on them right away."

"Four days from now, Del. What's going to happen?"

Fisher was still studying the information frozen on Jake's screen. "That's what we need to find out."

"Shouldn't you put an alert out or something? Isn't that what you guys do?"

"About what exactly? What do we tell people?"

"Oh, I don't know. How about calling for a holiday? National stay-at-home-and-board-up-your-windows day? Smoke some ganja, drink some beer. First day of spring, perfect time to chill."

"We'd start a panic."

"What's the alternative?"

"Figuring out where the fifty cells are based, what their targets are."

Jake glanced at the cryptic entries lining his screen. "I think your staff can handle that one."

"Maybe. But you're better. So keep working," Fisher said, and then pointed at the screen. "I want to know what those designations mean."

DAY EIGHT

CHAPTER **67**

Ben Kamal walked stiffly down Marseilles's Rue du Bon Pasteur, the Street of the Good Shepherd, in the center of the city's Old Port section, an area populated almost exclusively by Arab Muslims. Ben heard Arabic being spoken along the streets, no French whatsoever. All the women had their hair covered with scarves. Men in robes and sandals sat together in cafes watching Aljazeera or Al-Arabia news on satellite television. Kiosk-style newsstands sold dozens of Arab-language newspapers and magazines flown in on a daily basis. The Attaqwa Mosque in the middle of Rue du Bon Pasteur, he knew, was frequented by so many worshipers on Fridays that dozens are forced to kneel on prayer rugs laid out over the street in front of it.

In Baghdad the day before, with an astonished Colonel al-Asi standing by his side, Ben had contacted Israeli National Police Commissioner David Vordi from an American security station located on the ground floor of a walled former Republican Guard headquarters.

"Who's controlling these men?" Vordi asked, after Ben explained the situation.

"According to Ibrahim al-Kursami, no one now."

"You're lying."

"Who's controlling them is my problem, Vordi. Finding and finishing the soldiers of Black Sands is yours. Al-Kursami claims that passage was secured for them out of Iraq to Marseilles."

"We need more specific information than that, Inspector."

"We?"

"I have no agents in place capable of doing what must be done."

"So you expect me to track them down?"

"Based on prior experience, we can assume they're staying in a central location. We have intelligence assets who are quite adept at funneling tips to the Americans. Find that central location and I can have F-16s scrambled within an hour."

"We may not have an hour, Commissioner."

"I can push for an alert. That means they'll be in the air over the south of France, no more than twenty minutes from striking once they receive the coordinates."

"Furnished by me, of course."

"You'll have help, Inspector, technological as well as tangible assets."

"I thought you said you had no one in place."

"That's not exactly what I said. You'll understand in good time. For now, I'm going to give you the name of an Israeli colonel attached to the U.S. peacekeeping mission."

"I wasn't aware Israelis were part of it."

"Our files on members of the Saddam regime are much more complete than the Americans'. We have been granted advisory status. Unofficially, of course."

"I understand."

"This man will furnish you with the equipment you need to call in the strike."

"Assuming I'm able to find where these men of Black Sands are based."

"We have someone in Marseilles who can help you with that much."

"If that's the case, what do you even need me for?"

"You'll have to meet her to understand," said Vordi.

The equipment Vordi had spoken of had been waiting in one of Saddam's former royal palaces, now converted into the city's primary U.S. military headquarters. An operative spent several hours familiarizing Ben with its use. He and Colonel al-Asi then drove back to Jordan where Ben boarded a flight bound from Amman to Marseilles through Paris on Air France.

Now, as the midafternoon sun burned hot and bright, Ben found himself walking the Arab quarter of the Mediterranean city, a leather satchel slung from his shoulder. The equipment inside would be considered innocuous to all but the most seasoned eye. A camcorder that was actually a laser directional spotter. A digital camera with telephoto lens that doubled as an ultrasophisticated hundred-power binocular. A pistol made totally of plastic contained within the false bottom of a guidebook.

The legendary street crime of Marseilles had him holding the dangling satchel in hand to discourage the kind of attack for which tourists were prime fodder. He had no way of knowing if that crime extended into the port city's Muslim neighborhood and wasn't taking any chances.

The strange thing was how much he felt at home here in this enclave just north of the Old Harbor. The streets smelled of the grilled fish and meats so familiar to him from both the West Bank and Dearborn, Michigan. So, too, the lively street bazaars featuring energetic, friendly salesmen refusing to take no for an answer and loving to barter. But Marseilles bore some of the same painful scars as West Bank towns and cities as well. At Bellevue Pyat, a high-rise slum within easy view of the bustling markets, rising piles of fetid garbage attracted rats, roaches, and the kind of repetitive violence only poverty can bring.

Ben's path steered him well clear of that neighborhood. Vordi's cryptic instructions were to seek out a coffeehouse diagonally across from the Attaqwa Mosque on the Rue du Bon Pasteur. There he was to have his fortune told and all would become clear.

Ben could only wish that would be the case. He still hadn't been able to reach Danielle and the situation for both of them had become increasingly dire as a result of the last words Ibrahim al-Kursami had spoken to him: *The threat came from the soldiers of Black Sands and I made sure to tell one of my inquisitors everything I knew about them, which was everything that existed.*

Ben shrank from believing the identity of the man al-Kursami had referred to as one of the high-level moles left stranded with the collapse of the Soviet Union, but he had no choice. Much of what he and Danielle, at least initially, had uncovered made perfect sense now, but it also magnified the desperation of their predicaments. Was that why he had been unable to reach her? Had she been caught unaware, just as he nearly had?

Ben dreaded the answers. He found the umbrella-shaded outdoor tables of the coffeehouse packed with locals sipping from cups and smoking from their water pipes. The inside was deserted, save for a table occupied by a single woman with a deck of cards aligned before her.

Get your fortune told, Vordi had instructed. Could this be what he'd been referring to?

Ben approached the table tentatively, waiting for the woman seated there to at least acknowledge him. As he drew closer, she gathered up her cards and began to shuffle them. Her empty eyes never glanced at Ben.

"Would you like to see your future?" she asked.

The woman was blind, Ben realized, explaining David Vordi's cryptic references.

"Only if I'm in a position to change it," he said.

"That depends."

"On?"

"On what I'm able to see."

"Black Sands," Ben said.

"Sit down," the blind woman said, continuing her endless shuffling. After Ben did as he was told and slid his chair under the table, she spoke again. "Now, place twenty dollars to my side of the table in case anyone is watching."

Again Ben obliged.

The blind woman retrieved the bill quickly, folded it up, and stuffed it in her pocket. "You are Bayan Kamal?"

Ben started to nod, adding, "Yes. I was told you may have information for me."

"Indeed I do, Inspector, about the future. Now pay attention, so we can do our best to change it."

CHAPTER 68

The woman began to lay cards out in the pattern of a five-pointed star. "My name is Jamila Lalliou and it's been quite some time since I've been contacted by my control officer, for obvious reasons, of course."

"When did you lose your sight?"

"A few years ago. Let's say it has severely cramped my value as an asset. I stay here because after so many years, where else would I go?"

"You've been briefed as to what I'm after, I assume."

"You're looking for a hefty complement of Iraqi agents who managed to flee their nation before last year's war started. Part of a plot known as Al Awdah. I'd like to tell you that I've seen them, but, well . . ."

"I'll settle for any information you may have."

"I've heard talk. That's what I do these days—I hear things. All you have to do is to know what to listen to. I've trained myself to tune into certain conversations while tuning out others."

"Important skill."

"Unnecessary for the most part if you can see. Are you familiar with the Iles du Frioul?"

"No."

"Common name for the neighboring islands of Ratonneau and Pomeques located a few hundred meters west of the Chateau d'If. But, unlike the Chateau, Pomeques has been conveniently closed to all tourist traffic since some stray ordnance, left over from World War Two, was found in the remnants of German fortifications that dot the island."

"You think somebody put the ordnance there to chase potential visitors away?"

The old woman nodded, continued shifting the cards about until the ace of diamonds was faceup in the center.

"That's a good sign," Jamila Lalliou said, feeling along the edges of the card to make sure she had chosen the right one.

"I can use it. What else can you tell me about Pomeques?"

"I've heard talk from several local boat captains about ferrying men to and from the island on a regular basis."

"Exactly what's on that island that makes it stand out?"

"The largest German fortification in the region, just a stone relic now but originally a walled fortress built to accommodate hundreds of troops. You'll never be able to get inside."

"That's not the plan anyway. I'll need a reliable boatman, someone you trust."

"This is Marseilles, Inspector Kamal. Trust exists only in a relative sense."

"Then that'll have to do."

"I think I can accommodate you."

CHAPTER 69

J amal Jefferson approached the bench where Franklin Winters was sitting in the center of Rock Creek Park, not far from the offices of the State Department.

"Thank you for coming, Mr. Ambassador."

"You said it was important, Major."

Jefferson stopped directly in front of Winters, shoulders square with the sun.

"It concerns your son, sir."

Winters shifted uneasily on the bench. "Go on."

"Are you familiar with the role of a procurement officer?"

"They handle the supply line."

"And in war their contribution is crucial. They're the ones responsible for making sure there are enough tankers to keep the vehicles gassed and enough transport trucks to keep the troops fed. A misjudgment in either case and you've got men stranded hundreds of miles from the nearest depot with their tanks, or their stomachs, empty."

"This is all out of the manual, Major."

Jefferson stiffened. "Procurement officers are also responsible for arranging KIA transfers."

"Killed in action . . ."

"That's right, sir. A sad business no one likes to talk about much, but I don't have to tell you how important it is."

Winters rose to his feet to look Jefferson in the eye. "What exactly are you telling me, Major?"

"I've been doing some checking. My office has access to

confidential memos, requisition forms, flight manifests—all dealing with shipments in and out of the theater."

"The Iraqi theater in this case."

"There's an anomaly, Mr. Ambassador," Jefferson continued, "in a shipment of KIA transfers from the siege of Baghdad. Specifically, eleven more seal crates were signed for than were listed on the manifest out of Brandenberg."

"Coffins," Winters realized.

"I did some checking but apparently the anomaly only showed up that one time in transit."

"You're saying eleven unidentified bodies were shipped home."

"Unidentified and unreported as KIA."

"Something not in the manual."

Jefferson hesitated, choosing his next words carefully. "Assuming, just assuming, a Special Forces A-team was wiped out while on a secret mission behind enemy lines. The army would want to bury that at all costs. It might go unreported. The dead soldiers might continue to be listed as MIA. Kept off the books so far as the world was concerned."

"There are twelve men in a Special Forces A-team, Major."

"I'm aware of that, sir."

"You're telling me one member of my son's unit survived, aren't you, Major?"

"I'm telling you that eleven of them died."

"But one remains unaccounted for. You can confirm that much."

"Only so far as the transition reports allow. I was hoping to provide you some closure, a sense of finality."

Winters took a step closer to Jefferson, lowered his voice. "How do we find out more about these eleven bodies, Major?"

"Mr. Ambassador—"

"Who do we call about identifications, officially or unofficially?"

Jefferson shrugged. "I know some people in dispatch who

are expert at handling below-the-board transfers. They might be able to provide more details."

"Give me their names."

"They won't talk to you, sir."

"I don't want you risking your career."

"I wouldn't have a career if it wasn't for you, Mr. Ambassador," Jefferson said, and started to turn around.

"I need to know, Major. You understand that."

"Yes, sir," Jefferson replied, holding his ground. "I do."

CHAPTER 70

J amila Lalliou sent Ben to the Old Harbor in search of a fishing trawler called *The Chanot*. He found the boat in a berth set off by itself, a barnacle-ridden relic that at first glance hardly looked seaworthy. Ben handed the ship's captain the ace of diamonds and asked if *The Chanot* was available for charter. The captain, a man named Villechese, grumbled, scratched at his beard, and nodded. No price was discussed. His fee would be paid by Lalliou upon completion, in keeping with procedure.

They didn't set out until after dark on a moonless but clear night. The island of Pomeques was located only three miles west of the Old Port. Villechese brought *The Chanot* to within a half-mile of Pomeques's rocky shoreline before dropping anchor and casting his fishing nets. Only then did he reveal to Ben the inflatable rubber raft camouflaged in the trawler's stern.

Together they lowered it off *The Chanot*'s port side, using the trawler's bulky frame for cover. Ben had expected an outboard engine and was disappointed to find a pair of oars inside the raft instead. When he asked about a waterproof pouch to keep his equipment safe from the churning waves, Villechese produced what looked like a common garbage bag and fished through his pockets for a twist tie.

Fort Pomeques, as it had come to be known, had been chosen by the Germans in large part thanks to its natural fortifications that rendered the fort invisible from the sea. The island itself was basically one giant boulder chiseled away by time and the elements. As a result, the fort was built amidst the layered stone, watched over by twin rock-layered sentinels that rose into the night like opposite prongs of a pitchfork. The formation on the eastern side of the island, according to Jamila Lalliou, offered a better spot for landing, with more footholds and pathways for an easier climb.

Ben's plan after reaching the island was to claim the highest ground he could safely attain. Then he would contact Vordi and target the fort to assure its total destruction by the American F-16s that would be in the air even now.

Once inside the raft, the currents cooperated with him until he was swept within reach of the eastern shoreline. Here huge rock formations that would have eaten the bottoms of any boat venturing too close poked out of the sea and created havoc with the waves. Ben found himself paddling feverishly just to avoid losing ground before surging forward a few precious yards when a brief calm arose. He was panting with exertion by the time he leaped out of the raft into thigh-high water and tied it down to a boulder on the rock-encrusted shoreline.

He removed his satchel full of equipment from the garbage bag Villechese had provided and shouldered it, then began making his way awkwardly across the island's slippery rock surface for the eastern stone tower that overlooked the fort. The going eased a bit as the stone surface grew less slippery farther from the shore. But this brief respite ended as soon as Ben began his ascent up the rock formation. The going was easy at times, precarious mostly, and at times treacherous. Although he never had to struggle finding hand-and footholds on the sheer surface, the climb grew so steep in places that it was all he could do not to slip and slide downward. In the dark, progress came agonizingly slow and on more than one occasion, a dead end forced Ben to retrace his steps downward and find another path.

The top of the stone face, he soon discovered, was unreachable and unnecessary for his purposes. He stopped his ascent on a wide ledge affording a clear view into the ruins of Fort Pomeques below. At first glance, through his high-tech binocular disguised as a camera, Ben thought Jamila Lalliou's information must have been wrong. There was no sign of life inside the ruins, much less movement of any kind, and what was left of the fort itself seemed utterly uninhabitable. But Ben reminded himself of the caves of Afghanistan, where remnants of al-Qaeda and the Taliban had lived for months on end, and the bunkers of Baghdad, where some loyal to the Saddam regime were found months after the city itself was finally taken.

Ben had no idea what lay beneath the fort's ruins, what complexes of bunkers and tunnels the Germans might have constructed to defend themselves. But he wanted to be sure, wanted some sign that this was in fact the hiding place for the secret army Ibrahim al-Kursami had called Black Sands, a key component of Al Awdah.

Ben rotated the extended lens of the camera slowly from side to side. On the fourth pass, his patience finally paid off when he caught a slight flicker of light followed by a wisp of smoke rising. A guard perched on the remnants of an ancient parapet had lit a cigarette. Ben twisted the lens and zoomed in. The man sat cross-legged with a Russian-made assault rifle shouldered behind him. He puffed his cigarette lovingly, gave no notion he had any idea the sanctity of the island had been compromised.

Black Sands . . . So they are here, after all. . . .

Ben pulled the satellite phone from his satchel and hit the preprogrammed Send button.

"Vordi," the familiar voice answered.

"I've got their location in my sights."

"You know what to do."

"So long as the equipment works."

"It'll work. Aim the designator at the center of the target and hold it for ten seconds. That's all the F-16s need for acquisition. Stay on the line until I receive confirmation."

Ben kept the satellite phone pressed against his ear, as he felt through his bag for the laser target designator. It fit easily into his palm and was surprisingly simple to operate. Just line up a target through the cameralike viewfinder and press the button. As per Vordi's instructions, Ben focused on the center of the ruins, then pushed the button inward until he felt a click.

He expected to see a bright beam of blue light, like something out of a video game. But the laser designation being relayed to the F-16s cruising high in the sky was invisible to the naked eye. It didn't even radiate any heat. Nothing.

Ben counted slowly to ten, then removed his finger. A wave of both euphoria and expectation washed over him. He had done it! The village of Bureij had been avenged, averting a much worse disaster looming in the offing.

"We've got confirmation of target acquisition," Vordi told him. "I'm terminating this call. Enjoy the show."

Ben listened to the sky, waiting for the telltale roar of the F-16s as they banked into their attack run. Perhaps they did so from so high up that he'd never hear them, not even know they were here until their bombs impacted on the old fort below. He returned the camera binocular to his eye, as if to reassure himself he had done everything properly.

A number of figures were visible on the surface now. He turned the focusing wheel, concentrating on the small group moving for a cavelike entrance at ground level of the fort, prepared to descend into its bowels.

Ben froze, lost a breath and then a heartbeat, having caught a glimpse of the impossible in the lens:

Danielle Barnea.

CHAPTER 71

Danielle remembered little after being gored by the bull at the Arena in Nîmes. The two remaining gunmen had approached and crouched alongside her. Then they'd hoisted her upward, pretending to be rescuers.

She knew the effects of a drug-induced haze well enough to realize she'd been the victim of a mind-numbing drug that had blurred time. Had they tried to question her already, discern what she knew, who else she had spoken with? It didn't matter. Although she now knew the shape of the plan in its entirety, she had shared that knowledge with no one.

As four escorts dragged her across the ruins of some ancient fortification, Danielle tried to figure out exactly where she was. They hadn't taken her a great distance, she felt certain of that much. Meanwhile, the fresh clean smells and view of a nearby coastline she had managed to glimpse narrowed the setting down to somewhere still in the south of France. A port city. Marseilles, if she had to guess.

Danielle had woken from her trance numerous times in the last several hours, finding herself laid out on an old mattress in a room guarded by a pair of men standing on either side of the door. Each time, she was able to cling to consciousness only briefly before it slipped away again. Now that she had regained it fully, she assumed they were taking her somewhere else in the fortification, probably to be questioned.

Danielle tried to sharpen her senses by recalling the final

moments in the Nîmes museum office when the computer had provided translation of the last prophecy's final line:

> And each of the fifty stars shall slide from their heavenly perch, never to find the same sky again.

The line made no sense in and of itself. But when placed in the context of the entire quatrain, Nostradamus's vision was terrifyingly clear.

> In an age of two's four, in a land of many
> An army rises from midland afar on a day of equal light and dark
> Beneath the flames of the bringer of fire, a darkness will reign eternal
> And each of the fifty stars shall slide from their heavenly perch, never to find the same sky again.

She understood it all now, what the United States was facing, the terrifying form the attack barely three days from now was going to take. But she still lacked the specifics, and clung to the hope that Ben's pursuits had brought him closer to them than hers.

Her escorts led Danielle down a set of stone stairs into a flood of chilly air. A single ceiling-mounted light, probably battery powered, glowed at the foot of the steps. Danielle took a series of deep breaths, checking her strength, her reflexes. Were they sufficient to mount an attack and try for an escape? No, her four escorts were all armed and spread too far apart to overcome in her current condition. She might be able to do something about her bound hands, but not quickly enough to do her much good against an opposition formidable in number as well as skill.

Danielle resigned herself to being patient and descended farther into the bowels of the fort.

CHAPTER 72

K amal," David Vordi snapped, "you shouldn't be operating on this—"

"You've got to call the strike off!" Ben interrupted, shouting the words into his satellite phone.

"What? Did you say—"

"Listen to me, *Danielle's here!* They've got her prisoner!"

"It's too late."

"No, you told me it would take ten minutes, probably more.
You still have time to raise the F-16s, have them recalled."

"I can't."

"Vordi, you're not listening to me! Danielle's—"

"I am listening. I'm telling you, it can't be done."

"You bastard."

"I'm signing off, Inspector."

"For God's sake, call the Americans! Tell them to—"

Ben heard the click, stopped talking.

Damn Vordi! Credit for this strike would take him out of
National Police and back into the Ministry of Justice.

How much time had elapsed since Ben had designated the
targets, how many minutes were left before the night exploded in the fury of five-hundred-pound laser-guided
bombs?

Some. Enough.

Ben lunged to his feet, yanked the pistol from his satchel
along with a thin yet high-powered flashlight. Depending on
how far away the F-16s were when they received their target

designations, he could have fifteen, twenty minutes at most. How long had it taken him to get up here?

His mind calculated feverishly as he began his descent of the rocky formation overlooking the fort. He quickly abandoned the pointless effort and concentrated on the route before him in the darkness, slowing only to negotiate the steepest, most precarious parts. A few times it might have been safer to backtrack and retrace his steps over safer ground. But he didn't dare waste the precious moments that would take to manage. He slipped and fell twice, the first time plummeting ten feet down a slippery slope to a ledge; the second, landing face first on a weed-infested embankment.

At the bottom of the rock formation, Ben checked his watch. The glass was shattered, the hands frozen from a previous impact. He thought he could hear the distant whine of the fighter jets speeding into their attack approach, hoped it was the wind.

Ben rushed across the rocky ground, using only the night to conceal himself from the guard he had glimpsed in one of the parapets, along with any others. The front of the crumbled fort was open to anyone who wanted to enter; tourists almost exclusively until recent months when new tenants had taken up residence here.

The fort came into clear view in the darkness, as the sound of jet engines echoed through the night breeze. Ben tripped, landed with a thud, and regained his feet to find the guard he had seen earlier through his long-range lens turning his way. Ben yanked his pistol free, fumbled with it briefly, which allowed the guard to get his assault rifle steadied first.

Something sizzled through the air, trailed by a wailing hiss and sharp screech. The first laser-guided bomb impacted just short of the parapet and blew it apart. The guard disappeared in a huge shower of chunks of rock and stone. Ben was spared from the debris's onslaught by the cover provided by the still-whole entry archway to the fort, the heavy barricade door removed long ago.

Ears ringing, he threw himself into motion again just as another five-hundred-pound bomb struck the rear of the fortress. A third blew him into the air. He landed on layers of jagged stone, his spine numb, the feeling gone from his legs. Around him Ben heard men screaming and shouting, voices struggling to rise over the percussion of more bombs exploding with dizzying regularity.

Dazed, Ben somehow managed to regain his feet and surge onward, listing to one side and limping. He remained fixed on the position of the stairs down which he had seen men take Danielle. The explosions had coughed up smoke and dust that stole the stairs from view. Fires from the blasts lingered, providing glowing light that pierced the stained air.

Ben heard another whistling whine and hit the ground covering his head. More missiles came roaring in toward the fort. Ben risked a climb back to his feet, feeling the entire ground shake beneath him, and realized the last few missiles must have been of the bunker-buster variety, burrowing beneath the fort's rocky surface to the rooms contained below before detonating.

The ground quaked. The rocks beneath his shoes shifted. Ben staggered on, closing finally on what remained of the stairs down which Danielle had disappeared minutes before. There were no stairs left that he could see, yet an opening remained between the piles of rock and the crumpling ceiling.

Ben threw himself over the pile, pushing with his legs and hands. The air at the bottom was cleaner so that he was able to expel the dust-soaked debris from his lungs. Another blast shook the fort and a portion of both walls and the ceiling collapsed on a pair of bodies felled by the initial attack wave.

Ben ducked and turned sideways to move through a narrow fissure that had once been a corridor. Only then did he yank the Mag-Lite from its clip on his belt and switch it on.

"Danielle!" he shouted. "Danielle!"

No response.

Ben emerged on the other side of the fissure into a section of tunnel still intact, leading to a heavy door that had been blown inward. Another two bodies lay just beyond it and he looked at them only long enough to assure himself neither was Danielle's.

"Danielle!" he called again, peering inside the room.

An uneven, irregular pile of rock and stone, rubble from the blown-in walls and collapsed ceiling, filled the room. Ben stumbled across the lower-most stacks, searching for some hint of Danielle, praying she hadn't been crushed by the largest section of rubble which stretched almost to the ceiling. He nearly tripped on what he thought first was a rock. Gazing back, though, he saw it was a woman's boot and he dropped to his knees, feverishly grasping rocks and chucking them away.

Gradually, a human form became visible beneath him. He wasn't sure it was Danielle until he uncovered her hair. He shifted the remaining stones from her body and gently turned her onto her back, listened for breath.

Nothing.

Felt for a heartbeat.

Nothing.

Terror bottlenecked inside him. Above, the percussion of another attack run's bombs shook the walls and Ben leaned over to shield Danielle's body from more blast-ridden stone.

CHAPTER 73

The Mag-Lite rested on the floor to Ben's right, bathing the darkened chamber in an eerie white glow that barely reached above floor level. Enough, though, for Ben to prop Danielle's head back and breathe into her mouth while holding her nose.

"Come on! Come on!" he urged, pausing to gulp some air before the next two breaths.

Again and again he pushed air into her lungs, felt her chest rise to accept it, yet that seemed to be the only response. He felt down her breastbone, prepared to pump life into her heart. Suddenly she moved convulsively, coughing a stream of chalky dirt from her mouth. She continued to retch, face turning scarlet from the exertion, as Ben eased her gently to a sitting position.

"You're all right, you're going to be okay," he comforted. "Just take it easy."

Her retching slowed, picked up again, finally stopped. Danielle collapsed in his arms, tried to speak, failed.

"Catch your breath," Ben told her. "Just concentrate on breathing. Don't try to talk."

He saw her face tighten determinedly. She seemed to be swallowing. Her breathing slowed, became more regular. She swallowed again, as if trying to remind herself how to use air to form words.

"Are you all right? Does anything feel broken?"

She shook her head, muttered, "No."

He looped an arm over her shoulder to help her walk and led her out into the tunnel beyond. The route back up the stairs to the fort's ground level was totally blocked, leaving the tunnel as their only option for escape. It banked downward, leading deeper into the earth's depths. This was good for the added cushioning it would provide from any further explosions; bad for what it meant if the tunnel didn't provide another way out.

"Got to hurry," Danielle rasped. "Hurry. The United States . . ."

"Don't try to talk. Save your strength."

"The plan, the plot . . ."

Ben shined his Mag-Lite forward, carving a luminescent path through the dark, sooty air. They passed several doorways that looked still whole, the bunkers located beyond them undoubtedly reinforced. Clearly the sleeping areas, what passed for a barracks, in the fortress were located somewhere else. This section had housed Nazi ordnance during the years of the Reich's occupation of France.

Ben felt a faint breeze against his face. The air seemed less dense, less chalky, indicating an opening of some kind not too far ahead.

"Thank God," he said softly, taking a deep breath.

Danielle stopped and sank back against a wall. He held her as she slid down it, feeling her strength ebb and drain. Her breathing was raspy and hot, her face still frightened. He grasped her hand and she squeezed his in response.

"I know now, I know what's going to happen," she said between breaths. "We've got to stop it."

"Stop what?"

" 'And each of the fifty stars shall slide from their heavenly perch' . . ."

"I don't understand."

"The prophecy," she jabbered on. "The last line. Why Bureij happened. Why the old men from the 121st had to die in the United States."

"Take it easy. We can talk about—"

"Fifty stars, one for each state!" Danielle persisted. "On the flag. The American flag. That's the plan. Fifty states attacked, all at once."

CHAPTER 74

Ben and Danielle emerged into the cool night well away from the now smoldering fortress. Stubborn flames continued to lick at the air. Gray-black smoke climbed for the sky from chasms blasted out of the rubble-laced ground. Ben could see no one stirring. The pinpoint strike had clearly decimated the forces of Black Sands.

"How do you feel?" Ben asked softly.

Danielle sat cross-legged on the ground, trembling slightly. "Alive."

"That'll do for a start." Ben sat down alongside her and wrapped both his arms around her shoulders.

"Who were those men?"

"The last vestiges of the Iraqi Special Republican Guard. How many of them did you see?"

"What does that mat—"

"Just tell me."

"A dozen, maybe a few more."

Ben felt a chill slide up his spine. "They're already in place then."

"Who? *Where?*"

"The Iraqi agents who managed to sneak out of the country before the war started. They're the ones who are going to attack the United States, as part of an operation called Black Sands run by Sharif ali-Aziz Moussan."

"But I captured Moussan in Somalia. He's in custody now."

Ben recalled the words of Ibrahim al-Kursami. "Someone else has picked up where he left off."

"Who?"

He looked away.

"Who, Ben? Tell me."

He turned back toward her. "I was right about the bombing at the U.N. compound in Baghdad, Danielle. There are Soviet moles in high-level positions in governments all over the world. They're rogues now. Cut off, isolated, in communication only with each other, but still motivated by hatred for the West and a desire for vengeance against those responsible for the destruction of their way of life."

"And these moles have taken over Black Sands?"

"This plot you uncovered belongs to them now," Ben told her.

"But how could they have learned of the existence of Black Sands?"

"Because the head of the Iraqi secret police betrayed the existence of this covert army, part of a plot called Al Awdah, to an interrogator he's certain was one of the moles." Ben waited for his point to sink in before finishing. "Alexis Arguayo."

"WE NEED to get back to Marseilles," Danielle said.

"I've got a rubber raft tied down to the eastern side of the island. A fishing trawler brought me into the shallows, but the captain might have taken off once the bombs began falling."

"Let's find out."

As BEN suspected, the trawler was nowhere to be found, and he resigned himself to rowing back to the harbor.

"I'll take a turn," Danielle offered.

"No, you won't. I want to hear about this plot now, this, what did you call it, a prophecy?"

Danielle nodded. "Written by Nostradamus. The 121st Evacuation Hospital dug a whole manuscript of his lost prophecies out of a trench at Buchenwald in 1945. That's why they were all murdered. Because one of the prophecies mirrored this plot to strike the United States and the perpetrators couldn't risk being exposed."

"You're telling me you believe Nostradamus really *could* see the future?"

Danielle shrugged. "I don't know what I believe in. Maybe that's why I've started to think it could be true. Maybe even something like this to believe in is better than believing in nothing."

"That's not true, not about you."

"Isn't it? Unwelcome in my own country. An outcast disgrace to the legacy of my family."

"The circumstances were beyond your control."

"I created those circumstances. Maybe I got what I deserved."

"Tell me about this plot aimed at America."

"They're going to shut the country down, Ben, bring it to an absolute standstill."

"Not if we can stop them."

"How?"

"Let's ask Alexis Arguayo."

DAY NINE

CHAPTER 75

**LOGON COMPLETE
ALL STATIONS CONFIRMED ACTIVE ON-LINE
ENCRYPTION PROCEDURES IN EFFECT**

MESSAGE RUNNING

From: FRANCE
X-Priority:
Sensitivity: Company-Confidential
To: ALL
MIME-Version: 1.0
IM secure status: active
X-MailScanner: Found to be clean

**WE HAVE CONFIRMATION FROM OFFICIALS IN
MARSEILLES. THE FORT WAS STRUCK BY A
MASSIVE AIR STRIKE. BETWEEN TWO AND
FOUR AIRCRAFT WERE INVOLVED. MINIMAL
NUMBER OF SURVIVORS, ALL BADLY
WOUNDED.**

From: GERMANY
X-Priority:
Sensitivity: Company-Confidential
To: ALL
MIME-Version: 1.0

IM secure status: active
X-MailScanner: Found to be clean

THE AMERICANS AGAIN.

From: UNITED STATES
X-Priority:
Sensitivity: Company-Confidential
To: ALL
MIME-Version: 1.0
IM secure status: active
X-MailScanner: Found to be clean

THE FIREPOWER, YES. BUT NOT THE INTELLIGENCE.

From: RUSSIA
X-Priority:
Sensitivity: Company-Confidential
To: ALL
MIME-Version: 1.0
IM secure status: active
X-MailScanner: Found to be clean

CLARIFY YOUR RESPONSE.

From: UNITED STATES
X-Priority:
Sensitivity: Company-Confidential
To: ALL
MIME-Version: 1.0
IM secure status: active
X-MailScanner: Found to be clean

OUR INTELLIGENCE SOURCES INDICATE THAT CENTRAL COMMAND WAS ACTING ON HARD CONFIDENCE TIP FROM THE ISRAELIS.

From: GERMANY
X-Priority:
Sensitivity: Company-Confidential
To: ALL
MIME-Version: 1.0
IM secure status: active
X-MailScanner: Found to be clean

ISRAELIS?

From: JAPAN
X-Priority:
Sensitivity: Company-Confidential
To: ALL
MIME-Version: 1.0
IM secure status: active
X-MailScanner: Found to be clean

ONE ISRAELI, YOU MEAN.

From: FRANCE
X-Priority:
Sensitivity: Company-Confidential
To: ALL
MIME-Version: 1.0
IM secure status: active
X-MailScanner: Found to be clean

**WE HAD BARNEA IN CUSTODY. SHE WAS
APPREHENDED WITH LITTLE DISTRESS AND
WAS BEING HELD AT THE FORTRESS FOR
INTERROGATION.**

From: GERMANY
X-Priority:
Sensitivity: Company-Confidential

To: ALL
MIME-Version: 1.0
IM secure status: active
X-MailScanner: Found to be clean

HAUPTMAN'S REPORT CONFIRMS THAT MUCH.

From: RUSSIA
X-Priority:
Sensitivity: Company-Confidential
To: ALL
MIME-Version: 1.0
IM secure status: active
X-MailScanner: Found to be clean

**THEN WE ARE LEFT TO WONDER WHAT HAP-
PENED.**

From: UNITED STATES
X-Priority:
Sensitivity: Company-Confidential
To: ALL
MIME-Version: 1.0
IM secure status: active
X-MailScanner: Found to be clean

**PERHAPS NOT. BARNEA WAS IDENTIFIED LEAV-
ING PARIS ON A FLIGHT BOUND FOR AMSTER-
DAM. SHE WAS TRAVELING IN THE COMPANY
OF A MAN WHO HAS SUBSEQUENTLY BEEN
IDENTIFIED AS BAYAN KAMAL, FORMERLY OF
THE PALESTINIAN POLICE.**

From: CHINA
X-Priority:
Sensitivity: Company-Confidential

To: ALL
MIME-Version: 1.0
IM secure status: active
X-MailScanner: Found to be clean

HER LOVER.

From: UNITED STATES
X-Priority:
Sensitivity: Company-Confidential
To: ALL
MIME-Version: 1.0
IM secure status: active
X-MailScanner: Found to be clean

**AND FELLOW UNITED NATIONS INVESTIGATOR
ALSO ASSIGNED TO THE RECENT MASSACRE.**

From: RUSSIA
X-Priority:
Sensitivity: Company-Confidential
To: ALL
MIME-Version: 1.0
IM secure status: active
X-MailScanner: Found to be clean

**WE WERE GIVEN ASSURANCES THAT
INVESTIGATION HAD BEEN CONTAINED.**

From: UNITED STATES
X-Priority:
Sensitivity: Company-Confidential
To: ALL
MIME-Version: 1.0
IM secure status: active
X-MailScanner: Found to be clean

**THE INVESTIGATION, YES. NOT KAMAL. LIKE
BARNEA, HE MANAGED TO SURVIVE OUR
ATTEMPTS AT EXECUTION WITH HELP FROM
AN UNEXPECTED SOURCE. THE ISRAELIS.**

From: GERMANY
X-Priority:
Sensitivity: Company-Confidential
To: ALL
MIME-Version: 1.0
IM secure status: active
X-MailScanner: Found to be clean

**SOMETHING WE NEVER COULD HAVE
ANTICIPATED.**

From: UNITED STATES
X-Priority:
Sensitivity: Company-Confidential
To: ALL
MIME-Version: 1.0
IM secure status: active
X-MailScanner: Found to be clean

**NOR COULD WE ANTICIPATE A VISIT HE MADE
TO THE FORMER HEAD OF THE IRAQI SECRET
POLICE.**

From: FRANCE
X-Priority:
Sensitivity: Company-Confidential
To: ALL
MIME-Version: 1.0
IM secure status: active
X-MailScanner: Found to be clean

YOU'RE SAYING KAMAL WAS RESPONSIBLE FOR THE STRIKE ON THE FORT.

From: UNITED STATES
X-Priority:
Sensitivity: Company-Confidential
To: ALL
MIME-Version: 1.0
IM secure status: active
X-MailScanner: Found to be clean

HE IS CLEARLY MORE RESOURCEFUL THAN WE HAVE GIVEN HIM CREDIT FOR.

From: CHINA
X-Priority:
Sensitivity: Company-Confidential
To: ALL
MIME-Version: 1.0
IM secure status: active
X-MailScanner: Found to be clean

THIS CONTINUED SERIES OF MISJUDGMENTS AND MISESTIMATIONS IS OF GROWING CONCERN TO US. IF KAMAL AND BARNEA HAVE GOTTEN THIS FAR, PROMETHEUS CAN NO LONGER BE CONSIDERED SECURE. AND NEITHER CAN OUR OWN IDENTITIES.

From: UNITED STATES
X-Priority:
Sensitivity: Company-Confidential
To: ALL
MIME-Version: 1.0
IM secure status: active
X-MailScanner: Found to be clean

AS PREVIOUSLY STATED, POSTPONEMENT IS NOT AN AVAILABLE OPTION.

From: RUSSIA
X-Priority:
Sensitivity: Company-Confidential
To: ALL
MIME-Version: 1.0
IM secure status: active
X-MailScanner: Found to be clean

WE ARE NOT ADVOCATING POSTPONEMENT. WE ARE ADVOCATING CANCELATION.

From: UNITED STATES
X-Priority:
Sensitivity: Company-Confidential
To: ALL
MIME-Version: 1.0
IM secure status: active
X-MailScanner: Found to be clean

THAT IS NOT POSSIBLE.

From: GERMANY
X-Priority:
Sensitivity: Company-Confidential
To: ALL
MIME-Version: 1.0
IM secure status: active
X-MailScanner: Found to be clean

I AGREE WITH RUSSIA. IT IS MORE THAN POSSIBLE, IT IS PRUDENT. ACCORDING TO OUR INTERROGATION OF JACQUES MATHIEU, DANIELLE BARNEA HAS MANAGED TO

DECIPHER THE REMAINDER OF THE
PROPHECY. THAT MEANS SHE KNOWS THE
EXACT SUBSTANCE OF THE PLOT, NOT JUST ITS
EXISTENCE. THIS PLACES ALL OF US IN
JEOPARDY. THE RISK IS NOT WORTH IT.

From: UNITED STATES
X-Priority:
Sensitivity: Company-Confidential
To: ALL
MIME-Version: 1.0
IM secure status: active
X-MailScanner: Found to be clean

YOU FORGET THAT WE ARE STILL INSULATED
BY THE TRUE SOLDIERS OF PROMETHEUS.

From: FRANCE
X-Priority:
Sensitivity: Company-Confidential
To: ALL
MIME-Version: 1.0
IM secure status: active
X-MailScanner: Found to be clean

EVEN WE ARE NO LONGER CONVINCED OF
THAT.

From: UNITED STATES
X-Priority:
Sensitivity: Company-Confidential
To: ALL
MIME-Version: 1.0
IM secure status: active
X-MailScanner: Found to be clean

**I SUGGEST CONTACT BETWEEN US BE PUT OFF
UNTIL A LATER TIME WHEN THE TRUE EXTENT
OF DAMAGE CAN BE ASCERTAINED.**

From: GERMANY
X-Priority:
Sensitivity: Company-Confidential
To: ALL
MIME-Version: 1.0
IM secure status: active
X-MailScanner: Found to be clean

**NOT ACCEPTABLE. THE RISK IS SIMPLY TOO
GREAT. WE MUST INSIST THE OPERATION BE
TERMINATED.**

From: FRANCE
X-Priority:
Sensitivity: Company-Confidential
To: ALL
MIME-Version: 1.0
IM secure status: active
X-MailScanner: Found to be clean

WE CONCUR.

From: RUSSIA
X-Priority:
Sensitivity: Company-Confidential
To: ALL
MIME-Version: 1.0
IM secure status: active
X-MailScanner: Found to be clean

THERE IS NO OTHER CHOICE.

From: FRANCE
X-Priority:
Sensitivity: Company-Confidential
To: ALL
MIME-Version: 1.0
IM secure status: active
X-MailScanner: Found to be clean

U.S. WE AWAIT YOUR RESPONSE.... UNITED STATES, PLEASE RESPOND.

From: MAIN SERVER
X-Priority:
Sensitivity: Company-Confidential
To: ALL
MIME-Version: 1.0
IM secure status: active
X-MailScanner: Found to be clean

UNITED STATES HAS LOGGED OFF

MESSAGE TERMINATED

The Hague had seemed the perfect site for the International Criminal Court since the court's very inception. Already the seat for the Permanent Court of Arbitration and renowned for its hosting of a series of landmark peace conferences, The Hague enjoyed both the status and the credibility to provide the International Criminal Court with instant acceptance from the international community.

The Hague also served as the seat of government for the Netherlands, the offices clustered in a striking series of brick and stone buildings along an artificial lake called the Vyver. The vast offices and space required for the court's smooth function was created by relocating a number of governmental headquarters to the outlying provinces, decentralizing state government in favor of further boosting The Hague's international appeal.

With the International Criminal Court's ceremonial, if not official, opening scheduled for today, diplomats and dignitaries had been streaming in for days, led by United Nations officials responsible for charting the court's course and its general oversight.

"I could get used to this," Ben said, as Danielle wheeled him through Amsterdam's airport.

It had been her idea to use the wheelchair as cover, obtaining one as easy as having a flight attendant call ahead from the plane to request it be waiting at the gate. She had to assume that the enemy forces behind this plot had put out alerts for them all over Europe. Short of elaborate disguises, Danielle knew, the best way to avoid detection was to slide through the dragnet utterly ignored by those watching for something else entirely. No one pays attention to wheel-chairs, much less one occupied by a man being pushed by a woman.

Ben wasn't convinced at first but fell into the ruse easily, not abandoning it until Danielle pretended to help him climb into a cab bound for the area of The Hague's government complex.

"We still have to get to Arguayo," he reminded.

"Leave that to me," Danielle smiled, taking his hand in hers.

DETERMINING ARGUAYO'S interview schedule had been as easy as knowing the proper phone number to call, not here in the Netherlands, but at the general's office in New York where duplicate copies were kept. That phone call had yielded Danielle the information that two journalists from a major German newsmagazine, a male and a female, had been given the final slot of the morning.

Danielle then called back pretending to be Arguayo's Hague-based assistant with a request for the reporters' contact number. The general was running late, Danielle explained, and needed to push the interview back until the afternoon. A third phone call to the Germans canceled their interview altogether, leaving Ben and Danielle only the task of acquiring press credentials. That was hardly difficult considering the multitude of media personnel about and the relatively lax security precautions employed to match names and faces with actual identities. All Ben and Danielle had to do was wait for two journalists to emerge from the building and discard their credentials, their assignment complete.

THE OFFICIAL seating of the eight judges of the International Criminal Court, while not a huge media event, had still managed to attract hundreds of journalists from all over the world. Not surprisingly, the area around The Hague's government complex was crowded with both tourists and press members, all kept back behind hastily constructed security barriers until the official convocation. Even at that point, only a few members of the public would be allowed through, and before it United Nations officials were busy giving background interviews in suites of offices overlooking the Vyver.

As chief of U.N. security, much of the responsibility for cases to be heard by the new court fell upon General Alexis Arguayo. Accordingly, he had a full slate of interviews booked throughout the morning in half-hour blocks.

The questions for the first several hours proved to be strictly run-of-the-mill and Arguayo had encountered no difficulty answering them in a refined, scholarly manner. His eleven A.M. interview, his last until another series began in the afternoon hours following the official convocation, was with a pair of German journalists. He managed to squeeze in a few minutes of paperwork in the lag between one interview ending and the next one about to take place. He heard the door open and his assistant usher the Germans inside.

Arguayo capped his pen and looked up smiling, rising politely. "So nice to make your—"

He stopped, freezing halfway out of his chair.

"Good morning, General," greeted Danielle Barnea.

B en held his position by the door while Danielle continued to face Arguayo, watching his hands. He had, after all, been a legendary fighter long before he entered the world of diplomacy.

He scowled at Danielle, then focused his gaze on Ben. "I thought you were dead."

"Sorry to disappoint you."

"It's finished, General," Danielle warned in Russian.

Arguayo's eyes bulged. He tensed, then slowly relaxed as he smiled thinly at Danielle. "Most impressive, Inspector Barnea. I see the esteem in which I held you was justified."

"Unfortunate that's going to lead to your undoing."

"Have you managed to smuggle a gun into the building, Inspector Barnea?" Arguayo made a show out of gazing down at her hands. "Then again, with your legendary prowess, you don't really need one, do you? You should have stayed an assassin. It's what you do best."

Arguayo slid a hand into his pocket. Ben and Danielle both stiffened, relaxing only when Arguayo's fingers emerged holding a cigar.

"Sorry to disappoint you both, but I'm unarmed," Arguayo said, lifting a lighter and puffing his cigar to life. "I assume we can dispense with the pleasantries."

"It's time for you to go home," Ben told him.

"A difficult prospect when one has no home. Everything I

knew in Russia is gone. But it will all come back. It's happening already, slowly, behind the scenes."

"And once the United States is decimated by this attack . . ."

"Exactly, Inspector," Arguayo agreed, gloating.

"Too bad that's never going to happen," Danielle said.

Arguayo rested the cigar on the sill of his ashtray. He sat back leisurely in his chair. "I was warned about the two of you, you know, warned about your penchant for flaunting procedure and making up the rules as you went along, warned that we did not need your kind in the U.N."

"And yet we ended up assigned to investigate the very massacre you perpetrated."

"You were assigned to investigate the massacre before I was able to intervene. You have twenty-five minutes, by the way, before security comes to escort me to the convocation."

"Plenty of time."

"You think the two of you can stop Prometheus?" Arguayo chuckled under his breath, shaking his head.

Danielle took a step closer to his desk. "With you helping us, yes."

"And why would I do that?"

"Out of concern for your family, of course."

Arguayo pulled the cigar from his mouth, the smoke drifting toward the ceiling. "My family is dead, Inspector."

"Is that why you've been making regular monthly deposits in Venezuela's Banco Commercial?"

Arguayo smiled tightly. "My congratulations."

"I like to know who I'm doing business with," Danielle told him.

"And what do you intend to do, Inspector Barnea? Track my wife and children down, then come back still looking for answers I can't give you?"

"Not at all," Danielle said quite calmly.

"We intend to tell the truth to the Venezuelan rebels you

so forcibly put down," Ben followed. "Let them find your family."

Arguayo's lower lip began to tremble, as he watched Danielle slide a cell phone from her pocket.

"The rebel leader's name is Guillermo Paz," she said, showing him a Venezuelan exchange already keyed up on the screen. "Paz was recently paroled in an amnesty agreement worked out with the government. He's standing by right now waiting for my call. So, General, should I hit the Send button or not?"

CHAPTER 78

Y ou'll pay for this," Arguayo muttered, seething.

"Not before your wife and children do," Danielle said, still holding the cell phone.

"There's nothing I can do to help you, Inspectors. No threat can change that."

"You can tell us who the other moles are," Ben told him. "And where we can find them."

Arguayo almost laughed. "You think I know that? I've never met or spoken with a single one of them. All of our correspondence has been . . ."

"Go on," Danielle prodded.

"Our correspondence has been via e-mail the last few years. Encrypted reference points. Impossible to trace."

"And coordinated by who exactly?"

Arguayo remained silent, watching as she hit the Send button and eased the cell phone to her ear.

"Please hold, Mr. Paz," Danielle said, covering the phone's microphone with her hand as she continued to glare at Arguayo. "General?"

"All right! All right! The coordination was handled by the American agent."

"You brought him Black Sands after your interrogation of Ibrahim al-Kursami revealed its existence," Ben concluded.

"I brought the plot to the entire group. The opportunity to make sure it went forward was deemed too wonderful to pass up."

"With these Iraqi dissidents functioning as part of Al Awdah, receiving the blame," Danielle picked up.

"The perfect scenario," Arguayo acknowledged. "The United States pays a terrible price while our existence remains cloaked."

"Until Bureij."

"I never imagined you would trace the origins of the massacre to Buchenwald, to those old men and the prophecy they uncovered."

"So everything unraveled because of this prophecy?" Danielle wondered, shaking her head.

"Much more than just a prophecy, Inspector, as you have apparently learned. We couldn't take the chance that someone who could hurt us would notice. Eliminating the links was deemed the safest choice."

"In the paranoid world you grew out of, I suppose it would be," Danielle said. "How fitting you should destroy yourselves instead."

Arguayo didn't seem fazed. "The plot can't be stopped, Inspector. It's too late. I know nothing of the specifics."

"But you can help us get to someone who does, General."

"And who is that?"

"Sharif ali-Aziz Moussan. Better hurry," Danielle continued, removing her hand from the cell phone's microphone. "Your friend Guillermo Paz is waiting."

Mary Winters had set the dining-room table with three settings of their best china. She looked over her work proudly, not seeming to notice that the plates, bowls, cups, and silverware were misarranged.

"Jason told me he was coming for dinner," she said, shuffling past Franklin Winters back into the kitchen.

Normally Winters would pass the statement off as another of the delusions typical of the disease ravaging her. Since yesterday, though, he'd thought of nothing other than Major Jamal Jefferson's claim that eleven bodies likely belonging to his son's A-team had been found, leaving one unaccounted for. So today he followed Mary back into the kitchen where she was peering into the refrigerator in search of something she had already forgotten.

"Mary?"

She didn't seem to hear him, just kept staring blankly forward at the collection of food.

"Mary."

"A roast would be nice, but I don't know what's become of it. The damn maid must have stolen it. I told you to fire her."

Winters grasped his wife at the shoulders and eased him around toward her. "When did you see Jason, Mary?"

"Yesterday in the backyard. While you were out."

"In the backyard," Winters repeated.

"He must have forgotten his lunch box again."

"He spoke to you?"

"He's growing up fast. Looks just like his father. My husband. Said he missed me." She twisted out of Winters's grasp and turned back for the refrigerator. "Now, what am I going to make him for dinner. . . ."

The doorbell rang and Winters left his wife staring at the lettuce. He excused himself even though he knew Mary wasn't listening.

"We need to talk, sir," Jamal Jefferson said, as soon as he opened the front door.

"Come in, Major."

Jefferson gazed back toward the street before entering, made sure the door was closed behind him before walking past Winters.

Franklin Winters followed him into the study. "You've learned something."

Jefferson took a deep breath before turning. "The eleven corpses were all shot in the head execution style. Their bodies showed significant evidence of additional wounds, including those associated with torture."

Winters's throat had gone bone dry. "Was my son one of them?"

"The identifications were unofficial. Nothing on paper. Nothing anyone would admit to on the record."

"Was my son one of the dead?"

Jefferson pressed his lips briefly together. "No, sir, he wasn't."

It took a moment for Jefferson's words to sink in. Winters's legs suddenly felt rubbery. He took a few steps sideways and leaned against the bookcase. "He survived. . . ."

"We don't know that, Mr. Ambassador."

"Yes, we do. Otherwise his body would have been counted among the others. There'd be twelve instead of eleven."

"If he was alive, there'd be some record of him somewhere. A paper trail I could find."

"There weren't paper trails in the case of the other eleven."

"It's a lot harder to hide the living than the dead, sir."

Winters imagined his wife still crouched in front of the open refrigerator, the food inside slowly warming. "I think he's back, Major. I think he's here."

"Mr. Ambassador, I can't find any record of—"

"This is my son we're talking about. Special Forces team leader. You think he couldn't do it if he wanted, find a way to subvert all this record keeping? Make it back under the radar?"

"I'm hoping not, sir." Jefferson frowned.

"Why in God's name?"

"Because the eleven dead soldiers were shot with a single weapon: a Sig-Sauer nine-millimeter pistol. Standard Special Forces issue."

"You're not saying . . ."

"The bullets, Mr. Ambassador," Jefferson continued, expression tightening. "They were traced to your son's gun."

CHAPTER 80

"W ell?" Delbert Fisher asked, closing the door to Jake Fleming's office behind him.

Jake's eyes were transfixed on the screen. "Give me a sec, will ya?"

He was holding a wireless joystick balanced in his two hands, jerking it up and down, left and right. "Man, I never played any of these games with a computer this powerful before."

"Our system doesn't run games," Fisher said, striding over.

"You mean, it didn't used to. It does now. I downloaded a whole bunch."

Fisher gazed over Jake's shoulder at an alien creation being decapitated by a laserlike death ray. "How'd you pay for them?"

"I didn't."

"Pardon me?"

"It's easy. I'll teach you how, if you want."

"So the U.S. government has now broken every copyright law on the books."

"Actually, I did it on the government's behalf. Lighten things up around here," Jake said, as the monitor flashed "Game Over." "Shit. I can't get past Level Seven on this thing." And he leaned forward to reboot the machine for another try.

Fisher took a deep breath. "What about those designations on the incoming messages?"

A copyright notice flashed across Jake's screen. He clicked on "Accept" under the Conditions tab and winked at Fisher.

"Did you hear what I just said?" Fisher asked him.

"Sure. The designations. I couldn't decode them because they're not written in code."

"What?"

"Not encrypted. Do I have to draw a picture for you?"

"When did you realize this?"

"This morning. By accident. I was playing another game and—"

"You didn't think to buzz me?"

"I figured you had everything under control, Del."

"Assume I don't, Jake."

"Safe assumption, by the look of things."

Delbert Fisher placed himself between Jake Fleming and the computer screen. "You're telling me you know what the designations mean?"

Jake slid his chair sideways so he could see his screen again. "Not yet, dude, but I'm getting close."

CHAPTER 81

W elcome to Cuba," the pilot announced over the
loudspeaker, as the private jet rolled to a halt on
the runway at Guantánamo Bay naval base.

Both Ben and Danielle had already unfastened their seat
belts, eager for the meeting General Alexis Arguayo had assured them he'd set up with Sharif ali-Aziz Moussan. They
also insisted that he provide the Gulfstream that was one of
ten private jets in the United Nations fleet. The Gulfstream
had managed the flight without a single refueling stop. With
the time difference, this allowed Ben and Danielle to arrive
in Cuba while the afternoon sun was still burning high and
hot. They saw a Humvee speeding along the Tarmac, a pair
of soldiers inside, and could only hope they were coming to
escort them to Moussan.

The jet's copilot opened the Gulfstream's door and lowered the landing steps. A flood of heat instantly invaded the
Gulfstream's climate-controlled cabin. Ben and Danielle felt
the assault of a tropical breeze as soon as they set foot on the
top step outside. The sun was scalding, and the air around
the jet's cooling engines seemed to glow.

A marine officer standing at the foot of the stairs saluted
when Ben and Danielle reached the bottom. "Inspectors Kamal and Barnea, I'm Captain Anderson, United States Marine Corps. My orders are to escort you to your meeting with
Sharif ali-Aziz Moussan. Has anyone been over the ground
rules with you?"

"No."

"I'll brief you on the way. Now, if you'll follow me . . ."

He escorted Ben and Danielle to the waiting Humvee and held the rear door open for them before climbing into the front and nodding toward the driver.

"We're going to the primary intake and interrogation center," Anderson announced, turning his body so he could face them in the Humvee's rear seat. "Are you familiar with that, Inspectors?"

"Not at all."

"The building was constructed specifically to address the needs of the POWs whose care we're entrusted with. Before being permitted to speak to any prisoner, your identifications must be double-checked and confirmed. Since you are non-military, a prisoner may not be forced to speak to you or to do so without the company of a base representative or adjutant. The prisoner may request the interrogation be recorded, but no tapes, either audio or video, are permitted to leave the base without prior permission. Is all this clear so far?"

Ben and Danielle both nodded.

"The prisoner may choose to end the interrogation at any time. He may refuse to answer any and all of your questions. He will be behind security glass the entire time. Do not attempt to hand him anything or accept any material through the pass-through. Should you require any such exchange, please consult with the officer in charge. The interrogation rooms are secure. No representative of the military will be present, unless the prisoner requests it. The interrogation will not be recorded unless you or he so requests. Is this clear?"

"Yes," Ben and Danielle said together.

Captain Anderson nodded to himself and turned back around to face forward. "Then welcome to Guantánamo Bay."

CHAPTER 82

The intake and interrogation center was a square steel and concrete building that bore the signs of being built for function over form. The building lay inside a fenced-in perimeter on the eastern side of the Guantánamo property, effectively a base within a base constructed to hold men purported to be among the most dangerous in the world. The prisoners' cells, originally contained in mere outdoor kennel-sized shelters, were now housed in an ever-expanding series of buildings similar in design and construction to the intake center. A trio of guard towers had been added for good measure and sentries patrolled the prison complex's perimeter on constant watch. Additionally, all prisoners were fitted with an ankle bracelet that served as a locator as well as being capable, according to rumor, of injecting a sedative via long-range remote control.

Captain Anderson led Ben and Danielle into the building where they were subjected to both a manual and photo X-ray search to scan for any weapons they might have been carrying. From there they were escorted into a windowless interrogation room that featured a long steel table running down the center of its entire width. A glass wall had been installed from the top of the table all the way to the ceiling. There were no holes in the glass for a voice to travel through, but Danielle noticed tiny wires built into the glass, indicative of wireless microphones and a single envelope-sized slot through which materials could be passed.

As they took their chairs, a door on the other side of the glass wall opened and a pair of soldiers led Sharif ali-Aziz Moussan into the room, followed at a discreet distance by a third wielding an M-16. As the armed soldier stood vigil, the other two locked Moussan's arm shackles into slots built into the table and his leg irons into bolts driven into the floor. Satisfied he was restrained, the soldiers retraced their steps from the interrogation room, followed out by the armed sentry just as they had come in.

Moussan watched them go, then stared through the glass at his latest inquisitors. His eyes narrowed when they fell on Danielle. He snickered hatefully and then yanked on his chains as he tried to rise, seeming to forget they were there.

"You," he sneered.

"I understand you're cooperating, Moussan."

"Not with you." His voice emerged a bit mechanically through an unseen speaker.

"Not yet, anyway." Danielle glanced at Ben. "Inspector Kamal and I want to hear about the operation you were prepared to launch against the United States. The centerpiece of Al Awdah."

"It would have been glorious," Moussan pronounced proudly.

"Then why were you running when we met up in Mogadishu?"

Moussan looked surprised she had figured it out.

"We know about your base of operations being raided in Germany," Danielle continued.

"I've already told the Americans all this."

"Now tell us."

"Much intelligence, many resources and assets were lost. One of my men managed to erase all electronic data, so the Americans would not be able to find our Al Awdah agents. Unfortunately, though, neither would we. We needed to regroup, rebuild. That was why we sought to acquire the weapons in Mogadishu, an exchange your presence there ruined."

"What if your agents in the United States never got the message?" Danielle asked him.

"Of course they did. You speak the words of a fool."

"No, Moussan. Inspector Kamal and I believe someone else has taken over your operation, that it remains active today."

"Impossible!"

"We believe it's going to be put into effect on schedule the day after tomorrow."

Moussan's chains rattled on the other side of the glass. His face paled. "How do you know this?"

"Right or wrong?"

"That was the original date chosen, yes, but how did you *know*?" Moussan demanded again.

"Because it's all spelled out in an ancient prophecy that's about to come true unless we can stop it. Would you like to help us stop it?"

"Why should I? If you speak the truth, this is a blessing. I will thank God when it comes to pass."

"You'll never know, because you'll be in solitary confinement here for the rest of your life. Forget about gaining privileges, perhaps even your eventual release. If you don't help us, you will never see the sun again."

"Who are these men, Moussan?" Ben demanded. "How can we find them?"

"Their real identities are useless to you," he replied, addressing himself to Danielle. "And I don't know where to find them—by design, I might add."

"What about the targets?" she asked.

"I couldn't tell you that even if I wanted to, because I never knew; no one did, other than the individual operatives. They were provided with parameters, no more. Also by design."

"Parameters," Ben echoed.

"A school in one state, a hospital in another, a movie theater in a third," Moussan said, pride lacing his voices. "Just examples, you understand."

Danielle's eyes bore through the glass. "These were your *targets*?"

"A restaurant, a shopping mall, a post office," Moussan continued. "A subway tunnel, a railroad, a bridge, an interstate highway, major electrical switching stations and processing plants. There were hard targets of opportunity on the list, yes, but our purpose was to strike the Americans in the soft places they have so long taken for granted. We wanted to change their very way of life forever, make them live in fear. How long would it be before they would go back to a restaurant, send their children to school, leave their homes? They recovered from the effects of September 11. They would never recover from this."

"Have you seen the way prisoners are treated who don't cooperate, Moussan?" Ben asked him. "Of course you haven't. You're not supposed to; no one is. But you've heard, I'm sure you've heard."

"I am telling you what I know!"

"Then tell us how the cells contacted each other."

"E-mail, always e-mail!" Moussan insisted, repeating what General Alexis Arguayo had told Ben and Danielle.

"Then there would've been an activation code."

"Yes."

"As well as a termination code."

Moussan shook his head slowly. "There was no need."

"Why?" Danielle demanded.

"Because the agents were not to launch their strikes until word of the first success reached them. We called it the triggering event, something that would set the entire operation in motion."

"Tell us the triggering event."

"I don't know what it is."

"Bullshit!" Danielle roared, slamming the glass divider so hard that Moussan jerked backward.

He calmed himself quickly, let a smile linger on his lips. "You'd like it to be bullshit, but it's not. I don't know what the triggering event is because I didn't choose it. And I can't tell you how to find the man responsible because I don't know myself." Moussan clamped his lips together, then changed his mind. "You want his name?" he asked, staring at Danielle. "Hassan Tariq. I believe you know him."

"But he was with you in Mogadishu."

"And then he must have returned to his post in America. If what you say about the plot is true, Inspector, he would have gotten the word via e-mail. He'd be in position by now."

Danielle felt herself grow cold, recalling the deadly assassin she had last seen fleeing into the warehouse back in Mogadishu. "Don't think this glass could stop me from killing you, Moussan."

"How does it feel to be scared for your world?"

"Where can I find Tariq?"

"Somewhere on the East Coast. That was his only instruction. It will happen sometime early in the day of the action, no later than noon. After that even you will be powerless to stop the chain of events that follow."

"How can we identify Tariq's target?"

"Final confirmation by e-mail, containing target specifications, was required prior to activation. His confirmation would be the top one on the list."

"And this list?"

Moussan frowned smugly, stopping just short of a smile. "So far as I know, it was destroyed in Germany."

The door to the interrogation room opened to reveal Captain Anderson standing there rigidly.

"Inspectors Kamal, Barnea, the two of you need to come with me immediately."

Ben and Danielle looked at each other, then back at Anderson.

"What is it?" Ben asked.

"Please, Inspectors. Now."

They rose and moved toward the door, followed the whole time by the cold gaze of Moussan. A pair of soldiers waited in the hallway, M-16s leveled and ready.

"I have been ordered to take you into custody, Inspectors," Captain Anderson told them.

"*Us?* Why?" Danielle demanded.

"Please turn around, hands behind your backs."

"Not until you tell us what the hell is going on."

The two soldiers brought their M-16s into firing position.

Anderson nodded grudgingly. "A few hours ago, the body of General Alexis Arguayo was found in his office in The Hague. The two of you are being held on suspicion of his murder."

CHAPTER 83

"They're *what*?" Delbert Fisher asked, not believing what Jake Fleming had just told him.

Jake sat behind his desk, the gorgon creatures replaced on his screen by the fifty confirmations, each accompanied by its own combination of letters and numbers. "GPS notations. Precise latitude and longitude figures."

"Locations?"

"Yeah, that'd be my guess. You got one of those navigation things in your car?"

"No."

"Well, if you did, you tell it you want to get from Point A to Point B and it plots the most direct course. Warns you if you miss a turn or something like that."

"That much I understand."

"But computers, and that's what these navigation systems basically are, have their own language, their own code. You plug in a street in a city, the computer immediately converts that to a specific locale expressed in global positioning satellite terms. You never necessarily see the code, but it's there. It's how the system makes sense of stuff."

"So you're telling me what we've got here is fifty different hard locations."

"That's what I'm telling you."

"How accurate are they?"

"Very. Down to a specific address, or a city block in certain cases."

"*Fifty* targets," Fisher realized, "not just one."

"Yeah, that was my reaction, too."

"So to figure out where the terrorists are going to strike, all we have to do is match up the places with these designations."

"We?"

Fisher nodded. "Get to work, kid. You're on a roll."

CHAPTER 84

Ben and Danielle were placed in a room considerably smaller than the one in which they had interrogated Moussan. There was no glass wall, only a single smaller table, accompanied by the same bolts and slots to fasten the shackles that had been attached to their ankles and wrists. A guard remained in the room with them at all times.

"This is crazy," Ben whispered. "Didn't anyone check the cameras, the video? Arguayo was *alive* when we left him."

"It doesn't matter," Danielle said, surprisingly calm. "The people behind Arguayo need us out of the way. They sacrificed him to make sure that happened."

"This charge won't hold up long."

"It doesn't have to, Ben. Just forty-eight hours. That's all they need. We're the only ones who can stop Prometheus. With us out of the way . . ."

Danielle let her voice trail off as the heavy steel door rattled open and Captain Anderson entered the room.

"You're going to be returned to your plane and flown to New York," he announced matter-of-factly.

"I'm an Israeli citizen, Captain," Danielle said staunchly, "and Inspector Kamal is an American. We have rights."

Anderson looked at them emotionlessly. "Not here."

They were driven across the Tarmac to the Gulfstream in the center of an armed, three-vehicle convoy. Four of the soldiers escorted Ben and Danielle onto the plane. Then, under Anderson's direction, they affixed manacle holds into a pair of seats and snapped Ben's and Danielle's wrists into place.

"Myself and three of my men will accompany you to New York, Inspectors, where you will be turned over to United Nations custody," Anderson explained. "I suggest you make yourselves as comfortable as you can. It's going to be a long flight."

The Gulfstream rose through the air, still climbing toward its cruising altitude when the lights of Havana flashed below. Ben and Danielle had been seated three rows apart from each other, rendering even eye contact between them impossible. Ben noticed that the soldiers who had accompanied them on board were paying far more attention to her than him. Obviously they'd been warned of her prowess and, by connection, his lack thereof. He thought this might provide some sort of opportunity for him. If they let their guard down . . . if they began to ignore him totally . . .

What would I do? What could I do?

Danielle was familiar with these kinds of situations, not him. Their lives might not be in any real danger, but what prominent official at the United Nations in New York could they possibly get to listen to them under the circumstances? By the time they landed, the plot Alexis Arguayo had called Prometheus would be barely thirty-six hours from activation.

Ben gazed out the window, studying the lights of Havana which were dwindling as the Gulfstream climbed from the city. He had the odd sensation that one of those lights was actually rising toward the jet, an illusion, he thought, until something slammed into the Gulfstream's fuselage just behind the left wing, causing a violent shudder.

An alarm began to scream. The jet shook and then pitched downward, nose first. The three marines, who had not been seated, went flying in all directions, slamming into walls and bulkheads. Anderson, who was seated, had left his seat belt unbuckled and was thrown against the cabin wall. He bounced off and somehow landed back in his chair, bloodied but alive.

Smoke filled the cabin and Ben could feel the heat of nearby flames as he thrashed against his manacled wrists.

"Danielle!" he called out, as the Gulfstream continued its deadly descent.

The whine of the free fall grew to an ear-wrenching din, and then an oxygen mask dropped down from the console over his head. Instinctively, Ben tried to reach for it before remembering that his hands were shackled onto the hand rests. His teeth ached from the impact of gravity. He could feel his eyes bulging.

Outside the window, the lights of Havana began to burn bigger and brighter.

"Danielle!" Ben called again.

"I'm here," she said over the deafening roar that was shaking the cabin apart. "Almost got myself . . . free."

Suddenly the plane seemed to level off slightly, righting itself. In that moment, Ben believed there was a chance they were going to make it.

Until the ground came up fast and tore the consciousness from him.

CHAPTER 85

B en, can you hear me? Ben, you've got to wake up. Come on, wake up!"

Ben forced his eyes open to find Danielle kneeling over him.

"Thank God," Danielle muttered.

He turned enough to see the smoking wreckage of the plane twenty yards away. "The soldiers," he managed.

"Two died, along with the copilot. The other marine, Captain Anderson, and the pilot, I managed to tie them up." She heard sirens, stiffening as she gazed about. "We've got to get moving before the rescue crews arrive."

Ben propped himself up on his elbows, wincing in pain. One of his shoulders was stiff and felt swollen. The shirt-sleeve on that side was torn, and one of his pant legs had balled up toward the knee, revealing a nasty gash down the side of his ankle. "Maybe, if we—"

"Listen to me, Ben," Danielle interrupted. Her face was scraped and bloodied and there was a welt across her fore-head. But otherwise she had emerged from the crash un-scathed. "The jet was hit by some sort of missile, maybe a Stinger. They tried to kill us and they'll try again as soon as they realize they failed. We've got to move."

"Where?" Ben managed, trying to wet his lips with his tongue.

A plane banked into a descent, heading for Havana Airport.

"There," Danielle told him.

USING THE keys she had found in Captain Anderson's pocket, she had managed to remove their shackles. Ben imagined her executing that feat in a smoke-filled plane on the verge of exploding. The thought made him realize his lungs still burned and his chest ached every time he took a breath. So he tried to breathe slowly, as they looped around to the front of the airport.

"We have no passports," Ben reminded Danielle. "No visas. Not even any wallets," he added, recalling that Anderson had confiscated those as well.

"We'll think of something once we're inside. A charter flight maybe. Something where we can blend in, lose ourselves."

More sirens screamed in the background, flashing lights now illuminating the crash area they had fled. They clung to the perimeter of the barbed wire–topped fence that enclosed the airport's entire expanse. The front of the airport, even at night, was an ugly appendage of chipped, fading concrete fronted by a series of parking garages made of the same crumbling façade. But there were people about here, anyway, eager and willing travelers filling the airport with luggage and dreams in advance of their destination.

Peering through the entry doors they bypassed, Ben and Danielle could see short lines frozen in motion at all open ticket counters. Cuban troops wearing green uniforms with submachine guns slung from their shoulders patrolled the airport's interior, posted every twenty-five feet or so it seemed. More soldiers than potential passengers.

Ben and Danielle were moving toward one of the entrances when an ancient Lincoln limousine, dating back to the fifties, passed them and halted fifty feet ahead among the tiny Fiats and Ladas. Ben watched the driver lunge out and throw open the rear door. A pair of men wearing sunglasses even though it was night emerged first, followed by a third man wearing a taupe-colored Italian suit. The man gazed about, as if to reassure himself no threats were present; his eyes passed briefly over Ben.

"I know that man," Ben realized. "I know him."

Ben began to jog ahead.

"Ben!" Danielle called, too late for him to stop.

He drew closer to the man wearing the Italian suit, as the man's bodyguards lifted suitcases from the limousine's trunk. Ben only stopped when he reached the curb alongside the limousine and saw the bodyguards had whipped out their guns and steadied them straight on him.

Ben raised his hands into the air, still eyeing the man in the Italian suit. "Do you remember me, Señor Salgado?"

It was only a week ago, a lifetime it seemed, that Ben had rescued Salgado's son from terrorists who had seized an elementary school in a Colombian village. He remembered the incredible look of unspoken gratitude on the man's face in the moment before Salgado lifted a single hand to salute Ben's success.

Now Salgado studied him again, looking past his bruises and shredded clothes. His eyes widened and surprise dawned over his features. Then he nodded slightly in recognition.

"You," he said, as if not believing his eyes. "You saved my son's life."

"I need your help, Señor Salgado. I need it badly."

"Anything," Pablo Salgado told him, not hesitating for even a moment.

Ben took Danielle's hand as she moved to his side. "This

is Inspector Danielle Barnea, also with the U.N.'s Safety and Security Service. We need to get out of Cuba."

Salgado smiled broadly. "Then you've come to the right place."

CHAPTER 86

I'm heading for my private jet now."

"We don't have any papers, passports, money . . ."

"The two of you will accompany me to the diplomatic terminal as my guests. I assure you that you won't be questioned or detained."

"This airport doesn't have a diplomatic terminal," Danielle remarked.

Salgado winked at her. "My point exactly."

ON BOARD Pablo Salgado's private jet, at least twice the size of the lost United Nations Gulfstream, Ben and Danielle were both able to shower and then have their pick of clothes from a pair of closets, one women's and one men's. When they emerged, the drug lord was sitting in a leather chair before a wide-screen television.

"Satellite TV at thirty thousand feet," he told them, holding out the sophisticated remote. "Two hundred channels at five hundred miles per hour. It's a wonderful world we live in."

"Not everywhere," Ben said.

"So long as you are my guests, we'll see if we can change that." Salgado turned his eyes to Danielle, letting his eyes linger. "I must say you're looking much better, Inspector."

"Thanks for the ride, Señor Salgado."

"Pablo, please. We are friends now, yes? In my country the opportunity to repay a favor is the greatest currency of all. It is my pleasure to assist you."

"We need to get back to the United States," Ben told him.

"I'd fly you there now but we have filed no flight plan and Americans are very restrictive about their airspace these days. I can get you there first thing tomorrow morning. Will that do?"

"Just fine," Ben said. "How's your son?"

"Very well, thanks to you. Attending a different school now." Salgado aimed the remote control at the wide-screen television and clicked it off. "Sources forwarded me your file after the regrettable incident that brought us together. I'm sorry for the loss of your family, señor."

"It was a long time ago."

"I've lost my share of loved ones to violence. I understand that the grief never goes away. That's why I am so thankful for your rescue of my son. I pledged to myself that things would be different for him, that I would keep him insulated from my chosen life."

"But you couldn't."

"No more than you could protect your family a decade ago, Inspector. We are both prisoners of the kind of men we are, for better or worse." Salgado turned his attention back to Danielle. "I imagine you have a similar story to tell, señorita."

"Very much so."

"You look at me and you don't judge. That is good, heartening."

"What a man does doesn't define what he is."

"Well said, señorita. I would like to think that applies very much to my case. For me, it is a matter of survival. Something else I'm sure the two of you can relate to." He rose from his chair, still looking at Danielle. "A nice fit. The clothes I mean, on both of you. Now besides clothes and passage to the United States, what can I offer you?"

"Secure communications," Danielle told him. "We'll need to make some calls as soon as we land."

"You can make them from up here if you wish. Perhaps save yourselves some time. I have already alerted my med-·ical personnel. They will be waiting at my home to give you both a full examination."

"We're fine," Ben assured him.

"Then the spa and massage therapist might be more to your liking. Since you are only going to be in Colombia for one night, you might as well make the most of it."

"Thank you," Danielle said.

"This is my pleasure, señorita. There is no reason to thank me."

"I meant for not asking any questions."

"Why bother when the answers are irrelevant? It is a gift from God to be able to repay a debt. I am grateful just for the opportunity." Salgado pressed his hands together before him. "Now what else do you need?"

"An army might be nice," Ben frowned.

Salgado flashed his already familiar smile. "I think we can arrange even that."

DAY TEN

S o what happens now?" Jake Fleming asked Delbert Fisher, looking up from his chocolate-frosted dough-nut.

"We get you back home as soon as possible."

"How long have I been here?"

"Going on a week."

"A week without smoking ganja. You know the last time I went that long?"

"No."

"Neither do I. Eighth grade, maybe."

"Anyone ever tell you it was illegal?"

"So arrest me."

"Tell me again about those fifty target sites and I'll let it go."

Jake went back to his doughnut. "I did a reverse search on Mapquest.com. Their software wasn't up to it at first but I'm good at tinkering. Man, this is fucked up. The Statue of Liberty, the Hoover Dam, an oil refinery in Alaska, Los Angeles International Airport—targets like those make sense. But what's with those schools, nightclubs, restaurants? First, I figured I must have the designations wrong."

"They want to shut the country down, Jake. Scare every-one to death," Fisher said, seeing no reason to hold back. "Every part of the country."

"Fucking blows your mind, doesn't it? Makes you want to smoke up big time."

"You've earned it."

"You drop me off, we could smoke a bowl together."

Fisher shook his head. "Maybe some other time."

"Hey, you take care of my grades like you promised?"

"Straight As. Won't be official until the end of the semester."

"No finals?"

"No need," Fisher said and started to turn back for the door.

"You guys hiring for the summer? I could use a job."

"You'd have to pass a drug test."

"That's a problem."

"We'll see if we can get you a waiver," Fisher promised.

Suddenly an alarm began to wail, filling the corridor beyond with a shrill screech.

"What's that?" Jake asked.

"Probably a drill," Fisher said, stiffening as he moved for the door.

"Wouldn't you know it if there was gonna be a drill?"

"Just keep the door locked," Fisher instructed, as he started to close it behind him. "And don't open it for anyone but me."

CHAPTER 88

The plane cut through the choppy air on descent for Miami. With no flight attendants on board, or even a working PA system, Ben and Danielle simply refastened their seat belts out of habit.

"I have a cargo plane going out tomorrow morning. Bound for Miami with Panamanian registry and flight markings," Salgado had explained when they were safe within the confines of his walled fortress the night before. Ben and Danielle had both showered, eaten, and had their wounds cleaned and bandaged by an on-site doctor inside the compound.

"In that case, I'll need to make that phone call now," Danielle told Salgado.

Major Tom Spears was still in his Pentagon office when she reached him.

"Working late as usual," she greeted. "It's—"

"Don't say your name," Spears ordered. "This isn't a secure line. It's not safe."

"Arguayo's murder . . ."

"You and your Palestinian friend were part of tonight's security briefing. They're done via e-mail now. Allows for easier dissemination of photos."

"How did I look?"

"This call might be monitored."

"Fine, then whoever's listening can hear that Ben and I are innocent. Arguayo was alive when we left him."

"That's not what the report says."

"You believe it?"

"Of course not, and that's what scares me more than anything."

"It should, Tom. Your country's about to be hit."

"Keep talking."

"Fifty terrorist cells, totally independent of each other and all scheduled to strike tomorrow. One per state. Soft targets and hard."

Danielle left it there, listened to the dead air on the line through the long pause that followed.

"You have proof of this?" Tom Spears finally asked, his voice low. She could hear his breathing after he had finished.

"What do you need?"

"Just tell me what you've got."

"Confirmation from a ranking Iraqi operative named Moussan in custody at Guantánamo that the plan used to be his, part of Al Awdah."

"Used to be?"

"Set in operation just before the start of the war. But someone else has taken it over, picked up where Moussan left off."

"Who?"

"A deep-cover Soviet mole left over from the Cold War."

"Relics don't destroy nations, Danielle."

"They do when their hate, their obsession, has never gone away, when they see the chance to finish the assignment they've never abandoned."

Danielle listened to Spears breathing rapidly on the other end of the line as he digested the information.

"All right," Spears said finally. "It's late, but I'm going to call around. See if I can find out who ran the original operation that knocked Moussan out of the box."

"It was German based."

"But I'm betting the intelligence was home grown. You want me to call you back?"

"I'll call you."

"Give me an hour."

DANIELLE HIT the Redial button exactly sixty minutes later.

"All right," Spears greeted. "The man who ran the operation that took this German cell down twenty-five days ago is a Homeland Security spook named Delbert Fisher. If anybody knows how to find these fifty cells, it's him. Man had plenty at stake that made things personal: he lost his brother and sister-in-law in the Bali nightclub bombing."

"And they still let him take point?"

"That's the thing, Danielle. They didn't know, because he didn't tell them. Soon as they found out, they transferred Fisher out of Washington into Homeland Security's northeast regional headquarters out of Nashua, New Hampshire."

"So he's there now."

"As far as I know. But it's not that simple."

"It never is, Tom."

"I'm talking about the Nashua substation. I'm talking about Delbert Fisher."

"I'm listening," Danielle told him.

ven Pablo Salgado lacked the resources to get Ben and Danielle safely beyond Miami. As soon as the cargo plane landed, they climbed into khaki-colored uniforms that matched those worn by airport maintenance workers. That way, once the plane completed its taxi, it would be easy for them to meld in with the other personnel loading trunk-sized wooden crates from the storage hold into a pair of rented Ryder trucks. Neither Ben nor Danielle bothered to consider what was contained inside those crates, or whose interests on this end were supported by those of Pablo Salgado's Colombian cartel.

They slipped away at an opportune time, still unsure what their next step could be. Salgado had supplied them with credit cards and plenty of cash. But they couldn't buy their way to Nashua, New Hampshire, and a Homeland Security operative named Delbert Fisher, especially with their pictures being freely circulated among law enforcement personnel. The worker disguise would hold for a while, though, even stand up to close inspection.

"This way," Ben said suddenly, tugging on Danielle's arm.

"Where?"

"I've got an idea," he continued, and gestured across the Tarmac toward a freight area where FedEx jets were being loaded.

Ben and Danielle climbed onto an unattended luggage cart and drove it to follow the yellow lines that swept safely around the runways. They worked the plan out on the way, using a steel clipboard found hanging from the cart's dashboard to help create the effect of a random inspection. The FedEx loaders, having nothing to hide, had no reason to suspect anything amiss and cooperated fully, providing unfettered access to the planes and loading area.

A glance at a manifest yielded the information that a New York–bound jet, still in the hangar, would be leaving in three hours' time. Ben and Danielle separated, then slipped away into that hangar where the plane was waiting. They climbed on board and hid themselves amidst the heaviest cargo concentrated in the hold's rear.

The heat proved oppressive until the climate control system was switched on once the jet was towed out onto the Tarmac for final loading. Ben and Danielle held their breaths through the early stages of the process until it became clear that the workers were only loading smaller packages that rolled up the ramp, organized geographically throughout the front sections of the bay.

Finally the doors were closed, plunging the hold into total darkness, and soon after the FedEx jet began to taxi toward its assigned runway.

"Next stop, New York," said Ben.

CHAPTER 90

Jake's ear actually hurt from keeping it pressed against the door for so long. He'd lost track of time now too. At first, after Del Fisher had left, he had heard sounds of commotion and running, a few muffled shouts. Then nothing, and nothing since.

Finally he eased the door open, just a crack, and peered out into the hallway.

Nothing. Not a soul in sight. No signs of some titanic struggle. Just a murkily lit hallway.

Jake took a deep breath and emerged from the office they had given him. His moccasins pattered softly across the tile and he felt the frayed edges of his jeans dragging sloppily. He stopped long enough to crouch to cuff them, bouncing back upward and brushing the hair from his face when he heard a door slam somewhere on another floor, followed by the heavy stomp of footsteps. He looked up, then down. Hard to tell where the slamming door had come from until more footsteps echoed directly overhead.

"Del," Jake called softly, feeling immediately stupid. Here he was doing exactly what Fisher had told him not to do, as if the guy could hear him anyway.

Jake continued to walk, no idea what floor he was on and whether he should be heading up or down to get out, even whether he should be getting out at all. He passed plenty of offices, all of them empty. Not just empty, but cleared of equipment and supplies. No computers or even telephones.

"Del," Jake called again, not caring how it felt.

He smelled coffee, strong and stale. Figured it must be coming from inside a room just over on the right, the door to which was cracked open. He liked iced coffee, not hot, and the smell was so sickeningly strong Jake couldn't wait to get past the room. Even picked up his pace a little, until a hand snaked through the door and grabbed his arm.

"KEEP QUIET," Delbert Fisher ordered, clamping his other hand over Jake's mouth to muffle his scream.

"What the fuck, Del?" Jake rasped, as Fisher yanked him into the coffee room and sealed the door softly behind them.

It was then Jake realized why the stench of coffee was so powerful. Pots of it had splashed everywhere: on the walls, the floor, and most on the head of an unconscious man whose whole face was red and blistered. He lay on the floor next to a second form in an identical dark suit, the second man's face indistinguishable amidst a sea of dried blood flecked with bits of glass from a shattered pot. Fisher had used extension cords to bind both men's hands behind them. Duct tape covered their mouths. Del himself, meanwhile, looked to be in bad shape. His face was battered and one arm hung awkwardly from its shoulder.

"We haven't got much time," he said, breathing hard. "They'll be back."

"Bad guys," Jake said. He thought of the offices he'd passed en route to the coffee room, desks gathering dust and cable leads with no computers to connect with. "What about the good guys, Del?"

"That's the thing. There aren't any. Well, me and a couple others, but they're already down."

"I don't think I heard you right."

"This installation's been mothballed. So have I."

Jake tried running it all through his head, too much to make sense of. "What about the SWAT team that raided my dorm room?"

"Locals. My ID still pulls some weight."

"Then all this . . ."

"I had my reasons, and I was right, more right than I ever dreamed." Fisher stopped and swallowed hard twice. "That's why I needed you." He lowered his voice, sounding almost embarrassed. "And why I couldn't turn the tech work over to my 'staff.'"

"I guess this means I'm not getting straight As for the semester."

Del Fisher smiled in spite of himself, then shrugged apologetically.

"They traced us here, didn't they?" Jake asked him. "Whoever's behind those fifty terrorist cells."

"I should have listened to you, what you said about leaving an electronic trail."

"Don't sweat it, Del. Nobody ever listens to me."

"I'm sorry, kid."

"What happens now?"

"We've still got to get word out about what's going to happen tomorrow."

"Okay," Jake agreed. "So let's get our asses out of here and do it."

"There's a problem. I can't walk, kid. My ankle may be broken."

"That's a problem all right."

"But I can guide you out. Rear door, not far from the woods beyond the fence line. You can make it."

"That's another problem, because I'm not leaving without you. And what would I do if I did?"

"I can give you routing points, contact numbers . . ."

Del Fisher stopped speaking when the doorknob twisted back and forth. He reached out and pulled Jake Fleming to the floor behind him, both of them utterly silent. The knob stopped moving. They looked at each other, still afraid to breathe when the door burst inward, shattered at latch level. A huge man stood in the doorway, silenced pistol grasped combat style in both hands. The man hesitated, unsure, it seemed, which of them to sight down on first. He steadied the pistol on Jake, started to curl his finger inward.

"No!" Delbert Fisher screamed.

The gun exploded with a roar. Jake felt his head go numb, eyes squeezed shut. Something all wrong, because no second shot came from the pistol. Jake opened his eyes just as the big man toppled over like a felled tree to reveal a woman standing in the hallway clutching a smoking gun in her hand. A man stood alongside her, holding a submachine gun.

The woman stepped through the coffee room's doorway.

"Which one of you is Delbert Fisher?" asked Danielle Barnea.

CHAPTER 91

U pon landing at LaGuardia Airport in New York, Ben and Danielle had made their way into the passenger terminal and boarded the first bus bound for the Port Authority Station in Manhattan. They learned another bus was leaving in just minutes for Boston, and they used a small portion of the cash Pablo Salgado had provided to buy a pair of tickets.

The ride ended five hours later in downtown Boston within walking distance of a Hertz rental car agency where they rented a car with one of Salgado's credit cards. The car came complete with a NeverLost navigation system to guide them to the former northeast regional headquarters of Homeland Security in Nashua, New Hampsire, where Delbert Fisher had been summarily reassigned to a mothballed facility. There, according to Spears, he had been given a token title and placed in charge of a skeletal staff just to keep him on the payroll.

It was past midnight by the time they reached the complex. The guardhouse was empty, the front gate swaying back and forth in the breeze. Ben climbed out to open it wide enough to allow their car to pass through.

"Chain's been cut," he said, closing the passenger door behind him.

"Got to figure Fisher would've had a key," Danielle noted.

They left the car on the road and proceeded inside the grounds on foot. Whoever had arrived before them had left a bay door accessing an underground parking garage open. Ben and Danielle crept down the ramp and found a quartet of innocuous sedans, three clustered together and one off by itself.

"The engines are all still warm," Danielle said, after running her hand along the hood and grille of the three cars near each other. "I figure eight, maybe ten men."

Footsteps echoed down a stairwell and Ben and Danielle took cover beneath the nearest car. She signaled him with her eyes, directing Ben to the man approaching from the right, talking busily into a cellular phone.

Danielle lurched upward when the two men reached the car one over, launching herself over the roof upon the other man while Ben circled quickly around the trunk. The second man had just separated the phone from his ear, swinging when Ben pounced. Ben then stood guard over their unconscious frames, while Danielle bound and gagged the men, using sliced strips of the seat belt and shoulder harness assemblies.

"Down to six," she said. "Maybe eight."

Armed now, they stayed together once inside the building, taking another three men totally by surprise before coming upon the huge gunman looming in the doorway of what looked like a staff lounge. Danielle hadn't intended to shoot until she saw him sighting down on the two figures huddled on the floor. The shot scorched her ears, and she was ready to follow up with a second when she saw the big man keel over.

Danielle noted two more of the attackers sprawled on the floor not far from the condiment table, bringing the count to eight. "Which one of you is Delbert Fisher?" she asked the two men who had been the big man's targets. One of them, she realized, looked more like a boy.

"That would be me," said the older one, his face badly bruised and his shoulder hanging free of its socket.

Danielle gestured toward the boy huddled next to Fisher. "And him?"

"Long story." Del Fisher struggled to sit more upright. "Who the hell are you anyway, and how did you know I was here?"

"The term Prometheus mean anything to you?"

"No."

"How about a strike to be launched against targets in all fifty states tomorrow?"

Delbert Fisher and Jake Fleming looked at each other before Fisher spoke. "All too well."

"That's good," said Danielle, "because we know how to stop it."

"THERE COULD be more of them coming," Danielle said from the doorway, holding the submachine gun now. "We've got to hurry."

Jake sat down behind the computer he'd been using for a week now, cracked his knuckles to get ready. "It'll just take me a minute to bring up the site," he said, as Ben and Delbert Fisher looked on from behind him. Danielle had managed to snap Fisher's arm back into its socket, but had been able to do nothing for his badly swollen ankle besides support him as he moved down the hallway.

"What time is it?" Fisher asked, grimacing, obviously still in agony.

"Almost three A.M.," Ben told him.

"Okay," Jake said, "here we go. First one on the list, you say. . . . Yup, here it is. Good news. It's in New England. Not too far from us. . . . Uh-oh. Bad news."

"What?" from Danielle this time.

Jake swung his chair around to look at them. "It's the Millstone Nuclear Power Plant in Connecticut."

DAY ELEVEN

CHAPTER 92

A call to Major Tom Spears at the Pentagon resulted in the immediate closing of the airspace within fifty square miles of the Millstone Nuclear Power Plant just outside of New London, Connecticut. Spears reported that an all-out defensive perimeter would be enacted, all but assuring the plot's triggering event would be aborted.

"Stay clear of the area," he had warned Danielle.

"Your people will never even know we're there."

"I'm flying up myself, and I don't want to see you or your Palestinian friend. Remember," Spears cautioned, "you're still fugitives."

"We're e-mailing you the remaining forty-nine target sites," Danielle explained. "Be warned, though; not all the locations are exact."

"We'll do our best to shut them down, get perimeters enacted. But stop the Millstone attack and we stop them all. That's what you're saying, right?"

"Let's hope so, Tom. Have you picked up the prisoners we left for you in Nashua?"

"Being interrogated as we speak."

"My guess is they're hired guns who won't know a damn thing that can help us."

"In that case," said Spears, "let's hope we don't need them."

"SO WHAT do we do with him?" Ben asked as soon as Danielle was off the phone with Spears, indicating Jake in the backseat. They had already dropped Delbert Fisher off at a hospital, the condition of his shoulder and, especially, his ankle making it impossible for him to travel.

"You're heading south," Jake said, before Danielle had a chance to respond. "I can figure that much out for myself. Get me back to New London and I can catch a bus or train to Providence."

"In time for midterms?"

"What's the difference?" Jake shrugged. "I wasn't exactly going to ace them anyway."

THE ACCESS road for the Millstone Nuclear Power Plant had been blocked off by a pair of Connecticut State Police cars parked nose to nose and backed up by a full complement of National Guard troops. Ben pulled the car they had rented in Boston over to the shoulder near the congestion of media vehicles and bystanders wondering what was afoot.

"I think we can get him to that train station now," he said to Danielle, looking at Jake Fleming in the backseat.

But she wasn't listening, her mind clearly elsewhere.

"Danielle?" Ben prodded.

"I was just thinking about that prophecy, what might have happened if the 121st hadn't found it all those years ago."

"You saying you believe in Nostradamus now?"

"Nostradamus?" Jake Fleming leaned forward until he was almost even with the front seat. "What's he have to do with all this?"

"Nothing," Danielle said, before Ben had a chance to respond.

"Because I had a course on him."

"There's a course at Brown on Nostradamus?" Ben wondered.

"Actually, I made it up. An independent study. You're allowed to do that at Brown. Anyway, he predicted the attacks on 9/11, you know."

"A hoax," Danielle corrected.

"No, one of those poem things of his."

"Quatrains."

"Yeah. There's one that goes, 'At forty-five degrees latitude, the sky will burn. Fire approaches the great new city. Immediately a huge, scattered flame leaps up, when they want verification from the Normans.' That's the French now."

"I know," said Danielle. "New York City doesn't lie at forty-five degrees latitude, though."

"No," agreed Jake. "But the approaching fire could be those two jetliners and the huge flame leaping up, well, I don't have to tell you what that is. And there was a warning issued by French intelligence the day before the attack." He watched Ben and Danielle exchange a skeptical frown. "Hey, I'm just the messenger."

"How'd you do in the 'class'?" Ben asked him.

"Incomplete. Haven't been able to get past that forty-five-degree latitude thing yet," Jake quipped, gazing at the GPS system the car had come equipped with, currently displaying the Millstone Nuclear Plant's exact location. "Uh-oh."

"What's wrong?"

Jake pointed at the digital readout, suddenly serious. "That's not right." He started fishing through his pockets. "The latitude and longitude coordinates aren't right, I'm sure of it. Last number looks wrong." Jake uncrinkled a set of pages listing the coordinates of the fifty targets they had e-mailed to Tom Spears. "Yup, I knew it. A zero instead of an eight."

"A zero instead of an eight?" Danielle repeated.

"Here, see for yourself," Jake said, handing the rumpled pages forward. He held his finger to the entry in question. "Right here. The squiggly line means it's a zero. That's what I typed in, not an—"

The boy stopped in midsentence. His mouth dropped, eyes tearing up, blinking rapidly. Suddenly he threw himself forward over the console, reaching for the GPS computer that had come with the rental.

"You mind telling us what you're talking about?" Danielle said, as he worked the GPS's controls.

"I fucked up. It *is* an eight, but I typed a zero. That's what happens when I go without ganja for too long."

Ben and Danielle could only look at each other, as the computer calculated the new input Jake had fed into it.

"You're saying this plant *isn't* the real target?" Ben asked incredulously.

"Yeah, that's what I'm saying."

"Then what is?" Danielle demanded.

"This," Jake told her, moving away from the tiny screen so they both could see.

CHAPTER 93

The Benny Dover Jackson Middle School was located in the center of New London, fifteen minutes away from the Millstone Nuclear Power Plant. Ben drove there furiously while Danielle tried in vain to reach Major Tom Spears.

"Stay down," she told Jake Fleming, as they pulled into the visitor's parking lot located alongside the school's main entrance.

A pair of New London police cars were parked nose to nose in the bus loading zone set before a long, narrow waiting area sprinkled with benches.

"At least our anonymous call accomplished something," Ben shrugged.

"Maybe," Danielle said, sizing up the situation emotionlessly.

She reached beneath the seat and handed Ben one of the two nine-millimeter pistols they'd taken off the gunmen in New Hampshire the night before. He wedged the gun into his belt, made sure it was covered by his jacket.

"Excuse me, guys," Jake Fleming said from the backseat, "but what happens if you and the cops can't pull this off?"

Ben and Danielle looked at each other.

"What I mean is, what if I could shut this whole thing down?" Jake continued.

"How?" Ben asked him.

"School's bound to have lots of computers, probably a lab

full of them. I've been doing some thinking. You get me inside the building, I got something I'd like to try out."

"Are you sure it'll work?" Danielle challenged.

"Well, not totally."

"Then stay here and stay out of sight."

Danielle climbed out of the car and waited for Ben before heading toward a set of glass doors at the entrance to the school. Signs instructing all visitors to proceed immediately to the office, accompanied by directional arrows, greeted them inside. A bit farther down the hall, off to the left, they heard the boisterous sounds of students eating lunch in a cafeteria.

Hands edging closer to their pistols, Ben and Danielle entered the main office. Behind a chest-high counter directly before them, a trio of receptionist desks sat unoccupied, the phones atop them in all likelihood disabled.

Danielle signaled Ben to take the left wall, while she took the right, creeping toward a door labeled ASSISTANT PRINCIPAL.

"Empty," she called, after twirling into the doorway.

"Here, too," Ben said from the door to the principal's office.

They moved back toward the reception area, passing a copy room where they noticed stacks from a finished print job sitting uncollected in the output slot.

"We pull the fire alarm, we empty the building," Ben suggested.

"Think machine guns in the second-floor windows or on the roof." Danielle shook her head. "No, we can't take the chance, not until we know how many we're dealing with."

She stopped when she saw a half dozen walkie-talkies charging in separate bays. She yanked two free and handed one to Ben.

"In case we have to separate," she explained.

He clipped it to his belt as they moved back out of the office, nearly colliding with a teacher dragging along a student with spaghetti sauce painting his hair. The teacher seemed not to notice them.

"Seven, maybe eight hundred students," Ben said. "That's what I'm figuring."

"I counted four exits on the side of the building we parked on," Danielle added. "Double that to eight, ten at the most."

"The windows open only at the top. Means breaking the glass would be the only other way out of the school."

"Makes this the perfect place to take hostages. Textbook."

"What about the cops from the cars outside?"

"We find them, the odds get a little better. But if the terrorists find them first . . ."

"I still say we pull the fire alarm," Ben suggested again, moving toward a pull station eye level on the wall. "Throw something into the mix the terrorists weren't expecting."

"We'll have to pick them off as we see them. Hope for clear shots."

Ben nodded, grasped the red lever and yanked. Felt it depress under the force.

Nothing happened. No shrill sound or flashing lights.

The fire alarms had been deactivated.

CHAPTER 94

W hat's that?" Danielle wondered, as three short beeps sounded over the school PA system, followed by two longer ones. Instantly, across the hall in the cafeteria the teachers working lunch duty began instructing students to leave their tables and form a pair of lines, one for each side of the room.

"The beeps we heard must be some sort of emergency code," Ben said. "A lockdown."

Danielle shook her head. "No, a lockdown means hold in place. This is something else. They're being taken to a central location."

As if on cue, classrooms at the far end of the corridor began to empty in an orderly fashion, throngs of students spilling out into the hallway and heading toward the far end of the school.

"The signal had to come from the office," Danielle noted.

"Something we missed?"

"Let's go take a look."

They headed back to the main office, found the door locked this time. Ben ducked down and extracted a pen from a pocket of a backpack lying amidst a dozen others against the wall. He twisted the top off and worked the thin cartridge into the single tumbler mechanism. Danielle hovered over him, offering cover for the fifteen seconds it took for Ben to spring the lock.

He eased the door open slowly and led the way in. There

was no sign of the teacher or the unruly student he had escorted inside. Danielle grabbed Ben's shoulder and pointed to an alcove located beyond the reception desks. She drew her pistol and led the way through a waist-high swinging door.

Ben saw the body of the teacher they had glimpsed earlier lying behind one of the receptionist's desk, a bullet hole carved in his forehead. The bodies of the two cops from the cars outside had been stuffed beneath the front counter, pools of blood widening beneath them. The boy with spaghetti sauce coating his hair sat in the corner, hands wrapped around his knees, shaking horribly. There was a doorway on the right, leading into a tiny closet-sized room housing the PA system. A man in a dark suit, the principal probably, sat in a chair in front of the controls, a figure looming behind him holding a gun to his head, his position obstructing his view of Ben and Danielle.

Ben yanked his gun out now too. But Danielle held his hand down before he could raise it, something else on her mind as she gestured for him to move to the side of the PA room's door.

Danielle moved to one of the desks and nodded toward Ben. Then she picked up the phone and pretended to press out a number.

"Yes, this is Ms. Barnea at Jackson Middle School—"

The gunman stormed out of the PA room, angling his gun on her before Danielle could say any more. Ben slammed him in the back of the head with the butt of his pistol. The man wobbled, legs gone to jelly, but didn't go down. Ben hit him again twice, watched his knees buckle an instant before he crumpled.

Danielle surged into the PA room and faced the terrified principal, blood running down from a nasty gash on his forehead. "The students, where are they going?"

"The gymnasium," the principal said, swallowing hard. "At the other end of the building."

"How many terrorists?" she asked, as she tore a phone cord free of the wall, prepared to use it to bind the unconscious terrorist's arms and legs.

"I—I—I don't know. I saw two, no three. I saw three." He swallowed hard, looked at Ben for the first time. "Are you the police?"

He had barely finished the question when two more New London patrol cars and three from the State Police tore into the visitor's parking lot with sirens screaming.

"No," Ben said, "but it looks like they're here."

"TARIQ'S GOING to wait until the media arrives," Danielle told him, knotting the phone cord twice around the unconscious terrorist's wrists.

"Tragedy covered coast-to-coast."

"Meant to set off the other forty-nine strikes, remember?"

"Which gives us time to stop it. I'll take the gymnasium," Ben said, and helped Danielle drag the now bound and gagged terrorist into the closet-sized PA room. "But the terrorists down there won't be the only ones in the building."

"Leave the rest to me," she assured him.

JAKE FLEMING watched the silent line of students filing down the hallway through a glass slab built into a set of double exit doors. The design of the building, and the doors, was pretty standard. Not much different than the kind he'd mastered jimmying open way back in high school, when sneaking back into the building was as much an art as sneaking out.

Jake waited until the parade of students was gone before he worked the doors opened and entered the building. Nice suburban school like this probably had a computer in every room, and all he needed was one.

CHAPTER 9 5

Ben emerged from the office and fell in step alongside the twin lines of students moving in silence down the hallway. He had tucked his pistol far back on his hip, undiscernible beneath his jacket. He knew the eventual need for the gun outweighed the risk of it being found on his person. Hassan Tariq's men would have no reason to expect any of the school's teachers or administrative personnel to be armed, almost certainly eliminating the need to search them.

A few of the students glanced his way, noting the oddity of his presence. They didn't recognize him, but he could easily be a substitute teacher, visiting administrator, even a parent.

The twin lines swung right down a long straight hall that dipped slightly at the outset en route to the far end of the building where the gymnasium was located. During his months working for a private security firm, Ben had become well acquainted with the procedures schools had enacted in the post–September 11 world. Depending on the nature of the danger, anything from a classroom lockdown to an all-out evacuation could be ordered. Central gathering points were selected specifically for catastrophic events like bioterror attacks. Mandated drills occurred regularly, and Ben guessed students and teachers alike assumed this was just another of those.

He could see a twin parade of students being marched down a parallel hallway on the other side of a courtyard that formed the center of the building. Once clustered in the gymnasium, it would take only a small number of terrorist gunmen to watch over the entire school population, in addition to complicating the logistics for any attempted rescue. But Ben also knew the terrorists behind this seizure had no intention of giving the authorities enough time to respond. This wasn't about negotiation, or making a political point. It was about achieving a horrific result that, when taken among forty-nine others, would change American society forever, the wounds so deep they'd never heal.

Ben intended to make the logistics the enemy was relying on for success work in his favor. Neutralize the small number of terrorists who would be in the gym, and he could focus all his attention on evacuating the school from a single central location. This while Danielle dealt with the remainder of the terrorists. Surprise was their greatest ally, their presence being the one factor the opposition's plan could not possibly have accounted for.

The hallway ended adjacent to a second cafeteria at the far end of the building. From there the trek wound left through a foyer and into the gymnasium that was already packed with children arranged in tight circles by classroom.

Ben moved off to the side, apart from the other teachers, pretending to herd the students along. A man standing similarly apart from everyone else, and making no effort to direct students, was speaking into a walkie-talkie.

The first terrorist.

Ben continued to gaze around the room, found another two men standing by themselves near the gym's rear, each stationed near one of the double-door exits that opened onto the school's outdoor basketball courts and playing fields.

Terrorists two and three.

Ben contemplated striking now, drawing his gun and opening fire while the restrained chaos of the stream of arriving students remained his ally. The two terrorists at the gymnasium's rear, though, were an uncomfortably far distance away to trust to his aim with a pistol and a gunfight would surely claim innocent lives in the panic that resulted. Ben considered the risk against the potential gain, decided he couldn't chance it.

The terrorist who'd been talking into the walkie-talkie moments before closed the double doors after the last students had entered. Ben watched him ease a chain out from a jacket pocket and twist it through the latches, locking the doors in place. Across the gym, the other two terrorists took this as their cue to do likewise to the doors near which they had been posted.

"Hey," a casually dressed male teacher called out, moving away from his assigned class, "what do you think you're doing?"

The terrorist with the walkie-talkie whipped a submachine gun out from under his jacket and fired a deafening burst into the ceiling. Screams rang out. Middle school students lurched to their feet, backing into what quickly became an indistinguishable mass of humanity.

"Sit down!" the terrorist ordered, his two cohorts on the other end of the gymnasium tearing identical weapons free. Like the other former Special Republican Guardsmen recruited for Black Sands, they all boasted a Western appearance and the speaker, anyway, spoke with no detectable accent. "Sit down where you were and don't move! Don't speak!"

The students hesitated until another submachine gun burst into the ceiling sent them scampering back to their places on the floor. One of the terrorists in the rear of the gym added his fire to the mix, and the spent shells rattled against the polished floor, the din echoing through the newly entrenched silence.

Ben fell in amidst a grouping of students that lacked a teacher. He began to question his strategy of not launching an attack when the opportunity had been there, of outthinking himself. Hesitation was the difference between the cop and the soldier, between him and Danielle, and he wondered if that hesitation would now prove costly indeed. Then again, at least two of the terrorists had expended a hefty measure of their magazines, turning the odds a bit more in his favor once he did strike.

Fearful of losing the element of surprise, Ben knew his best chances lay in acting now. Seizing these moments of ultimate chaos and fear to do the last thing the terrorists could possibly be expecting. He pretended to scratch at his chest, lowered his hand to his belt and then snaked it back for his pistol.

The door to one of the locker rooms burst open suddenly and a fourth terrorist emerged, herding a line of boys harshly before him. The first few stumbled over each other, nearly tripping. The Iraqi with the walkie-talkie approached, began placing the emerging boys amidst individual class groupings.

And then Ben saw why, his breath catching in his throat.

A belt had been tied around each of the boy's waists. Thick and bulky, rising up toward their chests. All too recognizable. Suicide belts, they were called in the Middle East. Packed with explosives laden with nails and shrapnel, likely wired to a single detonator.

Ben watched the boys, nearly thirty of them, being positioned and then pushed down throughout the gymnasium by the lead terrorist. Thirty human bombs, each with the potential to kill anyone within a twenty-foot radius.

Ben shivered, tried not to think of the potential carnage, focused instead on the gun tucked back on his hip and the walkie-talkie still clipped to his belt. Was there a way he could contact Danielle, alert her to the scope of the plot confronting them?

"You!" one of the terrorists yelled, angling toward Ben with submachine gun lowered. "Stay right where you are!"

CHAPTER 96

D anielle knew the television cameras were probably still several minutes, perhaps even a half hour, away. The plot called for maximum effect and exposure. And Hassan Tariq would be following it to the letter, his cell's action destined to start a murderous chain reaction that defined the Iraqi plot known as Al Awdah.

She eased the office door open a crack and peered out into the main foyer. A set of stairs climbed upward toward the second floor directly before her, empty now. The cafeteria lay down a short extension of the foyer, also empty. Hearing no footsteps, Danielle emerged from the office and sealed the door quietly behind her.

A rattling sound froze her. Danielle pressed her shoulders against the wall and skirted to the cover of a corner occupied by a pay phone. The rattling gave way to a soft clanging sound, and she slid along the exposed brick wall to the edge where it merged into the school entry hall. One of the terrorists had just finished lashing one set of glass doors closed with a chain and was moving onto the second.

He had started to fasten another chain into place when Danielle sprang. He heard her at the last, too late to do anything but relinquish his hold on the chain and go for a weapon inside his jacket instead. Not wanting to chance shots that would surely draw attention to the area, Danielle grabbed the chain the terrorist had left dangling from the door latch instead. Before he could draw his weapon, she had looped it around his throat and pulled hard with both hands, taking up the slack.

Danielle could feel the air catch in the man's chest. His hands flailed wildly, groping behind him in hope of finding some stray purchase upon her. She yanked him backward and the man's boots kicked out, cracking the glass of one of the entry doors. Finally Danielle felt his resistance ebb, his body slackening, and she dragged him across the floor into a nearby lavatory. He was dead by the time she tucked him inside a stall and closed the door behind her.

Danielle paused briefly before exiting the lavatory to catch her breath. Her plan was now to work her way across the school toward the gymnasium eliminating any terrorists between her and Ben on the way. That would leave only the terrorists in the gym for the two of them to contend with. If she worked fast, the element of surprise, or at least confusion, would remain on their side.

She hugged the wall, sliding her feet across the tile floor to avoid any noise her footsteps might make. This hallway ran perpendicular to the twin longer ones that ran the entire length of the school. Signs with directional arrows indicated she was heading for the science wing, and a set of chained exit doors ahead told her one of the terrorists had already covered this area.

Outside she could hear the screaming of more sirens, announcing the arrival of additional state and local authorities who would find themselves utterly helpless against the forces that had taken the school. Sure enough, as she neared the end of the hall, she gazed back and saw a pair of cops approaching the front doors, pistols drawn. One started to yank back on the latch while the other provided cover.

Danielle almost lunged out to signal them away, but it was too late. As soon as the latch gave, the tiny explosive charge affixed to the door exploded, blowing the first cop into the second and showering both of them with glass. A single scream rang out, then nothing.

The clatter of footsteps and sudden burst of voices sounded along the science wing. Danielle rounded the corner to find a pair of boys and girls, two couples who had been hiding in a room marked TERRARIUM, surging into the hallway. They held their ground, uncertain what to do next, when their eyes fell on Danielle.

"Get down!" she screamed, an instant after seeing the shadowy figure of another of the terrorists appear at the other end of the hall.

The man opened fire with a submachine gun, just as Danielle dove to the floor, steadying her pistol. She angled her fire upward over the students now hugging the linoleum. Her bullets punched the terrorist backward into a steel doorjamb where he slumped downward, eyes glazing over.

Danielle bounded back to her feet, discarding that pistol in favor of another she had stripped off the dead terrorist whose body lay in the lavatory stall. The four students remained prone on the floor and her heart hammered with fear they had been hit in the crossfire. But all four stirred as she approached them.

"Are you all right? Are you hurt?"

They seemed briefly unsure themselves, until she urged them back inside the terrarium, immediately bathed in sunlight pouring through a glass atrium roof. The room was lined with display cases exhibiting various reptile and insect species. Danielle glimpsed snakes slithering about along with colonies of huge fire ants, spiders, and black beetles.

"Hide in that closet," she ordered the students. "Don't move until—"

The heavy pounding of gunfire cut off her words. Fired from above, it punctured the atrium roof and sent glass spraying in all directions. Danielle felt it gouge her scalp and pierce her arms and legs through her clothing.

"Get away!" she managed to scream at the students before

she lost her footing and hit the tile floor hard, the side of her skull slamming against a table leg.

Above her, an entire section of the glass gave way and Hassan Tariq plunged downward.

CHAPTER 97

It had taken Jake Fleming all of two minutes to find the computer lab located on the school's second floor. Shiny black Dells ran off a master server somewhere else in the building, giving him the power he needed to pull off his plan.

The machines were all whirring quietly. But a password was needed to get into the system. Jake smiled to himself, wondering if the school tech teachers really thought that would keep someone like him out.

He was logged on and on-line in less than a minute, the sheet containing the confirmation codes from all fifty terrorist cells unfolded and smoothed out atop the Formica table just to his right. It took another four minutes to crack through the school's security firewall and then he began entering the addresses the terrorists had provided. Jake was under no illusion that those e-mail accounts were anything more than dummy sites that would reroute the message elsewhere. Nor did he believe there was any chance he could possibly trace them back to their actual source.

Nope, he had something else in mind entirely.

Jake finished keying in the addresses and began to type out the message he had composed in his mind. Had just finished when he heard the echo of heavy footsteps approaching the computer lab.

CHAPTER 98

The explosion echoing from the other side of the building had taken the terrorist leader's attention off Ben. The man stopped halfway to him and snapped a small walkie-talkie to his ear and jabbered into it. He waited for a response and when none came, spoke into the microphone again.

Danielle, Ben thought. Thanks to her, he guessed no response would be coming. He watched some of the hundreds of students begin to stir, shifting about.

"Stay where you are!" the terrorist leader ordered, kicking a few of those closest to him out of the way to clear a path.

Maybe it was the sight of the children doubling over in pain. Or the realization that this was all going to end soon and badly. Or maybe the sudden burst of echoing spits that could only be distant gunfire providing the final impetus for action he needed. Whatever the case, Ben yanked the pistol from inside his jacket and shot the terrorist leader in the center of the forehead.

The two terrorists in the gym's rear twisted their weapons toward him. Ben stood his ground, no time to angle himself for a crouching shot. He fired off a half dozen shots toward each man, even as their fire burned the air toward him. But a few students had lunged to their feet in panic to flee, distracting the terrorists enough to confuse their aim.

Ben's bullets dropped one of the men to his knees. He flopped forward while the second keeled over like a felled tree. The final terrorist had been rechecking suicide belts, distracted long enough for Ben to get off his final two shots before the Iraqi could unshoulder his weapon. One of the bullets took him high in the shoulder near the neck. He staggered briefly, then collapsed.

Chaos erupted. Students rushed in all directions. They packed the exits only to be turned back by the heavy chains. Some of the students who'd had the suicide belts strapped to their waists began groping about, trying to free themselves.

Ben shuddered, grabbed the first teacher he saw. "Help me stop them!"

"What?"

"The suicide belts! They have to be removed a certain way! Otherwise, they'll detonate!"

Ben had recognized the construction of the belt from his last days as a cop in the West Bank. Designed to prevent volunteers from weakening and changing their minds, the explosives would go off if the belt was tampered with by anyone without intimate knowledge of exactly how to remove it.

"What do we do?" the teacher asked.

"Bring the students wearing the belts to the center of the gym! Then get those chains off and evacuate everyone from the building!"

The teacher narrowed his gaze questioningly.

"I know how to deactivate the explosives," Ben told him.

TARIQ LANDED in a tuck two yards from Danielle and bounced quickly back to his feet. He held a detonator in his right hand and submachine gun in his left, his glare the same as it had been when their eyes had locked briefly nine days before in Mogadishu. Around Danielle the force of the ceiling's implosion had toppled glass display cases to the floor where they smashed into hundreds of pieces, freeing the creatures trapped within. She felt a small rodent pass lightly over her wrist as she groped for the pistol still in her belt. Danielle managed to free it, but Tariq launched a booted foot toward her as she started to fire and her shot flew wildly high into a still-whole section of the atrium roof above.

Tariq steadied the submachine gun upon her but didn't fire, choosing instead to hold his detonator out for Danielle to see. She watched him ease his thumb toward the button that would surely destroy the gymnasium where the school's students had been gathered and where Ben undoubtedly was. He grinned, savoring the moment, until they both heard a crackling sound from above an instant before a fresh section of the roof gave way and a blanket of glass rained down upon Tariq.

BEN FOUGHT the rush of students stampeding for the exits, intercepting two with belts strapped to their waists before they could flee the gym through one set of now open doors.

Removing the devices wasn't difficult, just a matter of unhinging a hidden clasp at the belt's rear that was impossible for the subject to reach without triggering the explosives. Ben spun the boy he had caught around so he was facing the clasp.

"Stand very still," he said, as calmly as he could manage. "I'll get this off you."

He traced the length of the hard-wired triggering mechanism and pulled gently on the clasp. The belt came free.

"Go!" Ben told the student, easing it from his waist and moving to the trembling boy on his right.

DANIELLE LUNGED headlong into Tariq's knees, spilling him to the floor. He went down hard and cracked his head on a table leg.

The detonator skittered across the shiny tile.

Tariq swept a hand for a pistol tucked in his belt, but Danielle's hand got there first and locked against it, wedging it in place. The terrorist twisted, using his superior strength to force her off him. He groped for the detonator and had almost grasped it when Danielle closed her free hand on the contents of a broken bag of powdered fertilizer and flung it into Tariq's eyes.

The terrorist wailed in agony, automatically drew his hand up to comfort his eyes. Danielle seized the moment to attack and was greeted with a blow to the head that stunned her badly. The fertilizer still stinging his eyes, Tariq swept the floor blindly for his pistol. His fingers scraped across it just as a black horde of fire ants swallowed the gun briefly and forced Tariq to jerk his hand away, knocking the pistol across the floor.

It skittered to a halt just five feet from her and Danielle lurched for it as Tariq lunged for the detonator.

ONLY AFTER shoving himself under the long computer desk on which his was perched did Jake realize he had forgotten to put the machine into sleep mode. Now, with its monitor glowing instead of dimmed, any terrorist walking through the lab would spot the live screen easily.

Jake breathed a sigh of relief when the man passed the lab

without entering. He waited a few more seconds just to be sure, then popped back up into his chair.

Just one task left to go and his plan would be ready to put into effect. All he had to do was hack into one of the most secure systems known to man:

The Federal Bureau of Investigation.

He'd done it before, after all. Simply a matter of recalling the process.

If only I had a joint, Jake thought.

STUDENTS RUSHED from the building in droves through glass doors broken open by state policemen reaching the scene. A few of the officers fought through the surging crowd to reach the gym where Ben Kamal had now piled a dozen suicide belts in the middle of the floor.

"Jesus Christ," one of the cops muttered, unsure whether or not to holster his pistol.

Ben unclasped a thirteenth belt and added it to the pile. A trio of teachers had managed to gather all the students wearing the belts together, easing another forward each time Ben discarded the explosives that had been strapped to the previous one.

"Who the hell are you?" one of the cops demanded.

"Someone who knows what he's doing," Ben replied, not missing a beat as he unfastened the next belt strapped around a boy's waist. "Now, come over here and give us a hand."

DANIELLE REALIZED too late that Tariq was closer to the detonator than she was to the pistol. At the last instant, she

altered her path and threw herself at him. Tariq lashed an elbow into her face, loosening her teeth as he whirled from the
detonator and slammed her head backward into the rim of a
black lab counter. The counter heaved upward, toppling contents to the floor including a welding striker that rattled to a
halt near her left hand.

Tariq closed a massive hand around Danielle's throat. She
could feel the muscles in his forearm contracting as he
squeezed, compressing cartilage and shutting off her air.
She forced her head upward, only to have it jerked brutally
back down. Danielle felt the back of her skull slam into the
floor, trying futilely to strip Tariq's grip free as clouds
spread over the world before her.

In that moment she remembered that his pistol had rattled
across the floor. She groped for it desperately, scraping
across shards of glass from the shattered terrarium roof and
smashed display cases.

The gun is somewhere over here. I'm sure of it. . . .

More glass gouged her palm. She continued to stretch her
fingers outward, scratching at the floor in search of the gun
when they closed on something hard and rubbery.

A hose, running up through the floor. But what . . .

Danielle realized what the hose must be and fastened her
hand around it, yanking with all her strength. The hose came
free in her right hand, while her left snatched the welding
striker up from the floor.

She could hear the hiss of escaping natural gas, the acrid
stench just reaching her when she touched the welding striker
to the hose's end directly in front of Hassan Tariq's face.

BEN HAD fallen into an eerie rhythm, all the time knowing
that the slightest misplacement of a hand or finger would
lead to the deaths of everyone still in the gym.

Only three boys with suicide belts draped around their waists remained. The rest had already joined the others outside, their discarded belts piled in the far corner of the locker room where the overall effects of any blast would be kept to a minimum.

"Oh, man," one of the cops uttered, as Ben stripped another suicide belt free and moved on to the final two boys.

He unclasped the second-to-last belt, then quickly reached for the final boy's. Felt for the clasp catch and tugged.

Nothing. It wouldn't give.

"Get out of here!" Ben ordered the cop.

"What about—"

"Just do it!"

He could feel the boy trembling, hear his ragged breathing, as he retraced his fingers for the clasp. It had been bent somehow, his fingers coming precariously close to the detonating wire as he tried to twist the clasp back into shape.

"Stay as still as you can," he said softly into the boy's ear. "I'm going to get this off of you."

The clasp still wouldn't give.

THE BURST of gas-fueled flame enveloped Tariq's face in an orange shroud. He seemed not to feel it for the briefest of instants after which his eyes bulged as he screamed in agony, flesh and hair suddenly ablaze.

The stench of burning skin reached Danielle and she recoiled as Tariq lurched to his feet, flailing desperately at the flames spreading across his torso and arms. Danielle watched Tariq slam into the wall, bounce off it, and collapse to his knees, the last of his screams dying in his throat as he keeled over.

Danielle started to breathe easier, until she saw the detonator resting directly beneath him, its trigger button about to be depressed under his weight.

BEN MANAGED at last to straighten the clasp enough to pry it free of its catch. He let the final suicide belt drop to the floor, scooped up the boy in his arms, and bolted for the gym exit where a pair of state policemen were urging him on.

DANIELLE LUNGED, half-diving, half-pushing herself across the floor. She thrust a hand under Tariq's collapsing frame, felt the blistering heat off his still-flaming body as her hand came up just short.

The last thing she saw was the red light above the detonator's button before it disappeared beneath him.

BEN HAD just pulled himself and the last boy through the door when the jet of heat found him. More of an aftershock really, carrying none of the deadly nails and shrapnel that had showered the gym in all directions, digging divots from the polished floor, pockmarking the walls, and shattering all of the lightbulbs dangling overhead.

He left the boy on the floor between the pair of cops who'd dropped down covering their heads, and rushed toward the front of the building and Danielle.

THE BLAST shook all the walls of the building. Danielle climbed back to her feet, shaking and fighting the despair surging through her as she stepped over the now smoldering body of Hassan Tariq. The percussion of the blast from the other end of the building rattled in her ears, heartache dragged with it.

Ben and I have failed. The plot's activation is now inevitable.

Danielle felt her insides knotted, trying not to consider the congestion of students caught in the blast. Had Ben been inside the gym when the explosion came? If so, was there any chance . . .

She imagined his voice in her head, calling her name. Then she realized it wasn't in her head at all, but coming from the walkie-talkie clipped to her belt.

"Ben?" she asked, squeezing the plastic against her lips.

"We did it," he told her. "Everyone got out safely."

"But the blast, the trigger, the other forty-nine cells . . ."

"I know," Ben said.

OUTSIDE THE building, the chaos of parents struggling to be reunited with their children made it easy for Ben and Danielle to slip away. Never looking back, they walked straight for the street and headed west in the direction of the nearest main road.

"What about Jake?" Ben asked.

"He'll be fine," Danielle said.

They had reached the first traffic light when the car they

had rented in Boston pulled over to the side of the road alongside them.

"Need a lift?" Jake Fleming greeted from behind the wheel.

"YOU DID *what*?" Danielle asked him.

"Hacked into the F.B.I.'s server," Jake repeated. "Not the ultrasecure network, just the routing lines, enough to make it look like the new message I sent to all the terrorist cells from the school originated there."

Ben nodded, understanding. "So the Iraqis would think they'd been talking to the F.B.I. the whole time."

"In which case," Danielle picked up, "they'd figure they were set up. No choice but to abandon their targets. Go on the run."

"That's the plan," Jake told her.

"You really that good?"

"I'm a walking commercial for ganja's mind-enhancing capabilities."

"In that case," Danielle said, exchanging a glance with Ben, "I think there's one more thing you can do for us."

DAY TWELVE

CHAPTER 99

Franklin Winters ushered Mary into the house and then closed the door behind her. She shuffled off into the kitchen, mumbling under her breath. It was the aide's day off which left all responsibility for the care of his wife on him, a task he neither relished nor loathed but simply accepted even as he dreaded the day when no amount of care would be able to help her.

He hung his jacket in the front hall closet and moved to follow Mary into the kitchen.

"Ambassador Winters?"

The unfamiliar voice coming from the study startled him and Winters turned slowly, noticing a man and woman standing in front of the couch.

"Who are you?" Winters demanded, moving to the room's entrance as he judged the distance to the nearest telephone. There was a cordless in the hall, but the handset had long since vanished during one of Mary's episodes.

"We're from the United Nations, sir," said the woman. "I'm Inspector Danielle Barnea. This is Inspector Ben Kamal."

"And did the U.N. give you permission to break into my house?"

"We thought it would be easier this way," said Ben Kamal.

"I'm calling the police."

"We considered doing the same thing," Danielle Barnea told him. Her mouth was still swollen, the residue of her battle with Hassan Tariq, making it painful to speak. "Decided against it."

"Pardon me?"

"Prometheus is finished, Ambassador Winters," Barnea continued.

"I'm sorry, I don't know what you're talking about."

"We traced you through your e-mail address," Ben said, thinking of the magical work performed by Jake Fleming after they had given him the information provided by Alexis Arguayo. "We know you ran the operation. We want to know where we can find the rest of the people behind this."

"I have no idea what you're talking about. And if you don't leave now, I'll have no choice but—"

Winters stopped when his wife shuffled past him holding a tray packed with open cookie packages and empty glasses.

"You didn't tell me we were having company," she announced, setting the tray down on the coffee table. "Would anyone like tea?"

"Mary," Winters started.

"I have the fancy kind that come in the pretty colored wrappers. I have them somewhere." She started fishing through the pockets of the overcoat she was still wearing.

Winters grasped her at the elbow, started to steer her from the room. "You get the tea started, dear. Call me when it's—"

Mary twisted from him, the suddenness of her motion surprising him. But surprise turned quickly to shock when he saw the pistol clutched in her hand.

"Mary, what are you—"

"*Stay out of this, you idiot,*" she seethed in Russian, her voice strong and vibrant, the empty gaze replaced by a resolute stare.

"Mary?"

"*Shut the fuck up!*" Mary hissed, pointing the nine-millimeter directly for Ben Kamal.

Winters held his ground, unsure how to respond, what to feel, stunned by what he was witnessing.

"I know who you are," Mary said to Ben and Danielle. "I've seen your pictures, read your files. Congratulations."

"We know who you are too. *You're finished,*" Danielle continued in Russian. *"This is over."*

"Only for now," Mary Winters told her, reverting to English but no longer bothering to hide her Russian accent. "There are more of us. Everywhere. We failed yesterday. We won't next time."

"We'll find you all."

"Not before I walk out of here," Mary Winters said, rotating her intense gaze between the two of them. "If you try to stop me, I'll shoot you both."

"Why don't you tell your husband the truth about your son, Mrs. Winters?" Ben suggested.

"What's he talking about?" Winters demanded. Then, to Ben, "What are you talking about?"

"Your wife raised Jason in her image, Ambassador. He betrayed his Special Forces team's mission in Iraq when they stumbled on a hiding place for artillery shells filled with bioweapons, shells with Russian markings," Ben explained, repeating what he had learned that morning from Ibrahim al-Kursami. "Your son executed each member himself once they were captured."

"You were right all along, Mr. Winters," Danielle picked up. "Your son *is* still alive. Hiding out in Iraq. Sooner or later he'll be found. And punished."

"Oh my God," Franklin Winters muttered, recalling the tale told him by Major Jamal Jefferson just a few days earlier.

"Shut up, *you ass*!" Mary snapped at him, then trained her gun on Danielle.

Just as her finger started to close around the trigger, Franklin Winters wrapped his arms around his wife and twisted her to the side. The pistol roared. The bullet dug into the ceiling and sent a light shower of plaster floating downward.

Mary Winters lashed out, screaming. Her husband tried to wrestle her to the floor, and Mary flailed to break free of his grasp. She scratched at her husband's face with the nails of both hands as he kicked her legs out, leaving her nothing to break her fall.

Mary Winters's head crashed into the coffee table and snapped forward. Ben and Danielle heard the thud, followed by the sound of something cracking. Winters pushed himself off his wife's inert body.

"Mary," Winters said. "Mary?"

Ben and Danielle came forward together and gazed down at her unblinking eyes.

"Oh, my God," Winters muttered.

S he's in a coma," Ben explained to Colonel al-Asi over the phone days later. "Irreversible brain damage. Not expected to recover."

"A life in hell then."

"Fittingly."

"Regrettable she won't be able to supply the names of her cohorts all over the world, though."

"There are other ways to track them down, Colonel," Ben said, thinking of the way Jake Fleming had traced an e-mail trail all the way to the Winters home.

"Which still leaves forty-nine Iraqi terrorist cells at large in the United States. Sounds like a task for you and Chief Inspector Barnea."

"Not anymore. Delbert Fisher has their approximate locations. He's agreed to keep us out of it."

Al-Asi hesitated briefly. "Where are you calling from, Inspector?"

"It'd be better if you don't know."

"But Chief Inspector Barnea is with you."

"She's here."

"You'll give her my best."

"Of course."

"Everything can be fixed, Inspector. You should keep that in mind."

"Fixed, but not changed, Colonel."

"True enough. The three of us, we are prisoners of our own sensibilities."

"I'm tired of being a prisoner."

"I don't blame you."

"Good-bye, Colonel."

"*Salaam-aleikum.* Go in peace, my friend."

Ben pressed End and saw Danielle walking toward him, having just finished her jog down the beach. Sweat glistened in small beads atop her skin. A tan had already sprouted.

"Colonel al-Asi sends his best," he called to her.

"Did you tell him?"

"I told him. He thinks we'll be back."

"He's wrong."

"I know."

She sat down on the chair next to Ben and stretched her legs comfortably, squeezing her eyes closed.

"One question," he said. "Do you think Nostradamus really envisioned all of this?"

"No, because in the end it didn't happen. Prophecies are supposed to come true."

"Makes you a nonbeliever."

"Nothing new there," Danielle said, opening her eyes to look at him. "But I think I've finally found the only thing I need to believe in."

"Hmm," Ben uttered.

"What?"

"I was wondering if there might be a prophecy in that lost manuscript about us."

Danielle smiled, ignoring the pain in her jaw. "I'll be here when you wake up tomorrow morning. Need to know any more than that?"

"Not at all," Ben said and leaned back under the sun.